RESERVOIR OF CORRUPTION

This book is fictional. The characters, businesses, agencies, names and events are products of the author's imagination. Any likeness to actual persons, places or things is coincidental.

Published by Racing Thoughts, Unincorporated. Printed in the United States by Total Printing Systems using partially recycled, Forest Steward Council certified paper and petroleum-free ink.

Cover and interior design: Daniel Yeager bookserv.com nu-images.com
Cover illustration: Vladan Nesovic
Contact info: reservoirofcorruption@gmail.com

ISBN: 978-0-615-51147-3

This book is dedicated to my family and friends. An extra special thank you goes out to my mother, Francine, my father, Kenneth, my sister, Jennifer and Debbie Burke.

RESERVOIR OF CORRUPTION

D. L. MORRISON

Racing Thoughts

Northern Virginia

The sun was gone, temperatures were fading. The twilight was just bright enough to make artificial light ineffective. For two days the acidic secret had eaten away at her, but after talking it over with a sympathetic ear, Nancy Watkins felt relief. She tucked the phone away and with a renewed resolve continued along the woodland path. Conscious of her slight stature, Nancy stayed aware of her surroundings. Instead of the dark dirt lot, she had parked her car curbside under a lamp. The sight of the convertible made her cringe. It had been a present from her ex.

In minimal light a couple approached. The woman broke the silence in a friendly tone, "Hey, Nancy…what a surprise. What are you doing out here?"

Initially startled, Nancy relaxed when she recognized the pair from yoga class. "Just out for a run. How about y'all?" she replied, unable to remember their names.

Catching the headlights of an approaching vehicle, Nancy moved to shepherd the group onto the sidewalk. In a burst of clarity Nancy sensed something amiss. Her intuition spoke up forcefully. She attempted to run, but the man blocked her path and grabbed her under each arm with incredible force. Nancy shrieked and tried to break his vice grip. She screamed louder when he took two steps, planted his feet, and shoved her into the path of the oncoming van.

The impact of the five thousand pound battering ram striking Nancy was sickening. Traveling at forty miles an hour, the vehicle launched her body thirty feet. The metal grill snuffed out her fragile life with no remorse. The driver of the white panel van didn't touch his brakes. Seconds later it was out of sight.

John and Jane surveyed the area to check if there were any unwanted witnesses, but there was no one else around. John went over to make sure the job was done. Once up close, the murderer realized he didn't need to check for a pulse. The grotesque pile of bone and tissue was no longer a living being.

John yelled, "Make the call," as he pretended to give CPR. Now there was a plausible reason for his DNA or clothing fibers to be present on the victim's body. He quickly located the problematic cell phone in a pocket. John scoured the impact area for any incriminating pieces of Roger's van that may have broken off.

"Nine-one-one. What is your emergency?" recited the dispatcher.

In a hysterical manner Jane Doe exclaimed, "My husband and I just saw a hit-and-run. A woman desperately needs an ambulance near the entrance of Peaceful Oaks Park. Please hurry!"

"Were you able to see what type of car hit the woman?"

"Yes. It was a late-model black Suburban. We saw it clearly but couldn't read the tag," answered Jane describing one of the most common vehicles on the road.

The call went out to local law enforcement agencies immediately. All available manpower mobilized and started pulling over bewildered housewives in their SUVs across eastern Virginia, southern Maryland, and the District of Columbia.

KENAI PENINSULA, ALASKA

An hour before the murder of Nancy Watkins took place, a bright red floatplane landed on a pluvial lake surrounded by serious mountains. The pilot silenced the growling radial engine and it got real quiet. The two men climbed out onto the floats to inhale the impressive scene. Despite an age gap that spanned two generations, Scott Horne and Zell Fergusson had personalities that meshed well.

"*Homo sapiens* existed organically for hundreds of thousands of years without a trace…look at us now. In a single day one modern person creates more everlasting debris than entire ancient cultures. What happened?" wondered Scott Horne. "Sorry, I have a tendency to fixate on the destructiveness of humanity while in untainted places."

"The natural world took a backseat while those with cash or credit became obsessed with accumulating the material American dream," offered Zell Fergusson, a no-nonsense bush pilot. "The humble house with a white picket fence has transgressed into a gated mansion filled with anything and everything."

"Capitalists tricked consumers into believing bigger is better, more is merrier," responded Scott.

"Mother Nature will counterattack. Yin and yang…cause and effect. Nastier diseases, worse floods…longer droughts. The hubbub is about protecting the environment…the battle cry should be "Save the people." Send the message that humans are an endangered species. The planet will survive forever in some form…it's the people who might not," plainly stated Zell.

"Maybe dinosaurs developed machines that changed the climate to the point that it killed them off?" asked Scott in an effort to lighten up the conversation's trajectory. "Who knows? Undiscovered societies may have already flourished and disappeared here on Earth."

"Interesting concept. We definitely still have a lot to learn about this place. We need to revamp the way we do just about everything, but it's not too late. The silver lining is that retrofitting infrastructures and creating alternative energies can be the engine to rehab the sagging economy. No other country is better equipped to lead the charge to sustainability," suggested Zell.

"I'm doing everything I can to treat the planet in a responsible manner," pointed out Scott, trolling for a compliment.

"You're a capitalist, but at least you take a clean approach to creating profits. The dramatized images people see on the talking box ignites a desire for those freedoms and lifestyles worldwide," reasoned the gritty man. "We should be using the airwaves to broadcast positive ideas. I fondly remember the era before TV dominated people's time."

"You're right...TV has had a negative impact on humanity...but humans are greedy by design. It's a carryover survival mechanism from our wilder days. Admittedly America has taken materialism to absurd levels. Consumerism has become as big a part of the American legacy as freedom. Our star power undeniably accelerated the urges the less-developed countries were bound to have," said Scott. "But individuals have a heart...multinationals don't. Giant corporations are the ones physically destroying the planet," argued Scott Horne.

"That's the main problem...too many individuals. Over the course of my life I've watched Earth's population explode. Corporations are just meeting demands. Don't blame them," said Zell.

"Yeah, but that doesn't mean conglomerates should operate without a conscience...disregarding the long-term impact of their money-making."

"It's too early in the spring...and too late in the day to be standing around yapping like this. Are you about ready to skedaddle while the visibility and sunlight are still good?" asked Zell Fergusson. He climbed back into the floatplane without waiting for an answer.

"Listen to you. It's getting cold and dark? It sounds like it might be time for you to retire," said Scott in jest.

"I'm hungry. The raw fish you brought us for lunch looked more like fishing bait than table fare. To me, cooking seafood is not optional," Zell suggested.

"No worries...let's ride out. I just wanted to hang here for a bit. For whatever reason, I've always loved this basin," answered Scott Horne. "Growing up I felt an unexplainable magnetism toward Alaska. The unparalleled magazine with the golden border fertilized the fantasy."

"I felt that same thing. I remember reading about Alaska as a boy and thinking "That's the place for me," said Zell.

10

"As a kid I had too much energy to sit still in school all day. The only learning material that interested me was the outdoor world. Temporarily memorizing facts for a test didn't seem beneficial in the long run."

Sounding slow and throaty, the DeHavilland Beaver idled as they made a visual check for traffic, though they hadn't seen another plane or person nearby all afternoon. The pilot shoved the throttle all the way to the stop, transforming the nine-cylinder radial engine into a snarling beast. The floatplane responded sluggishly for a few seconds. As the lumbering craft began to build up speed in earnest, the flight controls came alive, the wing wanted to fly. After letting the velocity climb a tad higher, Scott Horne gently pulled back on the yoke and became airborne. In a violent spray the wind blast scoured water off the pontoons. Instead of establishing a normal climb, Scott dipped the nose back down and flew parallel to the lake, gaining airspeed rapidly at the takeoff power setting.

At one hundred and fifty knots and only five feet off the lake, the owner of the plane was getting nervous. With decades of extra flying and life experience, Zell got ready to verbally intervene. Zell's only hesitation came from the fact that Scott Horne was his most profitable client. Possessing a sizable yet brittle ego, Zell knew Scott would find a reprimand irritating.

Fortunately Scott had gotten his kicks and pulled into a steep climb. The daredevil leveled off just before too much airspeed was lost and the wing stalled. "Your flight controls," offered Scott casually, as if nothing unusual had happened.

"My controls…darn hot dog," responded a relieved Zell. "As the longtime owner/operator of Zenith Aerial Solutions, I don't believe in unnecessary risk-taking. Flying in Alaska is dangerous enough on its own."

"That's why you're the bush pilot and I'm a businessman. Bad decisions in my line of work can't get me killed," said Scott.

"Businessman? Is that what you're callin' yourself? Playboy is more like it…your business is pleasure. People have showed me your mug in those colorful magazines. All gussied up in fancy clothes and probably wearing makeup to boot," responded Zell while climbing out of the lake basin.

"I draw the line at face paint…but I'm guilty as charged. It's not my fault, Zell. I blame it on cable television and, later on, the Internet. My generation was overloaded with information. Naturally I wanted to do everything and anything I could," observed the childish adult.

"Give me a break with that bunch of malarkey."

"With all the new gear and activities available, today's hedonists have a rough time staying focused. I have ravenous eyes. They constantly demand new landscapes and experiences to feast on. My id has no lid," responded Scott. "Although I do respect the fact that you always shoot straight with me. The ability to administer honest but tough assessments aloud is a rare and admirable trait. In both my private and business life, I'm inundated by yes-men and -women."

"Well, unlike them, I'm not for sale. As to all the new gizmos...I like old stuff that's built to last and made to be repaired, not replaced. Old stuff and the old way of living...feel better...purer."

"That's cuz you grew up in a different era with different values. I'm old-fashioned in many ways, but I like to mix in highlights from the modern world."

"Like your whirlybird? You shoulda been one of those fancy-pants big-city defense lawyers with your silver tongue. Your pretty boy looks would've helped you win over jurors too," suggested the seasoned veteran. Zell's core attitudes were a result of his wartime experiences.

Tired of talking, Scott transitioned into sightseeing mode. In his logic, stress came from ground problems, and there was no room for excess emotional baggage when aloft. It's dangerous to have your head in the clouds when actually among clouds.

Zell is the perfect bush pilot...always thinking ahead of time and erring on the side of caution. Too bad I am not more like him, Scott reflected.

Scott Horne's eccentric imagination played a crucial role in his rapid ascent as a businessman. He had earned enough money with a series of adventure resorts across the globe to begin creating real, long-term wealth. Horne's innovative properties were off the grid and in tune with nature, utilizing all technologies to negate their impact on the surrounding ecology. In the last decade he'd matured into a venture ecologist, investing in salvaging, recycling, wind farms, solar arrays, saltwater farming, and reforestation efforts across six continents.

Northern Virginia

In the plush headquarters of Applied Leverage, a high-tech hive of electronics surrounded three talented men. To operate most effectively, the firm employed the best hackers money could buy. In the murky business of big-dollar lobbying, nothing is considered cheating.

A specific ring sounded notified Peter Zahn that he had an incoming call from the ground team. "Talk to me."

"She's still out jogging. I stayed in the van, but I'm ready if she tries anything," said Roger.

"Make sure you have a cell phone jammer at the ready, just in case. Where is she, exactly?"

"Right now she's winding her way towards the back of the park...looks like she's doing the same route as yesterday," replied the private detective.

"Stay in touch," advised Peter, before setting down the encrypted phone. His blood pressure spiked. His thoughts were a mixture of dread and curiosity. "What type of game are we going to play today, Nancy?" Peter Zahn asked the others. "I have a bad feeling about this...Nancy Watkins is going to cross the line."

Zahn reluctantly remembered the instructions from his boss if Nancy did, indeed, make the mistake of sharing secrets. Zahn could sense it, he could taste it. If he trusted anything in life, it was gut reactions.

Two days ago Nancy Watkins had been a bad girl. Hidden video cameras had caught her snooping around Alan Reynard's office not once, but three times. Mr. Reynard had been grooming the young woman professionally and socially for years and was understandably devastated by the video evidence. Peter's supervisor still held out a molecule of hope that it was a big misunderstanding, but after coordinating round-the-clock surveillance of Nancy, the guys in the basement suspected otherwise.

"Is this going to get ugly?" asked Peter of his coworkers.

SOUTHCENTRAL ALASKA

It was a beautiful day to be up. Not a cloud in sight, negligible winds, and a windshield full of the visual splendor that defines Alaska. The mountains were covered by a heavy snowpack, but occasional patches of baby-blue glacial ice broke the duality of white snow and brown rock. The sun, wind, rain, and gravity had sculpted the snow into geometric shapes of gigantic proportions. Razor-sharp spines lined the steep ramps.

"The lake may have defrosted, but in the higher elevations it's still winter. It looks like a giant putty knife loaded with sticky snow has been scraped across the ridges leaving huge cornices. The world is a cake, and snow is the frosting," said Scott.

Peering down at Cook Inlet, Scott remembered that the occasional wanderer became trapped at low tide. "Do people still get stuck there?" he asked.

"The mud acts like quicksand. Unless the authorities are notified in time the hapless victim gets to watch the bore tide roll in to drown them. The rescue method is blasting the area surrounding their legs with a high pressure water hose mounted on a hovercraft," said Zell.

The floatplane approached the coordinated beehive of Merrill Field and Lake Hood, two of the busiest general aviation airports in the world. The heavy jets going in and out of Anchorage International added traffic and turbulence to the cluttered airspace.

Zell made the landing on Lake Hood and was water taxiing when Scott realized he still hadn't checked in with his personal assistant.

"Can I borrow your phone?" Scott asked as he grabbed a small backpack from the rear compartment.

"You know I don't own a cellular phone. I only have the satellite job, and it's for emergencies only," replied Zell.

"You can put it on my tab. Where is it?" said Scott thoughtlessly.

"You rich folks think you can buy anything. I'll get it for ya, but make it quick," asserted Zell, wondering "What happened to patience?"

For reasons he couldn't fully grasp, placing phone calls made Scott Horne anxious, but at least the advent of satellite phones had increased the scope of his office. A contemporary businessperson can make calls and work online while deep in the wilderness. Reluctantly Scott dialed the number of his personal assistant.

"Erin De Sousa."

"Erin, it's me, we just landed. Sorry about not calling yesterday. I guess I just spaced out. And today I was only on the boat for a couple hours before Zell picked me up," said Scott. "At the moment it's relieving to hear the soothing voice of my chief problem-solver."

"Yesterday was Thursday. You were supposed to call me on Tuesday," responded his savior in her cheerful English accent. "So much has happened with the trash collection barge…I don't even know where to start. A woman named Lara from Virginia phoned on the oh-six-eight-four number. She's rung nine times in the past two days. The poor girl seems distraught and very eager to talk to you. Maybe you're going to be a daddy?" said Erin, casting a verbal stone to get even with her inconsiderate employer.

"If I can help it, that is never gonna happen. Give me the most recent number she left, please," Scott politely demanded. Lara was the name he'd told Nancy Watkins to use when calling him. Scott memorized the number and in his own way apologized again for his AWOL status, "I promise to make a bigger effort to act my age."

He pushed the little red button ending the transmission. After receiving stimulating news, Scott tended to let his imagination run free. Over a year ago Scott had hired investigators to search for a breach in Applied Leverage's armor, and now maybe he had found an opening. Lost in a reverie, curiosity trumped caution and he dialed the eleven digits on Zell's sat-phone, instead of waiting a few minutes and exploiting the anonymity of a payphone or using a redialing service.

"You called back...finally," said Nancy as her greeting.

"Sorry about the delay. I was offline...out of touch. I am beyond thrilled you called," Scott replied.

"I wish you were here. I caught my boss misbehaving," she confessed. "My family worried about my decision to take a job working for a lobbyist. They argued that big city folks were different and politics are dirty, but I wasn't naïve to the potential downsides...I was in love. Alan Reynard seemed debonair and generous. But they were right...he's a crook. I feel violated, lost, and angry. I wasted seven years working for a sleaze-ball."

"Nancy, he's a lobbyist. His job is to subvert democracy...of course he does morally questionable things. Reynard co-founded Applied Leverage. Their clientele creates untold collateral damage in their tireless pursuit for earnings. Manipulating government representatives better than anybody else has earned Reynard hundreds of millions of dollars. Rich, powerful, and arrogant...Reynard is on the inside of Washington insiders," consoled Scott, feeling the fuzzy first hints of delight stirring in his chest cavity. Nancy Watkins was the personal assistant to Scott Horne's carefully chosen archenemy. "What went down?" queried Scott, trying to sound calm.

"The day before yesterday Alan, walked into the office carrying a box with a bow on top. I thought it might be a present for me, so naturally I was curious," explained Nancy. "When he left, I went into his office to sneak a peek, but I couldn't find the gift. Later on, I asked Alan for his key ring in order

16

to work during my lunch break. I opened the locked drawer...and there it was. Inside I found ten bundles of used one-hundred-dollar bills bound with rubber bands. Two-inch stacks, not like the kind from a bank."

"It's probably for a gambling debt, I bet tha-," interjected Scott before being cut short.

"I was nervous, of course, but like you, I thought there could be an innocent explanation. After lunch Alan asked me to call the driver so he could run an errand. When he left he took the gift. Later that day I made a point to go down to the garage. I flirt with the driver regularly, so it was no trouble to find out where they went. Eric said he drove the boss to the yacht club to deliver a birthday present for Senator Cumming's wife. Eric said Alan didn't even get out of the car, that the Senator met them in the driveway to accept the package. I made sure to confirm it was the same box."

"Happy birthday! Truthfully, it's no surprise. You can't say I didn't warn you about Reynard. It's not admissible in court, but very interesting, nonetheless," exclaimed Scott jubilantly. He meant to ask her about the possibility of surveillance cameras, but he forgot in the euphoria of the moment.

"I still had his keys at that point...so when Alan went out for his afternoon highball, I searched his office again. There was no trace of the money anywhere. Was I thorough enough? I thought you would be proud of me. I wanted to show you that I paid attention to your crash course last fall," said Nancy.

"You did the right thing. It takes a lot of courage to do something like this. Somebody has to stand up against this guy. People like him are ruining our country," said Scott.

"I feel so betrayed...I might go to the media," revealed Nancy. "My physical relationship with Alan ended eight months ago, but I hadn't fully extinguished my emotions for him until he shattered my trust with the secret bribe."

The skeptic in Scott couldn't fully grasp what he had been told. "I know that Reynard is crooked, but to be that sloppy is unbelievable," said Scott. Suddenly fear shot into the forefront of his consciousness. He too, was being flippant about security. "Hey, what phone are you using? Please tell me it's not your work or home line?" asked Scott with a mind full of dire consequences.

"I did what you said. I only used payphones to call you. This number is a prepaid cell from a liquor store. I bought it with cash yesterday," said Nancy.

Relieved, but not satisfied that all of the danger had subsided, Scott asked, "Who else have you told of this? These people can be extremely dangerous." Inside his stomach he experienced a queasy sensation caused by anxiety of the unknown.

"Alan's bribe makes me nauseous. In hindsight he's done lots of questionable things, but you're overreacting. Alan Reynard still loves me. I find the notion of Alan harming me laughable…although he may already be suspicious of something. Alan refuses to look me directly in the eye lately," reasoned Nancy.

"You should get out of there right now. I'm serious. I'll send someone to get your stuff. You're underestimating the stranglehold that money and power have over certain people. Get in between them and their fame and fortune and…watch out. You can't go to the media, Nancy…you have no physical evidence. Applied Leverage will attack your character, blackmail you, or make you disappear outright," said Scott.

"Calm down. The reason I called you is because you were the one who had Alan pegged, and I knew you would be on my side. Whatever I decide to do, rest assured I am not going to let this slide. Let me get back to you tomorrow or the next day. By then I'll have made a decision about my next move. I'm out jogging right now and it's getting dark," explained Nancy.

"Not to be rude, but anybody familiar with special interests knows Alan Reynard is dirty. It would be more accurate to say that I am the only person you've met who is trying to do something about it. Please believe me, a stealth approach is the only way to get even with him. The thing to do is stay in place and act normal. I'll send someone there to bring you some equipment. When the next opportunity to get some hard evidence presents itself…we'll be ready. Be careful and please don't tell anyone anything….."

"Okay…you're probably right. Talk to you soon. Thanks for the concern. Bye," said Nancy.

"Cheers." After ending the call, Scott worried about the unintended consequences of what he had been told. On his advice, Nancy Watkins had put herself into an extremely volatile situation.

NORTHERN VIRGINIA

Guilt seeped into his psyche as Roger listened in on the conversation. After what she had just said, the beautiful young lady wouldn't be celebrating her next birthday. The Applied Leverage detective pulled a round dish out of the open window. The background noise had been no match for the sensitive parabolic microphone. The hired hand patched Nancy's side of the call to Peter Zahn on his cell phone. Roger had tried to use the cellular jammer but had been out of its functioning range.

Roger's fears were confirmed when Peter Zahn instructed the team to activate emergency measures. Roger watched Nancy head back towards her convertible at a faster pace. They needed to move fast. The detective turned around to describe the plan to a man and woman they nicknamed John and Jane Doe. "We'll beat her back to the car and I'll drop you off. Keep her occupied curbside until no cars are around. When I come through, throw her into the van. Got it?"

The Does exited the vehicle and completed the task with ruthless efficiently.

Later that night in his basement lair, Peter Zahn impatiently waited for the Does to finish making their statements to the police. He wanted to analyze the rogue phone and begin to track down the person Nancy had spoken with. Everyone feared that the man at the other end of the line was affiliated with a government agency. If the Applied Leverage empire ever came crumbling down, Peter suspected the underlings would take the hardest fall, since the board of directors always covered their tracks. The executives had seen what happened to peers in the aftermath of a public scandal. Exuding paranoia is considered a healthy trait at Applied Leverage.

Knowing Applied Leverage, more than one person will end up dead over that call, thought Peter. He tried to convince himself that he was absolved of guilt, because when Nancy went snooping around she had effectively committed suicide. He felt just as culpable as Roger and the Does, but not as responsible as the decisions-makers on the top floor. Ultimately, they were the powers that be.

Two hours later the phone arrived and remarkably still functioned normally. The call history listed only one call. The number wasn't even blocked. The number bore a 907 area code, which meant Alaska. Since procuring information from telecommunications companies was so easy, Peter fired off a coded message to an online admirer asking her to sniff around. He anonymously maintained a network of wanna-bes who did little jobs for him in exchange for tutorials.

After an hour, the results appeared on his screen. Peter now had a starting point for his search to find out everything he possibly could about the man. He doubted there would be multiple listings in the sparsely populated state. A breach of the Alaska Division of Motor Vehicles yielded the basic facts: age, Social Security number, and, most importantly, a recent picture. Once the hacker had the SSN, the job became easier. Utility bills, bank statements, and medical records would be easily accessed by the keyboard magician.

Peter marveled at the fact that Web users willingly post information for the Internet community to peruse. A community that includes parents, teachers, relatives, employers, advertisers, local police, Feds, sexual predators, kidnappers, and identity thieves. *People ought to be real careful about what they upload,* reflected Peter, a man who personally contributed to the dangers of the Web.

"This man is well known…his disappearance won't go unnoticed. It seems strange this Alaskan would be involved in corporate espionage. He has certainly expressed a lot of anticorporate sentiment in the interviews I've read. The public will demand answers if it doesn't look accidental…which makes dealing with this a highly risky endeavor," said Peter to a coworker.

"I don't think your job description includes anything about making policy judgments," responded the underling.

Six stories above the basement, Bill Jones solemnly paced around his luxurious office, running a hand through his salt-and-pepper hair. He was waiting for the guy they referred to as "the hunter" to return his call. Bill Jones had been Alan Reynard's best childhood friend. It was an odd pairing, considering Jones hailed from a working-class family while Alan Reynard came from an old-money, silver-plated gene pool. As teenagers Bill had saved Alan and his big mouth from beatings too many times to count. At well over six feet and nearly three hundred pounds, Bill's presence alone usually dissuaded any would-be attackers. Over the years Alan rewarded Bill's loyalty with a solid career as the head of Applied Leverage's internal security unit.

The unenviable burden of informing Alan Reynard about the accident involving his mistress and personal secretary fell on Bill's shoulders. The hour was getting late, and Alan didn't appreciate being interrupted during his free time.

GEORGETOWN, DC

Alan Reynard was three tumblers of cognac deep into the evening's drinking when the iPhone resting near the edge of the Jacuzzi began to play a digital melody.

"Hey, Billy boy…strange to hear from you at this hour," answered Reynard, raising his frail body halfway out of the hot tub.

"I don't know how to tell you this. Nancy is gone, Alan. Some lunatic ran her down on the street," truthfully explained Jones.

"What a shame. I tried to warn her about the dangers of running on roadways," replied Alan, feeling sincere sadness about Nancy's fate. Immediately, his mind went into damage-control mode, reminding him that Nancy had brought this on herself. It didn't work, he felt awful.

"All in all, it's an extremely sad story, but sometimes bad things happen. If you need anything at all, let me know. So far, the police have no leads. It's not likely they will be successful in finding out the identity of the driver. You could offer a reward for any information that can assist the police," responded a smug Jones, pleased with the cleverness of his idea.

"Good call. Organize a press conference for tomorrow afternoon. I'll offer a hundred grand. Also, I think I will do something for her brother. She sent him money every month…he's a mongoloid, or something. Anyways, I'm a little tied up right now. Stop by my office in the morning," said Alan before he signed off.

"What happened?" asked Trixie, one of a dozen high-priced escorts Alan regularly utilized.

"An employee of mine was out jogging and was killed by a drunk driver. It's a very tragic situation," replied Alan, expressing concern.

"That's so sad…let Trixie make it better," said the affection peddler.

ZIMBABWE, AFRICA

Geographically, Africa is rich in diversity. Its ecosystems run the gamut from bone-dry deserts to lush equatorial rainforests. From towering mountain ranges to broad savannas. Deserts, rivers, forests, lakes, and a few short-time glaciers provide habitat for the most glamorous land-based wildlife to have survived the squeeze of humanity and its technologies. Landlocked Zimbabwe's claim to fame is Victoria Falls and the gorges of the Zambezi River.

The brown crust of the arid lowlands baked in the afternoon heat. Both humans and animals sought shade during the sweltering part of the day.

An eccentric man suffering from heat exhaustion, anxiety, and impatience raised his rifle calmly and took aim from the cover of a dense bush. Tall and lanky with the lean look of a swimmer, his youthful physique stood in stark contrast to his alcoholic's complexion and dark sunken eyes. The man's life-style demanded that he keep his body ready for any physical demands that might arise, but his genetics demanded frequent chemical escapes.

Two hundred meters away, a female black rhinoceros ate branches, oblivious to any danger. Hunting rhinoceros is illegal because few remain. The so-called Big Five animals attract desperately needed tourist dollars to impoverished nations.

"Do it. Take shot," whispered Hondo, the guide and tracker. Hondo struggled with guilt about his role helping this strange white hunter in the slaughter, but it meant his five children would prosper.

"I need to make absolutely sure beforehand," said Dewey in a condescending tone to demonstrate annoyance at the remark.

Within three seconds it happened. All his criteria for taking the shot had been met. The time to fire was upon him. Dewey exhaled and pulled the trigger as smoothly as possible. The bullet left the muzzle at nearly three hundred meters-per-second and instantly closed the gap on its collision course with the targeted mammal.

The thirty-five-year-old rhinoceros knew a gunshot when she heard one and dashed deep into a thicket unharmed. The poacher hadn't been as lucky. The large-caliber projectile entered under the shoulder and blew out a section of the man's torso as it exited.

"Please, we go now. Rangers hear gunshot, too," implored Hondo.

Dewey ignored the bushman. He was locked into that surreal dimension that his endocrine system rewarded him with when he committed himself to heavy experiences. As double doses of chemicals were being pumped into his vital organs, a feeling of invincibility swept over him. It was a powerfully addictive, narcotic-like sensation.

Oddly, the human-hunter was assaulted by something resembling remorse. The seeds of regret arrived uninvited and rudely spoiled his high. He tried to dislodge the train of thought by reassuring his guide, "I wouldn't shoot someone hunting bush meat…but this guy only wanted the horn. If word gets around that there is a poacher poacher roaming the bush, others may think twice," said the naïve foreigner. "The guy probably has a family to feed and all that…but there are less than four thousand black rhinos left on the planet and there are more than seven billion humans. It's tough luck that he chose to hunt rhino today," explained Dewey.

It was a twisted case of logic from the warped mind of a man few people knew well. Dewey spent his free time avoiding the places where humans were entrenched. The way to accomplish that was simple, stay away from the roadways. "Let's get back to the plane," he ordered, now fully past the initial rush and back into his default mode of problem-solving.

"I wait for rangers. Me no like you sky machine," said Hondo in a stab at humor that did not succeed in diverting their attention from the dead tribesman. The naked truth was that he had aided a white man in hunting down a fellow Shona to shoot in cold blood. This turned Hondo's stomach and undoubtedly angered the spirits. *This man will have much to answer for in the afterlife,* thought Hondo, *but without famous animals, no tourists would come and more villagers would be forced to relocate to the city. Nothing in this life is easy,* thought the bushman as he ran alongside the fittest white man he'd ever encountered.

Their getaway vehicle consisted of a small engine powering a propeller located behind tandem seats, all of which hung from an oversized hang glider wing. The aircraft had no instrumentation of any sort.

"Get in quickly and put the helmet on," ordered Dewey as he jumped in the front. He stowed the rifle, flipped the hidden kill switch, and toggled the ignition. When the engine settled into a steady idle, Dewey went to full throttle. After a short rollout he pushed the triangular bar forward and the craft jumped into the dry air.

Dewey stayed inside of the dry riverbed. Flying below ground level would keep them hidden. Anyone who heard the noise from out of eyesight would assume it was a motorbike. After ten minutes of flying in the opposite direction of his destination, Dewey went into a steep climb.

Flat, colorless veld unfolded in all directions. Vegetation was scarce on the arid landscape. The sun was getting lower and less intense, but the heated earth still roiled the dry air. Light turbulence shook the small craft. Dewey climbed to six thousand feet before making a gradual turn and circling back toward his real course. After finding his waypoints, he looked back to check on his flight-weary passenger. Hondo gave him a big thumb up and a genuine smile. He preferred being way up in the air to navigating the twists of the wadi.

Back in camp, the duo enjoyed a dinner of *sadza*. The local cornmeal staple had been combined with a thick vegetable stew of squash and okra seasoned by smoke from the wood fire.

Nightly, Dewey numbed his faculties with round after round of painkillers, alcohol, and tobacco products. *How strange that, these days, all my drugs of choice are legal.*

"You worry that your sky machine die one day?" asked Hondo pointing upward.

"Winged aircraft glide fine with no engine power. The key to making a successful emergency landing is having enough altitude to find a safe place to try one. Losing power on takeoff is worst-case, because you're too low and slow to choose where you set down."

"Maybe you like fear?"

"I do, but I like overcoming fear more," claimed Dewey. "Hondo, how is Zimbabwe going to protect these rhinos? I can't keep doing this."

"Chase people who buy and sell horn. Strange times. Some whites help Africa now. Others steal still. Better in dese times, I think. More happy. Less pain."

"For centuries foreigners have arrived seeking to exploit the natural resources. If it had value, it was collected and shipped away to points north, west, and east. Africa has been simultaneously pillaged and neglected by the Westernized world for half a millennium. It's a shameful history," said Dewey.

"Tell U.S. government that, maybe sending more help," suggested Hondo.

"The scars of colonialism have yet to heal. Overpopulation, genocide, disease, civil war, famine, corruption, deforestation, diamonds, oil, and climate change present enormous challenges for African nations. Tribal populations struggle to compete in an increasingly complex, corporate climate that revolves around profits. Part of the problem is that Africa is divided...it has hundreds of tribes...speaking hundreds of dialects...it's easier to manipulate a fractured populace."

"Sad to say Africa need many help," admitted the bushman.

"Hondo, did you know that man?" A shake of the head was all Dewey got in return. "You are obviously suffering from regret...don't worry, that's normal. The stack of cash I lay on you will do wonders for your guilty conscience. I better call and check the weather forecast before I get too drunk."

Shakily, Dewey got up from the ground and went to retrieve the satellite handset from the ultralight. After reinserting the battery, Dewey turned on the power and was shocked to see an incoming call. Only one person had the number of his satellite phone. With excitement, the Hunter called the number back using a redialing service.

"I am returning a call from this number."

"Where are you? How soon can you meet for dinner at the place we ate the day you shot that moose?" asked a relieved Bill Jones from his home.

"Indonesia. I can be there within twenty-four hours. See you at our spot between seven and nine the day after tomorrow?" responded Dewey. He winced when Jones referenced Alaska, since he spends time there. An especially elaborate disguise would be needed because a couple people actually knew him there.

"Sure," replied Jones immediately.

"Come alone," advised the assassin before disconnecting. *Jones responded effortlessly which meant something very important needed to be done fast.* In Dewey's line of work, doing things without proper preparations was dangerous, and dangerous jobs weren't done cheap. Rubbing his palms together, Dewey loosened the reins on his imagination and allowed himself to fantasize about the looming payday. The job also meant someone would cease to exist, but that was merely an unpleasant afterthought.

"Hondo, pack up the gear. No tracking tomorrow. Something more important came up. I have to leave earlier than I expected. Don't worry…I will still pay you the full amount we agreed on. Wake me up at first light."

"Okay, boss, poachers lucky," replied Hondo with a toothy grin. The man was happy to get away from the darkness of Dewey while still getting paid.

"If I hear of more rhinos being slaughtered, I'll be back when my schedule allows," informed Dewey. "I understand why starving people kill for bush meat, but trophy hunting or poaching for parts enrages me. Hunters should team up with wildlife biologists. They could shoot animals with tranquilizers, at which point the scientists could take measurements and change the batteries in the radio collars," suggested Dewey.

"People like kill," stated Hondo, while wondering what kind of job the hunter did to earn money. He harbored a guess.

"In less-than-lucid late-night moments, I toy with the idea of going after the wealthy distributors instead of the destitute poachers. I might be crazy, but attacking doctors who prescribe illegal and rare animal parts as medicine… seems noble."

ANCHORAGE, ALASKA

Scott Horne spent the morning working. In his tailored world that meant sipping caffeine in a downtown café, flirting with the baristas, and catching up on phone calls and emails. A good part of his energy went into perusing various print newspapers.

After a while he rode over to the University of Alaska to meet up with poet and historian Jed Shern. As an eternally curious person, Scott was driven toward people who possess answers.

"On this visit I want to learn about the history of a tiny island I'm considering in Alaska's narrow southeast panhandle. Being a guy who subscribes to vibes, I want to check if the isle has ever been the site of something sordid."

"Ah, the life of a rich man," teased Jed.

"Part of what makes it fun to be rich is that I have the opportunity to indulge dreams that I formulated while I was poor."

After searching the archives without finding any references to the islet, Scott and Jed decided to take a late afternoon bike ride. They talked as they pedaled along.

"I'm one of those people who have to exercise regularly if they want to eat the foods they enjoy most. Plus I'm a fresh-air fanatic, which dovetails nicely with one of my other addictions. I love to be in motion. The paths of Westchester Lagoon are an ideal place to indulge my lungs and my restlessness," said Scott.

After the ride they admired the distant volcanoes while doing some dynamic stretching. The men used their hands to block themselves from staring into the sun. Brilliant columns of color were silhouetting the jagged massifs of the Alaska Range.

"That star is almost done shining on this part of the world for the day," commented Jed.

"I would live in AK full-time if it wasn't dark for half the year and bright the other half. The uneven sunlight distribution would unbalance my brain...which is naturally imbalanced. Living way up north is suitable only for people with an ironclad disposition," said a slightly embarrassed Scott. "If Anchorage were sited in the hospitable mid-latitudes...it would be a metropolis burdened by millions."

"Alaska is indeed a place inhabited by people who feel special, even a little smug about living at the end of the Earth. One overlooked perk about residing on top of the world is that it's easy to get to places in the Northern Hemisphere by flying over the North Pole," said Jed.

"Regardless of latitude, the city of Anchorage sprouted in a spectacular setting," said Scott.

"Even Alaska's biggest city is inundated with natural beauty. Immediately to the west is Cook Inlet. The east edge of the city crawls up the Chugach Mountains. To the south, fauna-rich Turnagain Arm has one of the strongest bore tides in the world and is a hunting ground for beluga whales. Dall sheep showcase their mountaineering skills right along the highway. Northward two mighty rivers, the Matanuska and the Susitna, flank the fertile Mat-Su Valley, with the Talkeetnas beyond. In the far west is the otherworldly Alaska Range," said Jed in summary.

"I admire the tough folks who live year-round in the extreme northern latitudes. Winters in AK, Canada, Greenland, Scandinavia, and Russia are hardcore," stated Scott.

"It's too moist today to see the tallest mountain in the world," said Jed. "It takes a particularly clear day to view Denali from Anchorage with the naked eye."

"Everest is the highest," replied Scott.

"You need to work on your listening skills. Not the highest, the tallest… measured by the elevation change from base to summit. Denali climbs from around two thousand feet above sea level all the way to twenty thousand, three hundred and twenty. Everest starts at around fifteen thousand and tops out at just over twenty-nine thousand. Side by side on equal footing, Denali would tower nearly a vertical mile higher. Is a five-foot man standing on a chair taller than a six-foot man?" asked the professor.

"I'm terrified by high altitude mountaineering. I like oxygen too much. Have you ever flown around McKinley with Geeting?"

"Yeah, I have stayed at the Ruth cabin a few times. You should call it Denali. The mountain has been a crucial part of Native Alaskan culture for eons, but politicians renamed it after President McKinley. It didn't take… Alaskans still call it Denali," said Jed, concluding his lesson. "You seem out of it today."

"I'm worried about a friend…she's playing with fire," responded Scott. Throughout the day he had been fretting about Nancy Watkins, even though she had said she might not call back until the next day. Tonight Horne was going to stay in Anchorage, but in the morning it was time for the nomad to go home.

NORTHERN VIRGINIA

"How could this have happened? How did someone get close enough to Nancy to convince her to spy on me without us picking up on something? I thought your main job was to keep an eye on our employees? I mean, come on. Our counterespionage budget is sky high. Isn't it?" asked Alan Reynard of his security chief, between sets at Applied Leverage's indoor tennis court.

"I'm sorry, Alan. We hadn't picked up anything on her phone lines or computer usage. Since you stopped being an item, we have been following her several times a week, as you requested. She hasn't been meeting up with anyone new, as far as we can determine. It appeared that she was living a very vanilla life. Boy, were we mistaken," admitted Bill Jones humbly.

"Has Peter been able to obtain the whole recording?" asked Alan.

"Peter's working on getting the other side of the conversation from the telecommunications company that handles the calls for that type of prepaid phone. Since you always say it's better to be safe than sorry, I made arrangements with the Hunter to meet me in Anchorage tomorrow," replied Bill Jones. He wasn't in a position to remind Alan that this whole ordeal would have been completely avoidable if Alan had used simple common sense. It was Alan that brought that box into his office, gave Nancy his keys, and then left her unattended.

"I don't want to know any details. Clean this up pronto, using whatever methods you need to, but keep in mind that this thing happened under your jurisdiction," said Alan. "I am not going to sit back and watch all of my hard work disintegrate because of this."

ANCHORAGE, ALASKA

The next afternoon Dewey touched down on a nonstop from Heathrow to Ted Stevens, arriving with enough time to do a little research before his meeting with Bill Jones. After doing some errands to assemble his kit, Dewey sought out something which had become an increasingly rare commodity in the cellular age, a functional public payphone. After finally finding one with a dial tone, he entered the number of a loyal snitch who worked the flight desk at Frontier Executive Air Services.

"Wally, it's your pal with a few screws loose."

"Don't fuss over your mental state…being crazy is in. Why haven't you had any work for me?"

"At this very moment I have five Ben Franklins burning a hole in my pocket. Go down to your work and get the tail numbers of all the private jets that arrived in the last twelve hours. I'm interested in one that came from the lower forty-eight. My guess is that it originated from somewhere on the Eastern Seaboard," explained Dewey.

"It's nice to hear from you after such a long lull. There's no need to go down to the airport, I just got home from work. As of half an hour ago, there were only two jets on the tarmac. One is owned by a local oil exec and the other came from Baltimore. The jet fuel was paid for by START, Inc. They arrived at around eleven this morning. They only paid for one day of tarmac parking. They are scheduled to leave tonight. I happened to chat up the pilots. They said it's a cushy job, lots of exotic destinations," said Wally.

"How many souls?" asked Dewey.

"There was only one passenger. Older-looking guy...a true giant. I watched him descend the stairs and then he disappeared into a town car. Never came inside, which struck me as peculiar," said Wally.

"Go down there anyway and get the tail number for me. Then head over to The Alaskan Bush Company. Don't keep me waiting too long, or some of your money will end up decorating the G-strings of the hardworking ladies."

A half hour later, Wally arrived at the establishment and nursed a gin and tonic while making small talk with his cash-laden buddy. Dewey drank coffee and searched the talent pool for his next lap grinder. Wally wasn't normally a strip-club devotee, especially during daylight hours, but he had trouble ignoring the acrobatic aspect of the stage performances. After receiving the information and giving the snitch his payoff, Dewey eventually tired of scented body spray and asked his buddy for a ride to the airport. The two men left the club and headed outside.

"It's still weird for me to walk out of a darkened bar into the sunlight," said Wally.

"Why?" asked Dewey. "I see nothing wrong with it."

When they arrived at the departure terminal, Dewey hopped out of the car and said goodbye. Loyal to his habit of misdirection, Dewey waited until Wally drove off before catching a cab back to his motel to begin getting into a new costume.

East of Anchorage, Zell Fergusson and Scott Horne were back in the DeHavilland Beaver. Skies were gray and overcast, but Scott held out hope that sightseeing visibility would improve as the flight progressed. They were flying low to stay under a thick layer of clouds. At that moment, the red floatplane was crossing over the lovely town of Girdwood, home to the world's northernmost temperate rainforest.

"Alyeska is one of only a few ski areas with a base elevation of sea level. Considering its challenging inbound terrain, light crowds, and heavy annual snowfall, the resort has to be the best of the bunch," said Scott.

A few minutes further and the historic seaport of Whittier slid beneath them. During World War II, Whittier was the auxiliary port in case Seward got bombarded by the Japanese. The nook of a town is accessed by a narrow, one-way, two-and-a-half-mile-long automobile/train tunnel that changes direction every half hour. The lasting physical legacy is the abandoned military barracks, which are by far the biggest buildings around.

"Those abandoned structures are a bane to adults and a boon to teenagers," said Zell, scoping the crumbling concrete.

From five thousand feet up and at a hundred and twenty knots of airspeed, Scott Horne was studying the lay of the small port when he spotted a familiar catamaran.

"That twin-hull is stout but swift," said Scott.

"The one that conducts tours of glaciers?" asked Zell.

"It noses in so close that you can feel it when chunks break free and crash into the water, while you enjoy a cocktail chilled by glacial ice," remembered Scott.

In the distance, glaciers choked most valleys. Tall as a high-rise building and calving in enormous chunks, the frozen watercourses are Alaskan landmarks. Extreme pressures have pushed all of the oxygen out of the ice, resulting in a dreamy aqua-blue hue. Continuing eastward, the men compared the cabins and fishing lodges that dot the jumbled rock-strewn coastline.

"There she is. Back to your fairy tale," said Zell.

"I regularly try to convince others that materialistically I'm traveling lightly in life. I guess the navy-blue vessel we're approaching suggests otherwise."

"Your vessel appears to have been designed by a marine architect who had been heavily influenced by old James Bond movies. How long is it, again?" asked Zell.

"The *Arana* is a catamaran and measures eighty-five feet long and fifty feet wide, although each pontoon is a slender twelve feet wide and a squat ten feet high. Without deep keels, it can access places with as little as five feet of water...a rare luxury on a large sailboat."

"Oh, yeah, with a shallow draft you're able to explore rivers, lagoons, and estuaries."

"The spider-like central pod owes its styling to my affinity for air traffic control towers…and tree houses. The eighty-foot-tall mast is topped by a small crow's nest."

"I'll have to check it out next time. I have never seen anything quite like it," said Zell.

"The entire boat is recycled aluminum and was engineered with a "function before fashion" ethos. The port hull has the kitchen, a dining room/lounge, a bar, two heads, and six staterooms. The kitchen is a stainless-steel masterpiece with all the tools and appliances needed to create a gourmet meal for twenty. The rear of each hull is devoted to mechanical systems. The front houses a full music studio of actual instruments and digital recording equipment. The remaining space was kept open, except for a set of shelves that ride on railroad tracks that run along the ceiling. This enables the shelves to be compressed when not in use," explained Scott proudly.

As the duo approached the strange vessel, Scott asked, "Can I do a low-level flyby?"

"I'm not in the mood."

"Ten years ago you would have buzzed the bridge so close it would have shaken," said Scott.

"Pfffftt."

Zell took over the flight controls and established a slow descent by cutting back on the power while keeping the same angle of attack. With less speed across the wing, less lift was created and the plane slowly lost altitude. From two hundred feet, Zell could see someone heading over to the dinghy to meet them as he dropped the Beaver down below two hundred feet. The layer of clouds cut down on glare. With light winds and waves, the sea landing was smooth.

Scott thanked Zell and jumped into the waiting tender. After a mere two days, it felt comforting to be home. His growing sense of calm was especially welcome, since he still hadn't heard from Nancy Watkins. The nerve-bending situation needed to be resolved.

ANCHORAGE, ALASKA

At a quarter to seven, Dewey leisurely strolled the half mile to the rendezvous, periodically checking for a tail. In the past he had done jobs for Bill Jones and had no reason to suspect foul play from the man, but Dewey didn't completely trust anyone. The large door of the Ninth Street Café beckoned, but he spent a bit of time acclimating to the scene outside the restaurant. Satisfied that he was all alone, the paranoid man entered the establishment.

The girth and paleness of Bill Jones stuck out against the dark wood panels. Casually, Dewey took a seat with his back to the majority of the patrons. Dewey kept his coat, hat, and gloves on. The ambient noise of the after-work crowd would keep their conversation discreet and make it difficult to record.

"Geez...you really do have a knack for changing your appearance," said Bill, holding his drink up in a salute.

Possessing a set of forgettable facial features and an average stature helped the transformations. His sameness gave Dewey a blank slate for building disguises. "What do you got?" asked the Hunter.

"This needs to be done yesterday. This guy needs to have an accidental plane crash," softly explained Bill, as he slid an envelope across the table.

"Negatory. No plane crashes," plainly stated Dewey, disgusted by the method requested. Dewey handed the elderly man a slip of paper reading Bank of Liechtenstein, #8791424011. "I would never sabotage an aircraft."

"I remember you telling me you could do anything, but now you have all these conditions," Bill pointed out, testing the waters.

"Listen carefully to me. I will do it my way or not at all. If you guys know someone better, call 'em," said Dewey, bluffing. Currently Bill Jones was his only source for lucrative illicit work, but if times got really tight, Dewey could always return to his specialty of freelance blackmailing.

"Fine, just make it look like a robbery gone wrong or something accidental."

"It's going to be one hundred and twenty this time. Not only did you interrupt an important project...you want this done immediately. Two big-time negatives," countered Dewey, holding up two fingers for emphasis.

"That's not up to me," Jones replied honestly.

"I'll check the account in two hours. If there's a deposit, whoever it is inside this envelope will perish. If not…lose my number," concluded Dewey as he snatched up the man's scotch and slammed it down in one swig, careful not to let his lips touch the glass. Jones looked up and started to protest, but all he saw was the Hunter's back.

Dewey inhaled and exhaled deeply a few times, once he was safely around the corner. He had this persistent paranoia about Bill betraying him and having a squad ready to ambush him. After verifying he was still completely alone, Dewey pulled out a miniature digital recorder and replayed the conversation. After listening to Bill's responses three times, he decided the negotiation had gone well.

He jumped in a taxi and headed over to Frontier Executive to test out Jones's direction-following skills. Ten minutes later, Bill Jones pulled up in a taxi and rushed into the building. *That's a good sign, he came alone like I requested. Good job, Billy.*

Dewey walked the three miles back to his motel. The exercise and crisp sea air served to center his mind while fighting the effects of the recent time-zone shuffle. Back in the privacy of his room, he opened the ominous envelope with zeal. A surprised Dewey examined an enlarged driver's-license photo. After further inspection, the assassin recognized the face. Over the years, Dewey had crossed paths with the guy multiple times at remote lodges. He remembered admiring the man thoroughly, but Bill Jones represented his best income source.

Committing the address to memory, Dewey lit the corner of the printout with a Zippo and used it to light a cigarette before tossing the charred remnants into the toilet.

He spread a street map out on the bed and checked his watch. Dewey put on his coat, hat, and gloves and walked out to a pay phone in the lot. Using a redialing service, he placed a call to the Caribbean. After a woman with a sultry British accent verified the account number and his password, she explained that $120,000 U.S. dollars had been deposited twenty minutes ago. Dewey moved the money to a different account, the first of many evasive tactics he would employ to protect his loot from whoever might try to separate him from it. *If it was that easy to get one twenty, I should have asked for more. All in all, not a bad paycheck for an ex-bartender*, thought Dewey with a full-face smile.

The payment had been made, so the killer became serious. He scrubbed his entire body in the shower and shaved his head and face with a razor to cut down on rogue DNA. He dressed methodically in a brand-new, dark-blue sweat suit and extra socks to make up for his boots being two sizes too big. Gathering up his equipment, he couldn't help feeling like he was forgetting something. Two knives and a homemade garrote were the only lethal weapons he would carry. He decided not to bring a firearm, because he was confident he could surprise and overwhelm his target. Additionally, he was leery of the potential forensic pitfalls involved with guns.

With everything dialed, Dewey donned gloves and a skull cap and stalked into the crisp night toward his rental car a few blocks away. After stopping for gas along the Old Seward Highway, the killer headed south on the town's lone expressway.

PRINCE WILLIAM SOUND, ALASKA

"Usually we get on well, but at other times I've considered axing this relationship due to philosophical differences. There is one major thing we agree on. Both of us want to spend the rest of our days exploring the world, pursuing both remote and urban adventures," said the helicopter pilot.

"In my eyes, a person's life is measured by the tracks he's laid across the planet and the people he's touched, not in the wanton accumulation of objects. I'm not sure where things went off track," said Scott Horne.

"No offense, but in the U.S. what's with psychopaths opening fire on innocent strangers or coworkers. Is there something in the water?" queried Byron Richardson, a verbally brash fellow.

"Who knows? It's an ugly, uncomfortable question. One guess is cable television," responded Scott Horne.

"That's a cop-out. Violence on the telly does not cause people to commit horrible acts. No way mate…you're dead wrong on that one. On an individual level, humans have been getting less and less violent," said Byron.

"You misunderstood me. I meant watching too much television leads to an unfulfilling indoor lifestyle that can help certain people to snap. That and cheap, accessible guns, but it's not the guns, it's the people. If no guns existed, people would use a car or a rock to the same end. Some brain chemistries are destined to go berserk, others seem to need a catalyst, an emotional or physical trauma. I guess in the good ole U.S. of A. we have a knack for itching each other's trigger fingers," morbidly summarized Scott.

"I support gun control. A shooter has to keep a firm grip on a weapon when firing it. That's an interesting theory about the idiot box. I think it has more to do with people being frustrated by their inability to achieve the American Dream. Or maybe the chemicals in factory foodstuffs make them go batty. The grocery stores in the States look like gigantic bloody walk-through vending machines. It's truly…a circus atmosphere," criticized the New Zealander. Byron almost mentioned the prescription drug cartels and their pills-for-profit schemes, but he knew those were sore subjects with his boss.

"Corporations have bastardized food in this country to the point where it's unrecognizable. Starving dogs wouldn't eat most of the stuff children do. As far as negatively impacting public health for profit, food factories are in a league of their own."

"But people choose to buy the stuff," reasoned Byron.

"The argument that no one forces anyone to eat those foods is irrelevant, because those with low incomes are forced to buy the garbage. It's cheap and doesn't take any time or skill to prepare. Manufacturers of engineered, preservative-laden factory products own a large slice of the responsibility for the myriad of health epidemics plaguing America," stated Scott.

"Conventional wisdom would be that the country with the world's best farmlands would eat the healthiest food. In truth it's quite the opposite," added Byron, fueling the ire.

"If you were to take a random sampling of the shiny packages lining the aisles at the local megastore, grind it up, and add some water, you would have a better chance of embalming a body than nourishing one," weighed Scott.

"Why doesn't the government protect the public from toxic foods?"

"Money. Lobbyists. Look I'm tired of trying to explain the unexplainable to inquiring foreigners. Curiosities about the ironies of Uncle-Sam-Land are understandable…but your questions are the same ones I ask myself. More often than not, I have no logical answers, only guesstimates. Who nominated me as press secretary?" answered Scott.

"Get over yourself, mate," suggested the Kiwi.

ANCHORAGE, ALASKA

It was a clear, cold night. The hired killer parked his rig a half mile away by road after checking out the neighborhood. By cutting through some Black Spruce trees, it was only three hundred yards to the target's home. The waning moon reflected enough light for Dewey to navigate quietly. He approached the cabin cautiously, since Alaskans love their guns.

The saddle-notched log cabin stood two stories high. It was surrounded by evergreens and dense blackberry bushes, and it looked to be over a half century old. Tall trees blocked the moonlight, which Dewey initially interpreted as an unnerving harbinger but quickly dismissed the negative thought. There wasn't a single light burning or any cars in the driveway.

The agile man climbed onto the carport to gain access to a second story, but the window was locked. Dewey used the butt of his knife to bust a hole in the glass, unlocked the latch, and removed the dowel that prevented the old wooden window from sliding open. Climbing into the bedroom in darkness, Dewey operated under the assumption that somebody could be behind any corner. He searched the house with the night vision function on a handheld camcorder. Heat radiated from the wood-burning stove and the distinctive smell of cooked caribou hung in the air. *He must have just left.*

The cabin was decorated in a minimalist, almost museum fashion, but what was there was impressive. Giant hand-carved hardwood elephants, a jade Buddha, and a realistic suit of armor seemed out of place. Other smaller, more fragile artifacts lined a large built-in shelf. Native Alaskan art and wood carvings were predominant. Dewey was struck by the eclectic artwork of the cabin, which looked especially dramatic in the green hue of night vision.

Without an auditory warning, synchronized halogen lights invaded the cabin's serenity. *Somebody's home*, thought Dewey positioning himself for an ambush but feeling oddly apprehensive about it. *This guy is someone I genuinely admire and Bill is the kind of person I hate. Have I completely lost the plot? I already have the money. Could I take their cash and disappear?*

The sound of a deadbolt's tumbler cut short his process tree. Even when given time to fruit, it was a damaged tree that was several limbs short of being healthy. Frustrated with himself for being distracted, Dewey quickly reset his focus and stepped back into the role of executioner.

After steeling himself, Zell entered the cabin barrel first and locked the door behind him. "You better just come on out, varmint. We've got you surrounded," suggested Zell in an aggressive voice as he switched the lights on. Luckily for Zell, he had seen fresh footprints in the snow and mud that led to discovery of the broken window upstairs.

This time Dewey feared there would be no easy solution. He had lost the element of surprise. "Ah, sir, there has been a mistake," called out Dewey from the pantry.

"No problem, son. Everyone errs. Come on out with your hands held high."

Not having any other choice, Dewey came out palms up and found himself staring across the room into the business end of a small pistol.

"Listen here, we are going to take a little walk over to my neighbor's house to use the phone," Zell commanded.

"Can't we work this out without the police?" Dewey pleaded.

"No chance," plainly responded the angry homeowner.

A split second later, Dewey played his only card and broke for the stairs, gambling that either the old man wouldn't shoot or that the short-barrel's accuracy wouldn't be good enough at that range. The two loud explosions that rocked the room dashed the first hope. The latter theory also proved to be incorrect as Dewey experienced two horrific impacts in the central torso. He went down to the ground and struggled to breathe.

"Look what you made me do," screamed Zell as he cautiously approached the withering intruder lying on his stomach. In over seven decades, this marked the first time Zell truly couldn't believe what he was seeing. "I'm going next door to call an ambulance...you're going to be all right, son."

"Please roll me on my side, I'm choking on my own blood," begged the gunshot victim.

Keeping the gun in his right hand, Zell got down on one knee. As soon as he grabbed the man's shoulder, the intruder spun around in a flash, grabbed Zell's wrist, and pushed it away. Zell fired twice, but both shots harmlessly lodged in a cedar cabinet.

With his free hand, Dewey stabbed the elderly man in the bicep of the arm with the handgun, causing him to drop it. Dewey was stunned and breathless, but alive and with cunning had turned the tables on the old man. If it weren't for his bulletproof vest he would have been dead meat.

The two men struggled to get control of each other's limbs. Finally able to get his good arm free, Zell punched the burglar in the nose several times and landed a knee to the groin. This stunned the burglar enough that Zell was able to wrestle the knife from him by gouging his left eye. Just as Zell stood up halfway and sensed the fight was turning his way, he was hit with a surging force. Instantly the scrapper became immobilized and fell limply to the floor with the heaviest part of his body leading the way. Dewey reached over and zapped him again with the 200,000-volt stun gun, to be absolutely sure the lion was completely incapacitated.

After securing Zell, a severely shook-up Dewey grabbed the pistol and considered his options. Following a quick survey of the scene, Dewey decided that with his DNA splattered everywhere, he would have to torch the place. The weakened man went outside to retrieve his jug of gasoline. He thoughtfully spread three gallons of ninety-one octane around the cabin and then opened all the windows and doors to give the blaze better access to oxygen.

With all of his pre-fire preparations made, Dewey stuffed a gas-soaked rag into a bottle of Zell's whiskey. After lighting the wick, he tossed the Molotov cocktail violently against the floor. When the glass broke, the flammable contents spread out and then ignited a split second later. Aided by the accelerant, the old wooden cabin was swiftly submerged in flames.

PRINCE WILLIAM SOUND, ALASKA

One hundred miles east of Anchorage, the *Arana* pulled defiantly on her anchor as a huge tide receded. When the captain made an announcement on the P.A. that Byron had a personal phone call, it unsettled him. Everyone who had the number had been told to use it only in a serious emergency.

Byron entered the pod and gave a nod. Captain Dan gestured toward the handset resting on the counter and then walked out to give the Kiwi some privacy. "This is Byron Richardson speaking."

"Hello, Byron, it's Marissa," said the caller morosely.

"Hey, sweetie…is everything all right?" asked Byron Richardson. He and Marissa were in a long-distance relationship in both the emotional and physical sense. Scott Horne had sent Byron to romance Marissa so he could get close to her best friend, Nancy Watkins.

"Sorry to bother you…I know you didn't want me to use this number, but there has been a dreadful accident."

"It's no trouble."

"Nancy Watkins was hit by a car while jogging two nights ago. She didn't make it," explained Marissa painfully. The last few words were spoken through sobs.

Byron felt dizzy. He had been so worried about something like this happening, it gave him night terrors. After a long pause he finally managed a response. "Sorry…I am in shock. Why did you wait so long to call? What happened? Who hit her?" Byron wanted the five W's answered, hoping that somehow it might have been an actual accident.

"Some maniac mowed her down right next to her car and didn't even stop. A couple saw the whole thing. Thankfully the police have really mobilized on this. They are checking every registered Suburban within two hundred miles. Nancy's boss personally offered a one hundred thousand dollar reward for information leading to an arrest," explained the distraught woman.

"Wow." Inside his screaming mind Byron plotted revenge. A realization bounced into his head. "Marissa, I hate to cut you short…but I have to fly right now. I was in the helicopter when you called. Let me call you back in a couple hours. I am very sorry about your loss, the loss in general. A beautiful soul has been taken back way too early," consoled Byron. "Try to fight off the sadness with exercise. Talk to you later, darling."

Generally Byron Richardson was a reasonable man wielding a temperament not prone to violence. However, if severely provoked, he had the potential to go aggro like anyone else. Byron needed to exact a prompt reprisal, and one of the people responsible for Nancy's death was conveniently located onboard. He stormed out of the bridge looking for Scott, finally catching him in the kitchen chopping mangos. Byron didn't consider the implications of the dangerous length of folded steel Scott wielded.

"You think you are so smart. You've done it this time," yelled the pilot as he approached Scott at a fast clip.

Scott believed Byron was messing around, as they had been chatting amicably minutes earlier. Sensibly, he set down the razor-sharp blade and balanced himself in case his pal tried something. Scott should have paid more attention to the available clues.

Instead of grabbing him, Byron threw a vicious right cross that practically knocked Scott off his feet. Confused by the sucker punch, Scott did what he always did when he found himself at a disadvantage in a fight. He shot in, grabbed a leg, and took the opponent down to the ground. Each man struggled for control of the other's limbs, but nobody gained a clear advantage. Byron was stronger, but Scott had the advantage of gravity.

At that moment the lead ski guide, Christian, walked into the kitchen. Initially amused by the spirited grappling match, he didn't realize it was a real fight until Scott broke free and postured up. Once he got his favored left arm free, Horne landed several elbows onto the forehead and face of Richardson.

Christian reacted in a flash, running over and grabbing Scott in a bear hug around the torso and dragging him off the motionless man. The second-to-last elbow had knocked the pilot's lights out.

"Why are you two fighting? What's wrong with you?" questioned the mutual friend.

"I wish I knew. Byron came up saying some nonsense and then sucker punched me. He might have broken my nose. He's lucky you saved him," Scott explained between deep breaths.

"Go to your cabin and keep your head tilted back. I'm going to get the captain to check out Byron."

"When he wakes up, tell him that if he wants to throw cowardly punches…he should become a bouncer," quipped a blood-soaked Scott, still fuming over the unprovoked assault.

"Give it up. You won the fight...get out of here."

After checking on Byron, the captain came by Scott's stateroom to suss out what had happened. After examining Scott's nose and determining that it wasn't broken, Dan stated, "I take a dim view of fistfighting on my vessel, but I acknowledge the need to defend yourself when attacked," and walked out.

Scott awkwardly tried to impose his own brand of logic on the thought processes of others. He couldn't grasp why his Z-land pal would attack him without provocation.

When needing a positive emotional nudge, Scott confronted the obstacle with music. A small digital device loaded up with thousands upon thousands of songs acted as an adult blankie. He hit the button and the Bob Marley album *Kaya* began recalibrating his disposition. *How did I ever function without these things?*

The blood flowing from Scott's nose eventually subsided. He smoked some painkilling flowers to ease the throbbing. The anxiety he felt about losing Byron as his helicopter pilot went up in smoke. Scott fell headlong into the reggae rhythms, but a half hour later a lazy knock on the door revived his alertness.

"Come in, but be aware I have a loaded gun pointed at you," bluffed Scott, who subscribed to using the abstract power of laughter to diffuse tension.

Byron entered the stateroom cautiously with his hands raised in the universal someone-is-pointing-a-gun-at-me position. The lumped-up man looked sadder than Scott had ever seen. One of Byron's eyes was bruised and puffy, and there were several knots on his forehead. For the first time since the bout, Scott experienced remorse.

Menacingly Byron still had rage in his eyes. The Kiwi broke the tense silence, "You killed her, mate...got her killed...whatever, same outcome."

Scott's nimble mind worked fast to digest the statement and consider the ramifications. Within seconds he understood what had caused Byron to attack him in such a manner. He didn't have to ask who Byron was referring to. "Nancy told me she had stayed off her regular phones. How could this have happened so quickly? Why kill the girl? She had been Alan Reynard's mistress. Fire her, sure. But end her life?" Scott Horne's normally optimistic outlook choked under a surge of self-doubt and guilt. "I debated whether or not Nancy was in immediate danger, but I decided it was an unlikely possibility. I blew it." It had been a difficult decision to make and would torment him for the rest of his days. Questions came into his mind rapidly, but Scott could only muster, "What happened?" before he choked up.

"They ran her down like a dog in the street. We, you and I, are going to avenge this. Marissa's brother could help us, as well," said Byron, leaving no wiggle room for Scott to slip through.

"I don't threaten to do things that I plan on doing. Prosecutors call it premeditation. Look, I was already going to sabotage Applied Leverage to the best of my ability, but now they've raised the stakes...and accelerated the timetable. I admit you were right all along. You warned me repeatedly to leave the girl alone...wish I woulda listened to ya, pal," Scott confessed to his friend.

Scott wondered how Applied Leverage had found Nancy out. He harbored a gut-wrenching suspicion that somehow Alan Reynard had monitored their satellite-phone conversation. In a revolting memory of that terrible call, Scott remembered using Zell's phone that day. *If Applied Leverage permanently silenced Nancy with such speed and audacity, they are definitely going to try to silence whoever they thought was on the other end. Nancy said she used a new phone, but she ended up dead anyway. Could they have listened in on the conversation using other means?*

Suddenly Scott brushed past Byron and ran up the stairs, across one of the struts and into the bridge. He found the satellite handset and dialed from memory the number of Jed Shern with shaky fingers.

"Pick up, pick up. Come on..." muttered Scott, determined not to be responsible for yet another death.

Anchorage, Alaska

"Jed Shern," mindlessly answered the comatose professor.

"Jed! It's Scott Horne. Zell's having an emergency. Get in your car and go over to his house. I will explain on the way. Bring your shotgun."

"My shotgun? Slow down, kid…what's going on exactly?" asked an instantly-alert Jed, while shoving the covers off. Jed grabbed his bird gun and loaded it with people shells.

Jed's wife of twenty-five years, Gina, awoke and became justifiably frightened by what she saw. "Jed, you're scaring me! What is going on? Who are you speaking with?"

"It's nothing, honey, go back to bed," lied Jed, as he headed toward the garage.

Scott tried to think of what to tell Jed, but he couldn't come up with anything the sharp-witted man wouldn't see through. Panic handicapped Scott's shocked mind from functioning at a productive level. "The clock is ticking. I can't tell you what's going on this second, but trust me, Zell's life is in grave danger. You still live Hillside?"

"I'm only a few blocks away," answered Jed, climbing into his car.

"Good. When you get there, tell him you need his help. Get him away from his house. If he resists, I'll talk to him," instructed Scott, whose desperation eased a bit. The night had gone from pleasant to tragic and still had the potential to deteriorate further.

Normally Jed operated his Subaru Outback with caution on the steep roads around his neighborhood. Tonight he careened around corners like a rally driver. "What in the…there are lights flashing everywhere. I can see emergency vehicles," soberly explained Jed. "I'm turning onto his cul-de-sac. Oh, no, it's all burned up! There's a smoldering pile where Zell's house used to be. It burned down to the ground. I'm going to go speak with the firemen. I will get back to you later, young man. You have a lot of explaining to do."

Back in the Prince William Sound, Scott felt the second onset of nauseating guilt burrow into him. He couldn't catch his breath. Earlier in the evening Scott had felt unstoppable. Now he viewed his entire life as a failure. It became easy for him to feel like everything he built had just collapsed on top of him. Physically he wanted to vomit.

After letting the doom sink in for a few hours, Scott began to mold his initial bloodlust into a viable system of revenge. He stayed up late visualizing the upcoming confrontation against Applied Leverage. Alan Reynard was without doubt a formidable foe and would sooner or later find out it was Scott on Zell's phone with Nancy, but Scott did have one significant advantage. Months ago he'd assembled a group of trusted private investigators to hunt for soft spots in the underbelly of Applied Leverage. The results from that investigation gave him a starting point from which to plot revenge.

After rejecting idea after far-fetched idea, Scott settled on an approach of deception. The concept was daring and dangerous and it entailed hundreds of variables, but a flawed, ambiguous plan is better than no plan at all. The possibility of losing everything, including his life, was a risk Scott would be willing, even eager to take.

After nailing down the incidentals, Horne would need to put together a first-class team of operatives to help him retaliate. Throughout the night he scrutinized known facts against vague details until the outline of a rough draft materialized. He went to the bridge and dialed from memory.

"Hello."

"Erin? I'm having a gigantic emergency and need Jack Welker in Alaska as soon as possible. As of now that's your only priority."

"Next time, how about…'Good morning, sorry to have called so early'?" suggested his assistant.

"Find him, please…everything has fallen apart," he said before hanging up.

Northern Virginia

The underground nerve center of Applied Leverage is a 24/7/365.25 operation. On this particular night, Peter Zahn had instructed the watchman to record all 9-1-1 calls to the Anchorage, Alaska, emergency call center. After a quiet night of minor-league incidents, the techie had listened in as calls of distress start pouring in. Neighbors reported an out-of-control house fire at the residence of Zell Fergusson. The overnight tech recorded calls for the rest of the night, to be thorough, but figured that the fire had been the important event.

Hatcher's Pass, Alaska

At a remote spot east of Willow, Dewey closely examined the two plums on his aching chest, using the reflection of a window since there were no mirrors in the simple trapper cabin. One had struck him square in the heart and the other in the upper stomach. Unabated, either one of the projectiles would have ended his life. Tender and puffy, the colorful bruises were endearing reminders of the fact that those two bullets had been stopped cold by his trusty Kevlar vest.

The two contusions weren't the extent of his injuries. The elderly brawler had gouged his eye viciously and struck him repeatedly in the nose and groin. *If I hadn't had a stun gun, that old man would have killed me. What an animal. That man must have been unstoppable in his prime,* thought Dewey.

"You know, if you wouldn't of had that zapper, I'd 'a' won that fight," pointed out Zell, alive and full of vinegar, although the high-voltage shock had caused him to fall on his head, leaving him with a permanent headache. The knife wound to his bicep hadn't been very deep, but it still added to his general discomfort.

Dewey had changed his mind at the last second and carried Zell out of harm's way before he set the wooden cabin ablaze. Dewey loaded the unconscious man and some valuables into Zell's pickup and then abandoned it.

Somehow Dewey had managed to convince Zell that he had only broken into the house to snoop around. Conveniently, Dewey failed to mention that Zell's hand-hewn cabin filled with personal treasures was now a worthless bed of ashes.

"Where did you learn to fight like that?" asked a humbled Dewey.

"I was a pilot in Vietnam flying the O-two."

"I am not too familiar with that aircraft."

"Not many people are. The Skymaster was a relatively slow, twin-engine aircraft with a unique push-pull propeller configuration and a twin-boomed tail. I served as a forward air controller flying unarmed at low level…directing bombs and ground fire into enemy positions. I'd compare it to running into the center of a riot wearing a straitjacket. Anyway, frustration over the war led to widespread fighting among the servicemen. I lost my first few fights, so the next time I was on R&R in Thailand I bought a few bottles of whiskey and befriended some Navy SEALS. They taught me a coupla tricks."

"Decades later you still got it. Tell me, why would someone pay me to dig through your house?"

"Since ya told me, I've been racking my old brain. I honestly have no idea. I've said some bad stuff about oil companies. I keep to myself more or less…no real enemies that I know of…not that kind of enemy, at least. I have no children, no life insurance policies. I managed to stay married to the same woman for twenty-five years, but we divorced on friendly terms in eighty-nine."

"The people that hired me to search your house are connected and powerful. I don't know if it's a private company or what, but I intend to find out. How about your personal computer or cellular?" asked Dewey.

"I hate them…never owned either one of those things. I own a satellite phone for emergencies deep in the bush."

"From the moment I saw your picture, the whole gig felt strange. I recognized you right away as a bush pilot I'd met several times. Do you have any powerful clients that confided in you about something important...a shared secret about their work or confessed to some sort of wrongdoing?" asked Dewey.

"I thought I recognized you from somewhere when you came out of my pantry. No important people come to mind...I fly a coupla big wigs around, on occasion. My best customer is actually a very successful businessman, but he's a tree hugger...and he's been my close pal for fifteen years," reasoned Zell.

"Who is it?"

"Scott Horne."

"The crusading environmentalist? When was the last time you were in contact with him?" asked Dewey incredulously. He followed Horne's environmental activism with interest and had a hard time believing he was in cahoots with Bill Jones.

"I dropped him off at his sailboat near Valdez the day before yesterday. Come to think of it, he did borrow my phone to make a few calls earlier in the week," remembered Zell.

"That has to be it. That's the connection," stated Dewey with confidence. "That has to be the thread." *What could have been said that could motivate somebody to kill? Something was said that put whomever Bill Jones works for into a state of action. Could they have mistakenly assumed it was Zell on the line?*

"We need to find out who Scott Horne called," stated Dewey.

"Why don't we ask him?" suggested Zell.

"For now it might be better to let everyone think you're missing. That way we retain the element of surprise. What do you think?" asked Dewey.

"Serves him right...but I need to reassure my ex-wife and a few friends, at least. She's a worrier, but she can keep a secret. What's your background anyway? Military...police?"

"Mixology."

Eastern Sierra, California

Risk is everywhere. Some embrace the challenge of the unknown. Others sip conservatively at life, plodding along safely immersed in their routines. Jack Welker gulped fearlessly at any and all opportunities within his grasp. He viewed his approach as binge living.

It was after midnight when Jack walked over to the tiny spring to get some water for the wood-burning sauna. Again he felt the uniquely disconcerting sensation of being watched. He dismissed his intuition and went about his chore until he heard a sizable twig snap. When Jack got back to the small sauna, he considered his limited options. *Should I make a run for my gun or hide here and wait? Maybe it's just an animal.*

Jack Welker is a risk-taker's risk-taker and decided to try to sprint the forty feet to the cabin where his Ithaca shotgun patiently waited. He only got a half step out of the sauna before the first bullet struck his torso. More rounds followed, leaving his chest and side soaked in red fluid. He instinctively dropped to the ground, but there was no cover. The plastic paintballs continued to strike his body in the darkness.

He was both angry and amused that someone was able to sneak up on him that easily. After the barrage ceased, Jack stood up and dusted himself off. Seconds later he detected the approach of the sniper.

Erin De Sousa emerged from shadows and strolled casually into the moonlight. She greeted Welker with a boastful quip, "I thought you were going to end up surprising me. I felt reasonably confident that you wouldn't start shooting live bullets without first seeing an attacker, but after that poor performance, who knows? I thought you were the woodsman of the group."

"Whatever…you got lucky."

"You let a city girl born and raised in London sneak up on you," bragged the woman. "Scott will be pleased I was able to track down and then ambush the elusive Jack Welker so easily."

Welker continued assessing the twelve or so new welts on his body, opting to ignore the comment. "The truth of the matter is, I was caught off-guard because I ruthlessly attacked my sobriety with a volley of Stoli shots."

"This place is a fully equipped resort and it's free of charge?" asked Erin.

"The doors stay unlocked to those in the know who are willing to make the nine-mile hike. This camp was left behind by an old mining operation. Decades ago, new technology ruined the mine's profitability and it was deserted. Savvy locals refurbished the cabins and turned it into a vacation getaway. A leave-it-in-better-condition-than-you-found-it mentality prevails among the lucky few who know of it. This pride of knowledge results in a property that is maintained better than most urban real estate," explained Jack.

"It looks like you have been staying fit," remarked Erin, complimenting Jack. In his boardshorts, Jack displayed a boxer's coiled physique. His compact height and build served him well in sports where being small and strong is an advantage. "Your body resembles a wild animal's."

"The boss said none of us can try to sleep with you, so comments like that in a setting like this are discouraged," said the perennial jokester. "Horne declared that his employees were off limits…not to be courted, flirted with, or anything else."

"Don't flatter yourself, J-Dub. Scott told me that's the name to use when you're drinking or drugging excessively. I am in a happy relationship, as you know. Anyway, the reason I tracked you down is that Scott has requested your presence up in Alaska, pronto. He said it's very important," explained Erin.

"King Horne beckons? I'll drop everything and come running. What… is he feeling blue? Needs to hang with someone poor to make him feel better?" responded Jack. "I'll hike out tomorrow and take my rental car back to the biggest little city in the world."

"That's a good idea. Most people would be stoked to get offered a free trip. Try showing a little respect every once in a while, OK, Jack. OK? It would go a long way," suggested Erin. "You're booked on the ten o'clock Alaska Airlines red-eye from Reno to Anchorage tomorrow."

"Scott can afford to send a private jet to fetch me, but I'll be sharing space with who knows who in a sealed germ-incubator breathing secondhand air."

"That's right, I forgot about your terminal OCD," answered Erin.

"I would rather live one more month as me, than live out the rest of your life. I was kidding anyway, private jets are ridiculously wasteful. I'll be at the airport on time tomorrow night. Regarding your cowardly attack on an unarmed, half-pickled man, I strongly suggest that you blaze outta here tonight...unless you want to wake up getting pelted by paintballs," warned Jack as he headed back toward the *banya*'s soothing heat.

"You wouldn't do that," De Sousa said.

"Try me," challenged Welker, without turning around, as he climbed back into the warm wooden shed. For Jack, a sauna is the premier place for deep contemplation. The exhausting heat cuts out any extraneous physical energy and mental chatter.

Erin suspected she was too fatigued to hike down nine miles of crumbling switchbacks and scree fields in the dark. She pretended to hike down the trail, but then circled back and slipped into an outlying cabin for some much-needed shut-eye. Carefully, the brunette wedged a chair under the room's only door. She secured the windows and disassembled the paintball gun. Erin felt secure in her defenses and drifted off into a deep, nourishing sleep.

Only six hours later, an irritated Erin rose with the sun because an east-facing window had an inadequate white curtain. Upon opening her eyes she looked first towards the door and was relieved to see the wooden chair snug under the knob. Erin grabbed her reusable metal water bottle and took a long draw, but as she screwed on the cap she noticed that something was awry.

She would have sworn she'd taken off her hiking boots and set them next to her bed. A quick search of the room confirmed her fears. Several of her things were missing. Jack Welker had taken her only pair of shoes and pants. A more thorough investigation of the cabin led to her finding a small hatch in the floor she hadn't noticed the night before. Erin cut a threadbare sheet into a make-shift skirt.

Hours later and about halfway into the hike she found one of her boots. After another couple miles, she saw a lone shoelace dangling from a low-slung tree branch. She tore the duct tape fastened fabric off her sore and blistered left foot and replaced it with the newly laced boot. De Sousa never found her pants or the other boot.

NORTHERN VIRGINIA

Peter Zahn and a coworker sat in the plush employee cafeteria at Applied Leverage, egotistically discussing their mutual talent.

"I'm telling you in the twenty-first century computer hackers are the modern alchemists. We possess a rare talent. There are a finite number of brains that are wired like ours. Having the ability to defeat computer systems is a priceless advantage. Our fingers are like an invisible sports car on the information superhighway," suggested the technician.

"If you look at the facts, I'd say you're right. When hackers are caught, they are usually offered sweetheart deals in exchange for doing consulting work for Uncle Sam. In other cases, paroled keyboard craftsmen can find work at corporations like this, working to protect companies from malicious peers. We are too valuable to sit in prison like the other lawbreakers," bragged Peter.

"On a more serious note, how are things going with the mystery caller?"

"Someone was dispatched to take care of the problem, but they did it in a way that left too many questions," said Peter. "The guys upstairs were in such a rush…that mistakes were made. Anyway, forget about it…having a good memory is a serious liability around here."

Four years before, Peter's life had been forever changed by the lobbying leviathan. The story of how Peter Zahn came to work for Applied Leverage was a simple tale of blackmail. Four years ago, as Peter Zahn sat in jail waiting for his next court appearance, he received a visitor who withheld his name. Guards led

Peter away from the visitor's area and to a private corner of the jail where he was led into a small room with a mammoth man. Peter decided to be very careful.

"Hello, Mr. Zahn, pleased to meet you. Bill Jones. I represent a firm that would be interested in acquiring your unique set of skills."

"Sure, guy, just bring me a cake with a hacksaw hidden in it and we're all set," joked Peter. Inwardly his pulse began to quicken.

"Let's see here. By your early teens you proved to be an expert at breaking down digital barriers. You were so good that you stole more money online as a teenager than most people make in their lifetime," stated Bill.

"The thrill I experience from a flawlessly executed cyber crime can be compared to the high from the best street drugs. Unfortunately I spent the loot too freely and drew the attention of the local authorities. I landed in juvenile hall for my last two years as a minor. After my release I redirected my skills into legal programming and secured a well-paying job at a leading international bank," countered Peter.

"Which didn't go so well either. This time your scam involved writing secret programs to cheat bank customers. A nickel here, a nickel there, added onto normal fees and deposited into an offshore account that you controlled."

"I can't talk about the case. My lawyer said not to believe anything anyone says," said Peter.

"Once a month you would transfer a couple million nickels into an accommodating bank with lax depositing procedures. But the scam imploded when you slipped up to your girlfriend one tequila-soaked night. She confessed the secret to her dad, a New York City firefighter. The Feds were notified and quickly set up a sting to catch you in the act. Even though they knew what you were doing, the authorities had a hard time unraveling the complicated layers of deception. Eventually they caught you using a payphone to call the bank. You were arrested a few days later."

"You can read."

"Let me guess. After failing to find a replacement rush, the promise of instant excitement drew you back to cyber crime. The cult of criminality is addictive, but it was the easy money that really drew you back. It seemed you were once again ticketed for an early retirement on the private island you looked into," said Bill.

"Talk about bad luck. I'm facing up to ten years in a federal penitentiary and that is if I accept a plea bargain. Now I have to listen to you rub it in?" asked Peter.

"Here, I brought you a carton of reds," said Bill Jones, handing over the cigarettes. "What if I told you I could get your charges reduced if you came to work for us? Your starting salary would be five grand a week," enticed Jones.

"Are you a spook or something? Must be a Fed to have that kind of juice with the Department of Justice."

"Not a chance. I am not associated with the intelligence services, or any other government agency…the pay is peanuts. I work for people who work closely with the upper levels of government," explained Bill truthfully.

"If you are serious about that offer, I would need a written guarantee that I could never be recharged at a later date," responded Peter, wary of any hidden stipulations that might be lurking.

"Of course, you'll have to surrender the seven million dollars you have at the Central Atlantic Bank. I am a very busy man, so I need to go. Sleep on it, enjoy the cigarettes. I'll call you tomorrow." Bill Jones stood up and stared down into the seated inmate's eyes and asked, "What other choice do you have? Are you really going to spend the rest of your youth caged up with a bunch of animals? We are not talking about white-collar misfits. These are hardened street criminals…violent, frustrated men with no options and dismal futures. If you ask me, any other option has to be better than that. Take a chance with us, young man."

Zahn sat in stunned silence, his analytical mind computing facts.

"If this were a detective trick, why would you let me know where you think the money is? You have done your homework. You must be a powerful man. Maybe you really could get me sprung on time served. I know I don't want you as an enemy. You can't be all bad, considering you brought me a brick of cowboy killers," said Peter.

"Think about it. Pleasure meeting you," said Bill before leaving.

That night a guard informed the defendant he would be changing cells. Upon arrival at his new, private cell, he noticed a large brown paper bag. In jail anything out of the ordinary is very exciting. He opened the bag straight away and found a Styrofoam carton which contained a rib eye steak, whipped yams, Brussels sprouts, and a six-pack of Guinness cans. The bag contained Peter Zahn's favorite meal, his favorite beer, and his favorite magazine. A typed note was affixed to a copy of Hustler magazine.

"I hated to see someone of your caliber eating slop with the rapists and killers. Enjoy the girls and the ale. Be extra careful with the yams! Your pal, Uncle Bill."

Peter set the box on the bed and probed the orange mash with his finger. False-alarm chunks of roasted garlic teased of treasure, but then he felt a small cellophane-covered parcel the size of a pea.

"Mr. Jones, you shouldn't have," sarcastically whispered a smiling Zahn as he carefully opened the delicate package. Peter shaved a sliver off with his nail and rubbed it against his gum. The alkaline substance instantly numbed his flesh. Peter pulverized the narcotic into a pile of powder. The notion that Bill Jones was a lawman was long forgotten. The computer burglar gleefully tucked into his first line of the Andes brain candy. This treat rotted dopamine receptors, not teeth. The food lost its luster and sat untouched as he paced about the cell, chain-smoking and drinking. Peter Zahn's mind would not permit him sleep that night as it reeled with visions of once again working his digital voodoo. Two weeks later he was a free man, or as free as anybody indentured to Applied Leverage could be.

CHUGACH MOUNTAINS, ALASKA

The roar was deafening. Visibility was nil. The screaming mechanical bird freed itself from the loose snow and rose vertically and slightly backward before abruptly spinning around and accelerating down the slope. The man-made maelstrom dissipated quickly. The landing zone was the size of a pool table. Two men gingerly strapped in to their snowboards.

Scott Horne broke the silence, "The Chugach aren't particularly high. But they receive some of the heaviest snowfall on Earth, combined with a maritime climate that creates an abnormally well-bonded snowpack. That's what's special. In springtime it's a powder wonderland with millions of acres available per skier. And it's still dark enough at night to see the northern lights."

"If I had some kryptonite this is where I'd stash it. Why did we have to get crazy nasty on our first run? It makes me feel better that you're scared, too," responded a frustrated Jack Welker, while tentatively gazing down from the peak.

"I am scared, but it's not because of this run. I've been snowboarding all morning. This is your first run. On a serious note, I'm worried about a problem I am having with this suit. There's this lobbyist who wants to see me dead or in jail. Unfortunately, he's got the juice to make it happen. I'm sure you realize that if I die or get locked up…everything will disappear. The boat, the heli…the traveling. I need your help to turn the tables on him," stated Scott bluntly as he melodramatically motioned to the snow, ice, and rock as if Alaska itself would cease to exist upon his demise.

"Sign me up. I've always told you to ask if you ever needed anything. So now you're asking. You know I'm down for whatever," Jack responded without missing a beat. The ugly reference to a lifestyle derailment got his attention.

"I really appreciate that. I'm not thrilled with the way I need to use you, but you are truly the best fit for the role," explained Scott. His hunch that he could count on Jack had proved to be accurate.

"But if you want my help…you'll need to get me off this peak in one piece. Let me see the camera," demanded Jack. "I'm more comfortable on mountains of unfrozen water."

Scott Horne lingered over the camera's display and handed it over. He had taken photos of the face from the helicopter. Once on top of the mountain, he studied the photos upside down to help find his line and memorize landmarks. This would keep him away from unridable sections.

"This is nothing compared to stuff we've ridden together. Keep your head on a swivel. Always check what's happening behind you. Stick to the smoother ramps and make sure to stay skier's left of the largest spine. Watch your speed for the first couple turns," encouraged Scott. He was feeling uncharacteristically paternal, since he had fully orchestrated the danger.

Scott slid to the edge and was relieved that he could see where he'd make his first turn before the slope rolled over out of sight. The colorful helicopter sat parked on the snow and at that distance looked to be the size of a fly. He pressed his hand to his chest to double-check that his transceiver was set to transmit. The small unit broadcast a digital heartbeat to his teammates, giving them a better chance to make a successful rescue using probes and shovels. He also made sure the mouthpiece of his other lifesaving device was perfectly positioned. The Avalung moved a buried victim's deadly, carbon-monoxide–rich exhalations away from the facial area to the lower back. However, suffocation is only one of the ways a winterized mountain can kill.

"Okay, boys, I'm ready to drop," Scott alerted his crew on the two-way.

The lead guide, Christian, was stomping his feet to stay warm in the shade of the valley and beginning to wonder what was taking so long when the walkie-talkie cackled to life. "Watch out for that cornice to your right as you drop in. Ready when you are, we're rolling," he advised.

Standing over a vertical mile above his entourage, Scott took three deep breaths, twisted his hips, and let gravity work its magic. The first turn came quick and put him onto his toeside. Under-board the snow felt slow and soft as he glanced up over his front shoulder, checking for movement below him. *Okay, good. Nothing is letting go.*

60

The layers of snow seemed to be firmly bonded, so Scott opened it up. He swung the nose straight downhill for a second. At forty miles an hour he edged into a sweeping heelside turn creating a twenty-foot plume. It wasn't a slam-on-the-brakes whip-your-tail-out powder puff. This spray resembled the rooster tail thrown up by a snowmachine speeding through fresh snow or the wall of water thrown up by a big wakeboard turn. Within the gut of the gully, Scott glanced uphill to check the amount of snow he was loosening with his elongated sixty-mile-an-hour carves. Part of him was frightened by what he saw, but the other side felt challenged. His snowboard scraping against the steep mountainside had started a small surface slide of only the top inch or two of fresh, but within a thousand feet the sluff's force multiplied to the strength of a small avalanche. The steep snow river could sweep him into an area of treacherous cliffs, rocks, or ice.

The prudent move would be for Scott to find an elevated island of safety. He could stop and allow the snow to flow by harmlessly and then resume his descent, but on this day Scott wasn't interested in avoiding danger. He wanted to access his inner stash of euphoric chemicals that the human brain self-administers when its owner desperately needs help.

The snowboarder took another quick look back and knew that he would have to stop making turns to win a race with the man-eating wave. He straightened his trajectory and tried to stay smooth while steadying his legs against the increased forces of a higher velocity. His pants and jacket were already flapping wildly, but he went faster. His brain shifted into hyper drive which slowed things down, allowing Scott to correct little problems before they became unmanageable. The intoxicants flowed through his body, giving him confidence and strength. *I can do this...I'm going to pull it.*

The steep face eventually fizzled out to a lesser grade. He had outrun the cascading snow by going straight. An ollie over a lip in the glacier and Scott Horne was safe until the next time. He stopped a few hundred feet uphill from the chopper to catch his breath and to privately savor the waning effects of the sharpness he felt from his fingertips to the end of his toes. The rush momentarily eclipsed the guilt he felt over the death of Nancy Watkins.

From past experiences, Scott had learned that when he was overcome with rage, the best response was to participate in aggressive activities. Physical endeavors acted as a pressure release valve for his internal boiler.

Blind rage led to blind actions. Scott preferred to let his anger simmer, allotting time to rationally plot revenge. Plus he liked to give his brain a chance to consider different angles in various frames of mind. He believed making decisions based on emotional instinct was a sign of weakness.

Scott rode down the last hundred yards and greeted the crew. "I think I'll call that one...The Funneling Runnel. That got a little loose...let's get out of here before I get killed," Scott admitted to his congratulatory crew. "That's why I was forced to buy my own helicopter...in order to regularly ride outside of my ability. Not that you can't have tons of fun without getting crazy. It's a misconception that you must be an expert to participate in helicopter skiing."

"Paying clients are taken to runs that are skill appropriate. Guides select terrain based on what the least skilled person in the group is capable of descending safely," said Christian. "Stronger groups get taken to more exposed runs after proving their ability but intermediate groups can easily find suitable terrain."

The boys left the chopper at the airport and went into town for beer and groceries. "This town is right out of a storybook," said Jack.

"Valdez rests snugly between a narrow fjord and a towering ridge of mountains. Old Valdez was destroyed by a tsunami following the 1964 Good Friday earthquake. It was the one of the strongest ever recorded, measuring an estimated 9.2 on the Richter scale. The quake triggered a submarine landslide, which created a giant wave that bounced back and forth across the narrow fjord and repeatedly swamped the old township," explained Christian.

"I didn't know that."

"In more recent times Valdez has been better known to Outsiders as the terminus of the oil pipeline from Prudhoe Bay and as the site of an ecological calamity. In 1989, after only a decade of operation, an oil spill occurred...again on a Good Friday."

"What actually happened?" asked Byron.

"A liquored-up supertanker captain delegated the helm to an unqualified crew member during the most dangerous leg of the journey…even though their radar was inoperable and it was nighttime. The roughly eleven million gallons of spilled crude caused a collapse in the local sea and shore life that persists to this day. The once-dominant herring fishery has never recovered," said the longtime local ski guide.

"On a lighter note, today the town of roughly five thousand is famous for a substance completely opposite of dirty black oil…clean white snow. A seasonal community has emerged from the black ooze. A number of roadside helicopter-skiing companies operate out of snowy Thompson Pass, drawing powderhounds from every corner," said Scott.

"The cities of Haines, Cordova, Juneau, and Girdwood also have top-flight helicopter chauffeurs. A springtime pilgrimage to coastal Alaska is a priority for big-mountain skiers and riders that favor the steep and deep," said Christian. "Valdez's new calling card blankets the steep peaks around town. The snow-saddled mountains, combined with powerful light helicopters and a maritime snowpack, create an unmatched destination for the snow slasher."

"Usually heli-skiing is a glitzy affair catering to an upper crust clientele with expensive packages, full of nonessential perks like luxury accommodations, spa treatments, and gourmet cuisine. If the highbrow heli-lodges of British Columbia offer a champagne-and-caviar experience, then Alaska serves up a whiskey-and-smoked-salmon vibe," said Scott.

"Skiers with no coin for heli-drops can hitchhike to the top of the pass and enjoy Road Runs. Hikers can pick a roadside mountain to ascend with man power. When weather and/or snow conditions get bad for days, even weeks, on end, these nuts develop a case of Val-disease. Symptoms include binge drinking, delusional thoughts, and temporary insanity," added Byron.

Scott was eager to get back to his self-contained sphere to speak with Jack Welker privately. Four cases of Alaska Pale Ale heavier, the sleek EC-135 twin turboshaft helicopter streaked south-southwest and into the sound. The waning sun shot its last rays directly into Byron's face as he flew along above the dark water at one thousand feet. Tinted goggles provided some relief for the pilot's eyes, but mainly he flew by instruments, looking up only to scan for traffic.

For the passengers, the show was a bonus, not a hazard. The curved windows framed panoramic views. Peninsulas of mountainous alpine terrain and evergreen forests made a stand against the seawater. Rocky beaches were bathed in a soft orange-red.

"Sunset is the consolation prize for losing the heat and light until the next day," said Jack.

"That spill proves that accidents can and will happen. People that support new drilling up here irritate me. It's like a degenerate gambler searching for new loans or additional lines of credit instead of addressing the root problem," said Byron Richardson. The rest of the squad became visually captivated and preferred not to be bothered with the nuisance of conversation.

Back on the sailboat, Scott baked himself in the sauna, passing the time stretching and meditating while organizing his proposal to Jack. He didn't feel right about asking Jack to do something that had a good chance of landing his pal in jail or even worse, but it was a role that Scott couldn't do himself. The task required someone reliable enough to get it done but also reckless enough to be creditable.

More than most other people, Jack Welker was an enigma. The young adventurer could survive in the wilderness for weeks with almost nothing, could speak intelligently on most topics, and voraciously studied history. Yet he couldn't pay his bills on time, hold down a steady job, or even return a phone call. In truth, Jack Welker excelled at certain things and faltered at others with no discernible pattern or explanation for which was which.

After dinner Scott exited his Swiss-chalet-themed stateroom and knocked on the door of Jack's quarters.

"Yes."

"Grab a jacket. Let's check for the aurora borealis topside," said Scott with a faint authority.

"Sir, yes, sir," teased Jack, who felt Scott Horne was a control freak.

Outside, the unfrozen seawater kept the air from getting ridiculously frigid.

"Hey. This pesky layer of stratus clouds is obscuring any northern lights that might be dancing across the sky."

"What are the most common colors?"

"Umm…green, white, and yellow displays are common, but red, pink, orange, and purple can make appearances, too."

"What causes it?," asked Jack.

"The different colors are caused by the varying composition of solar flares whose charged particles clash with Earth's upper atmosphere after being drawn into the poles by the magnetosphere. The natural sky show can last seconds, minutes, or hours."

"Dang, is it cold up in these northern realms," said Jack as he rubbed his palms together.

"There is nothing in science that says North is up. The universe is three-dimensional. The reason North is on top is that mapmakers were from Europe," replied Horne.

"I dig that map at the airport in Auckland, New Zealand, showing the flipside, with Antarctica on the roof and Oceania up top. Cape Horn of South America and Africa's Cape of Good Hope stand proudly upright. The major landmasses look as if they've succumbed to gravity, slid downwards, piled up on themselves," described Jack.

"It makes more sense for Antarctica to be on top. It has one sterling quality that sets it above the other six continents. It's human-less," said Scott with a smile.

"I want to see some northern lights."

"There's another directional snub. The southern lights, aurora australis, don't get as much attention as the aurora borealis because the world is biased toward all things North. I guess that's cuz the majority of land masses and humans are located in the Northern Hemisphere."

"Yeah, but in the Southern Hemisphere nobody lives super-south. Cape Horn is only at fifty-five degrees or so. That's roughly the same latitude as Amsterdam or Moscow. Only the scientists on Antarctica are well positioned to see the southern lights."

"True…true, that's a good point; I never considered that. It's too darn cloudy here to see anything. The winds are supposed to push them inland later tonight, according to the National Weather Service. Who knows?" appraised Scott as he handed Jack a pewter flask.

"What is it?" asked Jack.

"Coffee and Kahlua."

Jack knew better than to fall for that old trick and raised the metal container to his nose. The familiar bouquet of Wild Turkey greeted his nostrils, but he took a large swig anyway, out of courtesy and compulsion.

"I knew you had the ability to make it down that mountain with no trouble," offered Scott, greasing Jack up a bit with a compliment. "How did you like that Winterstick seven deuce?"

"That Tom Burt is super stiff…it felt good at speed."

"Yeah, that board, the Jones and Lib Techs are the only boards I have. It looked like you had a fun run."

"When the sluff started building, I cut onto something high and waited it out. I admit I was very scared rolling in…but I had a great time," said Jack. "Don't forget…that was my first heli-run this season."

"It's like riding a bike…down a giant mountain. Unfortunately it's time to discuss the reason I invited you here in the first place. Let me give you the scope of what I need you to do," said Scott, getting down to business.

"Make it quick or give me the Wild T back, because it's cold as all heck and I ain't got no long johns on, son."

Scott handed the sauce back. "Let me start off by saying that, in the event of a complication, I would set you up with the best lawyers available. But there is no need to worry about that, because you are too slippery."

Scott only explained Jack's own role and gave no indication about the overall scope of the operation. He really couldn't get into the actual plan yet, because there wasn't one. First, Scott had to assemble a team before he could formulate the details. Also, if he told Jack the whole story, it would be overwhelming.

A few minutes into the discourse, Jack was no longer cold, he was scared. Under normal circumstances, he enjoyed the sensation of fear, but if things got twisted he would be serving hard time in prison. The part of the plan he did like was that he would be playing himself, a role he had perfected.

After ten more minutes, Scott finished up his briefing and asked, "What are your thoughts, buddy?"

Jack Welker simply nodded his head. "I guess it's time to stop taking my mood stabilizers. Going off my meds cold turkey usually leads to trouble, but since trouble is what you are looking for…it's on."

"Exactly…I knew you would understand that this plan hinges on you. Your contribution won't go unrewarded financially. You do your part and I'll do mine. Afterward we'll take a trip to Brazil or something. Heck, we might have to go into hiding. Anyway, I am exhausted…gonna hit the rack," said Scott before he headed below deck.

"I will hold you to that, Horne. You know I have a fetish for Brasileñas… Latinas in general," said Jack with conviction. The reference to a long vacation and a big payday succeeded in diverting Jack's attention from the severe danger he faced.

Early the next morning, Scott met with Captain Dan alone on the bridge to lay out the schedule before he took off. "I'm on my way to stir up a hornet's nest back east. Head down to Cali at best possible speed, but stay out of the Inside Passage. Monitor everything. Radar, sonar, infrared, the radios. Keep the crew on full alert, twenty-four/seven," ordered Scott.

"California is a big place. Anywhere in particular?" asked the captain.

"Bay area. Someplace stealth. Be careful, these guys want me dead and they might think I'm onboard the *Arana*. These jokers are well connected with government officials, so don't be surprised if the Coasties hassle you. Expect to be searched, but it's no sweat. We have nothing onboard that's illegal."

"That's true. Don't worry about us. It sounds like you need to lay low and take care of yourself. People get real weird about money and power. I'll head way offshore out of the shipping lanes. If they want to know where I am, they'll have to use a satellite," boasted the captain.

"Good luck with everything. I have to go catch my flight in Anchorage," Scott explained before abruptly giving Dan a hug, a rare move for the normally unaffectionate man.

The turboshaft started up with a high-pitched electric whine, followed by the turbine spooling up to idle. The beating of the rotors increased until enough lift was created to overcome the weight of the aircraft. With Scott at the controls, the helicopter left the deck, yawed sideways, and sped away. The colorful machine had been covered in color-changing paints to replicate a hummingbird.

Once the chopper disappeared, Dan couldn't stop from morbidly speculating that that might be the last time he saw Scott Horne alive.

ADAMSTOWN, MARYLAND

Scott Horne was wasting no time in getting the rebuilding process started. He borrowed an estate to ensure privacy for the moment when he'd make a bold proposition to Marissa Ehrlich's brother. The pair had spent the afternoon together doing things befitting a millionaire trying to persuade someone to do something.

With the now-or-never moment upon him, Horne became queasy. Up until now his plan had been just an idea floating safely in the privacy of his consciousness. The pragmatist in him knew that if he proceeded, there could be no turning back. This was the point of no return. If the man sitting across from Horne didn't want to be part of his team, it was game over.

"One of the mottoes I subscribe to is that life can and will throw anything and everything at you. When things are going good, I make a serious effort to savor it. Everything has an expiration date. To be living with good health, piles of money, large blocks of free time, and a valid passport sometimes seems greedy and selfish," said Scott.

"That's a good problem to have," said his guest.

"It has taken only one misstep to demonstrate how fragile the human experience can be. The murder of Nancy Watkins has caused my entire psyche to come crashing apart."

"That is just a theory at this point. You have no evidence of any wrongdoing."

His guest was nervous and having a hard time controlling his anxiety. "When I received a phone call from a rich businessman claiming he needs my help, I was flattered, yet I was decidedly apprehensive as well. I've read of your wild side, Mr. Horne."

"I know it was unorthodox asking you to come here in secret, but I didn't think you would want to be associated with me. I recognize that we are both inherently...distrustful of one another," offered Scott.

"Mr. Horne, your hospitality has been great. The helicopter ride around the capital was an eye-opening experience. And this indulgent lunch is fit for a king. I hate to admit it, but it feels like you have been fattening me up for the slaughter. As you know...my time is also very important," responded a man who was almost old enough to be Scott's father.

Scott looked away, took a deep breath, and verbally plunged in. "The real reason I brought you here is to propose a partnership. Would you be interested in helping me expose a group of corrupt government puppeteers?"

"Nobody in Washington is crazy enough to tackle the lobbyists. I thought you invited me here because you wanted me to give you advice on a new business venture of yours. If you have real evidence of specific misdeeds by somebody, you need to follow the normal channels and contact the Department of Justice."

Scott cut in, "The reason the men and women of the House and Senate avoid this problem is that even the people who have nothing to hide have peers who are guilty. Nobody wants to be a whistle-blower on members of his own party. What about out-and-out criminals in Congress? Don't you think they are going to fight a corruption investigation? It would never happen. Nevertheless, there is an alternate course of action," suggested Scott.

"If you are about to say something illegal, please let me know so I can leave," declared the man, whose curiosity wouldn't let him storm off. "The things you are saying are true, but my career could be jeopardized by talking to you about things like this."

"We should go after the people who control them," said Scott, pausing for dramatic effect and then adding, "a certain lobbying empire."

"I'm starting to think the media are right about you. You are not sane. Applied Leverage is the unethical hired gun for companies that are more powerful than the government. Don't be naïve...they'll kill you if you attempt to interfere with their cozy relationship with the legislative branch," warned the man.

"These people have killed two people already and they will kill again, but let me worry about my own safety," Scott answered. "Unless you agree to help or at least try to help, I can't explain my plan."

The silence was thick and heavy like the air. Scott had expected an initial non-reaction, but it lasted too long. He reloaded, "Are you going to let America continue to be manipulated by a few thousand oafish individuals? This country has become what our founding fathers were fighting against... global bullies. It has become an oligarchy where only a tiny percentage of the population benefits from American policies. The masses have been subjugated by the super-rich."

"That's partially true, but it's irrelevant to this discussion," said the man.

"Per capita, Americans are the leading users of just about every category of resource. We use one-fourth of the oil and represent one twenty-fifth of the world's population. Conglomerates make billions from all this waste. Large businesses have hijacked our democracy. Voters need to wrest control from them. For the most part, Americans are good-hearted, and cleaning up our democracy is a surefire way to show the world our true intentions," said Scott Horne.

"Our image is definitely in need of a makeover," agreed the man.

"Historically American policies have been dictated by business interests. Look at the mess that has created. Having recently deceived international investors with our unregulated financial system and imploding the world economy…the time is right to redefine our objectives," concluded Scott Horne, who'd spent hours rehearsing the pitch.

"You make a good argument, but how much change do you think one man can really make?"

"Every revolution needs a spark, and I am not just one man. Let's show the world that private citizens using unconventional tactics aren't afraid to take on the people who manipulate our lawmakers," stated Scott in conclusion.

Both men were quiet for several minutes, silently contemplating the consequences of a partnership. Everything they had ever achieved would be at stake. Finally Scott witnessed fear changing to resolve across the features of the man's bony face. A decision had been made.

NORTH PACIFIC GYRE

A helicopter skimmed the sea on its way towards an enormous rig covered in solar panels and wind turbines. On this flight, Scott was using low-level flying to try to excite these first-time guests. Then he would attempt to transfer that buzz into enthusiasm for the project.

Large swells stretched across the horizon, but the structure stayed quite stable. Waves broke around the cylindrical towers instead of lifting them like a conventional boat hull. The hollow center of the legs could be pumped full of seawater to lower and stabilize the structure in bad weather. Unlike an oil rig, this was a floating, unanchored platform and could be pulled by tugboats in calm seas. It functioned as a research laboratory and collection center for the Great Pacific Garbage Patch.

Riding in the back of the helicopter were two journalists. One was from the BBC and the other from the *New York Times*. They were conducting an interview from the backseat. "Where did the idea for this originate?" asked one of the reporters.

"Wind and ocean currents have been concentrating non-biodegradable debris in a convergence zone east of Hawaii and west of California. Uninhabited atolls look like garbage dumps. In the middle of the ocean there are bits of plastic everywhere. Species of bird and marine life are being choked by ingesting miniscule toxic bits. At this stage nobody can do much about the tiny pieces, but I thought we could clean the shorelines while researching the problem from a floating laboratory," explained Scott Horne, who unabashedly courted attention from the international media.

"What made you take the plunge from concept to project?"

"I decided this would be my primary contribution to making the world a healthier, cleaner place. I know I can't clean up the ocean…I'm not completely delusional. The key is getting the citizens, the voters…the taxpayers of the world to fight the industries and systems that cause the pollution. Accidentally or intentionally, littering is going to happen. Let's make everything non-toxic and biodegradable. It is awfully arrogant for our species to be manufacturing anything that continues polluting forever. Humans have been behaving belligerently toward a planet we are just beginning to understand," explained Horne. "Our aim is to dramatically slow the flow of fresh petro-plastics into the ocean while researching the effects of what is already in the water."

"People have accused you of being an idealist, a dreamer. Do you have anything to say to your critics?"

"I am a dreamer, a very successful one. If I can inspire others to take action, at some point a drop in the bucket will become a bucketful of drops. I can't wait for the day when the wealthiest men and women of the world compete to have the most imaginative sustainability projects...as opposed to owning the most expensive house, car, gemstone, or other material trappings."

"Can you give me a rundown of the operation, please?"

"It's a mother ship...a floating laboratory that supports tenders that double as tugboats. Visible trash is collected and analyzed. Each vessel collects trash and then brings it to the barge to be sorted and studied by scientists. The rig is also a seaborne testing platform for alternative energies and boating technologies," said Scott smugly.

The pearl-white helicopter made a slow loop at two hundred feet, ensuring the passengers got a three-hundred-sixty-degree view of the behemoth before heading in for a landing on the helipad. As Scott approached his baby, he swelled with pride and became giddy. It was a rare, welcome break from his ridiculing conscience.

Sitting shotgun was Rokurou Yanagi, a billionaire bon vivant who embodied Japan's detail-oriented but pleasure-seeking populace. Considering Rokurou's love of the seven seas, Scott hoped the man might donate more generously if he saw the place in person. Both Horne and Yanagi were fanatical spear fishermen and strong advocates of creating sustainable methods of harvesting ocean delicacies through habitat protection and careful fishery management. Yanagi wanted his grandchildren's grandchildren to have the opportunity to enjoy all of the same seafood he did.

After touching down, Scott introduced the group to their tour guide. "I have some quick business to attend to, but I am leaving you in capable hands. This is Jill Hutton...she's on loan from the Scripps Aquarium and is an award-winning scientist specializing in the effects of plastics on marine bird life. She works in our state-of-the-art marine hospital/lab. I'll meet with the three of you a little later for lunch, at which point I'll answer the rest of your questions. Thanks, again, for making the long trip out," announced Scott.

"On behalf of everyone involved with Pacific Plastic Purge, I would like to formally welcome you aboard the first and only vessel designed specifically to study and remove pollution from our precious oceans. I thought we would start our tour by visiting the heart of the vessel, the power exchange room. The amps created by the turbines and photovoltaic panels are used to charge the batteries. This way, everybody; please watch your heads at all times," Jill began, as she led the eager group down a narrow steel corridor. "Wind and water turbines and the solar panels provide more than enough juice for the mother ship, the tenders, and the cargo ship. Huge lithium-ion batteries are charged and then placed wherever needed by boom cranes. Any questions so far?"

"Is labor a big part of overhead?" asked the correspondent from the AP.

"Yes and no," said the guide. "Out of necessity, the captains and crew are paid professionals. The rest of the workforce are volunteers. Primarily we host international students who receive college credit. When the barge is positioned at the western edge of its patrol area, volunteers get to take multi-day excursions to clean reefs and the shorelines of uninhabited islands. The amount of plastic fishing line and nets is heartbreaking. Any shallow areas act like a comb and snag debris. Returning activists raving about spending time rehabbing remote islands and reefs have proved to be an effective recruiting tool."

"What is a normal day like?"

"We grow seventy percent of the food we need in onboard greenhouses, so that accounts for a lot of the work. Volunteers also spend time in the sorting decks, affectionately called "the pits." The work is repetitive but not dull. Every day brings a few interesting finds that add a bit of zest to operating the machinery and sorting through the catch. Old glass buoys make popular keepsakes, as do messages in bottles. And we have satellite Internet."

After leaving the group, Scott headed in the opposite direction toward the bridge. After saying his hellos to the captain and officers, he followed a maze of corridors that led to a door labeled Greg Herge, Director of Environmental Protection.

"Knock, knock," said Scott as he rapped on the partially open door.

"If it isn't the man with an ego so big his neck can barely hold it upright," chided Greg. "A man with such brass ones, he thinks nothing of marooning his good friend in the Central Pacific."

"I've stranded you on a groundbreaking floating laboratory stocked with college girls. What a jerk I am," responded Scott.

"I'm too old for college girls. Things are coming together here. I solved, for the most part, the problem we were having with the solar incinerators used to dispose of human waste. It was just a matter of adjusting the temperature in the burn chambers and changing the pH in the flush water before it gets to the reed pond. Also, the lithium-ion batteries are no longer developing rust on the terminals. Mike designed a very creative Velcro sheath that protects them when not in use. Also I ha—"

Scott interrupted him. "As you know, I can talk technical minutia for hours. But we can do that on the phone. I came here in person to discuss something a little more delicate. You never can tell if someone is listening."

"Maybe you should choose your enemies more carefully."

"I needed to come out and host Yanagi in person, too. I was wondering if you could help me locate a radical-minded friend of yours," confided Scott.

"Are you suggesting that I keep company with an ecoterrorist?" asked Greg with mock irritation. "I have absolutely no idea who you are talking about."

"Nobody said ecoterrorist. I was referring to an environmental freedom fighter…a certain bird-like character," clarified Scott.

"I happen to know where the Owl is nesting. He's laying low at the moment. Big surprise. He's worried about an indictment coming down. He's no fire starter. That investigation is modern-day McCarthyism. People that question government and corporate policies in unorthodox manners are automatically labeled subversive. I think the biggest reward in being out here is the lack of popular media," said Greg. "You can find the Owl on the Oregon Coast. It's not far from Newport. Take a surfboard. See if you can sneak up on him. I'll pull up the exact spot on Google Earth."

WASHINGTON, DC

"It's good to see you. How long has it been?" asked Ambrose. Gunnlick as he walked along the National Mall.

"Over a decade. Tell me about your new gig," prompted his old colleague, Steve Olton.

"As you know, following 9/11 a new domestic counterterrorism task force was established, known as the Counterterrorism Investigative Group and Reactionary Squadron, or CIGARS. The group is authorized to operate without a net, free from the bureaucratic oversight and infighting that bog down other agencies."

"The majority of your career has been spent as a federal prosecutor toiling in courtrooms."

"Charging after hate groups and domestic evildoers with gusto for twenty years caught the attention of the newest bureaucracy on the block. Years of analyzing defendants' lives while preparing for trials gives me a unique insight into their troubled personalities. I also relate to the majority of them on a recreational level," explained Ambrose

"I remember you were born and bred under the big skies of Kalispell, Montana. You fly-fish, right?"

"Bow hunter and fly-fisherman since I was knee-high. Forget these city-based environmentalists. Hunters and gatherers were the first conservationists."

"It's a lifestyle that underlines the need for keeping wildernesses intact. You had the opportunity to experience the life lessons any young person learns by exploring nature," said Steve.

"Unlocking the moody sky, the foreboding forests, the silent power of the rivers, and their timeless mysteries gave me a perpetual project. An unfortunate side effect of living away from population centers is that it is easy to view city dwellers with contempt. To some rural folks, traffic, crime, pollution, and disease seem like unbearable circumstances that only a moron would choose to endure," answered Ambrose.

"We worked on cases together where that elitist mentality gets the best of somebody. Self-righteous pride can turn ugly and even violent. That is the kind of person that ends up on your watch lists."

"The fringe groups I investigate tend to reside on the outer edges of society, both politically and physically, inhabiting the sort of regions where free time is spent doing something in the woods. A small percentage of rural folks see their remote settings as an opportunity to exploit illegal avenues," said Ambrose. "It's discouraging. With a similar background, I've proved effective at profiling rural criminals for CIGARS."

"I bet it's difficult to decipher which ones are harmless loudmouths and which are legitimate threats."

"It is, but instead of reacting to past transgressions and fighting courtroom battles years after the alleged crime took place, nowadays I get to pursue future evildoers. I relish being a proactive force within the justice system."

"What do you know about the Owl?" asked Steve pointedly.

"I first heard the name Curt Joddell in connection with a protest against the expansion of a Colorado ski area. The developers ignored the threats and started building a new ten-million-dollar lodge. Young activists felt strongly about protecting the habitat of the Canadian lynx and showed their teeth. One night while still under construction, the venerable wooden lodge went up in flames."

"I know the story. The ski area continued with the new lift but never rebuilt the fire-bombed lodge, right?"

"I felt that it set a dangerous precedent. The message seemed to be, 'If you don't want something built, try burning it down during construction.' Curt Joddell had been caught on video at an area convenience store the night of the destructive fire. This put him squarely in the government's crosshairs," said Ambrose. "Luckily for the Owl, a different group of activists took center stage. I'm still intrigued by Joddell, but at the time I had bigger fish to fry."

OREGON COAST

By western standards, the cabin was tiny, only two hundred square feet. As a consolation the hexagonal structure had a wraparound balcony and an excessive number of windows. The fading art of custom woodworking was displayed everywhere. Ornately carved animal motifs adorned the beams. Handmade furniture added more warmth and character. Views extended for miles, showcasing a snaking river bisecting a thickly treed valley.

The cozy cabin was the hideaway of Curt Joddell, also known as "the Owl" for his tree-living, scholarly ways and tendency to travel by night. He operated by finding frustrated environmentalists and offering them constructive ways to effect change. As the figurehead of COED (Citizenry of Earth's Defense), Joddell's extreme politics earned him scores of enemies in the halls of power. The underground organization didn't have an address or exist in any physically documented sense. The Owl was the only member of COED known to authorities.

As per his routine Curt Joddell was up early and enjoying a steaming mug of tea when a lookout radioed to warn him about a trespasser. When he finally espied the intruder approaching, he peeked around the corner to get a better look. Even from hundreds of feet away, Curt recognized the determined gait.

As the man closed the last few feet toward the tree, Curt poured his tea over the side so that it would barely miss scalding his unannounced guest, a gesture intended to let Scott Horne know he had been detected long ago. "Sorry, Scotty, I didn't see you down there. It can be dangerous trying to sneak up on a paranoid man in the woods."

"It's cool. I know how clumsy you are. I prefer to drink my tea rather than wear it. I take mine with honey," said Scott. "Did anyone ever tell you look and act like an adult version of the carrot-topped mascot from *MAD* magazine?"

"I do look a decade younger than my forty-one years. I'm of medium height and slight build…so obviously my large presence isn't due to physical stature. It's rooted in my charisma," said Curt.

"That mysterious, yet indispensable, personality trait found in politicians, CEOs, and cult leaders," responded Scott.

"It must be my lucky day. A surprise visit from a millionaire capitalist," teased Curt from his perch. He tried to judge others by the content of their character and not the character of their assets, but he had a hard time not disliking wealthy people. Scott Horne represented a rare exception.

As Scott waited for the rope ladder to be lowered, he eyed the steaming liquid as it absorbed into the forest carpet. *I wonder how badly I'd have been burned if that had landed on me.*

"I feel you have been…a reliable sponsor in the past…although you've never donated as much as you could've," teased Curt sheepishly.

"That's the problem. Our relationship is tainted by your jealousy over my money," responded Scott.

"I guess that's why rich people surround themselves with other rich people…to avoid awkward tension."

After climbing the ladder, Scott took a few moments to let the gorgeous Oregon scenery set in. "My flight landed in Portland last night and the drive out to the coast was in darkness," said Scott. Now the sun was shooting golden rays across the valley, illuminating a proud, forested ridge.

"Traditionally, in order to enjoy three-hundred-sixty–degree views a homebuilder needs a mountain or hilltop to lay a foundation, but nature has provided millions of solid foundations if you know where to look. I chose the tree for my nest by climbing up fifty of 'em. This was the winner. Its riverbank location had spared it the saw."

"It's a sweet spot. Who designed it?" asked Scott.

"The *Treezebo* is an ingenious system for suspending loads from above using cables and steel pipes. It was designed by arboreal abode pioneer Michael Garnier of Out 'n' About. He also coinvented an extraordinary bolt that is harmless to the tree, is able to support enormous loads, and gets stronger with age as the trunk grows around the collar. The Garnier Limb paved the way for bigger, higher, and safer tree houses."

"I need one of these," said Scott jealously.

"What is so important that it could lure you away from your beloved Alaska during the heli-boarding season? Let me guess. You came here to ask me to get some of my devotees to do something that eventually will benefit you," astutely hypothesized Curt.

Stifling a smile, Scott replied, "That's pretty close. Actually, it benefits everyone...me, you, the public, Mother Nature," said Scott pointing at the landscape. I know your tribe is ready and willing to assist you in defending the planet, but where are they? Do you have anyone in Brazil?"

"I do. My fanatics favor remote regions with accessible mountains or water bodies. Let's face it...people who engage the natural world are more likely to be motivated to protect it. I'll be candid. You have never done anything dishonest to me. But there's a first time for everything," said the Owl.

"Before you get your panties in a pinch, allow me to explain my entire concept. There will be a comment period afterward. I know my plan doesn't follow your usual M.O., but that is what gives us an edge."

"You're a great motivational speaker," suggested the Owl sarcastically. "Since you have dragged your fancy self all the way down here, I guess there is the off chance you might have something interesting to say."

Scott spent the better part of two hours explaining the lurid details. As requested of him, Curt Joddell patiently listened while making scores of mental notes. When he and Scott finally took a break from the gravitas, the Owl went inside to fire up the white-gas stove. While he brewed a round of fresh mint tea, Curt used the time to consider the proposition. The pit of his chest tightened. The physical symptoms of nervous anticipation had always fascinated him, and this time was no different.

"At one point I was convinced that your mania had once again gained the upper hand and was controlling you. At other points during the spiel, the genius of the scheme was readily apparent. I know you have many contacts, but I don't think you have the type of dedicated people needed for an operation of this caliber. Basically you need individuals willing to go to jail or even die… true believers," said Curt.

"I can't argue that."

"I have never done anything this crazy. I'll have to give it some thought alone, before I commit my people to something as serious as this. I have to admit I've been bored. The way I have been operating doesn't seem to be working. Maybe it's time to up the ante," Joddell responded as he handed Scott a hot mug.

Scott had correctly assumed that would be Curt's response, so he didn't push the issue. With such a sketchy plan, he couldn't expect Curt to make a snap decision. "The trash rig is doing sweet. I just came from there. It's cruising right along," boasted Scott, changing the subject in an attempt at politeness.

"Nice work. The first time I heard you talking about it, I wondered if you had finally gone off the deep end for good. In retrospect I realize it must have been a period of constructive hypomania," teased Curt. "You have to remember that your zealousness brings about a mixture of apprehension and envy."

"I had to do something flashy to get the international media lubed up," said Scott.

"If shoppers refused to buy and use products with toxic ingredients, market pressures would quickly force the offending companies to resolve those issues or fade into history. Consumers need to vote with their dollars."

"I subscribe to the belief that the government will never force corporations to adhere to sustainable methods. Those with purchasing power would need to voluntarily change their spending habits, but galvanizing consumers to adopt conspicuously eco-friendly consumption isn't easy."

"Our government is nothing but a bunch of nicely dressed, semi well spoken corporate puppets."

"Rating's are paramount, so sensationalism is the order of the day. Conservation is a doctrine that falls on deaf ears, blind eyes...and dumb minds."

"The challenge is getting a conglomerate-controlled media to not let advertising interests completely dictate their broadcast content. Another problem is that the handful of umbrella companies that own the majority of news outlets can be sensitive to stories that might be damaging to their other businesses."

"The bottom line is still the bottom line. But the public can direct their dollars toward corporations with good intentions," said Scott.

"Like salmon, I feel like we're swimming upstream," admitted the Owl.

"In handcuffs...which led us to embrace darker methods of persuasion," added Scott with a shrug.

"I formed COED to fight entities that operate outside of established ethical boundaries," explained the Owl.

"Let's go surfing," said Scott, changing the subject.

"Nah, I want to think on this alone."

"What's the hitter breakfast spot around here?"

"Which way you headed?"

"South towards Newport. I want to visit some friends at the aquarium."

"You're a meat eater. Try the Bonepile in Depoe."

"I'm an omnivore because I have sharp teeth," retorted Scott, showing his canines. "What's a good hotel for tonight, back toward P-town?"

"You'd like the Grand Lodge in Forest Grove. Most well-kept old buildings offer a formal, stuffy vibe, but this place bucks that trend."

"What's the story?"

"It's an old hotel with hip management and reasonable pricing, run by brothers who excel at rehabbing historic buildings in both...urban and rural settings. Plus it has a disc golf course surrounding their beer garden."

There was nothing left to say, so Scott shook hands with Curt. "Thanks for the audience." At the last moment, he took a large satchel out of his backpack. "Here's some seed money, if you decide to join the fray. If this thing isn't right for COED...use the cash for your Web site," relayed Scott with a neutral tone. "It isn't a bribe, I just wanted you to have the resources in hand if you needed them." When no reply came forth, Horne descended the rope ladder and trod off into the verdant forest.

Shortly after Scott left, Curt Joddell made up his mind. He would join forces with Scott Horne in attacking the outlaw lobbyists. With great concentration, he started to kick around ideas about who to use and how to use them. As far as he could tell, Curt felt the plan would be heavily dependent on the performance of his recruits. Needing some hard music to help him think, Curt located an album by gritty Portland rockers *Rendered Useless*. After mulling over the logistics for most of the daylight hours, he quickly packed his minimal belongings and called a friend to drive him to the Rose City. Curt battened the shutters and hatches to protect his pad against both human and vermin banditry. He couldn't do anything about insects infiltrating, they used the tree trunk as a vertical highway.

QUANTICO, VIRGINIA

A bank of supercomputers hummed while forty agents organized digital aspects of the federal fight against crime. The cyber laboratory coordinated fingerprint and DNA databases, among other things. One main function of the unit was to disseminate information relating to the FBI's Ten Most Wanted list. Post-Patriot Act, enhanced surveillance protocols had made life much easier on information technology agents.

"Believe it or not, the Owl just surfaced in Portland, Oregon, an hour ago. When the employee at an airport car rental desk uploaded Joddell's license into the computer, it was automatically checked against a list of felony warrants and persons of interest. Curt Joddell is indeed a person of interest," boasted a senior member of the Domestic Terrorism Cyber Taskforce, or DeTeCT. "Joddell's rental car has a GPS. I've already contacted OnBoard. I have a field agent on the way to get the security camera footage and ask a few questions," explained Agent 30 to his boss.

"Who?" asked a newer member of the task force.

"Curt Joddell is COED. He's an ecoterrorist who usually stays invisible. We think he ordered the torching of the headquarters of a fast-food empire. Additionally it's believed that he had a role in the arson of a ski lodge and dozens of anti-sprawl crimes…sabotaging construction sites in remote areas and making threats to developers," replied Agent 30.

"This smells funny; he's usually more careful. It's like he's creating an alibi," offered a superior.

"We'll check the video. If it's a positive match for Joddell, I will advise Agent Riley of CIGARS that one of his perps has exposed himself to our net. Rather sloppily, I would have to agree," responded the techno-cop.

WESTERN OREGON

The suburbs fizzled out as Curt continued south through the Willamette Valley on Eisenhower's interstate system. Interstate 5 tracks from the border with Mexico in San Ysidro all to way to Washington's border with Canada at Blaine via San Diego, Los Angeles, Sacramento, Portland, and Seattle. Even-numbered roadways run east-west, while the odd-numbered arteries are oriented north-south.

Listening to the *Roundtable MCs*, Curt Joddell excitedly drove his rented subcompact. Lately he had been immobile and he preferred not to allow roots to grow. In a moderate rain at seventy miles an hour, the circumstances necessitated his full attention, but instead Curt was struggling to activate the cell phone he had just purchased. The phone was a burner, a prepaid that wasn't registered. Using cash to pay for it provided some level of anonymity, but he couldn't avoid the closed-circuit surveillance cameras. *How long will it take Big Brother to figure out that I am not in hiding anymore? Are they wired into private businesses yet? They probably already know,* thought Curt. He saw conspiracies everywhere.

The prepaid card's print was so small Joddell had to hold it up to the overhead light while entering the digits and steering with his knee. After nearly sideswiping a Mercedes, Curt got the code entered correctly and dialed a number from memory.

"Hi, everyone. I will be off the grid until Tuesday. Leave a proper message if you want a response." Beep.

"Hey, Charles, it's me…I have a very lucrative job opportunity for you. Can you please meet me at our favorite course on the thirteenth? I need you on this one," said Curt, hoping his pal would check the message.

Curt's day job entailed exploiting the superpower of the Internet to educate the public on the specific practices of industries and individual manufacturers. His informational Web sites gave people the opportunity to make educated decisions on what products and companies they'd want to boycott. Of course, Joddell wanted people to buy and use less, in the first place.

WASHINGTON DC

The moon was visible through the low clouds and leafless hardwoods but didn't offer much light. Only the twisting gray concrete track stood out from the dirt and mulch. The scene was interrupted only by the rhythmic footfalls of a lone runner. Then the tranquility was destroyed by the ring of a cell phone.

"Agent Gunnlick here," answered Ambrose in a voice intended to convey annoyance. It usually took only one call to ruin a pleasant late-night jog through a quiet park.

"Hello, Gunnlick, it's your pal thirty from DeTeCT."

"What can I do for you?" asked Ambrose in a newly accommodating tone. Agent 30 helped him from time to time with tidbits of useful data, and vice versa.

"We got a hit from Curt Joddell in Portland five hours ago. Uncharacteristically he rented a car with his real license. We've already processed the video. It's a match; it's him for sure."

"It sounds like he wanted to be seen. No disguise?"

"That was our feeling as well, but who knows? He wasn't wearing a disguise. We're following him via the car's GPS. Right now he's headed for marijuana country on highway one-ninety-nine south. He's about to hit the one-oh-one," said the DeTeCT agent.

"The state of Jefferson is a hotbed of COED activists. Maybe the Owl is going to take a tour of Pelican Bay to get an idea of what it's going to be like once we pin something on him," suggested Ambrose.

Stifling a chuckle, the cyber-cop responded, "I'll send what we've got over to your guys. Happy hunting...stay safe, partner."

"I'd bet he's headed to the Lost Whale Inn for the night. It's a bed-and-breakfast in Patrick's Point."

"What is it like?"

"I imagine it's a favored perch of the Owl because of the cliff-edge views and access to a long, private beach. Thanks for the heads-up...you guys at DeTeCT are on it. I really appreciate all the help you've given me. Don't be shy, feel free to call any time," encouraged Ambrose Gunnlick. As a trial lawyer, he knew his way around conversational psychology and tried to utilize the power of genuine praise.

EDGEWATER, FLORIDA

Before too much time elapsed and detectives had a chance to sift through the ash, Dewey had escaped from Alaska. He stocked the hideout with supplies for Zell, returned his rental, and caught a flight to the Lower 48. He changed planes and identities two times before flying home. A decade earlier, when he had first gotten hold of some real money, Dewey set out to obtain a property where he could dock an oceangoing vessel in the backyard. While comparing real estate values versus offshore, inshore, and freshwater boating potential, northeastern Florida stood out. The warm, fish-rich Gulf Stream is within range of a day trip, and rural homes located directly on the Intracoastal Waterway were surprisingly affordable. As another bonus, the area has historically avoided the killer hurricanes that have annihilated other parts of the peninsula.

When arriving at his modest crash pad after being away for a spell, Dewey had a simple ritual. Day or night, summer or winter, he would lower a boat into the water and go for a joyride. It didn't matter which boat he took, where he went, or for how long, the idea was to let the water help him decompress. Dewey believed that while running flat out, the windblast would scour away the residual guilt from his latest transgressions and it usually did.

In the past Dewey had dealt with lowlights the only way he knew how, by hiding offensive memories in a remote corner of his mind. The immature but effective technique involved not allowing his mind access to depressing, confidence-killing recollections. Unfortunately the system had clogged Dewey's arteries to the point that the plaque had caused an emotional heart attack. His mission to Alaska had brought him quick riches, but Dewey had never been lower. *It's time for an honest assessment of the decisions I make. I'm sick of navigating through minefields of negativity and guilt every day.*

Only the dull orange glow of the town that NASCAR had built defined the horizon. Surface winds were lazy, causing only the slightest chop. A small amount of surface roughness is actually faster than a dead calm, because air pockets reduce hydraulic friction.

Tonight's boat ride felt different to the driver. Ripping along in the dark offshore at a hundred feet per second was amusing, but it failed to completely silence his abnormally vocal conscience. Tonight his high-priced toy didn't offer Dewey the satisfaction it had in the past, actually, the opposite was happening. Of late, his sour moods spoiled his spoils. The one-dimensional boat with its never-ending upkeep annoyed his new sensibility. The hunk of fiberglass was failing Dewey's new system of cost-benefit analysis. *Who owns who? It's time to squash my materialism.*

Dewey's newly emboldened inner voice was becoming a constant nuisance. *What's the next step? Cash in and disappear? Do the right thing? That might be a nice change.*

SAN DIEGO, CALIFORNIA

Jack Welker touched down at Lindbergh Field marveling at the fact that an alternate airport site still hadn't been chosen. Didn't bother him any; he'd grown up on the smooth streets of Point Loma and loved the short commute. The jets soured the sweetness of the peninsula in the ears of some, but he tuned the noise out.

When he returned to his hometown during the daylight hours, Jack always wanted to take a drive out to the end of the point first off. Traveling west on Harbor Drive and then hanging a left, he and his gal pal passed Fisherman's Landing and H & M Sportfishing. A variety of boats offered local and long-range Mexican trips year-round. Local summertime tuna and yellowtail runs caused a stir within the fishing fraternity, akin to the way a good swell will infuse the surfing community with enthusiasm. They climbed up to the spine of the peninsula and headed south past where the residences ended.

"The sacrifices of past and present military personnel should never be overlooked or underappreciated," said Jack. "The tombstones of Fort Rosecrans National Cemetery provide a reminder that freedom wasn't, isn't, and never will be free. I was just reading about wounded-in-action veterans struggling to get proper health care and benefits."

"…while fast-acting politicians and executives misallocated billions of taxpayer dollars. The American public got a chance to see where the loyalties of their government representatives are," agreed Jasmine.

"It's like a bunch of drunk drivers were having an unregulated road rally and caused a huge pileup on the freeway, injuring scores of innocents… but when the police showed up and saw who had caused the accident, they decided to get the drunk drivers new cars and more alcohol and to close down the freeway to other traffic," said Jack.

"…and then charged everything to broke taxpayers who don't even own cars."

"The people with nest egg on their face…the reckless executives, government policy makers, mortgage companies, and other assorted con men behind this avoidable disaster should be held criminally accountable…not rewarded with taxpayer bailouts," said Jack.

"Why commit small crimes with big penalties if you can recklessly gamble billions of dollars away with few or no consequences?" wondered Jasmine.

"Exactly. The way the financial collapse was handled makes me want to kill somebody."

"Don't say things like that, Jack. I mean it. It's not funny."

"The people should have taken matters into their own hands and exacted justice the old-fashioned way."

"Grow up," said Jasmine.

As the couple continued south toward the lighthouse, the view included the Coronado Islands located in Mexico. From the Cabrillo National Monument, it's a nicely packaged snapshot of San Diego. The bay, the boats, and the general dedication to recreation give clues to its municipal star power. Tepid weather and warm ocean water clinch the deal.

When returning to his old haunts, Jack's stomach instinctively yearned for a *carne asada* burrito. In a city where bargains are about as common as rainstorms, it's cheap SoCal cuisine at its finest. The comfort tube consists of sinewy beef bits, pico de gallo salsa, and guacamole, all wrapped up in a large flour tortilla. Starches, proteins, fruits, and vegetables are all represented. There is no need for utensils, as wax paper does the job. The crucial final element is a couple of thimblefuls of red or green hot sauce. Jack got their burritos to go and asked his girlfriend to go check the surf at the cliffs.

Tonight Jack was scheduled to meet up with a couple of Scott Horne's friends to rehearse, but at the moment all he needed to do was select the soundtrack for their lunch. Considering the locale, it was a no-brainer. Jack twirled his thumb and tapped until his choice appeared. The soothing sounds of local musicians Slightly Stoopid filled the small car.

"I love that they snubbed the corporate machine and kept complete control over themselves and built up a fan base the old way, by touring relentlessly and showing concertgoers a great time. Stoopid prospers by delivering a quality live experience," said Jack admiringly. "Their dynamic set lists meander from sing-along anthems to fast, hard tracks. They've created a devoted fan base that comes to their shows at every opportunity. No amount of studio money, corporate radio manipulation, advertising, or anything else can buy that kind of long-term loyalty."

"These days it's more about concert ticket sales and merchandising than selling albums anyway. The Internet has helped cut the suits out of the revenue stream."

"It's a crazy idea. Let artists be the ones who profit most handsomely from their art," said Jack sarcastically.

TERMAS DE PONZONE, CHILE

The drive from Pucon to the Termas traverses an eerie forest with twisting hardwood limbs angling to reclaim the roadway. Accessed by a short trail through moss-laden trees, a series of rock pools clog a narrow ravine. Open 24/7 and remote enough to keep crowds away, Ponzone rewards those willing to make the commute.

At Termas de Ponzone the man-made rock tubs range in size and temperature. The pools feel natural, with massaging pebbles underfoot. The top pool is the hottest and has a changing cabin that bears resemblance to a waterwheel mill. Stairs in the floor of the building lead directly into the hot tub powered by Earth energy.

"I can't wait to explore this zone in daylight tomorrow," said Maria.

"Pucon is an adventure tourism town that sits beneath a picture-perfect cone, Vulcan Villarrica. It draws tourists in with whitewater rafting, hiking, climbing, sailing, skiing and wine-related pursuits."

"How are the pistes?"

"The local ski area is small, but there are easy-access backcountry opportunities on outsize lava features," explained Mick. "No trees though."

"Mick, why do you love trees so much?" asked Maria.

"It's not the trees I love...its oxygen...atmosphere. I love to breathe clean air. Deforestation deserves some of the attention that fossil fuels have been getting...it's all connected. Slash-and-burn, for example, is a threefold problem. You have the smoke from the fires. Combine that with the loss of oxygen production from the forest. The permanent loss of native plant, animal, and human habitat is the coup de grace."

"They clear land to grow crops. People need food."

"I'm worried mainly about industrial-sized projects. Incinerating a small piece of land's biomass with fire is committing suicide in the long term. The majority of a rainforest's nutrients are tied up in its foliage...burn that away and it's gone forever. A farmer may get a few good harvests, but inevitably the sun and rain will turn the unprotected land into wet desert. Earth has plenty of deserts already," judged the environmentalist.

"I know those things. What I meant was…why do you make the rainforest your passion?" asked the lovely Chilean woman. She was helping Mick mitigate legal red tape in his quest to buy up tracts of endangered forests across the continent.

"The lungs of the planets are being destroyed to make way for farming and cattle grazing. Intentionally destroying Earth's forests is like a chronic cigarette smoker voluntarily removing a functioning lung, against all available medical advice," responded Mick while wading over to the edge of the pool.

"You can't buy all of Amazonia alone," she reminded him.

"I know that, silly. That's why I'm working to find ways to convince countries that their remaining wilderness areas have a greater value to them, as is. Making that work economically will be a challenge, but with ecotourism, sustainable logging, replanting, and new methods of energy production now available…I believe it is my generation's responsibility to start the process. Part of the answer is to sell emissions offsets…force large-scale polluters to buy up forested land to help clean the airborne damage their business inflicts."

"My father said fighting big business is like trying to stop the tides," advised Maria.

"Businesses have weaknesses. Successful private citizens should buy carbon credits, too. The land could then be used by the indigenous peoples who have seen their habitat shrink under a groundswell of dubious capitalist enterprises. The natives could return to living the organic existence that they had perfected until conquering Western Europeans showed up bearing gifts of disease, enslavement, and property ownership."

Abruptly Mick Nolls climbed from the steaming tub and nimbly crab-crawled over some boulders toward the adjacent rivulet. A crashing sound echoed as it funneled through the boulders. Before he had a chance to chicken-out, the masochist submerged his body in a shallow pool away from the swift current. Without fail, cold water will shock the human nervous system.

Involuntary flexing, followed by a period of stiffening, was how Mick's body dealt with the jolt. "Come on in, the water is great. Really cold water is a quicker, healthier alternative to caffeine and other stimulants."

His companion laughed and remarked, "Gringo loco." She began to swim in the shallow water as moonbeams made shiny her nude athletic body. Nolls slipped back into the tub and gave his body its second harsh shock. This time, the heat made his frozen limbs tingle enjoyably. Cold strikes at the body, whereas heat envelops it. "I'm confident that I am in no danger of a having heart attack, because I would have just had one in that river."

"I think we test your heart out in other ways," responded Maria, as she literally threw herself on him.

Bright and seductive, the night light was directly overheard and made them restless. The full moon subliminally controlled their minds and bodies. The gravitational force that moves ocean tides can also sway the decision-making process of human beings. Their premise of maintaining some discretion and maturity in what was technically a public setting was blissfully forgotten.

Oddly, a phone began to ring. Maria thought it must be some other patrons ambling down the trail, but Mick broke their embrace. He jumped out of the water and walked rapidly over to his rucksack. The gringo then pulled out the largest mobile phone she had ever seen.

After looking at the screen and extending a comical antenna, Mick answered the call, "Hola?"

"I'm not sure if this is the right number; sometimes I have amnesia. My friend Johan left me a garbled message Wednesday morning," said the caller.

"No worries there, I understand, but this is the wrong number," responded Mick before hanging up. His sharp mind translated the coded message and began to rearrange his schedule and assemble a to-do list. "Un numero malo. A donde ustedes?" Nolls queried as he slid back into the water, pondering the reason behind the call.

"How did a cell phone get reception out here, and why didn't you tell me about this phone? We could have used it many times when the other failed," responded a decidedly cooled off Maria.

"Come on, don't be mad. Come here."

"You are just like other Yanquis...only interested in one thing. Well, that thing just got taken off the menu," she said as she ascended the wooden stairs.

Nolls angrily slapped at the water with flat palms. Remorseful feelings about not leaving the handset at his rental cabin poisoned his thoughts. "Some feat of technological progress that was," Mick said to the darkness.

As a general rule, Nolls made it a priority to minimize unpleasant interruptions. After a run of savvy stock investments, Mick checked himself out of the finance game before the tech bubble burst and retired at the age of twenty-seven. Taking a cue from Steve Fossett, he dedicated the remainder of his life to adventure. After six epic years of living out all his purchasable dreams, Mick started to feel unproductive and vaguely guilty. His sense of worthlessness metastasized and eventually he decided to find a more fulfilling calling.

During the past half decade, Mick had utilized his considerable wealth and energy toward a less-self-centered goal. Reborn as a naturalist, Mick Nolls devoted himself to making a dent in deforestation and soil degradation worldwide, but particularly in the rainforests of the Amazon basin.

San Diego, California

The climate of Southern California serves up temperate winters and low-humidity summers. The Pacific Ocean is a playground for water sports, but it also cools the coast during the hot summer. On crisp winter nights, the ocean reverses roles and becomes a heater.

Jack knew that drinking had been banned on city beaches and parks and that police officers had quotas to maintain and promotions to pursue, but the law took away the last two public places to imbibe in a city with year-round outdoor drinking weather.

Compelled by stubbornness to behave the way he always had, Jack bought a pint of whiskey and set himself up to watch the sun settling into the Pacific. It turned out to be a $250 protest. Initially he tried to play dumb about the new law, but it didn't work. The San Diego Police Department and Jack Welker were no strangers. An officer recognized him, walked over to get a closer look, and saw the bottle. Jack would have been issued only a citation for drinking on the beach, but he didn't have ID on him. He got taken downtown to establish his identity. After being released, Jack called his girlfriend to pick him up.

"Politicians have severely mismanaged this city, yet they focus on drinking on beaches? Water shortages, sweetheart pensions for government employees, laughable leases on city properties, polluted storm runoff, horrible rush-hour traffic…the list of actual problems goes on and on," lamented Jack. "The whole ordeal is no surprise. I'm disgusted to be a native. I'm aware that paranoid police operate on the assumption that anyone who doesn't toe the line completely is a danger. This legal detour is yet another reminder to me that I should avoid spending time in places that are crowded enough to warrant police patrols. Limiting interactions with law enforcement is one of many factors that pushed me into embracing the wilderness. The opportunity to temporarily escape advertising is another motivator." He liked to dump things that were bothering him on Jasmine. Somehow her tender demeanor defused the pressure.

"Let it go, Jack, all that stuff has nothing to do with you. You should focus on things that you have a chance to affect," suggested his longtime sweetie.

"It does have something to do with me. I just got detained and fined! Blemishes have tarnished the shine of America's Finest City. Saying people can't drink on the beach is like saying people can't swim at the beach," continued Jack, who couldn't let it go.

"I don't know what to tell you, honey," answered his girl, knowing it was easier to let Jack rant when he got into a tilted frame of mind.

"Why not make drinking illegal only on certain beaches? I mean, dogs have their own beach, but not drinkers? That stupid ticket is another reason to avoid this crowded, superficial, over-priced desert. What's next? No drinking on private property…or in your own home?"

"Calm down, sweetie. I'll pay the fine," offered Jasmine.

"It's not the money. I don't want fat, ugly people on the beach. Let's make a law against that. And screaming little children…criminalize that too. There are always a few drunk people who are out of control, but isn't that what the police are paid to do? Handle the occasional troublemaker?" asked Jack rhetorically.

"You know it's more complicated than that," reasonably pointed out Jasmine.

"Yeah, rich, beachside property owners don't want the lower tax bracket enjoying themselves in their front yard. Maybe sporting events should ban drinking. Better yet, make it where you can only drink alcohol indoors, under controlled circumstances, at an accredited facility, with proper supervision… after passing a series of physical and psychological tests," said Jack, giggling.

"People in other parts of the world think I'm joking when I tell them that a couple can't enjoy a bottle of wine on the beach at sunset…or that a construction worker can't have a cold beer on the sand after a hard day on the job," said Jasmine. "I admit…it's embarrassing."

Amsterdam, Netherlands

Thirty-six hours after receiving the phone call at the Chilean hot springs, Mick Nolls found himself across the pond. At this early hour, bicyclists dominated the scene as he leisurely walked down a tree-lined canal. The city was filled with pedal-power commuters, which Mick found positively enchanting.

After several random detours, Mick reached his destination, Amnesia. As he always did before a secret meeting, Nolls arrived well ahead of schedule to study the scene for signs of surveillance. It wasn't that he didn't trust the man he was meeting; in truth, he trusted the Owl to a fault. The issue was that maybe Curt didn't know he was being followed. He had witnessed the lengths law enforcement went to to spy on Curt stateside.

After a while he yanked the heavy door open and entered the business, dressed casually in cargo pants and a dark gray hoodie. There was only one other patron, which had the effect of relaxing Mick a bit. Even when he had nothing to hide, privacy was always preferable. Nolls signaled the attractive barista. "Could I have a large bottle of water, no gas...and a Chai tea, please? And I need a gram of a tasty Indica, but nothing super strong."

"I have a local indoor...Indigo. It's nice this time of day," responded the girl in beautiful British English.

"That's perfect. Could I please borrow the tall yellow one? *Dank u*," responded Mick, thanking her in Dutch.

"Seventeen and one-half euros. I'll freshen the bong water for you."

"That's a classy move."

Nolls handed over a twenty-euro note, told her to keep the change, and grabbed the small pouch of dried flowers. He found a seat with his back to a wall, which allowed him to monitor the small room. Anxious to explore the character of the new strain, he dumped the nuggets onto the table. Beams of sunlight transformed the tiny crystals into glistening diamonds. The delicate structure of the flower brought to mind the jeweler Faberge.

In the jet age, anyone of means can change the season, climate, language, culture, and anything else they want to in a matter of hours. Curt Joddell had done just that, with an all-night airline flight. Once through customs, he boarded a train a short walk away. The train left quickly and pulled into the gray morning; Curt appreciated the easy airport-to-city transfer. Efficiency made him smile.

Thirty minutes later a renewed Curt Joddell exited the gorgeous train station, Centraal, and raised his collar up against a damp breeze. *Presto, new continent.*

As a Eurorail-ing teenage backpacker on his first visit to The Dam, Curt Joddell fell in civic love. The Van Gogh Museum, the red-light district, and everything in between still captivated him in a way few urban places did.

Bursting with culture, the city hosted ornate buildings and quiet, leafy neighborhoods. Narrow waterways radiated outward like the spokes of a bicycle. Docked along the canals were nifty houseboats. Locals possessed a healthy worldliness and exhibited a friendly demeanor towards travelers. A rare tolerance toward adult recreation drew freedom-lovers from stricter environs.

The brisk walk, combined with fond memories, began to erase the effects of his overnight flight. It wasn't an easy city to navigate, but Curt had it dialed. His navigational prowess was a remnant from spending half a year there once.

Mick Nolls was setting fire to his third b-load when he heard the heavy door squeak open. He innocently raised his eyes and made eye contact with his friend. Frustrated by the rate of progress he was able to make legitimately, Mick had been secretly donating money to Curt's less-than-legal protective efforts.

The Owl walked up casually and asked sarcastically, "What are you smoking?"

"Indigo," said Mick, before the pair enthusiastically shook hands.

"I'll try something different off the marijuana menu," exclaimed the eager American. For a brief moment, Curt found himself frozen with delight. "I just fell headlong into an Amster-trance. Geez, I am struggling to fight off the effects of my flight."

"The best way to counter jet lag from a red-eye is by getting red eye," suggested Mick, handing over a toke.

"You got it."

"Can you believe they scissored tobacco smoking in the cafes?" asked Nolls. "Sheer genius...I might have to buy a flat now."

"They stomped out my only complaint about the coffee shops. The delicate natural smells of quality pot used to get overpowered by laboratory smoke. Not to mention the vile secondhand aspect of factory cigarettes," answered Curt. "Cannabis is steadily gaining respect."

"Potheads have this reputation as modern-day lotus-eaters. Ignorant people picture stoners wiling the days away in a stupor. Most habitual smokers are self-medicating, opting to burn sinsemilla because it eases mental and physical tension better than anything the guys in white coats can synthesize. Mother Nature has provided millions of beneficial plants and herbs for humans to safely use," surmised Mick.

"Weed doesn't create tax revenue for the U.S. government. Plus it cuts into the profits of the prescription-drug and alcohol syndicates, so it has been demonized. America should rethink its federal marijuana policy, considering the example of alcohol prohibition. Between the tax benefits and potential savings in the criminal justice system, a debt-riddled Uncle Sam should face the facts. Forward-minded states have started a common-sense transition without waiting for the Feds' approval," observed Curt before snapping the bong load. He was intentionally trying to get Mick into a revolutionary mindset.

"You forgot about the huge benefits of hemp farming. Maybe Andean coca growers and Afghani poppy farmers would switch to cannabis if there was a lucrative and stable market," said Nolls.

"How many people are killed by prescription medicines every year? The general public ignores the dangers of over-the-counter medicines because the media does. Heavy pot use has adverse side effects, but so do the synthetic alternatives," added the Owl, using his knack for persuasively injecting truths with conspiracies.

"After this, shall we go for a walk so I can speak with you privately?" Joddell asked, flicking his eyes toward the other patron.

Twenty minutes later the two men donned their coats, returned the water pipe, thanked the barista, and headed outside.

"In Amsterdam pedestrians need to stay alert to the legions of bicycle riders. I nearly walked into a stream of cyclists absentmindedly," said Mick.

One pedal-pusher passed by and then took one hand off the handlebars and started speaking into it, "The subjects left together and are walking south down the Herengracht."

A decidedly less relaxed crew convened inside a crowded police substation a few blocks away. Three Interpol agents were monitoring the two men on the network of video cameras that blanket the city's hub.

"Get the biometrics on this new suspect...and check him against Schiphol International's database for the last four days. If you don't get a match, try Frankfurt, London, and Paris, in that order. Why would Joddell choose Amnesia? He must be aware of the camera coverage," said Simon Page, an Interpol detective specializing in terrorism. "Maybe he's not doing anything he feels the need to hide? You know the Yanks are bloody paranoid these days. I worry that we are wasting time on tourists, not eco-terrorists," said Simon aloud, answering his own questions. Over his career the lawman had watched the allure of his life's work suffocate under a mountain of paperwork, red tape, and personality politics.

Back on the canal, Joddell gave a regal wooden motorboat an extended stare. "Now that's a beautiful boat. I love old-school craftsmanship, because products were built to last. I think I'd fancy a ride on it," said Curt. He went over to a set of stairs that led down to an old stone quay.

"You gonna flag him down?" questioned a suspicious Mick. *Be ready, you never know when Curt will spring a surprise test.*

After the boat went past, it made an aggressive U-turn and headed for the dock. The elegant craft approached the stone quay carrying too much speed to dock safely.

"Don't get caught flat-footed. Let it pass by, and then we'll chase the boat down and jump on," Curt suggested, trying to hide a chuckle.

As the boat motored past, the two men began to jog. Once it was a good bit ahead of them, Joddell accelerated his pace and angled toward the vessel. He smoothly hopped onto the gunwale and grabbed the outstretched hand of the driver. When Curt looked up, he realized Mick Nolls was already seated.

Mick Nolls was naturally quick and coordinated and had the kind of free time that allowed him to stay ridiculously fit. Rarely did someone he was with outclass him in a challenge of athleticism. "What took you so long," he asked the Owl mockingly. "I didn't think you were going to make it."

"You'd be better off saving those kinds of silly observations for your diary," joked Curt.

The startled surveillance team stared at the monitor in disbelief as the antique boat motored down the canal at high speed. "What happened? Who was that in the boat? Did anyone get a picture of the driver? Did they make us?" demanded Detective Page, confused. "Why would Curt Joddell put on a big show like that instead of simply losing surveillance at the airport?"

"That must have been preplanned. The Owl made no discernible calls or signals…additionally, he kept checking his watch in the minutes before the escape. It's like he wanted us to see him and who he was with, but then he wanted us to not see him anymore," judged the street agent over the radio.

"Call the harbor police and have them see where they go," ordered Page. "This man has purposely put a cat amongst the pigeons."

They dropped the driver off a few canals over and aimed for the main channel. "How much do you know about the Itaipu Dam?" inquired Curt.

"I've been to Iguaçu Falls a few times, of course, and I've taken the tourist tour of the dam twice. I've seen the complex from a heli," relayed Nolls. He had expected to be hit up for a monetary donation, so the oddball travel question surprised him.

"Good. So you know the area a little bit….I need for you to fly to Buenos Aires. Proceed by land to Puerto Iguaçu, and then cross into Paraguay. Relax, do some shopping, whatever. A few days later, head across the border to Brazil on your real passport. Get established in Foz do Iguaçu as a normal tourist. Hike, raft, ride the train, go see the dam. In the future, information will come only from Sonya. There shouldn't be any problems, but if there is a serious issue, reach out to my site in a coded email," detailed the Owl.

The brain in Mick's skull digested information with one half while the other side began to worry. *Is the Owl having a Jim Jones meltdown? Could he really be thinking about attacking that facility? They would just rebuild it.*

"Why send me?" asked Nolls pointedly.

"You're my South Am guru. And you speak Portuguese," he replied plainly.

"Not fluently, but I'll do my best," said Mick. *I hope I didn't just drink the Kool-Aid.* Mick looked long and hard into the face of the Owl searching for a clue to something, anything, but came away empty. Curt Joddell had mastered control of his facial musculature. "It's hard to trust a guy wearing sunglasses on a cloudy day."

"People wear sunglasses because the sun's rays are bright and damaging, but there are some other benefits. Shades stop people from reading your eyes, give protection from flying debris, and allow discreet use of your peripheral vision. Don't worry, Mick, you can trust me."

SOUTH FLORIDA

Across the Atlantic, Dewey zoomed gleefully towards Dade County. What could have been a horrendous slog down the I-95 in an old Honda Prelude had been transformed into a thrilling trip on a Ducati sport bike. The absurdly nimble crotch-rocket handled better and better as it went faster and faster. Under full throttle, a rider enjoys the kind of forces normally associated with jet aircraft. Modern sport bike ergonomics are so user friendly that overconfidence is an issue for risk-takers, a category that Dewey fit into. The machine dared its operator to twist his wrist.

Acceleration is the sexiest force, but go-fast toys cost big bucks. A big part of what originally led Dewey to commit crimes was the fact that he wanted money to spend on adrenaline-producing vehicles. On land, sea, snow and in the air, Dewey loved recreational vehicles in all of their applications.

Heavy traffic gave Dewey a chance to play slalom. Instead of stationary flags from his childhood ski racing days, these gates were hunks of plastic-covered metal weighing thousands of pounds and being operated by strangers of greatly varying dexterity and lucidity. Banking the land speeder back and forth through the maze of red taillights was confidence building, even therapeutic. Dewey delighted in seeing drivers flinch with fear as he zipped within inches of their isolation bubbles.

On this mission the clear weather and thin late-night traffic helped increase Dewey's margin of safety. Near the airfield, Dewey pulled off the freeway and headed west away from the Atlantic Ocean to find a dive motel. As he silenced the engine, he experienced a sense of relief. Walking up to the bulletproof lobby window, he glanced back at the silenced beast and marveled at the fact that sport bikes were street legal in this safety-is-everything era.

According to the mandate, he could call only on business days between 10 and 12 A.M. Zulu or GMT. Greenwich Mean is five hours ahead of Eastern Standard, which meant that he had four hours to burn. More than anything, Dewey wanted to head to the nearest watering hole to celebrate the midnight run, but he would end up getting overserved. He needed a clear, sharp head in the morning, which meant that abusing alcohol was not a smart option. As a consolation he took a hot shower and ingested a couple of Ambien to throttle back and get some rest.

The timepiece strapped to his wrist beeped him into consciousness at half past five. A quick shower on full-cold gave Dewey enough motivation to brew a cup of motivation. The plastic wrapper claimed it as coffee, but he had his suspicions.

After letting his mechanized horse warm up for a minute, Dewey pressed down with his left foot and opened his left hand while twisting his right. After completing the short commute Dewey parked his prized Ducati in the short-term garage and headed into the terminal looking out-of-place dressed in a bright one-piece leather suit. He paged Bill Jones with the number of the payphone followed by his special code. The response was immediate.

"Hello."

"I have been really worried about you. You really should call more often. How was your trip?" asked Bill Jones, trying his hardest not to explode into a tirade of slurs and curses. This phone call had been causing him to lose sleep. Alan Reynard had been pestering him incessantly.

"Ran into a little trouble, as I am sure you've heard. It turned out okay in the end. It's all wrapped up. It's a done deal," said the fluent liar.

"That's good to hear. I've been a wreck since you never checked in. Let's meet up. Where are you?" Jones felt a weight being lifted off his shoulders as he regained his faith in Dewey and his previously unblemished work ethic.

"I'm at the *aeropuerto* in Miami on a layover…changing planes before I head to South America to go fishing," said Dewey, misleading his employer.

"I wish you'd reconsider. I have a great new opportunity for you to earn some big-time cash. It's the easiest job yet," baited Bill Jones, making a note to have someone check the origin of the call.

"Money talks, my friend, but I trust you're speaking the truth. You have been good to me in the past. I will cancel my trip and call you later this week."

To end the connection, Dewey slammed the receiver down and pocketed the pen recorder he had been using to tape the conversation. He walked off briskly with newly minted visions of dollars. The leather suit mixed with high heat and humidity made him feel like he was being poached. *Should I ride the bike all the way up to DC? Nah, that's asking for trouble. I'll go via small plane.*

Back in the parking garage, Dewey reignited the fire. The lightweight, ultra-high-revving motor sprang to life without hesitation, as if it couldn't wait to get back to work. In neutral, Dewey flicked his wrist a few times for kicks and caused several nearby car alarms to trigger.

After a heavy snowfall, everything gets a fresh start. Clean, cold, and beautiful, a blanket of snowflakes transforms even the drabbest landscape into a sparkling showpiece.

Eons of tectonic shoving matches and glacial erosion had crafted a broken landscape of rock, snow, and ice. A sharply angled snowfield sat untouched by sun, wind, or rain. An alpenglow formed following the sunset, turning the pointy mountains pink and soft. At the base of the slope were the inky, foreboding waters of a fjord. The deep blue liquid provided an eerie visual contrast against the virgin snow.

With a limitless supply of energy, Scott Horne dropped in aggressively, letting the contours of the mountain dictate where to paint his turns into the bottomless snow. Each change in direction of his snowboard dislodged tens of thousands of flakes and sent them exploding into graceful plumes.

Suddenly the entire slope lost its battle against gravity and broke away. Snow is mostly air mixed with a bit of crystallized water, but water is heavy and gravity is persistent. The self-triggered avalanche swallowed Scott immediately, offering no avenue of escape. The brutality and speed of the tumbling beat the breath out of him as he rag-dolled helplessly toward the frigid water. While swimming for his life, Scott didn't give up hope that he could cheat death one more time. *Not now, not today. I can't die yet. I have unfinished business.*

Cascading out of control while accelerating down the last few hundred yards toward the icy fjord almost had Scott convinced that this time he was going to perish. *If you die, you deserve it.*

A loud noise changed his focus. Over and over the obnoxious sound attacked him.

WASHINGTON, DC

On the fourteenth ring, the wake-up call finally succeeded in rousing a comatose Scott Horne. Though he yearned to be one, Horne had never been an early riser. He angrily picked up and then slammed the receiver back onto its cradle. *The option of hanging up a phone with authority is something conspicuously lacking from cellular and cordless varieties.*

The cold powder smoke stinging his bare face, the vibrant sky, and the fear he'd experienced in the violent spin cycle of the avalanche had seemed so real. The dream was a memorable one because he hadn't been able to dictate the outcome. Scott Horne usually had more control of his night flights. Typically, he didn't have total creative control of the content and could only make alterations to existing scenarios. Mid-dream course corrections were especially useful in dreams containing women he found appealing.

He attempted to use the content of his dreams to psycho-self-analyze his hidden conscious. He interpreted the avalanche to be a warning that he was getting into something over his head. *Am I ignorantly taunting an uncontrollable entity? Is this a reminder that even when things are going good, disaster can strike, or, in this case, strike again?*

If there was one thing that he always counted on, it was that people, places, and things will always change. Concrete plans shackle. Flexibility is the key to pulling off any complicated undertaking. *The wise man always has an alternate route, or three.*

Scott was still in transition into full consciousness when his drowsiness was stopped short by a handful of cold water to the face. With pride, he recalled yesterday's successful recruitment. Then he remembered what he had to do later in the day. His plan of revenge was already well into motion, so Scott felt the time was right to bring Alan Reynard and his cronies into the mix. The day's sobering agenda called for Scott to attend the memorial services for Nancy Watkins. It promised to be an emotional event for him, considering he had had a part in precipitating it.

Drawing open the curtains, Scott looked out at the Capitol Building. The multi-faced people that worked there made him angry. One part of his mind felt pride in the national monuments and museums of Washington. In the other lobe of his gray matter, Scott knew DC as the physical place where the hopes and dreams of average Americans got crushed by special interests.

BIG BEAR LAKE, CALIFORNIA

Ernesto Vargas believed in supporting things like farmers' markets. He liked having a relationship with the vendors and enjoyed feeling appreciated for being a repeat customer. It reminded him of his childhood, a time period when customers paid great attention to where their dollars went. The older gentleman leisurely surveyed the vegetables, waiting for something to stand out and beg to be purchased and devoured.

"Hey, Judge, beautiful day, huh?" called out a farmer.

"You said it," agreed Ernesto.

"I thought you only shopped at box stores," teased the farmer.

"No, thanks. I prefer that my hard-earned dollars stay in the community instead of contributing to some CEO's ludicrous salary or bonus."

"I hear ya. I only grow a few acres of top-quality produce. I'm not getting rich, but it feels good."

"Giant companies have steered the feeding focus onto high-profit, low-nutrition, highly-processed junk food...products that contain an ingredient list that reads like a recipe for homemade ant poison. It's sad that the public got hooked so badly."

"Sometimes it seems the ultra-rich are the royals, and we peasants exist primarily to further enrich them."

"I've spent my life pursuing justice and the rapidly growing disparity of wealth eats me up. Literally. It causes acids to flood my stomach," confessed Ernesto. The leash in his pocket began chirping. "Excuse me. My wife probably remembered something else she wants me to fetch." He took a few steps away and answered the call without looking at the caller ID. "Hi, honey."

"Hey, baby, I know I'm your fly-fishing idol, but I didn't know you had real feelings for me," teased Scott Horne.

"Is that you, Scotty? I thought you had forgotten about me. I'm glad I decided to always carry my cellular phone with me."

"What did everybody do before cell phones came along? I mean, they have only been around twenty-some years and now everyone needs to have one on hand every second."

"I guess they took responsibility for themselves and for their actions… an abstract idea these days, thanks to current interpretations of liability. On the other side of the coin, for an old man like me it's a comforting notion to have emergency services at the push of a button," replied Ernesto.

"Point taken, but the cell phone still gets my vote for being the worst invention to come along during my lifetime. And I had concluded that before they evolved into tracking devices." Scott couldn't resist making at least one controversial law-and-order comment to his buddy.

"Regarding that, I would submit that a law-abiding citizen has nothing to hide and therefore nothing to fear. How about you?"

"I've been better. How is your sun-drenched mountain lake town?"

"The twenty-plus million Southern Californians who use the San Bernardino Mountains as a drivable winter experience took a hit. A landslide just closed the main highway."

"It is one of the few places where it is possible to easily go surfing and snowboarding in the same day without flying."

"Have you skied here?"

"If measured by acreage, vertical feet, or snowfall, Snow Summit and Bear Mountain appear to be minor league, but the resorts were pioneers of snowboard park design and lift-accessed mountain biking. Years ahead of other resorts with far more resources, Summit and Bear used their abundant sunshine and close proximity to where most of the surf-skate-snow companies were based to accelerate the progression of a new type of snowboarding and skiing," said Scott.

"Locals are proud of that," said Ernesto.

"On modest slopes overlooking the lake, a style took root that utilized man-made features and drew inspiration from street skateboarding and motocross."

"Have you been staying out of trouble?" asked Ernesto in an expectant tone.

"It's funny you should ask that, because I am about to send you a package. I don't know how to put this, but it's one of those…"open only if I disappear" gigs. I know that sounds macabre, but…" mumbled Scott as his sentence structuring skills faltered.

"What's going on? What is this about?" asked a bewildered Ernesto. "Is this another one of your jokes?"

"Are you at the same P.O. box?"

"Yeah, but…."

"*Lo siento, amigo*," apologized Scott before hanging up.

"*Buena suerte*, Scotty."

A steady sound drew Ernesto's gaze skyward. Even on the busiest and most developed boulevard in Big Bear, there were enough trees to give the wind something to whistle through.

WASHINGTON, DC

Scott lubed up his courage machine with a double whiskey on the rocks at the hotel bar before heading down the street to mail the parcel. He found a taxi stand and sized up the drivers awhile before choosing one who seemed to be laughing and enjoying himself.

"Are you trying to make some money today?"

"No, I'm a bored millionaire. I drive this cab for fun," responded the cantankerous cabbie.

"Well, I need to go somewhere way out of town, and then I'll need you to wait a half-hour or so for me."

"We can go wherever you want, if you got the bread," confirmed the driver.

This was the kind of guy Scott wanted to find. He flashed a roll of hundreds and got into the front seat.

"Spend much time in DC?" asked the driver.

"Fortunately...no," said Scott plainly.

"With that nice suit and fat wad, I thought you'd be some big wig."

"Not a chance, but today I need to look the part," responded Horne.

"I love this country, but after the last decade I'm worried about us."

"On paper, our constitution stands tall among its peers, but in the upper levels of government, temptation is everywhere. Survival is programmed into human DNA, but many politicians allow ambition and greed to overwhelm them. Nearly every person is susceptible to some price, perk, or privilege," said Horne, venting.

"I drive their mistresses around. I hear all the juicy details," confided the cabbie.

"Questionable campaign contributions are usually at the heart of political scandals. Rich and powerful corporations and individuals donate generously through intermediaries to both candidates. This puts elected officials in a submissive position. They end up serving those who helped them get into office and can ensure they stay there," said Scott.

"The electoral process was designed over two hundred years ago. It's too bad the founding fathers didn't add something about updating the Constitution as the world changes. The technology is there for a national vote on key issues," said the driver.

"People are too busy to be interested in policy-making," said Scott. "I'm enjoying your insight. We should do something about our geriatric Supreme Court. In seventeen-seventy-six the average life expectancy was something like thirty-five or forty years. People live too long now. We need to amend the term to ten years for justices. Get some fresh blood in there."

"Trying to get things changed in this town is impossible, because everything is entrenched...it's like moving mountains," explained the cabbie.

Scott took a deep breath of smog-infused air and tasted the fact that he was out of his element. "I can feel the emissions of the delivery truck ahead of us inside my mouth. I wonder how long it will be before everyone starts wearing surgical masks," Scott mused.

As the taxi headed out of the metro area, the dense development thinned. The dull palette of leafless trees didn't contrast much with the bleak gray sky. At the guarded entrance of Applied Leverage, Scott and the driver were forced to show identification and sign in as guests. The size and scope of the barrier impressed them.

"Keep going straight. I want to enjoy these beautiful grounds a little, first," said Scott. "I want to get a sense of the place." *At least the visibility down low looks fine. We shouldn't have any problems.*

"It's your money, guy."

The taxi slowly wound its way through the campus, eventually arriving at a parking lot in the shadow of the main office building. The contemporary glass-and-metal edifice stood over a hundred feet tall and possessed sharp, clean lines. The décor of the structure and surrounding landscape intentionally screamed money and power, as did the assembly of luxury automobiles.

Less than a minute after they pulled up, a dark blue SUV approached from around the corner. The driver pulled in opposite the taxi.

"Can I help y'all?" drawled the sentry.

"Ah, yes, sir. We are looking for the Watkins funeral," responded Scott, trying to sound confused.

"The gatekeeper didn't give you a map at the front gate?"

"He did, but I'm no good with maps."

"Please follow me," said the guard, barely hiding his disdain for Scott's incompetence.

"Thanks for the help, officer." Scott lowered his sunglasses, looked square into the man's eyes, and presented an awkwardly wide grin.

The driver followed the guard back to the correct location and parked right up front as Scott instructed. A perennial briber, Scott pulled out three hundred-dollar notes. The rectangles of green paper made the driver's eyes smile.

"Can you do me a favor and please wait for me right here? I'll probably need to make a real quick exit," said Scott. He then tore the bills in two and handed the cabbie the right halves. "Thank you."

The wake was taking place at an outdoor assembly area. Applied Leverage had spared no expense in preparing for the event. Nancy's family had been flown out for the proceedings. The hundred or so guests were seated or standing around ten clothed tables under a heated tent. A throng of servers were circulating with lavish arrays of gourmet edibles. Trays of hot coffee and tea warmed the mournful crowd.

The spring chill was strong enough that most of the guests had left their hats and scarves on, which pleased Scott, considering he was a semi-recognizable figure. Dressed appropriately in a loose-fitting, jet-black Savile Row suit with a matching fedora, Scott waved to nobody in particular as he approached the covered pavilion. He slowly panned the crowd while restlessly tapping his thigh with a pocketed hand. The camera masquerading as a jacket button took several pictures with each touch. The thumb-sized battery and hard drive could hold over two thousand pictures. *Smile, everybody.*

SOUTHERN MARYLAND

CIGARS had been established in the government-could-do-no-wrong era following the airliner attacks on New York and Washington, DC. The concept had been to create a small group of unencumbered specialists working to locate foreign or homegrown domestic terrorists before they could carry out a strike. To stay free from oversight, the CIGARS budget was hidden within other agencies. Congress had only peripheral knowledge of its operations.

Agent Ambrose Gunnlick and a colleague discussed the circumstances. "Have you seen the intel from Interpol regarding Curt Joddell's antics in Amsterdam?" asked a CIGARS computer guru.

"Yep. I've strained my brain trying to figure out this puzzle. The problem is that the only pieces I have to work with are the Owl's erratic actions. I read the new suspect has been identified as Mick Nolls. What's his story?"

"Until now Nolls has been viewed only as a sympathizer and possible donor, but he's now considered an active Citizenry of Earth's Defense operative. Nolls doesn't match the standard profile of a radical activist. The guy comes from a respected Jackson, Wyoming, family and cruised through an Ivy League education. Nolls then had a brief but distinguished career as a hedge-fund manager. The most worrisome part of Nolls's involvement is that he's worth over a hundred million post-recession dollars. This case now stretches across Europe, North America, and South America," said the specialist.

"What?" asked Ambrose.

"Nolls flew down to Argentina from Holland and promptly disappeared into the traffic of Buenos Aires with an unknown female."

Ambrose stared blankly at the wall, befuddled by the report.

Agent Gunnlick decided it was the right time to take the developing situation upstairs. He began to mentally assemble his spiel. After the rough sketch became a polished pitch, he picked up the phone and pressed buttons.

"The director's office," answered a nauseatingly chipper secretary.

"Hey, it's Gunnlick. Does the big guy have any holes in his schedule? I need a few minutes with him," said Ambrose.

"He can see you briefly at quarter to ten. Try being early for a change," responded the secretary with the smug attitude of a gatekeeper.

"Thanks, Eddie," replied Gunnlick before he cut the connection. "Work would be great if it weren't for the people," he said to his office.

Later that morning, Ambrose took the stairs up the three floors, arriving ten minutes early.

"Hey, Ambrose," greeted Eddie. "The director is free. Go right in."

Gunnlick gave the man a thumbs-up as he crossed the room. He opened the door and entered his boss's enormous office.

"Ambrose, ole buddy. How come you never visit anymore?"

"You canceled our last two scheduled meetings."

"It couldn't be avoided. Anyway, you have my attention now. What can I do you for?" asked Morgan Higgins dismissively.

"COED's leader Curt Joddell is actively planning something. Here's a printed list of what I have put together so far, evidence-wise. It's all circumstantial, but something is up. What it is…I have no idea," summarized Agent Gunnlick, pleased with his compact persuasion.

"In the past few days, several guys have mentioned him to me. There might be something brewing. I will look this over and talk to the section chiefs. Then I'll get back to you. Thank you for bringing this to my attention. Do you have anything else?" asked the director. Morgan Higgins hadn't risen to this elevated perch by following the premonitions of others. He possessed gut reactions, and those were the ones he trusted.

NORTHERN VIRGINIA

Looking around at the reception, Scott recognized several prominent members of Congress in attendance. He noticed Nancy's friend Melissa talking to an athletic but pale-looking man wearing a sharp suit. *Ask her about that guy.*

Satisfied with his stock of photos, Scott set about looking for the face he had committed to memory recently. Finding him quickly, Scott reached back into his pocket, pulled out a cell, and placed a short call.

He approached the man. "Sheriff Roberts. Pleased to meet you, sir. Scott Horne," he said, offering his hand to the lawman. "I have a piece of important information that will interest you."

"Son...you can call me at my office. This is not the time or place to discuss...."

Scott cut him off, "Actually it is. I want to collect the hundred-thousand-dollar reward for providing information that leads to an arrest for the murder of the young woman we are here honoring."

"For your sake, son, you better not be pullin' my leg," promised the sheriff.

Scott started walking away from the sheriff, while over his shoulder he taunted, "Alan Reynard offered the reward. I want him to hear this. Honestly, I want as many witnesses as possible."

Reynard was glad-handing when he was struck by the purposeful, brisk stride of a tall, younger fellow. A long-standing coward, Alan gestured to Bill Jones, who promptly put himself into motion.

Scott played nice guy, extending his hand and a smile. "Mr. Reynard, what an honor. I am a huge fan."

Bill Jones relaxed for a second, but then Sheriff Roberts interjected, "This man told me he has information about the hit-and-run and he wants you to hear it. Okay, what gives, bub?"

The statement caused gasps among the Watkins family and a spike in Alan and Bill's collective blood pressure. Scott looked at Reynard and enjoyed the moment. Then he lit the fuse that would blast the funeral apart. "First, I would like to apologize to the Watkins family for their loss. Sheriff, the truth is that I don't know exactly who was driving the car that struck Nancy, but I can guarantee you that Alan Reynard arranged it. She called me right before it happened and told me she caught Alan bribing Sen...."

Bill Jones had heard enough. He lunged at the interloper, grabbed his neck, and attempted to pin the man's right arm behind his back. It seemed that the intruder had accepted an early defeat, since he didn't put up a struggle.

After letting Jones manhandle him for a couple seconds to establish a case for self-defense, Scott set his feet, twisted his hips, and launched a left uppercut. The sucker-punch caught Jones under the chin. The force of his jawbone impacting his skull caused the big man to lose consciousness and subsequently collapse.

After straightening his jacket, Scott deeply examined the astonishment on Alan's face. "I only legally defended myself. Alan Reynard bribed Senator Cummins with a box of cash, and Nancy found out about it. Someone pushed her into the path of that vehicle," blurted Scott to the sheriff before taking off. Full of adrenaline, Scott easily outran the Applied Leverage guards who gave chase. The taxi driver was waiting with the engine running and peeled out of the asphalt lot as soon as his fare jumped in.

"Nice work," managed Scott through heavy breaths, rewarding the driver with the three left halves and two whole C-notes. After catching his wind, Scott pulled out a cell phone and hit redial.

The cabbie and Scott were winding their way toward the entrance when the SUV raced up behind them, sirens blaring, lights blazing.

On a loudspeaker the pursuer reminded them, "Pull over right now! You're already caught. You can not ram your way outta that gate."

"He's right. Pull over. Just tell them the truth," said Scott after a couple of seconds. As soon as the taxi was going slowly enough, Scott jumped out. He ran through the dense bushes, rocks, and hardwoods that lined the lane and headed into the open meadow at full tilt.

The head of campus security cursed the ornamental trees and rocks that prevented him from following the miscreant directly into the field. A few thousand feet down the road there was a gap large enough to squeeze his gas-guzzler through.

"He's in the meadow heading south. Get some ATVs out here in case he makes it into the trees," yelled the guard into his radio, knowing his future employment status at Applied Leverage depended on catching this perpetrator. *If this joker thinks he is going to come onto my territory and embarrass me...he's kidding himself.*

The big V-8 delivered and sent the truck careening through the gateway into the meadow. He could see that the fleeing fugitive's pace wasn't going to be fast enough for him to make it into the woods. "Where are you going to go now, buster?" said the guard aloud.

When Scott took a quick glance backward, he saw that the deep-blue SUV and its angry operator were racing across the grass at a freeway clip.

Back at the pavilion, the initial chaos following the accusations had worn off. On wobbly legs, Bill Jones was being helped over to a limo bound for the ER. The family of Nancy Watkins reacted to the intrusion with more curiosity than anger. Nobody in attendance had missed how aggressively Alan Reynard's bodyguard had restrained the man. Applied Leverage was obviously very sensitive to the inflammatory statement.

Newly arrived members of Alan's security detail felt impotent and humiliated. They had let their guard down because they were on home turf.

That loudmouth just committed suicide, thought one bodyguard.

"We are very embarrassed and extend our greatest apologies to the Watkins family. The truth is, that man is an ex-employee who is in the midst of a severe mental health crisis. Again, we are very sorry about this tragic interruption. We'd appreciate it if everyone here could, please, keep this quiet. You'll have to excuse me...I am going to the hospital with Bill," explained Alan Reynard, weaseling away from the event.

In the meadow, Scott's pace was falling off. The four-hundred yard dash had drained him. Although Scott ran often, the extended sprint had taxed his body in unforeseen ways. Not a second too soon, he heard the music his ears desperately sought.

Abruptly Byron Richardson appeared above the east tree line. The Robinson 44 piston-powered, internal-combustion engine was lighter, more efficient, and quieter than the jet helicopters he normally flew. Needing to lose airspeed fast, he brought the nose up and used the bottom of the helicopter as an airbrake. The tactic was a clever, but aggressive, method of bleeding off airspeed without gaining much altitude.

Scott shed his jacket as he ran, revealing a chest harness. The rescue hook dangled fifty feet below the helicopter. Byron timed his flare perfectly. The metal cable swung forward as the helicopter transitioned into a hover. When the pendulum motion reversed, Scott was in position to slam an oversized carabiner onto the lifeline. He raised his fist to signal that he was safely attached.

Byron twisted the throttle while pulling up on the collective, which changed the pitch of the rotor blades into a climbing angle of attack. His other hand gently pulled back on the cyclic, which tilted the position of the rotor in relation to the aircraft's fuselage.

Already at full available power, Byron became worried that the normally aspirated engine might not have the guts to hoist Scott over the approaching treetops, but it was too late to stop or turn.

Trying to settle into the harness more comfortably, Scott saw the situation deteriorating. One second he had been celebrating his escape, and the next he realized he might crash into a dense row of scraggly pines. He felt confident Byron was aware of the impending collision and was actively trying to find a solution, but nothing happened. At the last second, Scott pulled his arms in, closed his eyes, tried to spin around, and braced for impact. It never came. Byron coaxed enough power out of the small helicopter to safely clear his cargo over the treetops.

Like oil and water, the stunned guests had naturally drifted into two distinct groups, the family and friends of Nancy Watkins, and Applied Leverage employees. Marissa Ehrlich now understood why Scott Horne had called her before the reception and warned her to ignore him. Nancy's best friend was shocked. She was mad…beyond mad. Never once had she liked Alan Reynard or thought he was good for Nancy. Nonetheless, Scott's accusation was hard for Marissa to fathom. *I know everyone distrusts lobbyists, but this is beyond the scope of my imagination. I mean, Nancy and Alan were lovers for years…but Applied Leverage has been convicted of lurid behavior in the past. I hope my brother will do something.*

The steady vibration of rotors interrupted the tense mood of the assembled mourners. In the distance a small helicopter followed the contours of the rolling hillside. At a hundred miles an hour, the wind tore at the fine fabric of his suit, but Scott was enjoying the ride. The baggy fit had been necessary to hide his harness. Wearing goggles, Scott could see that everyone was looking and gesturing. He put his arms straight out like wings. *It would be awfully silly to kill me now, Alan. Too many witnesses. You've probably told them I am a lunatic of some sort. At least they can see that I'm resourceful and sane enough to have a getaway helicopter standing by.*

Byron held an altitude that kept Scott about twenty feet off the ground. The crowd became more confused than they already were. They couldn't help feeling that they were part of something bigger that they didn't understand. Off to the side, Sheriff Roberts stood alone, staring at the dangling man. He wondered if his association with Alan Reynard was going to be his Achilles' heel. On more than one occasion, friends had warned him about cozying up to lobbyists.

Foz do Iguaçu, Brazil

Foz do Iguaçu (Brazil), Puerto Iguaçu (Argentina), and Cividad del Este (Paraguay) are gateways to a spectacular waterfall complex. A flooded basin abruptly drains itself with a dramatic horseshoe of cataracts creating a one-of-a-kind display of hydrodynamics. At seven pounds per gallon, the cascading waters roar as they crash down with never ending force.

"The World Bank and IMF have served American interests first. Why do American voters let capitalists manipulate their democracy?" asked the jungle guide between breaths. He continued slashing at the undergrowth while awaiting a reply.

While traveling in foreign countries, Mick Nolls stayed cognizant of the global impact his country had made, because people he encountered frequently wanted to talk about it. "The people with enough power to make changes are the same people that benefit from aggressive business models. They have personal financial interests to protect."

"We have the same problem. Why does America use much resources?" asked the guide.

"Over-consuming is as American as apple pie...or an air strike. The United States evolved into a fire-breathing, natural-resource bully searching for extractable commodities with reckless abandon."

"That's old news. I mean twenty-first century."

"America's bond with gasoline and electricity...with energy...is strong enough for the public to overlook the problems it creates. As the most prosperous nation of the twentieth century, we should be leading the fight to protect the natural world. America's record of innovation is unmatched in its quality and variety, but it was those same industrial practices and business models that put the rate of planetary damage into high gear," said Mick.

"Do Americans talk to each other about these things?" wondered the Brazilian.

"Individuals do, but as a society we don't quite get it yet. Okay, *amici*, twenty questions is over," said Mick. "I've tired of the subject."

"See the tapir?" asked the hawk-eyed guide pointing at a barely discernible tail twenty meters away.

The damp air surrounded Mick's body like an open-air wet sauna. Though it was located in the subtropics, the Parana sometimes hosted energy-wicking levels of humidity, especially to someone who grew up in a cold, dry environment. Mick Nolls protected rainforests and wetlands, but that didn't mean he was acclimated to them.

NORTHERN VIRGINIA

Sitting around an enormous mahogany table were the power players of Applied Leverage. At one end of the large conference room stood a few members of Alan's shamed security squadron. Enormous windows displayed a post-sunset twilight that mimicked the group's cumulative spirit. An HD projector played surveillance footage of Scott Horne's field trip from beginning to end. The sequences were on a loop, running over and over.

The normally smug mugs of the men and women displayed fear and shock. The majority of the group had just formally found out what really had happened to Alan's plaything, although most held private suspicions that Nancy's death had not been an accident. The bombshell that Applied Leverage was behind the highly publicized arson attack and kidnapping of a famous Alaskan didn't sit well either.

"I can't believe he used his real ID," expounded a livid Alan Reynard. "Horne wanted us to know who he was and that he isn't afraid. And now if anything happens to him ...we're the lead suspects. Thankfully, he wasn't trying to kill me or I'd be dead," Alan bellowed, aiming a harsh glare toward members of his security detail.

"Is there any chance he's working with the Feds? Are we the target of an investigation that we don't yet know about? Someone may have squealed. People are not playing by the unwritten laws of Washington these days," said a vice president.

"This is not a case of financial blackmail. Horne's loaded, according to the guys in the basement. Can someone here please tell me how an enemy of ours waltzes onto my campus using his real name, then proceeds to mortify me and attack Bill Jones…all before getting picked up by a barnstorming helicopter and performing a flyby?" demanded Alan Reynard. "I pay the people in this room top dollar to have answers to these kinds of questions. Let me reiterate how important it is for you to make this Scott Horne problem go away. It is too late to make him disappear. Let's concentrate on taking away his ability to make problems. Dig something up, or frame him for something. I really don't care."

"If it's too late to make him disappear, what can we do?"

"Remember, people…public knowledge is what you tell them…it's defined by what they see on TV, read in magazines, view on the Internet, and hear on the radio. We need to systematically attack this man's character and creditability using every sphere of influence we have. From here forward, let's be the ones to act instead of having to react. We are lobbyists, and good lobbyists find ways to solve tough problems," dictated a frightened Alan Reynard.

The powerful group had a muddled look to them like a previously undefeated team getting blown out at halftime. Nobody knew what to make of the unexpected dilemma. Normally they were the ones doing the intimidating, manipulating, blackmailing, or bribing. Nobody in the room liked the bitter taste of victimization.

SAN DIEGO, CALIFORNIA

There were two questions in Jack Welker's mind. How and where should he spend Scott Horne's money? Never one for playing dress-up, Jack opted for the beach vibe of Garnet Avenue and its parade of tan, toned women displaying their facets. To get the mood going, he dipped into the wet bar.

An hour later, Jack's taxi motored through the salty maritime air, one pair of headlights among thousands. A group of adolescent kids recklessly crossed in front of the cab on skateboards, which made Jack Welker smile.

"Little buggers came out of nowhere," said the driver.

"When I was a kid, I can't say I respected cars as much as I should have. Car drivers are safely protected in air-bag–equipped cocoons. Pedestrians, skaters, and bicyclists expose their flesh and bones," said Jack.

"All these new action sports have taken over. You never see a kid walking down the street with a baseball mitt or a football anymore," commented the cabbie and former third baseman.

"Beach kids tend to avoid sports with lines, referees, and scheduled practices. Grommets still dream of winning gold, but now it's at the X Games… not the Olympics."

"You from around these parts?"

"Yeah, I grew up in Point Loma, but I am over this place."

"Too expensive?"

"And crowded, but I'm also aware that lovely ladies converge on So-Cal from across the globe. Transplants full of that…in-a-new-place optimism make bar-hopping here exciting. I spend a good number of my days secluded in remote places, so the nightlife here offers favorable…conditions," concluded Jack.

"That's certainly true…if you have money to burn."

"I've got money tonight. You know what? I've changed my mind, sir. I want to get a few turns in before I get drunk. Can you please take me about halfway up Mount Soledad?" asked Jack while gesturing to his skateboard.

"No problem. I haven't seen a skateboard like that in twenty years. You got some big wheels on there," responded the driver, who liked it when passengers showed a level of respect when addressing him.

"It's an eighty-six Powell Peralta 'Tony Hawk.' I have it set up for bombing hills with Independent one-sixty-nines, Sector Nine wheels, and German bearings."

"I have no idea what you just said, but it's a tough-looking one anyhow."

"I should have tailored my answer to the person asking the question. You're right, though, it is a tough skateboard," agreed Jack. The comment made him smirk. "There are three reasons to downhill skate in affluent neighborhoods...less traffic, fewer police, and fewer potholes to snare your wheels," explained Jack as they began to climb the flanks of Mount Soledad, an exclusive suburb of million-plus custom homes.

About halfway up, Jack said, "Let's stop here before the hill gets too steep for bombing."

"That'll be sixteen even. Isn't it dangerous to skateboard at night?"

"Yeah, but at night you can see an approaching car's headlights from far away, which is useful when blowing through stop signs and red lights," said Jack as he gave the driver thirty bucks. Regularly he was a good tipper, but with Scott's money his generosity multiplied. As Scott had requested, Jack had been skipping his antipsychotic medication. His unshackled mind exploited the newly available mental energy. The abrupt change put his psyche in psycho limbo. By speeding up synapse impulses, his brain was probing its new boundaries.

Downhill skating is dangerous enough when sane and sober. Jack Welker took a moment to relax and envision the run before he positioned his board underfoot. One last check for cars and he jumped on. A few tic tacs across the road helped him find the perfect foot positions. Then Jack swung the nose of his vintage skateboard downhill. His large wheels forced the first turn within a few car lengths of dropping in. With each carve, his confidence grew as the sticky wheels gripped with sureness and sent him careening across the wide road. Akin to surfing and snowboarding, a skater can use turns to slow down momentum. Jack was engaged in a back-and-forth, slow-motion dance as he carefully adjusted his balanced crouch to guide his board.

Impulsively he lessened the sharpness of his turns, which sped things up. All of his brain's energy was focused on one thing, survival. To aid in self-preservation, his brain went into turbo mode, which had the effect of slowing everything down. Eventually the hill began to flatten, which prompted Jack to stop making turns altogether and tuck down into a lower crouch. When he started getting speed wobbles, Jack stood from his crouch and twisted his torso sideways to increase wind resistance and use his body's drag as an air brake.

Internally, Jack had started to celebrate, when suddenly a large animal darted out and stopped directly in his path. He swerved hard to avoid a collision with the Labrador retriever. The edge of the board bit into the front left wheel, causing him to lose balance and forcing a jump off the board.

The problem was that Jack was traveling at thirty miles per hour and the street was stationary. Futilely he tried to move his legs up to the speed necessary to run it out, but it wasn't possible. After two steps, he felt his body pitch forward. Years of being a volunteer crash dummy taught him to pull his arms in to protect his head and to try to keep his inertia parallel with the street instead of getting whipped against it. At the cost of his right hip and shoulder, Jack successfully kept his fragile skull from impacting the ground. Skin and bones heal, brains don't.

Standing up to examine his road rash, the tail-wagging dog approached him. "Way to go, Clifford. What are you, a crash attack dog?" he asked the canine. The black dog replied only with the content demeanor of a healthy pet.

The skateboarder was relieved to be only scraped and bruised, but he felt frustrated at the randomness of the incident. Having a fist-sized hole in the shoulder of a tar-streaked, white T-shirt wasn't how he pictured his triumphant descent into Pacific Beach's grand avenue, Garnet. The street has a slight grade toward the beach, so Jack had planned on making a gravity-assisted pub skate, but he became increasingly agitated. With each lungful of car exhaust he felt less social and more concerned about what Horne had asked him to do. Jack Welker preferred confronting nature's perils versus urban dangers.

"Why would he send me on such a heinous mission?" Jack yelled out loud to no one in particular, causing concern in a passing couple. The sector of Jack's brain that dealt with addictions had been promised more alcohol, so it sent out the appropriate impulses to ensure that it would be coursing through his veins in short order.

Considering his antisocial mindset, Jack decided to brown-bag a pint of hard bar. Enjoying the small rush that came from forming a desirable plan, Jack broke into a run, jumped up, and came down smoothly riding the board. In front of the liquor store a quintet of easy-on-the-eyes college beauties reminded Jack of why he had chosen PB in the first place. The shapely girls caused another quick swing in his mood pendulum. Jack gave the ladies his best smile and was ignored. "Bunch of teases," mumbled Jack under his breath.

In the past few days, friends and family members had voiced concerns about his appearance and behavior. Level heads may think madness strikes like lightning or that it hovers at a constant level. Whether it was disrupted sleep patterns, endless energy, or delusional thoughts, Jack understood the signs of an impending episode. The problem was that he didn't want to alter the way he felt. Jack had battled mania in the past and could sense something was amiss, but this time he was intentionally going to let it develop. After enduring the low side, why disrupt the fun part? It's a "take the good with the bad" approach. The enigmatic human machine can produce incredible highs and lows from its own biological stash.

While Jack Welker's brain undoubtedly was imbalanced, it was also highly functioning. Instability and genius are a dangerous combination. Each crazy quilt is unique, owing some of its character to non-genetic patchwork sewn after birth. Jack Welker categorized his own personal mental illness as being a positive, not a negative. Basically he interpreted it as a gift to be exploited instead of a burden to shoulder. If a chemical brain anomaly was the root cause of the epic lifestyle he cultivated, then he felt lucky to have an imbalance. He would rather be dead than suffer through the day-to-day drudgery the majority of people endure.

Foz do Iguaçu, Brazil

Mick settled into his new domain and proceeded to enjoy the best activities. He toured the falls from both the Argentinean and Brazilian sides, including a flight-seeing tour. Getting into an aircraft was the only way to fully grasp the sheer scope of the hundreds of waterfalls at one time. He also rode the Rainforest Ecological Train, but mostly he canoed and hiked while always searching for the elusive jaguar.

Today's plan was different; Mick was meeting up with Sonya to take a tour of Itaipu Binacional's hydropower plant. Mick couldn't help hypothesizing about the method to this madness. *Perhaps today I will learn the specific reason Joddell sent me here. He can't realistically be thinking of attacking the dam!*

From what Mick could infer, he doubted that Curt had taken part in the arson attacks attributed to him. Curt and Mick agreed that the best way to attack corporations was by going after the brass.

Mick arrived at the hulking facility early, but after scanning the loitering faces he spotted Sonya. She had dramatically changed her look. The woman had wrapped her long body in a grey pantsuit. Red hair had changed to black, and her eyes from blue to brilliant green eyes that betrayed a curious nature.

"*Ola, bom dia.* I hope you weren't waiting long," offered Mick, slipping in a Portuguese phrase.

"Truthfully it has been just a few minutes. Here's the story. We are about to get a private tour from Marianne Tireau. She's an engineer I befriended a few weeks ago. I told her you are a filmmaker doing research for a documentary on dams. Did you study the Web site we set up for the fictional project?"

"Yes, I went over it. It looked believable," dryly remarked Mick.

"Marianne's cool, yet...slightly self-conscious. She speaks perfect English. She is originally from Switzerland but lives like a Brasilena. Dancing, hiking, photography, and friends are her world. She's single. She mingles," said Sonya finishing her briefing. Then she gave Nolls a questioning look. "Do you have what it takes to sweep a girl off her feet?"

Nolls absorbed the speech with growing disappointment. This new assignment only led to more questions. *What has Joddell gotten me mixed up in? I hope this is about this woman and not about the dam.*

"Initially you should act genuinely interested in her work. Physically, I'd suggest you let her make the first move. Have you been expanding your knowledge of dams?"

"No need to. I have always been fascinated slash irritated by dams. Been following the Three Gorges project for years, and I spent some time last year fighting the new dams on the Bio Bio...in Chile."

"I know where the Bio Bio is...thanks, though. When she arrives, you should dial up your excitement level. You're about to get a behind-the-scenes tour. Mick Nolls, documentary filmmaker, would be thrilled," suggested Sonya. From the onset, she'd had doubts about Mick's commitment to the cause and had told Curt as much, insinuating that Nolls was better suited to writing checks.

Mick was rapidly losing patience with Sonya, but he didn't want to let his emotions become a hindrance. *Suck it up. Show some patience.*

"Okay, here she is. It's showtime," said Sonya as she put her arm around Mick's shoulders like they were old friends. "Ola, Marianne. This is the talented filmmaker I told you about, Mick Nolls."

"Mr. Nolls, pleased to meet you," said Marianne Tireau extending a delicate hand.

"The pleasure is mine. I really appreciate you taking time out of your day to show us around. The tourist tour was great and all, but..." Mick responded sheepishly. Sonya hadn't mentioned that the woman was beyond striking. The foxy lady had generous curves in places Mick appreciated. *Keep it together, buddy.*

"Sonya told me that, if I took you on a private tour, you would take us out to dinner," added Marianne with a touch of playfulness. The engineer wondered about the romantic status of this man who shared her fascination with hydrology.

"I thought I said that Mick would take us shopping and *then* out to dinner," Sonya said, joining in on the ruse.

"No problem. Why wouldn't I want to spend time with two beautiful women?" said Mick looking directly into Marianne's eyes.

"Let's start the tour. We have a lot to see and little time," suggested Marianne, changing the subject. "There are a few places you can't take photos, but I will notify you in advance. The dam is actually a series of dams that have been joined together and currently produces more energy than any other. We have the capacity to create fourteen gigawatts of electricity, which is shared by Brazil and Paraguay since the Parana River is the border between them."

SAN DIEGO, CALIFORNIA

After indulging in multiple drinks, Jack's buzz finally hit its stride. The depressant quality of the alcohol managed to deaden his brain's activity to a tolerable level. He had just arrived at yet another watering hole stocked with beauties. The skateboarding crash was a distant memory as his senses were now fixated on the thirty or so attractive women within his field of view. After a quick search, Jack became particularly smitten by a gal in a form-fitting San Diego Chargers tank top reading #21. Her mannerisms displayed a confidence that he enjoyed. Solid eye contact was his best pickup line, so Jack positioned himself favorably to see if he could lock up optically. *The female brain is just as wired to be attracted to physical attributes as the male brain. Females just hide it better. One of the many things women do better than men.*

The woman's curves were boldly displayed. Figuring his body could only help the effort, Jack shed the dirty T-shirt to show off a tank top of his own. When their eyes eventually met, Jack wasted no time and walked over to introduce himself. "Hi, I'm Jack," he said, extending his hand and a harmless facial expression.

"Claudia," responded the twenty-three-year-old student.

Recognizing the accent, Jack switched to Spanish, "*Mucho gusto. De donde eres?*"

Encouraged by the gringo's passable accent, she responded, "*Soy de Colombia. Por favor, no bromas de café,*" she said before getting lost in Jack's green eyes for a brief moment.

"I've surfed and sailed on both the Caribbean and Pacific coasts. It's such a beautiful country. So green and lush. Everywhere in Colombia seemed to have friendly people and great food and hot girls like you."

"I miss it bery much."

"You should go back and start a lodge or something. Right now there are great opportunities for ecotourism. Tourists avoided Colombia for decades, so it's less developed than the rest...a nearly blank slate. Can I buy you a drink?" asked Jack casually.

Again the fast-talking Yankee impressed Claudia. This fellow represented one of the few Americans she had met who was open-minded enough to have visited her home country.

"No, thanks, I'm driving tonight. What happen to your shoulder?"

"I was attacked by a Labrador," responded Jack. After seeing the confused look on her face, he elaborated. "A dog caused me to fall off my skateboard earlier tonight. You a Bolts fan?"

"I went to my first game last year. Is bery nice, but I love futbol... soccer. What about you? No wife?"

"In my experience, women auditioning to become a wife...are way more fun than actual wives. The same could be said of husbands," teased Jack in an attempt to find out the woman's romantic status.

"Me and my husband are bery fun. He's bartender here," she revealed.

"That's mean-spirited. Where is your ring? That's not fair, there isn't even a tan line," complained Jack.

This brought a giggle from Claudia. "So sorry, I no like to wear jewelry every day...*solamente para ocasiones especiales.*"

"No worries, señora, enjoy your city life," said Jack using the formal female address reserved for older women. After slamming the remainder of his screwdriver in a gulp, he went to retrieve his skateboard from the coat check. Spilling out of the bar, Jack was tempted to jump on his board and skate down to the ocean, but he hesitated. Asininely, skateboarding in the street or on the sidewalk is technically a crime. Jack cut over to Cass and coasted down to the boardwalk where the evil skateboard could be ridden legally. Arriving at Crystal Pier, Jack was reminded that he had still neglected to rent one of the rooms over the water. Breaking waves held a meditative quality for him, day or night. If he hadn't already had plans, he would've spent a night there right then.

It was past midnight, but the boardwalk flowed with an assortment of rollerbladers, bikers, skaters, joggers, pedestrians, and drunk pedestrians. The motion, combined with fresh salty air, proved to be exactly the tonic he sought. After a while Jack asked a passerby the time and then headed south, weaving in and out of the slower traffic with a practiced ease. Put a board under Jack's feet and he was instantly happier.

"Hello," said Jack to some girls on a private patio.

"Hey," yelled a girl liking the looks of Jack's sandy-blonde, unkempt hair.

Looking back, Jack Welker saw the two girls waving at him. The girls appeared old enough to consent, so he began to drag his back foot. He made a U-turn and headed back toward the pair.

"My friennnnn tinks you're cuuuute," slurred a girl with margarita breath, while swaying side to side, foot to foot.

"Does she do all of her speaking through you? I think both of you are hot. Are you from around here?" asked Jack.

"I'm in school here and she is visiting from Phoenix," responded the other, more sober girl.

When Jack heard the sound of footsteps in close proximity to him, he twisted his head to investigate. Two young men and a girl were walking slowly down the boardwalk. They seemed harmless enough, so Jack ignored them.

Jack's skate was lying right side up a few feet from where he was standing. As the trio of partygoers passed him, one of the men ran up, jumped on his prized board, and began making back-and-forth turns across the concrete path. At first Jack didn't mind, assuming the guy would turn around and return it. Instead he kept rolling further and further away.

"Excuse me, ladies," said Jack before taking off in pursuit of the caper.

Running past the man's friends, one of them shouted, "Don't mind Conrad; he's hammered."

The perpetrator looked back and saw Jack closing in on him. He stepped off the skate and kept walking. Jack reached his board and popped it into his hand.

When Conrad saw the man confidently striding toward him, he was surprised at first and then angry. "What are you going to do…punk? I will smash you." Conrad had grown accustomed to using his formidable size to bully strangers.

Conrad's friends saw the guy run at their friend with the skateboard held over his head like an axe. Conrad instinctively tried to put his arm up to protect himself. The horrified pair watched helplessly as Conrad collapsed in a heap. Blood began to pool under him.

Strangely, Jack had been caught slightly off guard at how easily the incident had escalated. In a daze he exited the boardwalk onto the nearest court leading toward Mission Blvd.

The couple rushed up to Conrad to offer aid. Hernan took off his T-shirt and pressed it against his friend's bloody head. "Somebody call nine-one-one. Keep this pressed firmly against the wound. He's losing too much blood to wait for an ambulance. My car is right here. I'm gonna get it," advised Hernan.

Jack didn't let negative thoughts impede his escape; there would be plenty of time for analysis later. In his experience, it was in the first few minutes following a crime that you either got away or got caught. After confirming that he had no visible blood on him, Jack tried to discern what kind of lights were on an oncoming car's roof. *Is that a cab or a cop?*

As it passed, Jack could see it was a taxi. He ran out into the street to get the driver's attention. Distraught, Jack tried to hide his face and the skateboard as he climbed in. "Downtown, please."

The ride was tense, but with each passing minute and mile he felt better. After getting dropped off at the Coronado ferry terminal on the Embarcadero, Jack walked out to the end of a nearby municipal parking pier. Within sight, Jack could spot only one other group of people. After they departed, Jack spun around, discus style, and slung the board into the dark waters of the bay. He was fairly sure the weighty metal trucks would sink the otherwise floatable wooden deck and synthetic wheels. His board quickly sank to the murky bottom.

Back at the crime scene, two cruisers had driven onto the boardwalk. The swiveling blue and red lights darkened the mood considerably. The only pieces of evidence of the attack were a pool of blood and the eyewitness account of an intoxicated young woman. The rest of the witnesses had disappeared into the night, preferring to avoid the hassle.

"Miss, I know you are in shock, but if you could please recap your story to me once more, it would help us enormously," explained a female SDPD officer.

"I told you twice already. Were you listening?" Elana answered in a voice that betrayed her frustration at the tactic of asking the same question repeatedly.

"It's the last part I am not perfectly clear on. You said the man who got struck with the skateboard...was named Conrad. That he regained consciousness and left with the other man in a car? A nineties black Mustang. The problem we are having is that the local emergency rooms haven't seen any patients with blunt head trauma. How long have you known these guys? Why don't you know their last names or addresses?"

"Like I said, I've only known them a couple of days. We met at the Green Flash earlier in the week. Maybe they know a doctor close by or something? I don't know. I am the one that called you. You people treating me like I did something wrong," Elana asserted.

"Nobody is accusing you of anything. This Conrad character probably has an arrest warrant. That explains him not wanting to go to a regular hospital. We really appreciate your help. Is there anywhere I can drive you?" asked the officer politely.

WASHINGTON, DC

As promised, Dewey contacted Bill Jones, but he insisted that the nation's capital be their next meeting place. He suspected that was where Bill Jones and his cronies were headquartered and wanted to confirm that theory. Bill hadn't liked the idea, but he didn't have much of a choice.

Dewey hired a friend to fly him up the coast in an older, single-engine Piper Cherokee. It was a slow but anonymous method of air travel. Dewey embraced the tortoise pace. He loved studying landscapes from slow-moving, low-altitude aircraft. They followed the coastline, costing them time and fuel but spicing up the scenery with dense pine forests, swampy wetlands, and saltwater tidal basins protected by sandy barrier islands. The lovely coastal environment also attracted human developments, mainly roads, parking lots, and rectangular structures.

At a motel adjacent to the small airfield, Dewey spent over an hour on his costume and makeup. This time he chose to emulate an older, heavyset man taller than himself. Dewey left his pal with the instruction, "Be ready to leave on a moment's notice."

Dewey planned an early-morning rendezvous because his disguise would be hot and stifling. Springtime temperatures had gained a foothold in the area. Energetic birds were singing as he walked toward his rental car. *I wonder if the other birds are jealous of the ones who sing well.*

The plan called for Dewey to meet Bill Jones on foot at the corner of J and Sixth, but that wasn't going to happen. After parking the rental in a pay lot, Dewey hailed a yellow cab.

"I need to pick up a friend first, please, on J just before Sixth. Then we're headed to the Lincoln Memorial. Thank you."

The driver nodded his head and relayed the information to dispatch over the radio. As the taxi pulled up to the curb, Dewey easily picked out the bulky man from the few people loitering on the sidewalk.

"Hey, Jonesy, let's take a ride," said Dewey, opening the heavy door and carefully monitoring his reaction.

Bill Jones recoiled at the sound of his birth name. He didn't know Dewey's real name or anything else about him. This put Jones at an obvious disadvantage. At first he squinted into the cab, but then Bill's eyes darted back toward the street.

Dewey followed Bill's line of sight and saw it settle upon a tall, sturdily built man walking with a homely woman pushing a baby carriage. The man responded to Bill's gaze with a barely perceptible shrug. Bill feigned a smile and got into the car.

The guy they referred to as "the Hunter" had on such an elaborate disguise Bill could hardly believe his eyes. "Every time we meet you've completely transformed yourself from the person I met three years ago in northern Ontario."

The Does were caught outside of a vehicle and Roger, who was parked across the street, couldn't make a U-turn quick enough to follow the cab, which left all alone.

"You know my name. What should I call you?" asked Jones.

"Jim," answered Dewey.

"Okay, Jim, what's the plan?" asked Bill, hoping his henchmen were in close pursuit. *This guy is a killer and he just intentionally lost my safety net.*

"Driver? Could you just pull over right here, please? Sorry about the change of destination," announced Dewey abruptly. The two men exited the car, and Dewey handed the driver a crisp twenty. "Keep the change."

Bill got out of the car and shrugged, "Okay, sport, where to now?"

"We'll take a walk around the mall," explained Dewey. "Bill, you were a bit reluctant to get in the cab with me. You have absolutely nothing to fear. I'm the one who should be afraid."

"I wasn't afraid," Bill said, heart racing.

"Okay, good. Sorry about the delayed check-in regarding the situation in Alaska. The old man ambushed me and shot me twice in the chest, but I had Kevlar on. Don't worry, it's taken care of. What's this new gig?"

"Since he hasn't turned up, I'll take your word. The next job is a simple delivery," responded Bill, relieved that the Hunter didn't intend to harm him.

"Why, when, where, what, who?"

"They haven't told me yet."

"Who are 'they'?"

"That's a good question, but I think you know that I can't answer it. I was only told that a small package needs to be planted on a ship sometime next week on the West Coast. Two of our other contractors will supply it to you," said Bill.

"No chance. You know I work alone," explained Dewey. *Have these people lost their minds?*

"I told them you would say that. I guess I'll deliver the package to you myself. I think it'll be in a few days."

"The payment is going to have to be in cash. The amount depends on what the package is and where it needs to go. Here's my new sat-phone number for the next few weeks," dictated Dewey. "Oh, yeah...tell your friends congrats on their fake baby."

"Good eye, Jimbo. I'll talk this over with the boss and we'll get this thing knocked out," promised Bill.

"On second thought, Bill, I want gold bars, please."

"See ya soon."

ZNOS, BRITISH COLUMBIA

Western Canada draws outdoorsmen of all shades. The gigantic mountainous province could swallow California, Nevada, and Oregon, but outside of Vancouver there are few residents. The jagged terrain, huge rivers, and numerous lakes don't lend themselves to highway systems and large-scale developments. The majority of areas stay isolated. The huge, sparsely populated geography is a paradise for helicopter skiing, fishing, hunting, trekking, and mountain biking. The moderating effect of the Pacific Ocean keeps BC warmer than its continental neighbors. Widespread damming has created long, skinny lakes in narrow valleys. In British Columbia, electrical power is referred to as hydro, as in hydroelectric. Their power is generated by water and gravity.

Having recently returned from densely populated Europe, Curt Joddell opted to drive ten hours from Vancouver instead of flying into Castlegar. Usually he didn't miss a chance to spend the day in what he deemed North America's prettiest city, but he took off straight away. The leisurely twists and turns through the trees gave him time to straighten his thoughts.

Physically close to the American states of Washington and Idaho but thousands of miles away ideologically, the historic town of Nelson, BC hugs a hillside above Kootenay Lake. As with many frontier towns, the exploitation of ore had led to the creation of the initial settlement. Nowadays locals used their natural resources in a sustainable manner. They enjoyed skiing, mountain biking, hiking, camping, and sailing in their substantial backyard.

If the city of Nelson (pop. 10,000) was too big, then the outskirt settlements were an option. They were located close enough to head into town for shopping and schooling, but they were out of the loop. About ten kilometers northeast of town, a string of cabins shadowed a shallow river. The small batch of structures was inhabited by a broad range of characters. "Small town" would be an understatement. The narrow valley's commercial district consisted of one hotel/restaurant/bar, a small convenience store, and a waterfront campground. A nearby mom-and-pop ski area served up thigh-burning runs of steep, dry powder. All-you-can-eat face shots were a specialty.

Every Friday afternoon—regardless of sun, rain, sleet, or snow—a group of friends met with the humble goal of enjoying themselves. They varied in age and occupation. Originating from all walks of life, most were transplants from faster places. Opting to eschew the popular cultural trap of asset and status lust, they took pride in the notion that local parents needed to worry more about wild animals or an avalanche than a kidnapping or gang shooting. Their common bond was a love for the out-of-doors and a special kinship with the peaceful valley. They'd decided that maximizing quality of life was the main objective.

The waning sun hid behind Kootenay clouds as the friends gathered at an abandoned mill site for their weekly game. A shiver-inducing rain drenched the riparian landscape. Some hide indoors from harsh weather and yearn for summertime, others barely notice foul climate. The not-so-gentle men were still in tailgate mode when Curt drove his rental onto the bumpy access road. The mini-SUV drew the attention of the group. A shiny, clean car meant tourist.

He'd met the group while living at Red Mountain for a winter working as a ski guide for Big Red Cats. Hearing of a group that played disc golf all winter long, he'd felt obliged to check it out. Curt drove into the dirt parking area, happy to see that the guys hadn't started to whirl. He laid on the horn. One eagle-eyed member recognized Curt Joddell from forty meters and alerted the others. A coordinated volley of discs flew towards the vehicle. Swerving away from the bulk of the fusillade, Curt took a couple of hits. With a smile, Curt remembered that he'd bought the supplemental insurance. He stomped on the gas and took aim at the posse, but at the last moment he cranked the wheel over, sliding the plastic box into a one-eighty. After his inertia was completely overcome by friction, he slammed the gear shifter into park and killed the engine.

"Nice wheels, Joddell…a fancy guy like you deserves a cute car. You finally marry for money, or what?" shouted someone. Nobody knew of Curt Joddell's alternate underground life. Everyone thought he was only a Web-site designer.

"Truthfully, Sid, I thought I would come and show you hillbillies how to properly throw a Frisbee. Actually, I came to drink outdoors without worrying about Johnny Law," explained Curt as he unloaded two cases of Kokanee from the backseat. He enjoyed the refreshingly youthful spirit of the group.

"You mean you can't even drink while disc golfing in the States?" asked Mike.

"It depends, but generally you can't drink anywhere except a bar or private property. I see you guys are still scaring all the girls away," teased Joddell.

"You always were an idiot. This is our time away from the womenfolk. But, yeah, Corey is still more or less keeping them away," responded John, the inventor of a gravity-fed backcountry firefighting hose.

Everyone exchanged sarcastic quips and questions of interest or insult.

The guys designed the course using baskets and tones. The target is a pole-mounted basket with a circular top that supports two sets of hanging chains. Getting the disc inside the basket is akin to sinking the ball into the hole in traditional golf.

The tones were made of spent artillery shells from avalanche guns. Perforated with hundreds of holes to expel explosive gases, the shells played a deep reverberating note when struck with a hundred and seventy grams of hard plastic.

The real reason Curt had made the long voyage was to speak with three thrill-seeking brothers. The adage "If riding in an airplane is flying, then riding in a boat is swimming" always reminded Curt of the Derels and their unique approach to being. The nickname was a derivative of their often-derelict appearance. The brothers Derel typically sported heavy scruff over sun- and wind-ravaged complexions. Their visual disarray was a result of prioritization. There was no time for manscaping when nature's bounty was right outside.

The brothers excelled at freeskiing and other exploitations of gravity. Sponsorships from ski companies paid the bills, but lately it was hang gliding, paragliding, BASE jumping, and wingsuiting that got the Derels out of bed in the morning. Unlike sports that are dependent on the prevailing conditions, these relied on gravity, and gravity is always available, day or night, everywhere on Earth.

On its own, the human body can create lift and track across the sky instead of just plummeting straight down, but the advent of the wingsuit has taken the sport of skydiving to new levels of aerodynamics. Free-falling has become free-flying. Technology finally has granted man's age-old wish for flight.

Unfortunately for Curt, only one of the Derels was present, but the other two were sure to be within a few hours' drive. Curt didn't know Lyle very well, so he decided to tell him as little as possible until his brothers were present.

"How did winter treat you? I saw you guys getting pummeled in late February. I was so jealous," admitted Curt.

"It was nipple-deep like five times. No joke. The kinda days where you have to time your breaths in between turns. Will under-rotated a front flip and dropped upside-down like twenty feet into ten feet of powder. If no one had seen where he landed…he would have drowned for sure. Good times," answered Lyle, gesturing wildly. Both men attributed a spiritual quality to periods of heavy snowfall.

"Been jumping much?" asked the Owl, getting down to the task at hand.

"Here and there, but not as much as I'd like. Summer is on the way and I'm going to New Zealand in August. Other than that, I'm going to fly as much as possible. I did my first ski BASE jump this winter. It was the off the scale!" said Lyle with gusto.

"After being teased with hoverboards and jet packs, we finally have an invention that softens the pain of all the useless modern merchandise. Sadly, I haven't taken my bat-suit out in a while. Soon though. Actually, that is what I wanted to ask you about."

"I got hooked up with a sick new wingsuit recently," said Lyle.

"Would you and your brothers be interested in doing some stunt work? It pays ridiculously well," delicately probed the Owl.

"It depends what it is and what it pays. I know I am real tired of being broke. The recession has crushed my income. Are you talking on-the-books money or…?" inquired Lyle. The brothers all had various sponsorships but subsisted on meager funds well below the poverty line.

"Tax-free casheesh. Your choice of Canadian or US dollars. It's a highly profitable arrangement all the way around. I wouldn't have traveled all the way here if you three weren't a perfect fit for the job," assured Curt. "There is one strange thing about it. Everything has to be kept ultralow profile…don't mention anything about this to anybody. If we can make a deal, I brought a cash advance," mentioned Curt offhandedly. He wasn't comfortable bribing people, but he needed these guys and they needed money.

SEA OF CORTEZ, MEXICO

There was no reason to make himself an easy target for Applied Leverage. Scott Horne headed across the border to lay low. He had taken the tourist train, "El Chepe," into Copper Canyon and spent two nights on the edge of the canyon. Afterward he headed southwest again and traveled to the site of a business venture. Scott had kept his investment in this particular farm a secret, and he felt certain that the integrity of his hideout was uncompromised.

While searching for new technologies to invest in, Horne had come across American innovator Carl Hodges. The scientist devoted himself to finding ways of growing food in regions not conducive to traditional agriculture. The result of his research was saltwater farming in coastal desert regions. Using seawater, arid regions could be transformed into breadbaskets that could help feed a crowded, hungry planet.

The *Salicornia* plant had proved to be the best suited to saltwater farming. The foliage of the plant could be steamed or eaten raw, and the nutritious seeds could be eaten or pressed into cooking oil. The plant matter could be dried and compacted into clean-burning briquettes to be used for heating or cooking.

Scott got up early in order to take a walking tour with the foreman before the sun caused the desert to shimmer. As they meandered, Scott was impressed with the progress made since his last visit.

"They look like baby seaweed scarecrows. What is the deadline for having all of the equipment run on biofuel pressed from the seeds?" asked Scott.

"Maybe next winter."

Squat adobe structures dotted the hills. The low-tech building material didn't fool Scott. He knew the semi-underground homes were solar-powered marvels of efficiency. "How much land does each family tend?"

"About twenty hectares," answered the honcho.

"Any problems?"

"They get free accommodation and utilities and are paid a share of what their plots produce. They're happy."

"The air compressors that produce potable water…how are they working out?"

"Sometimes okay, but they use lots of energy. We use desalinated water to supplement them."

"The shrimp add fertilizer to the salt water in the form of waste products, right?"

"The nutrient-rich shrimp sewage is used to directly irrigate the shallow basins filled with the *Salicornia*."

"Other shrimp farms return fouled water back into the Sea of Cortez untreated?" asked Scott.

"Sadly."

"I want to create some irrigated mangroves…restore some of the wetlands that were destroyed when the waters of the Rio Colorado got redirected."

"Nice dream."

"Hard landscapes develop tough characters. In northern Mexico an indigenous population has eked out an existence from this unforgiving desert," said Scott.

"Your heart likes this place?"

"I just came from the jewel of the Sierra Madre…*Barranca del Cobre*, Copper Canyon. Not as singularly grand as the one in Arizona, but it's not one canyon. It's a network of chasms. In recent years, melodramatic media coverage of drug smuggling and police corruption has scared tourists away. Using the same common sense that is necessary in any developing nation, travelers to Mexico can still enjoy budget adventures with amazing food and friendly hosts."

"There are dangers, my friend."

"Danger is everywhere. Mexico is a beautiful place whose progress has been thwarted by the drug addictions of a megalomaniac neighbor. Any country that bordered the massive United States cocaine market and was located on air, land, and sea routes from the Andes would have the same problems," said Scott. "Thanks for the tour."

Scott took refuge in a sun shelter. The downtime let his mind thoroughly explore the guilt it was suffering. The quiet solitude, hot temperatures, and fatigue allowed for a vividly painful recollection. Despite multiple pleas from Byron to leave the girl alone, Scott had paid for Nancy and Marissa to meet up with them in Argentina the past August.

Crowded around a basket of bread and two bottles of wine, four adults basked in the glory of a great day of skiing at Cerro Catedral. The storm had fully cleared out, leaving good visibility and a half meter of fresh. Everyone sported wind-chapped cheeks, which contrasted with the unblemished skin around their eyes. Their ski goggles had protected only part of their face from the sun and wind, creating a raccoon-like mismatch in color and texture.

"*El Boliche de Alberto* delivers some of the best red meat I've ever tasted off that hardwood grill. And with these delicious local wines you get another level of decadence. Are you two enjoying South Am so far?" asked Byron.

"Other than a few quick trips to Canada and Mexico, I've never traveled outside the States, so this is great. I can't thank you guys enough for inviting me here and showing me around this place. It's surreal, making powder turns in summer; I don't quite understand it," admitted Nancy.

"Throughout its elliptical orbit, Planet Earth lies at twenty-three and a half degrees off the vertical axis, creating the seasons. For half the year the top of the planet gets more sun while the bottom receives much less, and vice versa, creating opposing summers and winters for the Northern and Southern Hemispheres," said Scott Horne. He enjoyed reciting facts for others. "This tilt means nomadic snow-sliders can double down. Snow-starved denizens of the Northern Hemisphere have two options, New Zealand and South America. However, the ski resorts of the Andes are steeper, deeper, higher, closer, and cheaper."

"But New Zealand has more variety. Skiing isn't everything, mate," said Byron defending his country.

"It must have been a drag to wait around for us novices all day," said Marissa.

"Friends of Byron's are friends of mine. And I've always thought that it's not the person who's the best at something that wins... it's the person who is having the most fun. Today you two ladies shared the blue ribbon. The great thing about fun is that it's contagious. Your enthusiasm made me have a better time," responded Scott, getting in a manipulating mindset. He was hoping Nancy would become swept up emotionally. The great day of skiing, the quaint town, the food, and most importantly the wine could coalesce and work to his advantage when he approached her about spying on her boss.

"I can't believe how few people were skiing in the fresh snow," added Marissa.

"As far as riding out-of-bounds goes, it's mainly an issue of having the proper gear for powder conditions. You need fat skis or a long snowboard with the stance set back to float across snow that deep," explained Scott.

"I would like to propose a toast to Marissa and Nancy for showing amazing ability out there today. Especially considering this is an off-season trip for them," said Byron.

Following dinner the foursome ambled along the main drag, Mitre, to stretch their sore legs. "Considering the remoteness, Bariloche gives off an aura of affluence. The center of town has heavy stylistic influences from the European Alps. Touristy décor and signage juxtapose against world-class wood, metal, rock, and glass craftsmanship. The low-rent district is conveniently tucked out of sight."

On this night, students from Buenos Aires were in town for their senior trip. En masse the teenagers were holding hands and singing school songs in the street. Byron and the Americans found the impromptu pep rally quite amusing. The zeal of the adolescents served to remind the adults that, when looking to have a good time, singing with friends is a good place to start.

"Let's head to Berlina. I want to show everyone the building…it's amazing. It's run by three brothers…they're cool cats."

After a few drinks the group headed back into Bariloche at well past midnight to sample a discothèque. The ladies had a blast, grooving into the wee hours as a stream of confident men attempted to swoop in and win them over.

The guys had their own distractions. They had switched over to drinking whiskey, which fueled the intensity of their disagreement about Scott's intentions. "Trying to convince her to betray Reynard will be a delicate issue, made immensely more difficult since using cash would be ineffective. Her value system rules out trying a bribe," suggested Scott.

"I'll say it again. Leave her alone, mate. There are other ways to get at Reynard," said Byron.

"The next logical ploy would be to use sex somehow, but she is a knockout who can sleep with just about anyone she desires."

"She isn't cut out for spying. I never should have agreed to this," said Byron. "I feel guilty. I'm the one who led you to Nancy Watkins by seducing her best friend."

"I need to appeal to her on moral grounds. Create a clear connection between Reynard's actions and something she personally hates. The best way to convince a person to do something is to lead them toward the desired conclusion by artfully arranging your arguments and letting them think it was their idea," said Scott smugly.

"I've got an idea. Why don't you go after Reynard's son, instead," said the Kiwi, but his plea fell on the deaf ears of an egomaniac.

"At first I simply wanted to get inside Applied Leverage's headquarters. Nancy works in Reynard's office and was intimately involved with the weasel. Sorry, man, I have to try."

"You are an utterly selfish bloke!" yelled Byron over the bass before wobbling away. From his end the argument was close to getting physical and he wanted to avoid that. Byron hoped Nancy would ignore Scott's advances.

Once back at the cabana, everyone headed for the hot tub. The moonless night was rudely spoiled by porch lights needlessly blazing away on adjacent cabins. Otherwise, stargazing conditions were excellent. The cabin sat far enough out of town to have negligible light pollution. The clear southern sky was filled with constellations unfamiliar to the *Norteamericanos*. Below the cabin lapped the dark waters of Lago Nahuel Huapí. In the distance was mountainous terrain that resembled the jumbled high deserts of the North American Southwest. The difference is Patagonia is riddled with trout-laden, snowmelt-swollen rivers.

As he watched the others, Scott was pleased with Nancy's low level of sobriety. As long as he, too, was drunk, Scott felt it was a fair negotiating tactic, neither deceptive nor unscrupulous. While under the influence of alcohol, the majority of people stop projecting the image they want others to see and become the genuine item. For better or worse, interacting with a stewed individual provides a sneak peak at their true nature.

As his intricate plan came together, Scott savored the moment. Months of bouncing ideas around, scrutinizing details, and pouring tens of thousands of dollars into private investigators had finally led to him having a shot at subverting the personal secretary of Alan Reynard. The businesses represented by Applied Leverage harmed the planet, making them Scott's favorite enemy.

Ready to move his plan along, Scott firmly suggested, "You two lovebirds should get a room. Oh, wait, I rented a whole cabin for you. Why don't you go use it, Mick?"

Byron directed a long, disgusted look at Scott, but left wordlessly with Marissa in tow. Scott had toyed with the idea of assuming a different identity when meeting Nancy, but he'd eventually decided to just be himself. It seemed like she didn't know much about him anyhow.

"Visualize yourself sitting in a rocking chair looking back on your life. What kind of person do you want to see?" he asked Nancy through the steam of the hot tub.

The sun crested a ridge and reflected its bright light off the Sea of Cortez toward Scott Horne's closed eyes. The twinkling glare was strong enough to disrupt the bitter flashback and return Scott to reality. *What an idiot I am. Why didn't I listen to Byron? Now I'm putting people in jeopardy again. What is my problem?*

SEATTLE, WASHINGTON

A misty spring chill settled over the Emerald City. Angular buildings rose vertically and imposed themselves on the narrow streets. The Space Needle appeared ready to rocket-off at any moment. Once again Alan Reynard's gofer, Bill Jones, waited for his hunting buddy, Dewey. Having come straight from the jet, Jones found himself to be underdressed.

"At least it isn't raining," he said.

It was late at night outside the Experience Music Project, but Bill Jones didn't appreciate the impressive architecture. He was preoccupied with nerves and anxiety. Out in the open, alone and carrying illegal contraband, Jones felt as uncomfortable as he could remember feeling. Between the two packages on his person, he could be sent to prison for a long time. Out of nowhere a tap on the shoulder thoroughly startled Jones.

"It's just me, Bill. Are those for me?" asked Dewey with a slight grin, since he loved being able to sneak up on people. On this night the chameleon had dressed up as a street kid with a stained hood cinched tightly around his face.

"The ship arrives tomorrow morning. The vessel shouldn't be guarded when it stops at the recycling plant. The rest of the info is inside. Be especially careful with the top of the package. They planted a fingerprint on it," explained Bill. After handing over the two parcels he felt much better.

"What's in there? Drugs?" wondered Dewey as he slid both parcels into a small backpack. He had noticed the severely mismatched weight-to-size ratios.

"I don't know," said Jones dishonestly. "Your package contains sixty ounces of gold. We couldn't get hold of bars on such short notice."

"That's fine, boss, it'll melt down the same. You have my guarantee that everything will go much smoother this time around," said Dewey before walking off into the night and disappearing as quickly as he had appeared.

San Diego, California

At the other end of the West Coast the foghorn at the harbor entrance groaned in a single-note, on/off tempo sounding like an uninspired organist. The one hundred percent saturated air smothered the taller homes and trees. The advection fog formed offshore as the ocean sweated moisture into the cool surface air. Light onshore winds pushed the curtain ashore.

Following the run-in at the boardwalk, Jack had taken refuge at the hillside home of a trustworthy friend. The only time he left the premises was to go surfing at dawn. Since Jack avoided TV like it was TB, time passed in spates of pacing, push-ups, and racing thoughts. Unable to relax, he climbed onto the roof hoping the fog could mentally transport him to a realm with a more favorable set of circumstances. The old cedar shakes were damp and fragile as he crept along.

Maybe I should get out of town? How could I? What if the police already know it was me? I should eat something. I can't believe that girl was married. Why doesn't every house around here have solar panels on the roof? How is Scott's plan going to be affected by this? Does he think I have a death wish? I can't get over how that went down on the boardwalk....

For several days, questions had been flooding his head, making Jack regretful for not ingesting his mood stabilizers. *Who does Scott think he is? That shady plan of his is going to get me locked up. I should have brought a few beers up here with me.*

Nerve-racked, Jack eased back onto the tiers of slippery wood and tried to do some deep-breathing exercises, but the tranquil setting was spoiled by paranoia of both the rational and delusional varieties. Controlled breathing was no match for a manic mind.

Early the next morning after only a short nap, Jack flitted erratically around the living room awaiting a response from Scott Horne's assistant, Erin De Sousa. Jack had broken Scott's no-contact rule and left a message, conveniently leaving out anything specific about his problem.

Upon hearing a car door slam, Jack scurried to the window to determine the source. The unexpected jolt made him realize he should keep his shoes on in case he needed to make a run for it. Jack walked over, unlocked the deadbolt, and cracked the door a smidge.

"Cameras are everywhere, clear as day. So are the signs stating that the boardwalk is under surveillance," somberly announced Jasmine. She had been afraid to ask Jack what had happened when he asked her to go check that out for him. In the past week the unstable side of Jack's personality had arisen, scaring her and everyone else. Two nights ago, members of Jack's family had begged her to try to convince him to voluntarily check into a private psychiatric facility.

Jack wasn't surprised about the cameras, but the news unsettled him. The up-and-down cycles of the past few weeks were grinding him down emotionally. "This is a development that has to be addressed immediately. Horne told me he'd get me attorneys for the other thing. I hope that offer is still good. I shouldn't count on him completely. I'd better come up with a backup plan for my backup plan," said Jack, realizing the seriousness of everything. He directed his overactive brain to work at finding the best exit strategy.

"Sweetie…I haven't seen your meds around…" Jasmine gingerly prodded.

"Meds schmeds. Healthcare is all about profit," was the snide reply.

Asking Jack about his pills and whether or not he was taking them was a source of unparalleled annoyance. Jack frequently used the tactic of answering undesirable questions harshly to train the person not to ask the next one. "I appreciate you asking about that, but you don't know the whole story," he added reflectively.

"Did you get hold of Scott or anybody?" inquired the genuinely concerned woman. They had been high-school sweethearts, but only Jasmine still saw their relationship in that light. Jack viewed Jasmine just as his girl. He spent most of the year on selfish adventures, which didn't make for a healthy relationship.

"No, he's offline right now, but Erin will call me back for sure. Horne is selfish but Erin is reliable. Anyway, Scott needs me more than I need him. Trust me," stated Jack.

Across the bay at the SDPD's downtown headquarters, two detectives sat around a computer monitor watching the assault over and over. The telltale footage showed the perp clearly enough for the FBI's facial recognition software to make a match. The violent suspect now had a face and a name, Jack Thane Welker.

"Says he got ticketed last week. Got picked up on the beach drinking straight from a bottle. He claimed ignorance of the law. He had no ID, so we brought him here to establish his identity."

"Find the arresting officer and get him on the phone. What's the listed address for this kid? Is it local?" asked the senior cop.

"He has no current license anywhere that I can find. I couldn't find any email addresses or cell phone records in his name. I pulled up his info. The address listed on his passport is probably not current, but I'll have the Mendocino County Sheriff check it out anyway. The kid has traveled extensively…might be a drug smuggler? I've already notified the Transportation Safety Authority of the situation. He won't be boarding any airliners."

"Any priors?" asked the senior officer, guessing there would be.

"As an adult…two DUIs, a couple of drunk-in-publics, three assault arrests, and possession of less than an ounce of marijuana a number of times."

"With all that expensive foreign travel, Welker strikes me as a cannabis cowboy. Probably deals or transports. I doubt he has the patience to grow. He's an outlaw, but one smart enough to keep any charges against him small enough to stay out of prison."

"Well, this is one thug who's fresh out of luck. Premeditated assault with a deadly weapon and attempted murder…caught on film," answered the junior officer.

BIG SUR, CALIFORNIA

The omni-blue Pacific throbbed lightly under gentle swells and light winds. An occasional whale could be seen loading up on oxygen. A few jagged rocks, a ship now and again, but other than that it was a vista of only sea and sky. Located only sixty feet above sea level, the sturdy house would shudder a bit when the waves got really big. The dwelling cantilevered off a cliff and was sheltered from the roadway by a dense greenbelt of trees and bushes. The high-tech glass that made up the majority of the exterior of the small house let in low-angle winter sunlight while the overhangs blocked intense summer rays.

Erin De Sousa's grim mood couldn't suck the beauty out of the dramatic setting. The perch belonged to a friend of a friend. Scott Horne had advised everybody to avoid persons, places, or things that were associated with him.

The smartphone which had delivered the offending email now appeared ominous and evil. At any moment it could cry out again, notifying the arrival of more devastating news. In her entire life Erin had never felt less enthusiastic about making a phone call, but she pressed the Send button on the touch screen anyway. *Scott said that he was prepared for anything, but I doubt he envisioned a tragedy of this magnitude.*

"*Hola*," answered Scott in a dejected tone that hinted he might already have heard about the drug bust.

"*Que pasa?*"

"Let me see.......Some degenerate planted heroin on the Pacific Plastic Purge supply ship in Seattle and then tipped off the Coast Guard. The worthless Security and Exchange Commission has opened an investigation on me. The Coasties landed aboard the rig an hour ago. At least they haven't found anything so far. They'd better not," said Scott, sourly recounting the events of the second-worst day of his life.

"You warned me that you had become embroiled in a fight against a powerful and dirty enemy, but this is shocking nonetheless. I didn't foresee that someone would choose a harmless nonprofit as a means of revenge. What kind of sick people don't want volunteers to clean up the ocean? I can't tell you how sad this all is. What is really going on? Should I be worried for my personal safety?" asked Erin, feeling nauseous.

"At this point I don't know. You must keep it low-key. Only use cash; be anonymous. Stop using this phone and take the battery out," advised Scott, who knew the statement would add to her anxiety.

"This whole thing is too bizarre for me, to be honest. Who is going to monitor my check card usage...or my iPhone? If you are in trouble with the law, you owe me the truth. I'm not going to jail for anybody," said Erin, firmly laying out her parameters.

"That's reasonable. I'll have the bank wire you a generous severance package. I don't want to involve you in this any further. I honestly appreciate everything you've done for me. I'm sorry, but this still doesn't mean you can go back to your life. You still have to stay offline for another four weeks. I'm truly sorry you got dragged into this," concluded Scott, meaning every word.

"What is happening in four weeks?" asked Erin. After receiving no answer, she continued, "This is great. I've wasted five years of my life building an empire with you and up until recently everything seemed fine. Better than fine. I guess everybody was right, you really are insane."

"Honestly, considering what I have gotten myself into...I'd agree that my sanity has taken a hit lately," said Scott.

"Speaking of instability, Jack called needing money and legal representation in San Diego. What's that about? Were those your drugs they found on the boat? I have never known you to use opiates, but who knows after today? I mean, you sure have the addiction gene," said Erin De Sousa.

"Do me one last favor? Tell Jack I recently gave him a stack of money. If he already needs an attorney…he's screwed. Mine are busy. Tell him to hold tight for a couple weeks. I am terribly sorry…someday you will understand what this is all about. Goodbye, Erin," said Scott, severing the connection without remorse, feeling that on this front he was doing the right thing. He'd already caused enough collateral carnage and this wasn't her fight. Erin De Sousa was part of Scott's business life, not his militant agenda.

COOK STRAIT, NEW ZEALAND

"What are you doing?"

"I'm having a few Speights stubbies," said Byron to his young questioner.

"Why?"

"Well, I'm off work for a while and a ride on the Wellington-Picton ferry always excites me. I can't understand why most of the passengers stay inside," said Byron, gesturing to the scenery.

"Adults are always cold. What is your job?"

"I fly helicopters."

"That's a good one. I don't know what I want to be. Did you always know?"

"Certain people have a moment when they discover what they were meant to do with their life. I didn't…but luckily I figured it out ,while I was still unattached and flexible, which gave me a better shot at pursuing my perceived destiny. As a lad I fantasized about surfing a helicopter across the ground mustering livestock."

"I've seen those guys hovering just above the ground," said the teen.

"It's like crop dusting if the plants could run. By my mid-twenties a new prospect intrigued me more than maneuvering farm animals…shuttling skiers to mountaintops in the Southern Alps."

"So cool. You are so lucky," exclaimed the teen.

"I didn't luck into it. It took a lot of time, money, and sacrifice, but it's been worth it."

"Do you make a lot of money?"

"Nope. It's not about money. Satisfaction and excitement are more important. Helicopter skiing bothers my family. They wanted me to do something more structured and lucrative, but navigating a jet helicopter amidst rock and ice is so fun I would pay to do it. That being said, the world runs on money, so do good in school," advised Byron.

"Why is the boat so crooked?"

"The captain has to aim the bow about thirty degrees off course to correct for the stiff current."

"I thought it had something to do with the wind," said the kid.

"Water is denser than air, so current is more important, but if there were no current you would have to steer into that crosswind. Today the Cook Strait is living up to its reputation as a dangerous crossing."

"Where are you going?"

"Arthur's Pass."

"I got to go, mister. Bye," said the teen.

"Don't worry about a career yet, buddy. Enjoy being young, explore the world first."

Byron Richardson was returning home to ride out the storm Scott Horne had kicked up. Scott had only shared details of the scheme that pertained to piloting, which was fine with Byron. He more or less trusted Scott, but he also had a healthy fear of the ruling elite. Specifically he feared aggressive captains of industry like Alan Reynard.

On the horizon the distant Southern Alps made him nostalgic for the early eighties and the New Zealand of his youth, although it was hard for him to gauge which childhood memories were factual and which ones he romanticized. By studying his formative years, Byron believed he could better understand the man he was today and the one he wanted to be.

After docking, Byron found a shuttle to take him the rest of the way to Arthur's Pass. The next morning Byron went to see a high-school sweetheart. When Byron found himself home, he looked forward to visiting friends and family most of all. Most of his mates had settled into careers, marriages, mortgages, and baby production. Byron was edging toward forty, but he wasn't one for caving in to timelines. Approaching the door he could hear rugrats, but he went ahead and knocked anyway. In his estimation children represented the ultimate sacrifice.

"Hey, Byron, it's so nice to see you. Are those pretty flowers for me? How's life been treating you?" asked his old flame.

"Truthfully, I've been better. A friend was killed by a hit-and-run recently," confessed the man.

"Sorry to hear that, sweetie. Life is so precious. Speaking of that, I don't think you've met my newest little one," pointed out Sheila, scooping up a baby. "This is Rose. Here, take her. Maybe she'll jump-start your biological clock. Did you know that every time I see your mum she complains about not being a grandmother?"

"Get her to baby-sit for you. It's okay for people to not have children. It's not like the world is short on people. I can always adopt or have kids late in life," replied Byron. Sooner or later someone inevitably confronted Byron's wifeless, childless status.

"The fact that males can produce children safely at a later age than females is one of the biggest gender inequities. You are right, childrearing isn't for everyone, but, trust me, you would make a great dad. See...Rose likes you. Having a child changes you forever," said the proud mother of three.

"That's exactly what scares me about it. I don't want such a definite, irreversible responsibility. Do you want to know my single greatest obstacle to fatherhood?"

"Enlighten me."

"It's the dangerous nature of my lifestyle. If I had a moppet, I would be compelled to weed out any unnecessary dangers. It would be unfair for me to voluntarily put my life at risk if a little one was counting on me. Removing intentional risk-taking from my life is an unacceptable option at this point," said Byron defensively.

"I understand. I won't bother you about it anymore. So what negative thoughts do you have about the institution of marriage? Or long-term relationships?" asked the spunky woman.

"I'm in a relationship right now. On one finger, I am envious of the stability my married friends have arranged for themselves. On the other nine fingers, I feel living with the same woman and going to the same job in the same town every day would be lackluster. That type of drudgery would extinguish my spirit…the absence of variety would snuff it out," said Byron, deciding to fight sass with crass.

"I guess some things and some people never change. I hope you don't end up a lonely and bitter old man surrounded by strangers in a nursing home."

"That makes two of us," agreed Byron.

SAN DIEGO, CALIFORNIA

"Why did you contact us and not the Feds? I am sure you know that they pay for information, too. And they could easily arrange for any future charges against you to be dropped," Bill Jones asked bluntly.

"The way that the Feds would conduct an undercover investigation wouldn't work. They would end up getting me killed. For another thing, I knew you would believe me. Why do you think I waited until after Scott paid you a visit?" explained Jack Welker in a newly-calmed demeanor. The super-strength pharmaceuticals he had been ingesting bullied his overactive brain into submission.

"Why should I believe you're willing to turn on your friend over the minor matter of some bail money?" reasoned Bill Jones.

"Horne's gone off the rails and is going down either way. He's a lunatic on a sinking ship and I am jumping off. This is not about bail money. Horne turned his back on me in a time of need. Plus it's his fault I was down here in the first place. I should have been in the Sierras this whole time," said Jack wistfully.

"What's he up to?" asked Jones with keen anticipation.

"He's got it in his head that Applied Leverage murdered some innocent girl and then killed Zell Fergusson to cover it up. Scott Horne is a conspiracy theorist. He has all of these wacky theories, he believes electromagnetic fields cause cancer...he also thinks toxins in the air and water are making people crazier. The end of our friendship has been a long time coming," summarized Jack.

"Why would I trust someone who is turning against his best friend?" asked Bill Jones while trying to keep a poker face. The reference to the Alaska situation had knocked the breath out of him. Confidence is like ice, when thick enough it's strong, but when thin, the lightest weight can be shattering. Bill's sore jaw reminded him of the problem with becoming overconfident.

"First of all, we've only known each other a couple of years. I am definitely not his best friend. He's never treated me as an equal. I was someone with a free schedule to go traveling with. Look, I'm an opportunist more than anything else. But I also feel like I am more or less a decent guy. He's gone off the reservation and is planning to hurt people. I'm not gonna be a part of that," explained Jack.

"I understand that," said Bill.

"And it's not just going to be the bail money. You guys are going to give me a lot more money for what I can offer you. Scott Horne is planning something spectacular. After you guys bail me out, I'll get back into his good graces, then I'll feed you information that you can pass on to whoever you choose. Imagine the goodwill of being the heroes who helped the Feds avert a domestic terrorist attack!"

"Terrorist attack! How would that be getting even with us?" questioned a shocked Bill Jones.

"That's the problem. As of right now I don't know exactly what he is planning. Maybe he is going to attack you guys personally? It's too early to tell…either way, you'll want to know about it in advance."

"What do you know for certain?"

"Let's review the facts. When I saw Scott in Alaska, he was possessed. There was a look in his eyes that scared me. He acted agitated and excitable like a rabid dog. He gave me some money to secretly hire a welder for a big project. He's quietly assembling a posse of ecoterrorists. Add that up and consider his wealth and his resources…it's a scary combination," said Jack, angling to inflate his importance and subsequent value.

"Jack, I believe you and I really want to figure this thing out. But I'll need some definite proof…tangible evidence of what you are claiming. I'll speak candidly. Son, I have to remind you that we're having this conversation inside a psychiatric facility at which you are a patient," said Bill pointedly.

The unmistakable odor of industrial cleaning solvents permeated the dreary space. Indestructible, octagonal picnic tables and fluorescent lights welcomed visitors at the private inpatient mental health facility "Rejuvenations."

"Bill, Bill, Bill, shame on you. You think I would ask you to travel all the way out west without having a simple way to establish my claims?" Jack asked rhetorically, pointing to his temple. "I have valuable-enough information inside my head to appease everybody. This isn't easy. I'd be more likely to help someone being chased by the police than vice versa. I understand and respect the need for a police force, but excessive patrolling and profiling are un-American."

"I'm glad you decided to do the right thing...the honorable thing," offered Bill.

"This is hard for me. I've joined the good guys. Growing up, I rooted for the bad guys in movies. I found myself especially sympathetic toward Native Americans. I could never watch the endings," admitted Jack. "Give me your pen and pad. I haven't talked to Horne in about a week, but I will give you what I know," promised Jack. He wrote down enough to whet their appetite and then dramatically tore off the sheet and folded it up. "Take this and they will green-light me. After I turn myself in, arrange for my bail. It will be worth it. We both want the same thing," Jack stood up and offered his hand. He was careful to make solid eye contact. "See you soon." Jack turned around and walked away. A nurse buzzed him back into a secure area.

During the conversation, Jack felt like he was creating a second skin. Contacting Applied Leverage ran counter to most of his core principles, but he had been forced into it. In its own way, the sensation of being a turncoat felt oddly satisfying. Excessively bouncing among guilt, fear, and relief, Jack asked the on-duty nurse for an antianxiety pellet.

SANTA CRUZ, CALIFORNIA

The fairway consisted of a hillside corridor through trees with a slight downhill that ran alongside the access road. A semi-ceiling of arching limbs added difficulty to the short hole. A golfer wants a straight low shot. The yellow disc was launched quickly, accelerating in a few feet to a speed at which the airfoil created its own lift. The plastic projectile flew true, with a hint of a left fade. After traveling about two hundred feet, the disc broke for an ace run. With words of encouragement ringing out, Charles's throw continued its perfect trajectory. The group's anticipation reached a fever pitch.

Upon impact the chains rang as if struck with a baseball bat. Sadly, the thin disc splashed off to the right side and rolled down onto the asphalt out-of-bounds.

"Noooo," yelled Charles, drained from the three-second emotional rollercoaster. "It looked like it hit true. What a shame. I guess it wasn't meant to be."

"Fun to watch, at least," said Curt. The others left it alone. They knew the frustration that goes along with almost achieving something spectacular.

"It went from ace to a penalty stroke and a thirty-foot putt for par," stated Charles, still agitated from the disturbing sequence.

Hours later, on the last hole, Curt spoke up, "Can you guys play through so I can speak with Charles alone?"

"They call this one top-of-the-world because it offers sweeping views of the Monterey Bay National Marine Sanctuary. I love Santa Cruz because it blends So-Cal surf culture with, an organic Nor-Cal sensibility," said Charles.

"It's a fancy, yet funky, coastal gem. Eleven over par. What a pathetic game. It saddens me to play bad here," complained Curt.

"Frisbee golf has grown considerably since you introduced me to it a decade ago," said Charles.

"Nowadays the US alone has nearly three thousand courses. Disc golf makes sense. It's all ages, equipment costs are low, and, most importantly, it's usually free. And courses are often set in semi-natural settings that need little water or maintenance."

"What is so important that you had to interrupt my rehab?"

"Rehab? You don't have a drinking or drug problem. A physical rehabilitation?" he asked.

"Too much time in the city grind...I might've lost my mind. I was on soul rehab. Did a solo hike from Shelter Cove to Petrolia on the Lost Coast. It's an amazing trip. Have you spent any time out there?"

"I've done some sea kayaking off a friend's sailboat. I'd like to get some boot mileage in. From the water it looked raw. Anyway, I have an opportunity for someone to enrich themself while helping the world. They could be certain their efforts wouldn't be in vain," abruptly announced the Owl.

"You want me to rub out an executive?" asked Charles, who tried to lighten serious situations with awkward humor.

"No. I need you to gain the confidence of somebody. Of course, how far you take the seduction is up to you."

"It's a man?"

"He's young, single, fit, and supposedly outdoorsy. I should mention that I have a very rich sponsor on this one," explained the Owl.

With her stunning runner's body and delicate features, Ashley Charles said, "I'm put off that you still view me mainly as a sexpot spy. Conversely, I itch at the notion of going under. What do you need from him?" she asked.

"Let's see if you can get him comfortable with you. Then I'll relay some specific goals. Initially act disinterested in anything remotely related to his work. We'll stay in touch," said Curt excitedly.

"Why me? You know other girls willing to do your bidding," Ashley asked, wanting to hear the answer from her ex-lover.

"You are the hottest girl I know who's down for the cause and is also a savvy con artist. And I know you possess a bundle of hate for corrupt special interest groups."

"You should have stopped at 'hottest girl you know'…and mentioned something about me being a dynamo in bed," teased Charles.

"In beds, boats, planes, rooftops, beaches, mountaintops, and riverbanks," recited Curt with more than a hint of nostalgia in his voice.

SAN BERNARDINO MOUNTAINS, CALIFORNIA

In many small towns the local diner serves as more than just a place to eat. One Big Bear Lake eatery is, known for gigantic buttermilk pancakes and a cook with a playfully grizzly manner.

"In the twenty-first century the economic jungle is becoming overrun by a dragon, a tiger, and a bear. These booming economies have been catching up to us. China, India, and Russia were achieving solid annual gains until the US mortgage crisis kicked off a global recession. Our government has focused on costly foreign affairs while ignoring the looming crises at home. As the American economy goes, as goes the world…and they're sick of it," said one patron.

"The root of the problem is that people in the Far East save and people here consume, borrow, and then consume some more. China is happy to play banker to the United States for now because we sustain the enormous trade imbalance. But in the future, who knows?" reasoned Ernesto Vargas, loosely engaged in the discussion.

"I worry about crude oil being traded in something other than US dollars. It's possible," offered a diner sitting at the counter.

"I don't know if the members of Congress know anything about history, but empires that become too entangled in foreign affairs crumble. We need to focus inward on our own citizens. Screw building other nations…let's focus on our own country," said Ernesto. He couldn't focus on the discourse, because he was worried about his fishing buddy Scott Horne. The package had arrived and he had opened it immediately. After studying the contents he felt that Scott had cast his lure into dangerous waters. As a man of rigid convictions, Ernesto Vargas chose to fight institutional crookedness in an entirely different manner. He also knew that people who imperil moneymaking empires can end up having premature funerals.

To unwind after breakfast Ernesto took a hike with his wife, Julia. After reaching an elevated vantage, they quietly took in the surroundings. "As pretty as this vista is, one thing bothers me. The density of these trees isn't safe. The main drawback of this valley is fire…particularly when hot, dry Santa Ana winds are blowing off the Great Basin," he lamented.

"Human policies have contributed to severely overgrown forests," agreed Julia.

"For millions of years, natural wildfires ignited by lightning would roll through and burn the brush and small trees away. Ground fires wouldn't burn hot enough to set the older trees ablaze. Nature's controlled burn," he said. "Nowadays fires are suppressed to protect private property. This has caused tree density and undergrowth to get so thick that when wildfires do get started, they burn so hot that everything in their path goes up in flames," he said.

"Once it gets into the crowns of the big trees, the inferno is uncontrollable. As we witnessed firsthand a few years back, these super-fires create erratic wind patterns and do scary things. Why risk lives protecting homes and businesses that were knowingly built in fire pathways?" asked Julia.

MANASSAS, VIRGINIA

Barely two days after meeting with the Owl, Ashley Charles moved into a new apartment. A few enterprising male neighbors offered to personally welcome her to the area, but she politely declined. The vixen received instructions from one of Scott Horne's private investigators. She walked over to the picnic table and waited. An older man sauntered over.

"Good afternoon. Mind if I join you?" said the private eye with a thick southern accent.

"Pleased to meet you. Thanks for the help," said Ashley, recognizing the outfit he'd described.

163

"Here's the rundown. Peter Zahn is thirty-one, lives alone, and rides bicycles. Pretty normal habits. His trash shows that he eats healthy. No credit cards or debts. This is the best picture I have. The guy is sort of an anomaly. He doesn't really fit the mold of a hacker," said the sleuth.

"There are no molds, everybody's unique. Have you seen him with any women?"

"We've only been on him a coupla weeks. It doesn't appear that he has a steady girlfriend. The dancers at the local strip club seemed to know and like him."

"He's got money to spend…of course they like him. Any male friends? Does he drink?" asked Ashley dispassionately.

"He has a few buddies and goes out. We haven't seen him drinking heavily yet. We have to be really careful, because Applied Leverage conducts surveillance on him."

"Hobbies? Patterns?"

"Every day after work Zahn goes straight home, quickly changes clothes and leaves on a bicycle. Sometimes on a road bike, others a mountain bike. I'd say that's your in," suggested the private investigator. "You're a knockout; Zahn doesn't stand a chance."

"My condo is in the same neighborhood as his house. It'd be normal for me to be riding around and checking it out. What's the biking around here like?" said Ashley.

"It's a semirural setting of second-growth forests, large ranches, and suburban sprawl. He rides fast on the streets. Not too sure what happens in the dirt, but I imagine he gets after it."

"A guilty conscience can be very motivating. Anything else?"

"I hope your identity is bulletproof. These people seem real serious."

"I guess we'll find out. We've got some pretty good operators on our team, too. I'll call you if I need anything," she said with a smile.

"Since you're here, the boss said to pull off him. Stay safe."

"Bye for now."

TWIN FALLS, IDAHO

Lyle, Evan, and Will were bonded tightly and not only because they'd been born in quick succession. Lax oversight from alcohol-abusing parents forced the boys to mature early. On trips up to the local ski hill, the boys discovered that the camaraderie there could fill the parental void. The ski community became their de facto caretakers. As they began to stand out as gifted athletes, the attention and accolades snowballed. Learning to adapt to changing weather and conditions helped to prepare the youngsters for the constant flux of the man-made world. Having an unbiased medium to vent stress proved invaluable to the boys. The natural world operates with impunity and is impartial to wealth, appearance, race, religion, sexual orientation, gender, and politics; humans are treated equally by Mother Nature.

In the beginning the boys were nudged toward ski racing, but they purposefully underwhelmed coaches when skiing gates. Evan, Will, and Lyle wanted to ride in the trees while launching off obstacles into the fluff. They favored the type of skiing that is bounded only by physics, creativity, athleticism, and gumption. Other boys watched from the lifts while Will, Lyle, and Evan floated gracefully through the trees on hand-me-down skis and thrift-store wool. As teens they rebelled against the pot culture and weren't much for boozing either.

It didn't take much persuading for Curt Joddell to convince the Derels to participate. The cash Curt flashed was more money than they had ever seen and sealed the deal. Repeatedly to the point of awkwardness, Curt emphasized that everything was to be kept super-secret or the deal was off. He lied to them and said the stunt was going to be the introductory sequence for a big-budget ski movie. The boys came to US Highway 93 to practice for the upcoming stunt by leaping off the Perrine Bridge.

"Why do you think Curt would be the messenger for a moviemaker?" pondered Will.

"Who cares? Why do you have to analyze everything? I need that money, no matter what he needs me to do," advised Evan, the youngest and boldest of the three. "Rarely are corporate dollars used in ways that benefit people like us. Let's enjoy it."

"Give credit to Red Bull for sponsoring groundbreaking events and innovative athletes," said Will.

"The Air Race is hands down the most exciting spectator-friendly event to have come along in recent history. Red Bull has set the standard for productive, sponsor-athlete relationships. I keep waiting for their call," added Lyle.

"They helped subsidize the reigning daredevil of the twenty-first century…Travis Pastrana. One-ninety-nine can also race off-road with the best of them on two-or four wheels," said Evan jealously.

"The world has become so safe that those who crave risk have resorted to creating unpredictable situations via sports, sex, crimes, drugs…I became obsessed with the stunts I saw on TV and in movies. People across the world were recreating in bold new ways using sponsorship money, and I wanted in," said Will.

"My vice isn't sold. It's produced internally in reaction to what the mind perceives to be life-threatening circumstances…the miraculous human machine's version of nitrous oxide," said Evan.

Lyle was fed up with small talk, "If everybody was jumping off a bridge, would you jump, too?" He climbed up onto the railing and slowly tilted his body over the edge until he was committed. In the first second he fell about thirty-two feet, and about sixty-four feet in the next. Then he casually rotated a front flip. Stabilized in an arch, Lyle threw his drogue parachute, which yanked out his main chute. He had a clean opening with no tangled lines. (As the seasons had passed, the brothers had been able to garner a few skiing sponsors. When they had a little cash, they became experienced skydivers and began to dabble in BASE jumps. Today, all three brothers were rarefied aerialists.) The doting brothers watched until Lyle landed safely on the gravel bank over four hundred and fifty feet below.

"This bridge rocks. Kudos, Idaho. You're right, Evan, who cares? We all need the money, and the looming payday makes that fat bonus look like chump change," conceded Will.

A local teen rode up on a road bicycle. "How much scarier is that than skydiving?"

"When you jump out of an airplane, it's already traveling at high speed. You don't get to enjoy the full effect of gravity. When you jump off a static object, you experience those glorious first seconds of constant acceleration. It's the sensation of jumping off something into water, but by using a parachute, a BASE jumper gets to fall further and therefore faster, yet with a soft landing."

"So you hope," said the kid as he pedaled away.

Foz do Iguaçu, Brazil

Mick Nolls had a new problem to add to his collection of old ones. No longer did he worry about Curt attacking the Itaipu Dam. His current unease centered over the fate of Marianne Tireau. Blooms of anxiety had taken root and rapidly consumed his thoughts. Prudence cast aside, Mick had become smitten with Marianne. He wasn't the first person to have fallen in love inappropriately. With regrets about the false pretenses, Mick connected with Marianne on an emotional and physical level.

Riding around with aggressive cabbies while wearing no seatbelt usually appealed to Mick's rebellious nature, but his mind focused inward. *What is the point of this? Maybe I need to reorganize my priorities? How well do I really know Curt?*

Arriving at the sidewalk café a shade early, Mick settled into a table against the building and ordered a bottle of Chilean cabernet. His date arrived soon after, casually attired in a lightweight cotton sundress.

"You're drinking wine during the day...I like that. I've found an American who can learn to live properly," said Marianne. She enjoyed teasing her beau as a method of foreplay.

"Congratulations, you created a monster."

"What is your plan?"

"Today? Or...?" wondered Mick.

"I must travel to Las Vegas in a month's time. Perhaps we can meet up if you're in Los Angeles? You could be my 'plus one'," offered the engineer, inviting Mick with an intentionally casual demeanor.

For a variety of reasons the statement caused him to panic. "Why are you going to Las Vegas?" questioned Mick.

"I'm scheduled to represent the engineers of Itaipu Binacional at an annual convention. The International Hydroelectric Forum is held near a major dam every year. We hosted two years ago...this year is the Hoover Dam. It could be another VIP tour of a world-class facility. I'm in charge of planning the tour for my group," outlined Marianne.

"Sign me up. I would love to meet you there," replied Mick. He figured that response would be consistent with Curt's plan and that scared him. "What am I getting into?"

"In the daytime it's a chance for dam executives and engineers to coordinate with lobbyists and construction contractors. After dark it's more of a party than anything else. We will have fun together," promised Marianne.

"It's getting time for me to head back to the States anyhow. I have to get to work on my movie. A toast to Las Vegas," offered Mick as he dramatically raised his wine glass. It was a quarter-hearted toast. The word lobbyist had jumped out at him. Nolls knew the Owl preyed on lobbyists.

"To us, together in Sin City," offered Marianne. "It's totally optional, honey, you're not obligated to go. Stay here at my place if you like. But I thought your inner filmmaker would be excited at the opportunity," she explained, not wanting to seem clingy.

"No, no, I wouldn't miss a chance to spend time with you on my home turf. I have editing work to do in LA, so I'll head there beforehand," fibbed Mick. Nolls needed to go talk to Curt Joddell in person to find out what was really going on, before he got involved any deeper.

MANASSAS, VIRGINIA

On a warm afternoon Ashley Charles contentedly watched Peter Zahn leave on a titanium mountain bike. She had both types with her, but preferred the privacy of an off-road trail as opposed to the shoulder of a highway for making the first contact. The early stages of the hunt always thrilled her. The game of manipulation made her tingle with anticipation. She had been stalking her human prey for the past few days and decided how to go about meeting him. To her, people were projects. By doing her homework and putting in dirty work, Ashley felt she could decode and subsequently handle anybody.

The narrow single-track wove its way through dense forest in gradual turns that allowed Peter to pedal aggressively. He kept his speed up in order to ascend the short inclines while staying in a low, fast gear. His legs were pumping like pistons at a steady RPM. After spending long stationary hours in the basement, he needed to get outside and burn off some stress.

Over the past few years Peter had tediously cut out his on-again, off-again courtship of prescription drugs. Painkillers, benzos, sleeping pills…it didn't really matter. The addict gobbled or snorted whatever he could get his hands on. Now that he had rat-holed a pile of clean money, Peter wanted to live a long and healthy life. As his replacement fix, he turned to strenuous exercise. Recklessly exerting himself until he nearly threw up, sometimes he did.

Zahn was zipping along a sidehill when a feminine scream, followed by a crash, broke the woodland soundtrack. He came around the bend eyes wide looking for the source of the noise, but there was nothing to see. *Am I imagining things?*

Then he saw her. An attractive woman had fallen about fifteen feet down from the thin trail. Peter stopped quickly and set his bike off the trail.

"Are you okay?" asked Peter from above. *What do we have here?*

When she had thrown the bike down the hill and then slid down on her side to get dirty, Ashley hadn't foreseen the sharpness of the gravel. Two long cuts ran the length of her left thigh. "Nothing is broken, but I am pretty banged up. This is my first ride with clip-in pedals. I stopped and I couldn't get my foot free until it was too late," Ashley said. She stood up slowly and surveyed the minor damage while dramatically brushing dirt off her torso.

Without prompting, Peter boot-skied down the steep slope to help. "The same thing happened to me, but luckily I only fell onto my front lawn. I'm glad you're wearing a helmet. You could've been seriously injured. Let me take your bike up. Do you need a hand?" asked Peter sincerely.

"No, I can manage on my own. If you could carry the bike, that would be great," answered Ashley. She was an independent soul who didn't possess much natural humility in her emotional composition, but she could act with the best of them. "Thanks so much."

"No problem at all," he answered genuinely. The woman's allure had him reeling.

Back on the trail Peter checked her bike. "I deem it to be in good working order. Your accent gives away that you're not from around here. Do you work in government?"

"I recently lost my job out west, but I'm originally from Wisconsin. I am inheriting a condo nearby, so I moved here to make some improvements before I sell it someday," she explained. The story was intended to make Ashley appear middle-class, but with some ambition.

"Maybe we could be trail buddies…keep an eye on each other," suggested Peter, immediately regretting his choice of phrase.

"I appreciate your help and everything, but I just got out of an abusive relationship. That's the other reason I moved out here. Right now I'm not in a place where I can trust men," deceived Ashley. She'd decided that a vulnerable girl would appeal to Zahn.

"I was only suggesting that we ride bikes together, but I understand. Sorry to hear about your relationship. It was nice meeting you," concluded Peter. He faked a smile, threw his leg over the bike, and pushed off. He pedaled away wondering how he'd managed to mess that up so quickly. *I didn't even get her name.*

Ashley decided to replay the conversation on her digital recorder to check her initial reaction. She closed her eyes to heighten the function of her ears. After listening to the brief conversation three times, Ashley felt confident that she had positioned herself in the forefront of Peter Zahn's thoughts.

"I've got him," Ashley bragged to the indifferent forest as she began to pedal languidly.

NORTHERN VIRGINIA

A tense and frustrated Bill Jones sat in Alan Reynard's office awaiting a definitive answer. The two men were arguing over the contentious subject of Jack Welker's vague proposition.

"It seems farfetched. I mean, how can we trust this guy?" asked Alan. "I'm reluctant to pursue a relationship with this misfit."

"Peter hasn't been able to find anything online or anywhere else that contradicts what the kid told me. At the very least we should check out the information Jack gave us. What can it hurt? It will give us a fuller picture. I already have figured out the angle we can use," said Jones.

"We could run it by Morgan Higgins," conceded Alan. He picked up the phone and asked his new secretary to immediately set up a call. On his desktop he pulled up Applied Leverage's profile of the man.

"You won't regret it. This is a great opportunity."

"The problem I'm having is why this fellow would commit mutiny so easily," said Alan.

"He's in the midst of a mental health crisis. Let's use that to our advantage. Scott Horne is ignoring him because he's busy dealing with us. And Jack's scared of having innocent blood on his hands. Jack knows Horne is on a path that leads to nowhere."

"He could just disappear instead of turning on his friend," said Alan.

"Jack thinks we can get the charges against him dropped. And of course there's the issue of money, which is the ultimate motivator," summarized Jones, wanting to give Jack a chance to make good on his promises.

"Horne has plenty of money," pointed out Alan, who couldn't quite pinpoint the source of his apprehension.

"According to Jack, Scott Horne is cheap. The sucker gives his money away to environmental causes, not to his friends."

Bill and Alan grew tired of going back and forth on every point and sat in silence. The oversized phone on Alan's desk interrupted the stillness, "Director Higgins on line four, sir."

"Howdy, Morgan. I haven't seen you in ages. How are Cindy and the kids doing? Bobby is what…like, seven now?" asked Alan reading off his monitor.

"Everybody's doing great, Alan. I hate to rush you, but I have a jet standing by, ready to whisk me away. I'm on borrowed time, but your secretary said it was urgent and you have always been good to me so I made an exception," said Higgins, lying. There was no jet or any rush at all, he wanted to make Alan feel important.

"I'll tell you what, Morgan, I really appreciate the callback because Bill and I are in one heck of a pickle here. You remember Bill Jones, I'm sure. Let me put you on speaker," explained Alan Reynard.

"Hey, Morgan, thanks for such a quick response. The short version is that, for quite some time, Applied Leverage has been receiving threats from a group of ecoterrorists. Recently we were contacted by one of them who proposed a secret exchange. Information for cash. We agreed to it because it seemed like the best way to protect ourselves and our families."

"Bill, this is an unsecured phone. Let's get together when I get back to DC. Why didn't you tell me about this sooner?" asked Morgan. Applied Leverage could make or break his career, depending on their intent. He knew that dealing with them demanded caution and planning. "Who are these jokers, anyhow?"

"Our informant is in tight with Scott Horne and Curt Joddell," said Bill, anxious to see the shock value that the names held.

"Guys, I'm going to postpone my flight to meet up with you right away. Meet me in the dirt lot just before the Triple C at seven sharp. Thanks for bringing me in."

As Alan Reynard and Bill Jones drove toward the Commonwealth Country Club, they recognized Morgan's distinctive Cadillac CTS-V and pulled in. "What's the plan?" asked Alan.

"Jump in…we'll take a little drive," suggested Higgins. "It would be improper for me to be seen with you." Night had fallen and made it harder for passersby to recognize them, but he didn't want to take any chances. "It's roomy in the back."

Reluctantly Alan entered the rear of the luxury vehicle through the front door. Bill took the front seat to present the case.

"This is Bill's deal, since he had the chance to meet this guy and look into his eyes," said Alan.

Morgan eased out of the lot onto the rural lane. He cranked up the radio and rolled down the windows as a precaution against recording devices. Trust wasn't one of Higgins's stronger attributes. "Please continue," politely said Higgins.

"I can't tell you exactly who our source is. Let's call him Wayne, but through him we can relay valuable information to you."

"The two names you mentioned over the phone aren't exactly a secret. What do you really know about those guys?" said Higgins.

"This guy Wayne swears that Curt Joddell is planning an attack against innocent people, with Scott Horne putting up the money. Our only motive is to protect our employees and the general public…that's why we felt obligated to call you. He also mentioned a rich adventurer named Mick Nolls…and Brazil. Does that name ring a bell?" asked Bill, guessing it would after Higgins's reaction to the other two names.

"You two did the right thing, but CIGARS will have to take control of the informant. It's that simple."

"That's where it gets tricky. I pointed that out to Wayne when we met the other day, but he's paranoid about authorities. He believes you guys would get him killed. Honestly I think he'll go underground if the issue gets forced. Plus we can pay way better than you guys," said Bill. The remark added to his aura of oafishness.

"Or I could have the FBI arrest you and him for obstruction of justice." *These old men are in over their head,* thought the lawman.

"There is no need for trivial threats, Morgan. You have skeletons, too. Don't bite the hand that feeds. Like it or not, we're in this together and we will work together," interjected Alan, backseat negotiating. He'd correctly guessed that Bill would blow it and would need a verbal rescue.

"We have to keep this a secret for now, but I do know that at some point that's not going to be possible anymore. What else do you have?" asked Morgan regrettably. At the moment it sounded like he had no other choice than to join ranks with Applied Leverage.

Alan took over the reins of the conversation. "We'll keep you updated through a courier. I don't trust anything digital. Is that everything, Bill?"

"Wayne mentioned that Scott Horne seemed crazed and agitated. I'd like to point out that Horne has checked himself into psychiatric facilities four separate times in the past ten years," responded Bill, rubbing his bruised jaw.

"I wasn't aware of that. You both know that I will sit before Congress and deny everything if it ever comes to that, but for now we will work together on this," said Morgan sourly. When his secretary called stating that Alan Reynard urgently needed to speak with him, he suspected that sleep would be lost.

Northern Virginia

Peter Zahn was having a tough time at work. The stress kept him at redline. If Applied Leverage put any more pressure on him, one of his internal components would fail. Between the normal workload and trying to sabotage Scott Horne, Peter hardly left the basement for air. As usual the hacker turned to physical exertion as an after-work therapy. Almost finished with an extended road ride, Peter noticed an old CJ-7 lingering alongside of him. At the point when he was about to yell something, the classic off-road vehicle sped ahead and pulled off the road.

Peter couldn't quite believe what he was seeing. The woman from the trail crash gracefully dropped from the vehicle. He had been replaying the brief encounter with the girl obsessively. Peter had spent his adolescence indoors learning codes, playing video games, and exploring porn sites instead of figuring out how to act around the opposite sex in real life. Trying to hide his elation, he coasted to a stop.

After giving him a moment to catch his breath, Ashley Charles spoke up, "I'm glad I ran into you. I was already having a bad day and then I took that spill," explained Ashley with feigned humility.

"No problem, don't worry about it. I get irritated when I wreck. Everybody does," consoled Peter. He felt sweaty and self-conscious in his tight and bright road-biking getup. He thought she looked great in workout pants, fleece vest, and wool beanie.

"Anyway I've been regretful about my behavior and then I happened to see you riding down the street. I wanted to stop and formally apologize."

"Let it go. I didn't give it a second thought."

"I'd like to invite you over for dinner sometime this week."

"That would be nice. I can't cook for squat, but I make great ice."

"I owe you a home-cooked meal. Let me give you my number." Ashley went back to her doorless, roofless vehicle and returned with a slip of paper. "Do you have any plans for the day after tomorrow?"

"Pretty sure I'm free."

"Call me around five. Enjoy the rest of your ride."

"I live just around the corner."

"Me, too. Oh, my name is Ashley," she responded with a seductive smile.

"Peter," he said, pedaling away and attempting to appear nonchalant.

Ashley Charles climbed into the Jeep and sped away, beeping the horn as she passed her mark. Occasionally when manipulating people she felt guilt, but not this time. Ashley had done her homework on Applied Leverage. As a button pusher in their employ, Peter Zahn and malice were no strangers.

SAN DIEGO, CALIFORNIA

After his seventy-two-hour hold expired, Jack nonchalantly asked the staff at the psychiatric facility to call the police on him. The arresting officers had been polite and professional, respecting Jack's right to remain silent, after he reminded them about it. He was booked into the human kennel without incident. Although Jack declined any further treatment, he would have to speak with an onsite psychiatrist.

"Do you know where you are and why you're here?" asked the curious doctor. Welker didn't fit the physical profile of his average client. The kid had perfect teeth and looked to be in great health.

"We're inside a physical manifestation of the war on poor people...a wretched concrete monument to the prison-industrial complex. I'm kidding, we're at the downtown jail in SD," responded Jack.

"How did you end up here?"

"Cops drove me here."

"Yes, from Rejuvenations, but how did you end up there?"

"My girlfriend drove me there," answered Jack, having a little fun with the jailhouse quack.

"What made you check yourself into a mental-health facility?"

"I stopped taking my meds and my brain got stuck on fast-forward. I needed a time-out," said Jack honestly.

"Did mental illness play a role in the crime you're accused of? What circumstances led to you being here in jail?"

"The burden of a dynamic mind is difficult to gauge…things are always changing. Every brain is genetically unique…and then subjected to different experiences, pressures, nutrition, and drugs. With proper support an imbalanced brain can flourish. Neglected or ignored, someone with a mental illness can easily have one bad episode and end up a forgotten citizen in an overcrowded prison. As to the pending charges against me, my attorney has advised me to not talk about the case."

"How should a law-and-order society handle criminals?"

"The way it currently works, nonviolent offenders get thrown into general populations where they are preyed on by lifelong criminals. Inmates are forced into joining racially segregated gangs for protection and then coerced into committing sentence-lengthening crimes. Taxpayers subsidize these repeat-offender factories."

"What would be your solution?" asked the head doctor. "I'm intrigued by your insights."

"If government allows private companies to get involved in the correctional system, then it should be in exchange for inmate labor. Send first-time and low-risk offenders to work camps where they can be productive. The free labor could help subsidize the cost of feeding, housing, and guarding the prisoners."

"There are programs like that."

"Teach prisoners skills that they can actually use for future employment on the outside. When they are released, find them a job and a place to stay in a new city. Make relocation a condition of parole."

"Let's get back on track, Jack. Do you understand the charges against you? The potential sentence you're facing?" asked the doctor.

"I understand that when prisoners equal profit, everyone loses. Privatizing prisons was a horrible mistake. I'm sure you are familiar with scandals involving kickbacks to judges."

"Prisons had the same problems before privatization. It's just one big money grab, huh?"

"Inmates are people, and people make mistakes, especially when they're young. The current system definitely seems to prey on poor, urban minorities. What the government should do is give citizens with limited options a chance to learn a marketable skill before they resort to becoming a career criminal. Offer at-risk youth an opportunity to learn a trade. It would be a lot cheaper in the long run."

"There is some truth to what you're saying, but it's much more complicated. What about violent, repeat offenders? What would you do with them?"

"Fence them in and let them administer themselves. I guarantee that would deter some youngsters from committing crimes."

"I think you know that's not realistic."

"Okay, ship prisoners overseas to an inexpensive country with no unions," suggested Jack with a smile. "There are plenty of countries that would love the business."

"That's better than your anarchy idea, but still impractical. Are you willing to take your meds while you are here?" asked the doctor, ready to move on. The jaded professional had heard all the conspiracies before.

"Sure, but I am not going to be here long."

"What makes you think that?"

"Just a hunch. Anyway, I'm good, I'm not gonna cause any trouble here. You can sign off on me."

"Well, it's certainly been enlightening, Mr. Welker. Thank you for sharing your ideas with me."

Northeastern Florida

On a sunny Florida afternoon Dewey motored along the Intracoastal Waterway in his fancy cigarette boat, hoping the toy would help him to snare a gold digger at a waterfront bar. Cruising south back toward Ponce Inlet, Dewey could see the sandbar scene going off. He counted eight boats, ten guys, and over twenty girls. Dewey felt his fully stocked liquor cabinet would make a nice addition to the scene. He throttled back and angled his craft toward a beach landing. The rumbling supercharged V-8s drew envious stares from onlookers. He silenced the engines and gently drifted against the shore.

Immediately a teenage kid came over. "That is a sick boat, partner. It sounded like you got some big blocks."

"Blown five-oh-twos."

"Wow! Expensive, huh?"

"You said it. Hey, who are those bikini-clad girls with?"

"Whoever can take them home, I guess. I think some are local and some of the younger ones are on a late spring break."

"I saw you over there with them."

"Yeah, I was trying to pull something off, but they told me I'm too young. They are fun to look at anyhow."

"You said it. What are they drinking?" asked Dewey, assembling a plan.

"Captain-n-Coke, mostly."

Dewey grabbed a big bottle of aged rum from his stash and a bucket of ice. "Let's go make some friends," he said, leaping over the gunwale.

A grand entrance in a quarter-million-dollar speedboat had been a good start, but walking up with free alcohol actually caused the crowd to become giddy and animated. Dewey cracked the bottle, took a long pull, and then filled a cup to the top and gave it to his underage cohort. Then Dewey started pouring shots and spiking cocktails as his introduction. On closer inspection most of the women appeared to be in their mid-twenties, which Dewey felt was a bit young, but he could make an exception. Something about the combination of hard alcohol and women rendered his moral code indecipherable.

"You live around here?" Dewey asked a stunning brunette.

"Nah, I'm on vacation with some girlfriends."

"Doesn't your husband worry about letting a beautiful girl like you loose in Daytona Beach?"

"What husband?"

"Well, your boyfriend then?"

"What boyfriend?"

"I'm Dewey. Welcome to Florida."

"Mindy. Nice to meet you. I would've thought you'd have a boatload of girls with a toy like that." said the twenty-something gesturing toward the floating artwork.

"That's not my style. I'm a one-girl guy," replied Dewey.

"Shut up, I don't believe that for one second."

"But it sounded kinda good, right?"

"You know, evidence of loose spending can be a formidable aphrodisiac."

"I've heard that women don't see an actual speedboat. They see shopping sprees, spa treatments, and alimony checks with pretty numbers."

"Whatever…my first thought was that you are compensating for something. Does it have a bathroom?"

Dewey and the woman boarded the speedboat. When the woman emerged from below, he asked, "Mindy, do you want me to freshen up your drink?"

"No, thanks, the booze and the sun have already taken a toll on me. I don't know about you, but I've been drinking too much this week."

"I use alcohol and drugs daily, but at some point I'd like to address the problems that cause the urge to chemically escape myself."

"That's a little too much information. It looks like you are doing okay. You're fit, and you seem to be having a good time."

"This boat and other thrill purchases work in a drug-like manner. They provide a temporary rush, but eventually the buzz wears off and I'm back to square one."

"What do you need to escape from? Are you feeling guilty because mommy and daddy pay for everything?"

"I wish it was that simple. I guess you could say that recently I realized that, without finding a high level of inner peace, I will never be truly happy. People who accept themselves fully are the wealthiest, regardless of their actual financial status. I want that kind of comfort," explained Dewey.

"That makes sense, but I think you're being too hard on yourself. What's in the past is done and over. Focus on the present and the positive."

"Oh, I try to, believe me. The reason I study my past misdeeds is to help calibrate my future actions."

"That's a good thing, then. You are definitely a strange, but interesting, man. What do you do?" asked the woman.

"What do I do, like what are my hobbies, or what do I do, what is my job?"

"Job."

"Why not just ask how much money I make?"

"Don't be an idiot. I was just trying to make conversation…there's no need to get defensive."

"Sorry. It just bothers me when people ask that straightaway. It seems like they want to judge my job not…me."

"That makes sense…if you're crazy. It's a standard question. I don't care what you do or how much money you have. Honestly, I just wanted to use the bathroom. See you around," she said before climbing off the boat. "I think you might be having a midlife crisis."

"I think you might be right."

SAN DIEGO, CALIFORNIA

Considering the caliber of the men at the downtown lockup, Jack became aware that parts of his prison-reform theories were improbable. The condensed mass of humanity repulsed Jack's antisocial tendencies. He felt certain that every single disease or condition imaginable was represented in the cross section of men. His mind envisioned unseen maladies nonstop.

The sound of the big door opening had a Pavlovian effect on the inmates. Since it wasn't time for chow, the interruption meant somebody had made bail. Everyone, even those with no real hope of escape, scrutinized the correctional officers.

"Ronald Dunsfeld," announced the emotionless guard.

The guards had failed him again. Jack sulked as he shook his head.

What is going on? Why is Applied dragging this out?

"And Jack Welker."

"Believe it. Sorry to have doubted ya, Bill, ole buddy," said Jack to no one in particular. He had never lost confidence that Bill Jones was going to get him sprung, because he had given Applied Leverage valuable intelligence.

Jack changed into his street clothes, processed out, and happily walked out into the sunshine. *It's time for a stiff drink.*

A burgundy Ford was parked amid the squad cars lined up on the curb. The woman sitting shotgun was looking at a map and spoke up. "Excuse me, sir. Do you have a moment? We're lost."

"As a traveler I sympathize with navigation frustration. Let me take a look." are asked Jack. "Where are you trying to go?"

"Get in the car, Welker. Jones didn't want to come in person," said Jane Doe.

"My mom taught me never to get into a car with strangers."

"We're all on the same team, Jack. We've put our faith in you…return the favor," reasoned Jane Doe using a soothing voice to subdue his reluctance.

"That's a fair point," allowed Jack. He got in the car. "My mom would be appalled. Where are we heading?"

"It's not far. Bill Jones is waiting for us there," said Jane calmly.

"Everybody knows my name," stated Jack after a minute of silence.

"Excuse me, how rude. I'm Jane and this is John," deadpanned the woman while shaking Jack's hand. "We'll be working together."

"Besides driving, what do you two do?" said Jack, intentionally pressing buttons to see how they handled provocation.

"Don't be cute. Do what you promised, mind your own business and collect the money. It'll be much easier that way," forcefully suggested John as he wheeled onto the Pacific Coast Highway.

"Tell us about your hometown, Jack," suggested Jane.

"San Diego is an American city because of its bay. The Treaty of Guadalupe Hidalgo ceded the territory to us after the Mexican-American War. Uncle Sam made sure to keep possession of the pueblo when deciding how much of Alta California to retain. Point Loma and Coronado combine to create one of only a handful of natural deepwater harbors along the West Coast of the continental US. At a time when the might of a nation was determined by the power its navies could project across the seven seas, its strategic importance was obvious.

"In the twenty-first century the Navy continues to be the city's biggest player. The region is dominated by the military, as you would expect of a corner city with a great port. Mexico may lie ten or so miles south of downtown San Diego, but across the busiest land border in the world a truly exotic experience waits. The San Diego Zoo is the cornerstone of Balboa Park. It's a relic of the nineteen-eighteen Pan-American Expo. Today the space is home to acres of museums and gardens," said Jack playing tour guide.

"I'm an ocean-loving snob, so to me San Diego exists west of Interstate 5. The peninsula of Point Loma guards the bay with custom homes of all styles. Eclectic Ocean Beach and Sunset Cliffs confront the Pacific, while Loma Portal, Fleetridge, and La Playa face downtown, the South Bay, and Mexico beyond that. The California dream doesn't come cheap in La Jolla, Torrey Pines, Del Mar, Cardiff, Solana Beach, or Encinitas. The Scripps Institution of Oceanography operates a first-rate, bluff-top facility. As a boy, I dreamed of one day working at their private pier and getting to explore the adjacent underwater canyon. A poor effort scholastically derailed my aspiration early on," admitted Jack.

"It's a pretty city," said Jane.

A few stoplights down the road, John looked to his right and watched an arriving airliner come dangerously close to hitting a parking garage, "Why do they have a building on final approach?" he asked. "They need to tear that down."

"Developers own this city," answered Jack. "It's a ridiculous place for a parking garage, and the airport is too small for a giant city."

They turned into a fixed-based operation across the runway from the public terminals. The sedan drove straight onto the tarmac. "I guess rich people aren't to be troubled by nuisances like X rays and ID checkpoints," said Jack. He had a notion of what he had gotten into, but that didn't mean it wasn't going to be awkward. After climbing the stairs, Jack entered a realm of opulence he had never before experienced. Hardwood, supple cowhide, and gaudy fixtures covered all surfaces, but it all fell short of the flight attendant's beauty. Since he'd left the jail only moments earlier, the woman looked too good to be true.

"My man, Mr. Jones. Nice Gulfstream. Who cares that, efficiency-wise, traveling by private jet is like having a personal train or riding down the highway in a three-hundred-foot–long bus. I'm kidding ya. Thank you for moving so fast on this. You've realized the value I have to you," boasted Jack extending a smile and his hand.

"They fought me at first, but they came around. There's plenty of time to talk shop later. For now just sit back and enjoy the ride and a drink," exclaimed Bill Jones. He made a vague gesture toward the stewardess.

"Something to drink, sir?" asked the uniformed attendant with a coy smile. The new passenger's youth and good looks were a welcome change from the usual parade of geriatrics.

"Stoli and OJ on the rocks and a bottle of water, please," replied Jack, struggling to deal with the extreme swing from jailhouse to penthouse. "Where are we going?" he asked Jones.

"Rest easy, kid, we're headed to a relaxing ranch and vineyard outside of San Luis Obispo. You'll be back tomorrow. Later today we can ride horses or you can go surfing if you want. After dinner we'll formulate a plan. You need to prove yourself to the rest of the crew," briefed Jones, pointing toward the Does.

"How do you know I surf?"

"Jack, we've researched everything about you. I know things about you that you don't know. I'm sure you can understand the need for that."

"Is the stewardess coming along?"

"No, this is a fractional ownership jet. She doesn't work for us, not directly, at least," explained Bill.

Jack Welker shook his head with mock disappointment on his face, but under the surface his buried nervousness screamed. Getting into a car with strangers was one thing; boarding a private plane was something entirely different.

SOUTHWESTERN ARIZONA

By 8:30 A.M., the desert sun already had Yuma, Arizona, baking at 93 degrees. At 5000 feet above ground level it was a balmy 76 degrees.

"The warm ultra-dry air of the Southwest is harsh on the skin, but it's great for flying partially exposed to a hundred-mile-an-hour slipstream," said Scott over the intercom.

"One key to outdoor activities is understanding humidity's effect on temperature. High levels of water vapor make cold temps seem colder and hot ones hotter," responded the plane's owner.

"Few of life's pleasures tickle my spirit like open-to-the-air planes. Thanks so much for picking me up. What is this, exactly?"

"It's a new Waco YMF Super. It has the elegant looks and character of a nineteen twenties biplane but with modern engineering and components."

Earlier that morning Scott Horne had tested the waters by crossing back into the United States from Sonora, Mexico, on his real passport. He worried that the drug bust might get him pulled aside for an impromptu interrogation or worse, but he was waved through without a hassle. He arranged to have a friend meet him on the Nogales side of the border.

West of Yuma the graceful Imperial Sand Dunes broke up the drab landscape. Fun-loving desert rats were tearing across the sand on powerful off-road vehicles trying to beat the summer heat. "I remember riding dirt bikes at Buttercup and Glamis like it was last week, yet it was twenty-five years ago. Ever been down there?" Scott asked his friend over the intercom.

"Nope, but I'd like to check it sometime. I hear it's a raucous crowd."

"There are still adventurous folks left in the world. You just have to look a little harder to find them these days. Americans dominate the realm of recreational vehicles. Our landscape lends itself to exploration, and we've got gasoline running through our veins," said Scott.

The dunes flattened out and the land morphed into agricultural usage. A colorful flash drew Scott's eyes downward. A silver crop duster boldly strafed a huge field of alfalfa.

"Do me a favor and stay further to the north of Interstate Eight. It edges too close to the Mexican border. No need to raise eyebrows," said the owner of the plane.

"Sure, but true interstates run nonstop from one side of the country to the other. Hey, where is NAF El Centro?" asked Scott. "Do the Blue Angels still practice there during the air show off-season?"

"To my knowledge. It's a little further west and a bit north. I'll point it out."

"Those guys are amazing...unmatched in precision jet flying," said Scott.

The Tecate Divide and Laguna Mountains loomed in the hazy distance ten miles away. Scott started an early climb because high temperatures and altitude hurt the performance of an internal combustion engine. Way off to the north, they could see a shimmering body of salt water with a shoreline dotted by dilapidated buildings.

"It's hard to picture the Salton Sea's heyday as a popular vacation spot of the fifties and sixties," remarked Scott.

"My grandparents used to take waterskiing trips there."

"Have you ever seen a cougar?" asked Scott.

"Nah. They're down there, though. Mountain lions are mostly active at night," replied his pal.

"It warms my soul to think that man-eating predators reside just outside such a densely populated area."

"You are one sick puppy."

Scott took the plane into the Ramona airport located in the foothills of East County. He touched down a little heavy on the tailwheel. "I should have kept it up a little longer. Sorry about that."

"It's not an easy plane to jump into and grease a landing."

"I've mostly been flying my helicopter. Can you give me a ride to the Santee trolley station?" asked Scott while taxiing.

"I didn't think a high roller like you would ride the trolley."

"I love any mass transit, but I have always wondered why the San Diego trolley shadows the freeways. It should run straight down main boulevards at street level," suggested Scott.

"My big complaint is that it doesn't access the airport or the beach, even though it's already physically close to both," said the lifelong resident.

"Or North County…whatever, …anything that gets commuters out of cars is cool with me."

Northern California

Curt Joddell possessed a soul that persuaded him to spend most of his time in or near the wild. For the past week he had been staying in a yurt off a dirt road in northwestern Humboldt County. "Of all the trees I've encountered across six continents, *Sequoia sempervirens* is the reigning champ. The coast redwood stupefies me like no other species. It isn't just their dizzying size or the fact that a particular giant might have sprouted before the Dark Ages. It's the color scheme, the deep texture of the bark…the inviting shade, the intrigue… it's the whole package that seduces me," said the Owl.

They planned to traverse Redwood National Park in a long, two-day push. The California sun flexed its muscles, but tall trees blocked most of the radiation. A trailside stream contributed some evaporative cooling. Crashing ocean waves could be heard but not seen.

"As far as an ecosystem crossroads goes…old-growth redwood forest against the Pacific is hard to compete with," stated Mick. "After researching the globe, I'm certain that no other nation rivals the continental United States for geographical diversity. We've got low and high deserts, several mountain ranges, thousands of islands, lakes, and rivers. Volcanoes, hard- and softwood forests, grasslands, swamps, estuaries, and glaciers. I could go on."

"Include Alaska and Hawaii and it becomes even more lopsided," added Curt bragging.

"This is our best bit of forest left, if you ask me."

"Nationwide only four percent of old-growth anything is left. A tree hundreds of years old is not renewable. Forest owners are better off growing big trees. Older wood is better and more expensive anyway. They should harvest the weaker trees," said Curt.

"Anyway I was surprised you broke your nocturnal pattern in Amsterdam, and now it happens again in California. I'm getting comfortable with the newly confident you. Next thing you know, I'll see you yakking it up on CNN with Anderson Cooper," quipped Mick, squinting as they passed into a rare column of sunlight.

"It's all part of the master plan," said Curt dismissively.

"You annoy me with your purposely ambiguous statements. Look. I understand the need for secrecy and all that, but I am not some twenty-year-old radical. Don't forget I helped create you. You owe me an explanation," explained Mick. "I don't need to remind you of my past financial contributions."

"I know who you are and what you've done. I haven't signed you up for anything out of line," replied Curt cryptically.

"I'm already signed up. Don't get your golden goose incarcerated. If I get thrown into jail, they will seize my assets," stated Mick, reiterating the monetary implications.

"You are overreacting. Earlier in the week when you emailed demanding a meeting, I suspected you would demand details. I had hoped that moment would be later, but I agreed to meet…a choice I'm starting to regret."

"How much danger am I putting myself in by continuing?"

"If I were to explain everything, you would be in more danger. That's all I can say for now," answered the Owl.

"You have never given me any reason to distrust you, but there's a limit to my patience. I'll head to Sin City as planned, but you need to keep me updated," said Mick, frustrated that he couldn't tell Curt about his feelings toward Marianne.

"Check out that one. Wow. Lightning split it in two," responded Curt using his favored conversational trick, diversion. It was a majestic tree and did possess the ability to derail a train of thought. "I am glad you came to visit because I needed to give you these instructions in person. Marianne is planning the activities for the lobbyists and dam engineers. You need to contact her and explain how you can get her two free limousines from Sterling Charter Services for their field trip to the Hoover Dam."

"What's this all about?" asked an agitated Mick, whose nervousness had reached critical mass. "Why do you want to control their transportation?" he asked immediately, not liking Curt's assignment one bit.

"Take a couple of deep breaths, Mick. Sit tight, we'll find you some slippers for those cold feet. Soon we'll all be together in Vegas," assured the Owl, who felt a surge of guilt bubbling up from within.

"Who is we?"

"All of us. You, me, and everybody else who is coming," explained the Owl, delivering the typically enigmatic response without sarcasm.

SAN DIEGO, CALIFORNIA

After looking around for a minute, Scott Horne walked up to an oceanfront cottage at the end of Orchard Street in Ocean Beach. From the looks of the front yard, Scott was glad he hadn't put any money into the place yet. Broken surfboards, sodden wetsuits, stained towels, rusting beach cruisers, beer cans, bottles, cartons, cigarette butts, and piles of BBQ ashes were strewn around the small yard as if a miniature tornado had torn through.

Returning to the present, Scott waded through the debris and knocked on the door. "Yo, Jack, you here?"

Jasmine opened the door wearing a Betty Go Hard T-shirt and short shorts. "Oh, hi, Scott," she blurted out. "Sorry about the mess, hon, I didn't know you were coming by."

"I couldn't care less. You're the one living with it," pointed out Scott. "While I was studying the yard, the term 'beach bum' popped into my head with jealousy attached to it. I think I was happiest as a broke teenager who snowboarded all day, bussed tables at night, and partied after that. Maybe my mind has warped those recollections?"

"Those memories could be a product of youthful exuberance."

"Good call. You still working for that Web site? What's it called?" asked Scott.

"Jenlikes.com. It's going great. In addition to interior and exterior design, we're doing weddings, events, and some retail," answered Jasmine. "I'm surprised you remembered anything about my work."

"Is Jack in town?"

"Um…Jack is going through a tough time. He checked himself into a psychiatric facility last week and instructed the staff not to release any information about him. He called yesterday and said he'll be out tonight or tomorrow," explained Jasmine feeling embarrassed for Jack. "Over the years I've grown tired of making excuses for him."

"In the circles I run in, most everybody needs an occasional tune-up," said Scott, unperturbed by the news since he had literally been there before. His main concern was that Jack might have peaked too soon. He didn't need Jack to be at full-crazy, yet.

"For Jack to voluntarily seek professional help for substance abuse and…psychiatric problems is a good sign," she agreed.

"We prefer to say 'midlife crisis,' 'nervous breakdown,' or 'exhaustion,'" he said with an involuntary laugh.

"Those labels sound better than 'psychotic episode' or 'drug rehab,'" remarked Jasmine.

"Jasmine…do you have a car I can rent from you?"

"You can borrow my car anytime. I mean, you let me live here for free, practically."

"I haven't gotten around to rehabbing this place since property values have stayed low following the real-estate crisis," said Scott.

"San Diego County was hit especially hard because its properties rose faster and higher than most regions," added Jasmine.

"Honest folks who did nothing wrong have seen their equity evaporate into thin air due to the greed of deceptive borrowers, leading investment banks, and an insurance giant. Anyway…there will be no stunt driving this time. I promise," said the millionaire. Eight years back, Scott had rolled her Toyota RAV4 playing in Baja sand.

"I remember the horrible day you crushed Kermit. I should have known back then that you and Jack were nothin' but trouble."

"You should have known long before that. What are you rocking these days?" asked Scott, shifting her attention.

"A drop-top Mini."

"Where are the keys?"

Driving away in the updated British classic, Scott was impressed by the leg- and headroom. He began to compile a to-do list out loud, "Get a throwaway cell phone, hit an Internet café, go by the bank, call my tailor." The list sounded like an almost insurmountable challenge to a person who considered himself above running errands. His anxiety actually came from the future showdown with Applied Leverage. *I'm knowingly putting my friends into a volatile situation.*

Scott felt himself getting light-headed. "You wussy. Get hold of yourself. Take a few slow, deep breaths. Calm down. Focus on the goal."

MANASSAS, VIRGINIA

The ordeal of having been caught digitally stealing and forced to serve time as a minor haunted Peter's ego. He tried to repress the damage by writing it off to youthful indiscretion and the fact that he didn't have a father figure.

"America's major social problems stem from the breakdown of the nuclear family and how that affects the behavior of individuals. For the first time in history new generations don't worry much about upholding their family's honor when decision-making. It's pointless to worry about your family's standing in the community when making life choices if neither entity functionally exists," said Peter as he sparred ideologically with his new girlfriend.

"Local communities have definitely taken a hit, but I blame electronics. Consumers have been duped into an overly…indoorsy lifestyle that has complicated the human experience."

"You've lost it. The Web is the greatest invention ever," said Peter defensively.

"The Net is ok for some stuff, but I worry about its impact on kids. Impressionable children can be exposed to the culture of sexually objectifying and degrading women. Adult-themed entertainment is literally at their fingertips. This isn't 'boy finds a Playboy magazine in dad's closet.' There's free content online that any sane person would find repulsive…hardcore graphic imagery. This makes strong parenting and lucid role models more important than ever."

"There are parental controls for that, honey," responded Peter with a sneer.

"Regardless, all that stuff is a virtual reality, a simulation. It is a worrisome symbol of the times that millions of people opt to spend their real life pretending," she said.

"We're not pretending. We're playing. It's like watching a movie, but you get to participate and compete with people from around the world in real time," corrected the gamer.

"Don't get me wrong. I love all of that stuff…television, the Internet, video games. They are the main reason people stay inside and out of my way. Can you imagine how crowded everywhere would be if everyone spent their free time outdoors?"

"There ya go; you found the silver lining. I think you owe us an apology, you little brat."

Peter Zahn had fallen hard for Ashley Charles. Most of all, he adored her sassy confidence. Of the girls Peter had dated, he reckoned the majority had been drawn in by his spending habits rather than a natural attraction.

At his behest, Ashley had practically moved into Peter's house but hadn't tried to use him for money. Peter had never felt more validated as a man.

"I still don't understand what you do, exactly," she probed. First she attacked his virtual world, and now she wanted him to brag about it.

"It's all very top secret…indoor nerdy stuff. I can't talk about it," teased Peter while tickling the knockout under the covers. "I work in network security deterring any would-be thieves from accessing our computer systems."

"So you are Applied Leverage's answer to hackers?"

"Exactly. I don't care what anyone else says, you are at least somewhat bright," said Peter.

"Shut up. Tell me more about your special talents. I find it a turn-on."

"Why? Should I change your college GPA to a four-point-oh? Clean up your driving record?"

"Can you do that? How about messing with the jerk that left my sister pregnant and penniless?"

"That would be illegal, honey, but if it is important to you, we can look into it. Does your sister need some help financially?"

"I can't accept money from you for my sister…although I would love to register her ex as a sex offender, or something fun like that. Whatever you think you can get away with."

"Maybe he needs a suspended license or a few outstanding tickets? We could destroy his credit or cancel his Visa. With my skills, any online system is accessible."

"Couldn't we get in trouble for something like that?"

"I have a laptop I use for special stuff like that. I'll piggyback onto some sucker's Wi-Fi from in front of their house."

Ashley physically attacked Peter with forceful, deliberate kisses and caresses. When sleeping with men or women for ulterior motives, the first time was always the hardest. After that she became desensitized, and, depending on the individual's skill set, it could even be enjoyable.

SAN DIEGO, CALIFORNIA

At some point while Horne was out fighting traffic, Jack Welker returned to Jasmine's. Later that evening when Scott returned, he noticed someone had taken the time to clean the yard up. "No crashes, no citations, nada. That's a fun little car." On the oceanfront deck, Scott saw Jack, beer in his hand and bong on the table. He grabbed a cold one from the fridge and headed outside. "Have fun at the funny farm?"

"Ha-ha," said Jack, ignoring Scott's offbeat attempt at humor.

"That's the past. We need to focus on the future. How are you squared away for cash, J-Dub?"

"I need some. How much depends on what you want me to do," replied Jack, needing some concrete details.

"Did you make the necessary arrangements with the metalworker?"

"Yeah, I gave Josh a sufficient cash retainer. Do you have the blueprints?"

"Yes, I do. Tell the welder this thing has to be fabricated exactly to spec. It literally needs to be able to support several tons," explained Scott.

"He's game for whatever, if the money's right. I had him clear his schedule," said Jack, relieved by how easily the encounter was progressing. He'd expected to get hassled about his irreverent handling of the last batch of cash.

"Here are the schematics and here's twenty g's. I'm meeting the *Arana* somewhere near Half Moon Bay tomorrow, and you're coming with me. The whole squad is going to be there. It's a trust-building trip," directed Scott as he passed over the loot and a sealed manila envelope.

"Where are we sailing?"

"It doesn't matter. Just be ready mañana. Byron's picking us up at Montgomery Field at noon," Scott stated flatly. "Can you give me a ride over to where my faux-bra is being stored? I have the address written down somewhere. If I'm going to be plying the highways of SoCal, I need something nastier."

Traffic had dispersed to a tolerable intensity by the time Jack took Scott to retrieve the car that Erin De Sousa had shipped.

"I can't help feeling out of place whenever I drive around a large city," said Scott.

"Quit being a baby. One day of zooming along in an isolation pod with the other sheep isn't so bad. Just follow the signs and the lines."

"That's good advice."

"What's the plan for the rest of the night?" inquired Jack.

"I think I'm going to head downtown. It's time for me to dress up and throw some money around. It's not like I will be able to take it with me."

"With you where?" asked Jack.

"Wherever I am going," replied Scott with a smile. "Thanks for the ride. Go drop the schematics off right now, will ya? You'd better be ready at eleven sharp tomorrow. I'll send a taxi."

"Have fun tonight. Only drink beer, okay?"

"They must have given you some extra-strong pills at the quack-house. You can get only so drunk on beer. Tonight is going to be a whiskey night, maybe bourbon…" said Scott.

"I could chaperone. I've seen what your hard-bar nights turn into," offered Jack.

"No dice. I'm rolling lone star tonight. Are you feeling okay? I have never known you to play mama bear."

"I just feel like going out, too."

"Don't worry, I'll keep it upright, ba-zook. I'll see ya tomorrow at Montgomery. Pack for several weeks, you might not have a chance to get back here before we…ah…."

"Before what?" inquired Jack.

"Before we head to our final objective," said Scott looking away.

Jack made sure Scott possessed the correct keypad code to enter the storage facility before taking off. Welker's first order of business was to scope the blueprints. The plans depicted a curving metal ramp mounted on a dual-axle trailer. Perplexed by the design, Jack racked his brain as to what it could be for, but he could guess only that it was meant to launch a car over a guardrail or barrier. After making copies and driving to Oceanside to drop off the blueprints at the welder's workshop, Jack returned to Ocean Beach. He stopped at The Olive Tree to procure an adult beverage. All the chit-chat about boozing had provoked his inner alcoholic. Before heading in, Jack went over to the phone, put two quarters in, and dialed from memory.

"Yeah," answered the lifeless tone.

"Johnny boy?" asked Jack.

"Yes."

"Meet me at that same lookout...Del Monte." Click.

With a mind fluttering with dollar signs, Jack tried to keep his composure. In an effort to stay on the good side of his new partners, he hid the twelve-pack of Newcastle in the trunk. After the long and tense interrogation at the ranchette, Jack Welker understood the thin line he was walking with Applied Leverage. They trusted him about as much as he trusted them, which didn't amount to squat. He hoped that this installment of information would foster a newfound credibility.

Standing on the guardrail Jack watched the Does pull into the dirt lot. He walked over and climbed through the sliding door of their Volkswagen van.

"Way to go, Jack. Nice work with the bug at the house. We could hear everything," complimented Jane. "I want you to know that we are proud of you. You are doing the right thing. It may seem like you're selling out your friend, but a real friend wouldn't put you in harm's way."

"Here is a copy of the blueprints. I'm not sure what its purpose could be, but it looks like a launch ramp for a car or truck. You heard him say it needed to be able to support tons of weight. From here on out, Scott will be driving a primer-grey Cobra with an Alaska license plate," squealed Jack. "He's going out drinking downtown tonight. I don't know where, but he'll probably start off on the top floor of the Hyatt. I suggest you go take a look-see and witness for yourself what kind of loose cannon we are up against," explained Jack.

"That's not a bad idea. If you had to wager a guess, where would you say the attack is going to take place?" asked Jane.

"I still have no idea what he's planning or when or where. You heard Scott shut me down when I asked where we're sailing to. I bet the site of the attack is somewhere he doesn't frequent…somewhere he dislikes. That rules out anything coastal or mountainous. Where's the cash?" levied Jack.

"Remember, this operation is not about money. It's about doing the right thing and having peace of mind for the rest of your life," suggested Jane as she handed him a brick of currency. "Don't forget that Scott and his band of idiots are going to jail for a very long time, and you're not. That's enough of a reward in and of itself."

"Nobody accepts righteousness as legal tender. I'll stick with greenbacks. Thanks for the advice, though," said Jack. The jokester's quick wit and loose tongue had always been his biggest weakness. Jack decided to nullify the last comment. "I need the money to help my family out," he said, misleading the Does.

"Take this with you tomorrow. It'll allow us to track your movements," advised John, handing Jack what looked and felt like an unopened bar of bath soap. "Does Scott use counterespionage equipment aboard?"

"Not that I have ever seen or heard about, but his paranoia is noteworthy. It's certainly possible. It's not worth risking it…it's still early," explained Jack. I'm starting to realize you guys are going to twist my arm on each and every issue."

"At least take it in the helicopter tomorrow. When you get to the boat, throw it overboard if need be."

"Get someone at the National Reconnaissance Office to spy on us with their space binoculars."

"I don't know why you think we are so connected with government. Anyway, satellites don't work like that," retorted John, trying hard to contain his temper.

"Okay, fine, I'll take this gadget with me in the chopper, but that's it. You two have won this particular battle, but I'm not going to do something that gets me killed because of your perceptions of what I should do," responded Jack truthfully.

"Thanks, Jack. We need for you to stay safe. Of course you know the situation better than we do, but as time gets shorter so will your leash. Contact us using the same number as soon as you can do so safely," added Jane stoically.

"Tell Bill thanks for everything, but please remind him to work on getting those charges against me dropped."

Jack got out of the car and walked to the Mini. As the Does pulled out he gave them a big thumb up.

NORTHERN VIRGINIA

"Things are moving fast," said Director Morgan Higgins. "I've revealed to the task force that I have access to information from within COED's inner circle, but I haven't shared my source with the team yet. Probably everybody suspects it's a paid informant. Several agents have expressed lukewarm enthusiasm. I know that snitches can be either the best or worst sources. We know now that entrepreneur Scott Horne is the financial backer. This didn't surprise anyone. We've always had the impression that Scott Horne was a bad cookie. The brash millionaire was implicated recently in a narcotic seizure where his fingerprints were found on the drugs."

"I find that odd," said Agent Gunnlick. "Why would he be involved with that?"

"The circumstantial evidence accumulating against Scott Horne has grown strong enough for a federal judge to sign off on ramped-up surveillance tactics," said Higgins.

"What puzzles me is the fact that Horne hasn't tried to defend himself in the media as he's done in the past."

"He absconded to Mexico until yesterday, when he reentered the United States. On his first night back, Horne was caught by surveillance cameras behaving belligerently at a downtown San Diego nightclub."

Agent Gunnlick's limited street experience worked against him as Director Higgins overlooked him when naming a lead investigator on what had been randomly code-named "Operation Firefly." It didn't surprise Ambrose that he had been snubbed. He figured he was lucky to still be working the case. "So what's our next move?"

"Horne's sailboat is in central California. I wonder if he's been spooked and plans to make a run for it," wondered Director Higgins.

"Horne was already in Mexico and he came back. If he wanted to, he could disappear on his own in complete secrecy...not in a one-of-a-kind catamaran," said Agent Gunnlick. "I'm not buying that theory. Horne knows the Coast Guard would interdict them before the vessel crossed into Mexican or Canadian waters."

"I have learned that the attack involves a mobile ramp. The blueprints are being analyzed by computer-modeling software. The obvious conclusion is that Curt Joddell and Scott Horne are plotting to launch something off an elevated structure, such as a freeway, a bridge, or a parking garage," said Higgins. "Agent Gunnlick, your assignment is to pinpoint where the strike will take place."

"After spending the last few days researching everything I could find about Scott Horne...and considering his flashy style and flair for publicity...I'd say the Golden Gate and Bay Bridge are potential sites," said Gunnlick.

"I have reason to believe Horne will attack somewhere he dislikes."

"If that's accurate, it puts my Bay Area theory into question. I read an interview where he listed San Fran as his favorite American metropolis. I'll put my head to work and get back to you later today," said Agent Gunnlick.

Weighing data for a couple hours, Agent Gunnlick's mind repeatedly led him to a scintillating hypothesis. After carefully considering other locations, he walked upstairs to relay the idea to the boss.

"Hey, Eddie, does Morgan have a free moment? This is top priority."

"He'll be back in twenty minutes or so. Do you want to wait here? Or I could call you when he's available."

200

"I'll wait," answered Agent Gunnlick. If his theory was correct, the break would likely catapult him into the top tier of investigators. Agent Gunnlick wanted to be privy to all available data regarding Operation Firefly, considering he had insight that others didn't.

PIEDRAS BLANCAS, CALIFORNIA

Scott let Byron fly through the crowded, controlled airspace of coastal Southern California. After transitioning the large cylinder of atmosphere controlled by Vandenberg Air Force Base, they refueled and headed back out to the coastline.

"The stretch of Highway One from Cambria to Carmel clings to California's rugged central coast and is on my short list of best worldwide drives. The clash of sea and geology is a mesmerizing mixture. Somehow this breathtaking section of Cali has avoided heavy development," said Scott.

"Being located in a state with thirty-five million residents makes the desolateness even more remarkable," agreed Jack from the backseat.

"To drive the road on a clear day is to temporarily leave the man-made world behind and enter one that emphasizes nature. The sea assaults the shore while a spring-fed stream tumbles down a steep ravine."

Scott cradled his music box and manipulated it until the album *South of Heaven* appeared. He chose Slayer because he felt their music echoed the ocean in relentless beautiful aggression. The headsets would automatically mute the music if a radio call came in or someone spoke up, but Byron and Jack had learned it was best to omit any nonessential communications when the guy with the money was deejaying.

Two days prior Byron had returned to the States from New Zealand. His initial fury had been subdued by the passing of time and the tender touch of

Marissa Ehrlich. She had come down to New Zealand for a week of tramping in Milford Sound. Trekking the remote fjord had been cathartic for the couple. While away, Byron wondered about the type of retribution Scott had in mind. He still had a score to settle with whomever was responsible for Nancy's murder, but not at the cost of his own life or freedom. *I don't have a short-circuited brain like these other blokes. I can sleep normally and don't have addictions.*

"My flight controls," announced Scott. "Now that we're on our own, the little kid in me wants to engage in some stress management. Kill the transponder."

"You got it. It's gusty...be careful," advised Byron. "Judging by your music selection, you're probably in the mood to fly dangerously," said Byron sullenly.

"A sport helicopter is the ultimate make-your-own-track rollercoaster. The sensitive controls need only a minimal flick of the wrist or a nudge of the foot to change pitch, roll, or yaw. Following the contours of the erratic coastline would be thrilling with a conservative pilot. Give the controls to someone like me who likes to be scared, and the situation becomes unpredictable," teased Scott, even though he didn't plan on doing anything stupid. He started out by playing peek-a-boo with ground-bound sightseers on the roadway, popping in and out of their sightline like a metal dolphin. "As low-key as I claim to be, I am a closet showman."

Scott played a game where he tried always to stay within two hundred feet of obstacles, either horizontally or vertically...although at times the wind-gnarled limbs of Monterey Cypress seemed to be so close that the rotor might engage in some impromptu pruning, or worse.

"This scenery and soundtrack are stoking my pixilated spirit. Purposely creating dangerous situations...and then navigating unharmed through the challenge—releases toxic energy and builds confidence," said Scott as an apology. "Yanking and banking around these headlands gives me the chance to become fully immersed in the moment...and escape myself."

The two passengers weren't having as good a time. In Jack's mind, he was exposed to the same risk as Scott, but he didn't get the benefit of being the operator. It was kind of like riding on the back of a motorcycle, it's more thrilling because you have no control. Over the years, Byron had gotten used to Scott's eccentric aviating and always stayed ready to issue a forceful suggestion.

Eventually Scott tired of having to concentrate on operating the machine in such a manner and gave the controls back to Byron. The rest of the trip was flown in a straight line at a constant altitude to a background of Hendrix riffs. They ended up rendezvousing with the cat in Monterey Bay.

SAN FRANCISCO, CALIFORNIA

After leaving the Emerald Triangle, Mick Nolls motored down Highway One to California's foggy centerpiece. On the Sausalito side, Mick parked his motorbike and commenced his traditional walking of the bridge. In the pantheon of spans he had seen, none came close to the structural beauty of the Golden Gate. The red steel members and serious hardware conveyed the powerful elegance of 1930s construction.

Walking along the eastern side of the bridge gave Mick a panoramic view of the bay. A moderate wind whipped at the water, causing an occasional whitecap. A volunteer fleet of sailboats zigzagged about, making use of the clear, breezy day. Motor vessels tracked this way and that way with linear purpose. The City by the Bay sits on the southern peninsula, symbolically maintaining the gatekeeper role that the Presidio once filled. The steep hills that collectively constitute San Francisco mirror the city's diverse political landscape. Modern residents uphold the city's legacy as a hotbed of social restlessness. The civic-mindedness appealed to the activist in Mick Nolls; over the years he'd always made time for a visit.

Mick stowed his motorbike at a garage and took a walk along the Embarcadero. He tried to enjoy the sights, but his mind couldn't stop speculating about Las Vegas and why Curt Joddell wanted to provide transportation for the engineers. Deeper into the afternoon Mick met up with some friends for a late lunch at Alioto's on Fisherman's Wharf. Following the meal the posse decided to play a geographical drinking game, they would indulge in one drink per neighborhood. After half a dozen stops the rowdy bunch boarded a cable car to catch a lift uphill. The bay dropped away as they began to ascend Hyde Street.

For some, courage is proportional to things like how many of their friends are present, whether or not a camera is involved, and, perhaps most importantly, the amount of alcohol consumed. Several of Mick's friends decided to see who could hang out away from the cable car the furthest. As several tourists took photos, one guy used his upper body strength to hold both legs out perpendicularly from a pole.

The game seemed harmless to the guys, but their giddy behavior wasn't appreciated by the operator. "I'll call the police if you hooligans don't get off my trolley immediately," he threatened.

Hours later, in Chinatown, Mick's world started spinning. He slipped away from the group unannounced to avoid peer pressure and somehow checked himself into a nearby hotel for the night.

MANASSAS, VIRGINIA

After some effort, Ashley Charles got Curt Joddell on the phone. "True to his word, Peter Zahn cyber-assaulted the man who had supposedly wronged my sister. The problem for Peter is that I don't have a sister," said Ashley.

"Now we have something to blackmail Zahn with, but we'll need something stronger to scare him into switching allegiance," warned Curt.

"Considering Peter's hefty salary…it won't be easy."

"When push comes to shove, Applied Leverage is a force. The key is combining the emotions Peter feels towards you with the fear of getting prosecuted for committing dirty digital deeds."

"Unconditional love will distort an individual's judgment like nothing else. Exploiting that weakness has made me enough money to retire on."

"Do you still have that place in Panama?"

"Yes. A buffet of fresh fruit and muscular surfers awaits me. My surf camp will make for an idyllic lifestyle under the tropical sun. My main obstacle to retirement is my addiction to manipulating miscreants who think they've got it all figured out. I visualize myself as an ego-crushing fairy, flitting about righting wrongs by destroying people who have it coming," summarized Ashley.

"Don't get too cocky. The crux of your success is that you're an equal opportunity snitch willing to work for anyone with enough cash to pay your outrageous rates. Usually your considerable sex appeal is the only weapon needed."

"There isn't an easier mark than the married bachelor…a common fixture among the Type A's found in the boardroom. I've conned all sorts of scumbags…from drug dealers to crooked cops, but my favorite victims are college-educated, white-collar types who had other options," confessed Ashley.

"Wall Street robber bankers?"

"I love to undo sleaze balls who blend into society readily and are generally immune to prosecution because of their influence or affluence…the kind of person who has deluded himself and everyone else for so long that he no longer thinks that he's doing anything wrong."

"The world needs more people like you," said Curt. "Keep up the good work. Thanks."

SIERRA NEVADA MOUNTAINS, CALIFORNIA

Every spring the snowpack of a High Sierra watershed begins to thaw. The snowmelt flows downward and goes on to create one of the most spectacular displays on Earth. With the greatest concentration of mega-tall falls, the Yosemite Valley is an unmatched pairing of rock and water. The park is heavily used, but most of the visitors stay on or near the roadways. On this morning Mick himself only had time to suck in the beauty for a few hours. He took a short hike, shot some photographs, and then reluctantly continued onward after spending a couple of nights at The Ahwahnee Hotel.

Utilizing the recently opened Tioga Pass would save Nolls a lot of time, but as he climbed Highway 120 toward the divide, the air thinned and temperatures sagged. At the upper elevations of the pass the twenty-foot-tall roadside snowbanks acted as radiant coolers. Mick had to pull over and put some clothes on. When crossing the Central Valley a few days earlier, he had been warm while riding in a T-shirt. Now he had driven back into winter.

Nice and toasty in close-fitting fleece, Mick descended from the pass and turned south on Highway 395 in waning sunlight. Sourly he counted seven sheriff or highway patrol cruisers between Lee Vining and Mammoth Lakes. *I thought police presence was based on population. Where is the tax revenue for this kind of saturation?*

As Mick pulled into town he was treated to a visor full of Mammoth Mountain Ski Area. The hill was still totally covered in snow. The view was bittersweet to the lifelong skier. *I knew those corporate raiders were going to yuppify the old blue-collar resort.*

After grabbing some groceries Mick headed out to the foot of the Sherwins. The faint moonlight made Mammoth Rock glisten like a piece of gray chalk. The familiar view made Mick recall his college-era winter breaks of skiing and living hard. Reminiscing about those days made him realize how different his life was now. *Saying 'don't let money change you' is like saying 'don't let time age you.' One can make efforts to hide the evidence of either, but everyone else still knows it's there,* thought Mick.

The next day he slept past noon without intending to. The combination of long hours in the saddle and exhausting scenery had taken it out of him. The day's light was half gone so he decided to stay an extra night. Ironically, twelve hours of sleep had caused him to feel droopy. Mick felt drained, but he knew it was just a temporary lethargy. After going for a swim and getting a massage, his mind and body were properly energized and refocused. He reluctantly bought a disposable international calling card and sought out a secluded payphone. After he'd dialed scores of numbers and access codes, the familiar tone of Brazil's telecom system throbbed in his ear.

"Ola."

"Marianne, it's Mick. It's so good to hear your voice again," exclaimed Mick honestly.

"How's the big city?" wondered the engineer. Mick had told her he was in Los Angeles.

"I am on a little road trip right now. I took some great shots in the Yosemite Valley yesterday. That place never fails to give me goose bumps."

"Does it compare with Iguaçu?"

"It's different. Water doesn't just fall there…it freefalls for thousands of feet. The molecules alternately divide and coalesce in a graceful dance during their extended drop. The falls are paired with enormous walls and smooth granite domes, all garnished by pine forests and grassy meadows. Both places have been inducted into my personal Seven Wonders of the World," said Mick.

"How's the film business going?"

"Sometimes I want to just get a boat and go sailing for a decade."

"If you need a multilingual first mate, keep me in mind."

"You have already been on my mind constantly."

"How sweet. I would say the same thing, but I've already replaced you with a new man." Marianne paused to let the statement sink in. "His name is Davos. He's a four-week-old kitten I rescued."

"Always a joker. I have some good news. An old friend opened a limousine service in Las Vegas. He offered to give me a few free rides. I'm not usually into being chauffeured around, but I told him we might enjoy a complimentary trip out to the Hoover Dam and back."

"We should ride with everyone else in the minibus," responded Marianne, who was a little confused.

"He'll get us as many limos as we need for the whole group."

"I'll ask my boss if that would be appropriate. Sounds fine to me, I guess," explained Marianne. "Mostly I look forward to spending some time hiking the red canyons with you."

"We'll do a helicopter tour of the Grand Canyon."

"For an environmentalist…you seem to love helicopters."

"I've always maintained that it's more important to worry about the polluting habits of the masses than the behavior of a few well-intentioned millionaires," said Mick sarcastically.

"As interpreted by one of the millionaires," astutely remarked Marianne.

"I'm confident the hundreds of thousands of hectares of tropical rainforest I've protected will offset the effects of a ninety-minute jet helicopter ride," said Mick pompously.

"Nobody likes a braggart, but your generosity is an incredible achievement. I hate you more now. Sorry I need to cut this short…my friend is picking me up to go dancing."

"Remember to keep an adequate personal-space bubble between you and your dance partner," responded Mick.

"This is Brasil…clothing is the only barrier. I'll see you when I see you. Adeus," she said before hanging up.

Mick loved the way Marianne teased him using salty humor. Women he dated usually tried to portray what they thought he wanted in a wife. After the dreaded phone call he decided to treat himself to a sumptuous dinner at Convict Lake. Later that night Mick couldn't sleep because he kept picturing Marianne. *Curt Joddell better get his act together and assure me that she's not in harm's way.*

After a futile effort to stifle his rambling mind, he decided to hit the tubs. The region is an ancient caldera and still boils with geothermic activity. Multiple hot springs were available if you knew where to go. To fight the pre-dawn chill Mick bundled himself up before jumping on his iron horse and heading south toward the green church road. As far as Mick's priorities went, soaking in naturally heated mineral water while enjoying a vivid sunrise took precedence over 'most anything.

EASTERN PACIFIC OCEAN

Airborne moisture diffused the first beams of light entering the eastern sky. A layer of low clouds had formed overnight but didn't extend down to the water. The *Arana* sailed along under light surface winds looking the part of an eccentric millionaire's yacht. Curt, Jack, Scott, and Dan stood on the fly bridge. "How often do you have to use the generator?" asked Curt.

"The wind turbines on the bow can be swung down into the water. Underwater the propellers make energy using liquid instead of air. Between the solar water heater, the photovoltaic panels, and the turbines, we always have a usable charge on its lithium-ion batteries," said Dan.

"It depends what we're doing. Large amounts of juice are required for the three-hundred-horsepower electric motors, the restaurant kitchen, and the recording studio. If under way for a long time, you have to fire it up," said Scott.

"How fast can you go on the motors?" asked Jack.

"A leisurely five knots. Harnessing the wind is the only way to go faster. It's a little underpowered, but bow and aft thrusters on both hulls make parallel parking dockside a cinch," said Dan.

"It's got clean lines, except for the helipad," judged Curt.

"The elevated perch is located at the rear to keep away from the mast's supporting cables. The high position limits the amount of corrosive saltwater spray coming in contact with the sensitive machine," said Scott defensively. "When aliens from other galaxies see Planet Earth, I bet they assume that the dominant species inhabits the blue parts. The most adventurous *Homo sapiens* do live on the ocean. Whether you're of the moneyed set or a tough character of modest means, the seven seas are the best address."

"The genius of a level sea is that it's a single interconnected body. For nautical purposes…the world is flat," said the captain playing along.

"The wind is free…and with some local know-how and specialized gear you can harvest all the nutrients the human body needs from the ocean…also for free. With reverse osmosis, salt water can be freshened. For me the motion of the waves and salty air are a therapeutic combination," said Curt.

"When I was a boy, the idea that the ocean was a nondevelopable wilderness screamed out to my imagination. As I matured I became obsessed with living a liquid life. As much as possible I avoid compartmentalizing life into years, months, days, and hours. The timetable I follow is dictated by the seasons, the tides, and other prevailing conditions," said Scott conceitedly.

"To me it's a no-brainer. Enter at any point and go anywhere else, including major river systems, canals, and the newly defrosted Northwest Passage," said Dan, who understood that part of his duties as captain included entertaining the owner.

"I'm terrified about losing our ice," said Curt.

"It's getting late in the game," agreed Dan.

"Hey, we should fly the kite today," Scott said as a statement, not a question.

"If you want to, we could. The wind direction looks promising," acknowledged Dan.

"Good."

"Did you know Byron is scheduled to pick up Curt's friends this afternoon?" asked Dan.

"No," said Scott.

"They called from LAX late last night. I told them to catch the first Amtrak steaming northbound this morning," explained Curt.

"It should be a nice introduction to California for them. A tranquil train trip up the coast, followed by hanging out with you nutcases," teased Dan.

"From what I hear, they, too, like a good scare. If the ceiling gets high enough…us nutcases are going to get some skydiving in," said Scott while looking in the other direction. "I know that you and Byron prefer not to use the helicopter with the kite out, but I pay you to to minimize dangers, not avoid them. Tell you what, Dan. We'll flip a coin. Heads, we put the kite out. Tails, we fly the kite."

Dan grabbed the PA and announced, "Hear ye, hear ye. The honorable King Horne has decreed, 'Let there be kite.' Lower the main and stow the jib."

"Cool, I want to see that. How does it work?" wondered Curt.

"Kite surfers have the advantage of being pulled in any direction; a fifty-thousand-pound rectangular catamaran isn't as maneuverable. The *Arana* can only be pulled from the bow pulpit. The winch can pivot ninety degrees to the left or right. The kite looks like a parachute, except it has tapered ends, an inflatable leading edge, and two carbon fiber spars to resist collapsing."

"How do you control it?"

"It's controlled wirelessly by small actuators, similar to a kite surfer alternately pulling and pushing one side of the bar. The actuators manipulate the risers to control the flight of the wing. It is kept at a favorable angle to the wind by the boat pulling back against it. Altitude is determined by the amount of line out and the angle of flight. The more line out, the more pulling force created," outlined Scott.

"But extra line decreases control," said Dan. "With strong surface winds it can be launched directly from the pulpit with the winch. Today's light surface winds mean we'll have to create more relative wind across the wing to get it airborne."

Twenty minutes later Scott and Curt carefully dragged the tethered kite out on a small sled while trying to avoid tangling the risers. With about four hundred feet of line played out and no tangles in the lines, Scott radioed Dan to make sure they were lined up with the prevailing wind. The captain made the call and threw the throttles into full reverse. Once there was enough pull, Scott released the sled from the dinghy. When the kite showed signs it wanted to fly, he freed it remotely.

As soon as the kite left the sled Dan began taking in line with the winch at full speed. Between the boat backing up and taking in line rapidly, the wing raced upward. "That was the crucial moment. The trick is to not let it get erratic and crash back into the water," said Dan to the others on the bridge. "Now the kite is solidly airborne, so I'll stop taking in line and make a few corrections with the actuators. Since the kite is ascending slowly and in control, I'll put the engines in neutral."

"It is the moment of truth. Will the kite be efficient enough to outpace the conventional sails?" wondered Byron.

The answer came swiftly once Captain Dan found the right combination of vessel heading, altitude, and attitude. "The challenge for a kite sailor is to maneuver the boat to a position where, with the right amount of string out, the kite is as perpendicular to the prevailing wind as possible while the sailboat's vector is still productive."

On this sunny morning the bright kite flew at about eight hundred feet and was locked into the sweet spot, pulling the *Arana* along at a respectable six knots. Watching his kite system at work gave Scott Horne great pleasure. Since touching down on the *Arana* yesterday, he'd become less stressed about the upcoming operation. Morbidly he realized this could be his last sailing trip. *You have to get those thoughts out of your head. Visualizing things going wrong can lead to real mistakes. From here on out I need to put my lackadaisical mindset on hold and center my focus on avenging Nancy's death.*

Scott remembered he needed to make some travel arrangements. He wondered if his throwaway cell phone had the wherewithal to function offshore. Only after climbing into the crow's nest was he able to get sporadic cellular reception.

WASHINGTON, DC

The Titans of Charity Ball was one of Alan Reynard's favorite annual events. This year's coveted invitation depicted a scene from the Old West. The circular tables positioned close to the stage represented various fiefdoms of power and status: captains of industry, old-money scions, government representatives, media icons, and token celebrities. Alan was positioned front and center among cronies from the energy industry. Surrounding the movers and shakers huddled a who's who of Beltway losers and fakers. These status-famished hyenas and Johnny-come-lately vultures sat on the sidelines waiting for their chance to feast with the lions.

Philanthropy was a public way for Alan Reynard to right some of the private wrongs that had contributed to his income. Alan gave most generously to feeding America's poor and to researching colon cancer, a disease that ran in his family. Being around peers exacerbated Reynard's competitive nature. The conversation centered on the stormy topic of offshore tax shelters. "You can't trust government with tax revenues these days. Uncle Sam can't manage money anymore. Successful individuals can do better things for the world with those dollars privately, through charity," opined Alan with lips loosened by four snifters of cognac. "Expanded private equity and aggressive business practices built this country. We shouldn't overtax and overregulate in a misguided attempt at humanism. They call that socialism…and it suffocates an economy."

"I agree with part of what you said, but for businesses to take profits made in America offshore to avoid paying taxes is treasonous," remarked a colleague. "It's that kind of tunnel-vision greed that nearly caused the collapse of our free market. How much money do you really need, Alan?"

"It's called capitalism. You capitalize on anything that is profitable. That keeps the dream alive for all the lower-income folks that somehow they can join the ranks of the rich. That is why everyone continues chugging along," said Alan.

"Have another drink, Alan," encouraged Senator Cummings. The influential politician had stopped by to say hello and had caught the tail end of Reynard's rant. Cummings sat on the Ways and Means Committee and didn't need to be present while Alan made a fool of himself. Considering the conspiratorial nature of their relationship, Cummings aimed to distance himself from Reynard.

A server approached Alan and handed him a handwritten note. He quietly excused himself from the table and stumbled off. At the entrance to the hotel Alan was dismayed to see it raining steadily. He spotted the sleek Cadillac across the parking lot and begrudgingly picked his way through the puddles.

Reynard pulled on the handle, but it was locked. Morgan Higgins nudged the switch to open it. "Did you have to park way over here in the doggone rain?" demanded Alan slamming the door. "If my crocodile loafers are ruined…I'm sending you the bill. Couldn't this have waited until tomorrow?"

"We think we have figured out where they are going to strike," said Morgan. "The Hoover Dam. Get in touch with your guy ASAP and run it by him."

Even in his less-than-lucid state of mind, it all came together for Alan in an instant. "Scott Horne is going after Alan, Junior. Four of my top lobbyists are slated to represent Applied Leverage at a dam symposium in Las Vegas next week. My son is scheduled to tag along as a learning experience."

"Has your guy said anything about your son?"

"Wayne's still incommunicado. He's on Horne's sailboat until who knows when," Alan slurred. "I'm kind of out of it right now. Let me think this over in the morning and I will get back to you."

"Your guys need to get their act together over there. This is serious business…people's lives are at stake," exhorted Morgan Higgins.

"You're right. I'll drop the hammer on the team tomorrow. Now that we have a starting point, believe me, things will begin to happen," promised Alan, who couldn't think straight through the concern for his only child.

As Alan paced back and forth later that night in a luxurious suite, he and Bill Jones tried to understand COED's intentions. "Horne could have easily killed me at the funeral and didn't. He thinks that killing my son would be worse than killing me," stated the nervous dad. "And he is exactly right in believing that. I'm not going to send A.J. to Vegas to be slaughtered like a lamb. You don't think he is in any danger right now, do you?" questioned a sobered Alan.

"Not according to our intelligence. Remember that we have Jack to warn us in advance. If we spook COED this time around…they will disappear and present a continuing threat. We should handle them now and be done with it," pleaded Bill Jones.

"That's a valid point, but A.J.'s still a kid. He doesn't understand the dangers of the world. His mother was intent on raising a wuss…and she succeeded. I should have played a larger role in his upbringing," Alan lamented. "I view myself as a bold man. In the mirror I see a seasoned political veteran who has faced adversity and prevailed again and again. If we do this, A.J. will have to be kept in the dark. There will need to be an impenetrable safety net around my son at all times," established Reynard.

"Of course, Alan, whatever you want. Nothing is going to happen to your son. Sebastian will never leave his side," promised Bill referring to one of Alan's personal bodyguards, a snake eater from the French Foreign Legion.

"I recall you being at my side when Scott Horne dropped you like a hot potato," pointed out Alan.

SOUTHERN CALIFORNIA

To check the progress on the launch ramp and retrieve his Cobra, Scott Horne traveled back down to San Diego before heading to LA to meet with his lawyers to transfer funds, liquidate assets, and make some changes to his will before the big day. Following Jack's verbal directions Scott pulled up to a dilapidated Quonset hut in an industrial park. The door to the shop was locked, but he could hear death metal cranking from the stereo. Luckily the welder needed a cigarette and popped out.

"Josh? I'm Jack's friend."

"He said you'd be stopping by. James, right?"

"Yep. Nice to meet you," said Scott.

"Is that yours?"

"That is my one and only car."

"I'd have a Viper. I figured a guy building a ramp like this would have a warehouse full of them."

"Cars are for roads…and roads are where people and police amass themselves," said Scott.

"I never thought of it like that. Whatcha got in it?"

"I went with a small block three-twenty-seven for efficiency, but plenty of horsepower created with intake, ignition, and exhaust system upgrades. A gain-performance-by-cutting-weight approach was taken from tongue to tail."

"I bet that thing is fast," remarked Josh.

"It looks like a stock kit except for the full roll cage and seats, but beneath the outer skin everything is top shelf. I left it primer gray and kept the Bondo patches and rusty rims to quiet the appearance and hide its real value," admitted Scott.

"Smart."

"You want to take it for a spin? I'm going to wait for the LaLaland traffic to settle down before I head that way," said Scott, tossing the keys to the incredulous welder.

"I grew up in the sticks, can't stand gridlock," said Josh.

"My municipal anxieties have been provoked by San Diego, but now I'm heading to a much larger city. My urban angst is largely irrational, in that it's based mostly on perceptions, not actual experiences. Often fear turns out to be nonsensical and seems silly in retrospect."

"You can't change how things make you feel."

216

"Can I take a look inside?"

"You bet," said the unsuspecting welder as he headed toward the Cobra.

Scott entered the shop and laid eyes on the almost-completed masterpiece. To see the ramp in person gave him chills. Its physical presence alone was threatening.

Scott Horne left North County at half past seven. By the time he hit the 405, the freeway was functioning. The crowd-shy man had timed the traffic patterns of the suburbanopolis perfectly. There weren't enough cars to slow the flow, but there were plenty of speeders to blend in with and share the risk of a ticket.

Scott opted to stay downtown for convenience. *I need to rest up and strategize. The components of my plan are meshing together, but that doesn't mean I can afford to be smug. It's the unsinkable ship that sinks. People, agencies, businesses, industries, nations, and anything else that becomes complacent against uncertain dangers are on borrowed time.*

Prone in his hotel bed, Scott tried to visualize the variables, but it was like playing with a Rubik's Cube with no matching colors. *Trying to understand and predict the behavior of people is a frustrating and futile exercise, but I have a goal to achieve and certain people need to be manipulated accordingly.*

Weary of running mental simulations, he turned off the light and tried to sack out. After twisting and struggling for two hours, he got irritated and gave up. Lying in the darkness, Horne knew from experience that it was already too late. It was almost four and his appointment with the lawyers was scheduled for nine. *Going to sleep now will just make me more tired.*

Abruptly Scott stood up and went over to the window for some city air. Sloppily, he had encouraged the sleeplessness by concentrating on stimulating topics late into the night. To carry out his plan, a degree of madness was necessary, so a sleepless night could be a good thing. Suddenly an idea shoved its way into the forefront of his thoughts. Picking up the cell phone, he dialed a number from memory.

"Da," managed a drowsy woman.

"Dominika, this is Scott Horne...sorry to call so late," he said deceptively. "Visions of your dancer's body forced me to attempt it."

"No, you're not. It's the middle in the night here. Why you made a stranger of yourself?"

"It's just past four. I'm at the Hotel Figueroa...in downtown LA," said Scott, testing her temperature.

"Come by if you wish."

"Are you still staying in that same guesthouse?"

"Yes, I do. See you soon?"

"I'm on my way." Click.

Filled with alertness, Scott quickly dressed in a suit and gathered his minimal belongings so he could go straight to his meeting later that morning. The front desk clerk noticed that Mr. Horne checked out with a bounce in his step. Sleepy CIGARS agents began barking back and forth over the radio. Scott used a hand towel from the hotel to wipe the dew off his seat. The interior of the roofless car had been sprayed with the rubberized product that's typically used to protect pickup-truck beds. The minimal instrumentation and racing seats were also waterproof.

A twist of the key and the Cobra angrily came alive, but it quickly settled back into a rumbling, throaty idle. The stiff sound and vibration from side pipes acted like caffeine for Horne's brain.

An off-and-on insomniac, Scott Horne made a habit of driving or walking around cities late at night when the streets were dormant. On this night the lack of traffic inspired him to adjust his route. On a whim he decided to include a side trip through a particularly twisty section of Mulholland Drive.

DEATH VALLEY NATIONAL PARK, CALIFORNIA

At dawn, Mick pulled himself away from Mammoth and headed south on Highway 395 through Bishop. At Big Pine he turned off onto Highway 168 and headed east, opting to take dirt roads into the rarely visited northern extreme of the park.

The globetrotter got a kick out of the fact that resident-rich California offers some seriously lonely places. The best time of year to visit Death Valley was during the dead of winter, but presently Mick wasn't in a position to tailor his sightseeing agenda to seasonal fluctuations.

Since he had gotten an early start, Mick had plenty of time to tour the park's highlights, but he especially enjoyed the Devil's Golf Course and the Artist's Palette. At the end of the long day Mick found himself too tired to make the three-hour ride to Vegas. Though he could afford to stay the night at the Furnace Creek Inn, he hatched a better idea. In darkness, Mick gingerly walked down to the bottom of the Ubehebe Crater with his Wiggy's sleeping bag and a Thermarest to catch a long nap. Death Valley gets frigid at night, especially at the bottom of a crater. Cold air sinks to the lowest point.

Though Ubehebe is just a baby compared to Arizona's Meteor Crater or Utah's Upheaval Dome, Mick loved landmarks where a meteor strike had smashed the earth. He located a relatively flat spot and climbed into his cocoon. Mick's restless eyes searched the star-filled panorama for movement, trying to witness Earth's invisible shield burn up incoming galactic artillery. The irony of trying to spot meteors from within a crash site wasn't lost on him. The gash forced Mick to contemplate a frustrating, but endlessly fascinating, topic. Outer Space. To Nolls, pondering the universe was mental quicksand. *Where does it begin and end? Are earthlings a product of one-in-a-trillion circumstances unlikely to be repeated in other galaxies? Or do the known boundaries of space represent just a trillionth of something else?*

The rhythmic bleeping of his watch alarm woke Mick hours before sunup. He didn't want to run into any of Smokey's rangers. A toasty sleeping bag has one drawback. When the time comes, it's hard to climb out of. Mick manned up, unzipped the bag, and de-mummified. After stuffing the sack, he ascended the loose rock of the crater's west side. He went over to where he'd stashed his bike and discovered that his only water had frozen stiff overnight. The thirsty man stormed off thinking he should have kept the bottle inside his sleeping bag. A dose of adrenaline, courtesy of the aggressive riding, made his freezing extremities and parched lips irrelevant. The only thing that really mattered was the line he was going to take through the next turn.

A few hours later a vice oasis erupted from the desert with clusters of colored lights. The neon mountain range created a false dawn. Rings of cookie-cutter developments laid siege to the central circus. After waking up in a meteor crater, driving down into the Las Vegas bowl was a surreal change of atmosphere.

Los Angeles, California

CIGARS had had Scott under blanket surveillance ever since he had come ashore. No less than five cars of agents were always nearby to rotate in and out of coverage. A Los Angeles County Sheriff's Department helicopter orbited in case the ground units needed to pull back.

Two plainclothes CIGARS agents watched Scott Horne briskly exit a prominent bank escorted by an armed security guard. He loaded a hefty satchel into the passenger foot well before climbing in and recklessly pulling into a steady stream of midday traffic. Since CIGARS had a beacon on the car and the informant emphasized Horne's paranoia, everybody followed at a safe distance. When the Cobra abruptly entered an underground parking structure, the team hesitated. They were afraid to enter blind and potentially blow their cover. The agent riding shotgun spoke into his encrypted handheld radio, "The subject entered an underground garage. Should we follow him in?"

"Get in there. Worse comes to worst, he'll assume we're following him because of the drug bust," explained Director Higgins from a circling Sheriff helicopter.

The agent pulled in and pushed the ticket button, but it was already too late. The Cobra came around the corner, got a bit crooked, and then straightened out. The agents could see that he now carried a passenger.

After handing fifty cents to the attendant, Scott tore out of the parking garage. The car had wide, low-profile tires and Positraction, but Scott's full-throttle second-gear scratch caused smoke to pour off them. The Cobra slithered back and forth across crowded lanes of traffic.

"He's got a passenger now. White male...maybe 25? Medium size. He's wearing a blue T-shirt. I sincerely doubt they still have the money in the car."

The Director couldn't believe his luck. "Are you telling me that a million dollars in cash and who knows what else has just been transferred to terrorists while ten federal agents were within a four-block radius? Horne knew we were on him the whole time. That's all there is to it. He used the underground parking structure to negate the helicopter. Pull back. We'll keep an eye on him from up here. Nice work, everybody," chastised Director Higgins.

Channel Islands, California

The *Arana* floated lazily in a secluded anchorage on the northeastern coast of Santa Cruz Island. After what had happened to Pacific Plastic Purge's cargo boat, the crew stayed on full alert around the clock. They had nothing illegal onboard and wanted to keep it that way. Radar, sonar, infrared, motion sensors, spotlights, and bulletproof glass were incorporated, but the biggest advantage was that each hull and the bridge could be locked down completely and rendered impregnable to anything but explosives.

"What's the deal with Scott? This boat is a lightweight fortress. Is he paranoid, or what?" asked Lyle.

"After one of his role models was murdered by modern pirates in the Amazon, Scott cultivated fantasies about counterattacking waterborne raiders," said Curt, not liking the direction of the conversation. "International law favors pirates by prohibiting law-abiding ships from possessing equivalent weaponry. Scott decided homemade flame-throwers were a devastating secret weapon."

"That's hard-core. He's definitely a bit strange."

"There is no doubt that ultrarich people are out of touch with reality. He has the crew train regularly for various attack scenarios. Daytime, nighttime, anchored, underway, and feigned-distress counterambushes are practiced. One team attacks the catamaran and the other defends it using less-than-lethal projectiles."

"Seems a little excessive," said Will.

"With all preparations for the big day having been made, are you guys enjoying your paid vacation?" asked Curt. He intended to change the subject away from Scott Horne's violent side. The Derels knew nothing about Horne's plan. Even Curt didn't know all the dirty details.

"This has been insane. The best were the trips ashore to hike and explore. Plus the crew has helped me to step up my fishing and freediving skills," said Evan.

"It's Groundhog Day. Every morning at sunrise we enter the kelp forests. I would never have guessed there is such beautiful diving off California," said Will.

"I think of Baywatch when I picture this part of the world, but this is ridiculous," Evan added.

"The dense mop of aquatic plants teems with life, huh? Calico bass, sheepshead, lingcod, opal eye, Garibaldi, rock lobsters, spider crabs, sea lions, and elephant seals inhabit the brown tangles. Type-A predators patrol the fringes from time to time, adding a level of trepidation," said Curt. "Later today when the tide is right we'll tour some sea caves in kayaks. Refracted light does breathtaking things inside the limestone caverns. You'll see some vivid colors not normally associated with seawater. The quarter-mile-long Painted Cave is the showstopper."

"What's the story on these islands?" asked Lyle.

"The Channel Islands depict Southern California's original coastal characteristics before the Europeans arrived. The Chumash subsisted on the bounty the sea offers to those who respect and understand it. When the Spanish arrived with the concept of land ownership, Santa Cruz Island became an island ranch. Over time, escaped pigs and sheep became feral and overgrazed the island, severely disrupting the ecosystem. At one point it was used as a stocked hunting preserve. The chemical DDT decimated the bald eagle population, which opened the door for the golden eagle that fed on native foxes instead of fish. The nonnative animals wreaked havoc on the native flora and fauna until The Nature Conservancy stepped in to eradicate them and preserve endemic plants and animals. The three-decade restoration has been a resounding success and serves as a model for rapidly repairing man-made damage through hard work and good science," said Curt showing off his scholastic side.

At that moment, Curt decided a reward was in order. The Derels had unwittingly committed to a very dangerous undertaking, and Curt felt guilty. Since Will, Lyle, and Evan were at an age where it wasn't inappropriate to chase college girls, Curt wanted to introduce them to Isla Vista. He had a pal whose son attended University of California Santa Barbara, and the outgoing youngster would make a good host. After getting the student on the phone, Curt presented the young man with a challenge. "I have an opportunity for you. If you can find a good place to throw a rager tomorrow night…I'll anonymously donate two thousand dollars for beer and alcohol."

The elated kid responded immediately, "We'll throw the party here…at our house. I can probably get a few bands to play. We'll do a cover charge at the door. Five bucks for guys…chicks free," said Chris. He had met Curt several times and admired him.

"How's IV these days?" asked Curt, who knew the area from recruiting activists there.

"Loaded with honeys, that's for sure," confirmed Chris, describing the infamous square mile directly west of campus.

"That place is a trip. It's blighted and trash-strewn…yet it's inhabited by wealthy residents."

"Mommy and daddy pay ridiculous rents so their precious baby can walk from party to party and avoid the scarlet letters D, U, and I," responded the sharp kid.

"Getting tagged with a boo-ey is still a possibility. The fact that riding a thirty-pound bicycle drunk can result in a penalty similar to driving a bone-crushing motor vehicle intoxicated sends the wrong message to heavy drinkers."

"The fine isn't as bad, but, yeah, it's illogical. As you know, applying logic is often a waste of time in this world."

"I once saw a cop straight-clothesline some guy riding a bicycle. Never knew why," remembered Curt.

"He must've been holding his cup upright. The rule is you have to flip your keg cup upside down when you're off private property. Sneaky coppers hide in the bushes," explained the student.

MOJAVE DESERT, CALIFORNIA

Even though it was out of the way, Scott chose to session Highway 2 through Wrightwood. He opted for the longer, more challenging route solely for entertainment purposes. "Sorry about the detour, Jackie, but a curvy mountain road combined with a sports car is an opportunity I couldn't bypass," said Scott.

"No worries, I love this thing. Have you always liked Cobras?" asked Jack.

"The 1967 Shelby Cobra has been my favorite car since I was a little boy. It was a limited-production street-eater with a rare blend of brawn, agility, and beauty. The groundbreaking design was low, narrow, short, and light and came with no frills. It was a true performer made for racing, and it dominated the track in its day."

"Why not get a real one?"

"I could have bought a real one, but they are too precious. I got a fake because then I can accidentally fishtail into a curb or guardrail and laugh about it. It feels good to be away from the concrete," confessed Scott.

"Like San Diego, LA has a lot of positives…nearby national parks, Mexico…ocean water sports, and sunshine. One huge advantage sits twenty miles offshore…Catalina Island. Regardless…it always feels good to escape SoCal," said Jack.

"I agree. My ability to quickly adapt to the bright lights scares me sometimes. Single women, fancy hotels, museums, concerts, and quality vittles all appeal to me. Once in a big city I usually dive headlong into those luxuries. Sometimes I worry about getting bitten by a city-bug and relocating to a high-rise human hive," joked Scott.

"It's easy to picture you eating synthetic foods and exercising indoors," said Jack. "The measure of a metropolis is its effectiveness as a magnet for beautiful women. In this all-important category, Los Angeles is unrivaled stateside even by New York."

"I don't know, bro'. Even if that's true, it's because the climate lends itself to looking good…but in other civic comparisons New York reigns supreme. The Big Apple is the national stronghold for the arts. The City of Angels is the epicenter of pornography and reality TV," said Scott jokingly. "In fairness, LA does host Hollywood, which brings…influence, prestige, and jobs. For better or worse, movies and television are satellite ambassadors."

"Powerful people carve up the world from Manhattan. Greater Los Angeles is so vast it's a region rather than a single city. Its growth came after the era of the automobile…which led to an emphasis on roadways and parking lots," said Jack. "Separating businesses and residences makes absolutely no sense. For thousands of years humans chose settlements on harbors, rivers, valleys, et cetera. The horseless carriage came along, and now all that's needed for a town site is an off-ramp."

"I hope investors, developers, city planners, politicians...and anyone else responsible for the homogenization of America...cry themselves to sleep in shame...only to suffer through nightmares haunted by the ghosts of craftsmen and mom-and-pop proprietors," said Scott while aggressively guiding the car through the tight turns of the mountain road. "The desert is probably going to be scorching. Let's stop for a leisurely outdoor lunch in this cool, high-elevation air."

Los Angeles, California

Inside a highly modified, but outwardly normal-looking tractor trailer, several CIGARS agents discussed the latest bit of data from what had turned out to be a bad morning. Video proof had arrived showing that Scott Horne had walked out of a downtown bank with over a million dollars in cash and the unknown contents of a confidential safety deposit box. The footage showed an agitated Horne gesturing rudely at the bankers. Agents were interviewing employees and hunting down the serial numbers of the bundles.

"For a supposedly smart guy, Horne is making a lot of sloppy mistakes," remarked one investigator. "Or maybe he is planning on not living long enough for it to matter?"

"Before leaving the bank he electronically transferred some liquid assets to various causes. He contributed about three million to condom distribution programs, The Nature Conservancy, and National Geographic Society. He must think there's a good chance he is going to die," assessed Higgins. "Our CI suggested that Horne is experiencing some type of manic episode."

"I have a crazy brother-in-law. When the madness gets into him, it's like he is a very different person…it's night and day. It's a very scary condition," said an agent.

"Of course he's having a mental health crisis…he's planning on killing innocent people. I still can't believe he managed to transfer that loot to his cohorts. My professional experience combined with this latest batch of evidence reiterates the need to neutralize COED at the first opportunity. This is a very capable, very dangerous suspect," said Higgins. "Every man in this room is dedicated to keeping Americans safe, and we're not going to give these COED lunatics a chance to harm anyone."

VICTORVILLE, CALIFORNIA

"The pitfall of living in a climate with mild weather is that you become acclimated to heavy doses of melatonin. This makes it hard for the sun-soaked to travel to other places. The weather elsewhere seems horrible," pointed out Jack. "I know about it from personal experience."

"People get SAD without their sunshine. In cloudy climes it's a special event when the sun finally breaks through. In SoCal it's daytime," agreed Scott. "Spring's teeth are getting long. When directly overhead, the sun's rays pass straight through the protective gases, but when they strike obliquely the atmosphere blocks more radiation. Since we're headed east, the later it gets, the easier it will be on the eyes. That's why I wanted to lag."

"Sunbeams at obtuse angles transform into that beautiful golden color associated with the presunset or postsunrise. I remember when we were in Alaska, the sunlight was that rich, yellow hue for the entire day," replied Jack.

When the fun driving was behind them, Scott offered Jack the opportunity to drive. While going up the last part of the Cajon Pass, Jack got into a little something with an older Porsche 911. Both cars bobbed and weaved through traffic going about fifty miles per hour faster than the law-abiding citizens.

"The Carrera ended up winning the race because that lady started utilizing the shoulders as passing lanes. Did you see the driver?" asked Jack giggling.

As the car pulled away Scott said, "I didn't have a chance because she smoked you. That thing must have been turbocharged to have performed like that in this hot, thin air."

"At the very least that car has undergone some heavy aftermarket upgrades," said Jack. "I hate to lose at anything."

"Do you think you would've won if I wasn't in the car?" questioned Scott, eager to test Jack's honesty.

"I would have at least stayed right with her until we hit the straightaway. This roll cage and these seatbelts make me feel invincible. Whenever I drive this thing I feel like those joyriding mechanics in *Ferris Bueller's*...like it's this huge one-time opportunity," replied Jack Welker with no spin.

"This rig is geared for low-end acceleration...and throttle-induced fishtails, not freeway antics. High speeds in a straight line never did much for me. That type of high-risk, minimal-skill situation turns me off. I prefer the braking and accelerating dance of negotiating tight turns. Of course, I'd rather be carving three-dimensional patterns into the sky."

"Well...most everybody isn't as lucky as you," replied Jack.

"It's not luck. I always think about Chuck Yeager when I'm in this area," stated Scott. "The legendary Army Air Corps/Air Force pilot flew out of Muroc Field, known today as Edwards Air Force Base. He chalked up twelve point five aerial victories in the P-Fifty-one Mustang over Europe. Then in forty-seven he climbed down from the belly of a B-twenty-nine, strapped into a Bell X-one rocket plane, and proved that the speed of sound is not a barrier."

"Sounds like he had one of the better rides of the twentieth century," acknowledged Jack.

The thought of Yeager's fast living provided a mental spark. Scott remembered a game that he and a daring nurse had invented that would make the long drive go by faster. "Since we're headed to lost wages...shall we start the gambling early?"

"What did you have in mind?" asked Jack. "I'm sensing it's something that's either a bad idea or an outright bad idea."

"As your attorney, I firmly suggest we play Side-seat Driver!" shouted Scott, mimicking a toddler.

"You are definitely not my attorney...and I'm not in the mood to play games anyway," said Jack, smiling at the *Fear and Loathing* reference. His feigned reluctance was an attempt to bump up the purse before committing.

"Pick a category," said Scott.

"British Classic Rock."

"If you can outlast *Pink Floyd's Echoes* off *Meddle*, I will give you ten grand," offered Scott, who frequently used music as a timekeeping device. He had only worn a watch three times in his entire life.

"Come on, that's over twenty minutes. How about *Zeppelin's Kashmir* off *Physical Graffiti*?

"Six thooousand."

"Passing cars or staying in the slow lane?" asked Jack, wanting to define the parameters of the wager.

"Passing the slow cars," responded Scott. "I try to be fair."

"For six I'll do...*Gimme Shelter* by the *Rolling Stones*. That's a good deal," encouraged Jack.

"Okay, even though it's less than five minutes," agreed Scott jovially. Pleased with the negotiation, Scott unlocked the glove box and took out an iPod, headphones, and an eye mask used for sleeping in bright conditions.

"Don't be lying about when the song is over. I know what five minutes feels like fool," reminded Jack. They only had one music player and one set of headphones, and the car's only sound system was the exhaust pipes. Jack took one last look and then blinded himself with the satin cover.

Almost a minute went by before Scott needed to make the first correction. "Speed it up a tad, your direction is good. Use the sound of the exhaust to keep your RPMs steady," suggested Scott.

"This is a teamwork exercise similar to falling backwards into a friend's arms, except this game involves endangering the lives of the other drivers," remarked Jack,

"No one is in any danger. What is it with you lately? What did they give you at that nuthouse? Estrogen?" asked Scott callously.

Jack won the first round, but lost it in a double-or-nothing bet. After switching places while they were still driving, Scott drove blind for twenty-four minutes. "My commanding ability is appropriate. It's my car and my game," stated Scott to console Jack.

Six thousand feet above and slightly behind the little convertible flew an unseen Predator, but this bird of prey had no teeth. It was unarmed and therefore incapable of shedding blood. On domestic flights, unmanned aerial vehicles were used only as surveillance platforms.

After shadowing the Cobra with ground assets to limited success, Higgins borrowed one of Homeland Security's precious Predators off the Mexican border to keep a bird's-eye view on things. Scott Horne's jet helicopter and bottomless bankroll made him more elusive than the average domestic terrorist suspect. The UAV was being controlled from a mobile unit that resembled an ambulance in looks and stature. The young man at the flight controls was barely old enough to legally drink and gamble. The die-hard gamer never would have guessed that the ten thousand or so hours he'd devoted to video games would turn out to be perfect job training. The controls for the seventeen-hundred-pound flying robot resembled the high-tech flight simulators he'd ritually manipulated as a boy.

"Look at that. The suspects just switched drivers again while motoring down the freeway at seventy miles an hour. Coupla of idiots is what we got here."

"They're lucky to be driving through the Mojave and not a Middle Eastern desert," said the pilot, meaning that in a theater of war, an air-to-ground missile already could have thwarted any malicious intentions.

ALEXANDRIA, VIRGINIA

Ashley Charles struggled to cope with the confusing assignment. *I'm considering flagging this whole endeavor and disappearing. The money is great, but the excitement factor has waned. I have larger reserves of cash than patience, which doesn't bode well for Peter Zahn. Peter has attractive qualities, like a sharp wit and being well-traveled, decently athletic, chivalrous, and generous to a fault. He stocked that young homeless couple with healthy foodstuffs. At times, I pity the guy. He has become enmeshed in Applied Leverage's gill net and can't escape. Why does Curt keep the money flowing even though I haven't been able to obtain any valuable information from Peter? It doesn't make sense.*

Her cell phone rang. It was him.

"Hello."

"Hey, Ash. I called to invite you to lunch. I have some exciting news."

"Our usual spot? How about twelve-thirty?" suggested Ashley.

"See you there," said Peter.

Two hours later Peter offered a toast, "I'm grateful to be the guy sitting here with you."

"Thanks, honey. What's on your mind? I can see something percolating in that brain of yours."

"Ever been to Vegas?"

"Once or twice…why do you ask?" Ashley asked cautiously.

"Would you be interested in accompanying me there? I'm not sure of the exact days yet, but it's soon. Some people don't adapt easily to the rigors of travel and the unfamiliar surroundings, accommodations, and schedules. I need to test you out," said Peter with a smile.

"Please. I will out-travel you any day," said Ashley.

"The frequent delays and exhaustion, combined with the abrupt absence of one's possessions, family, friends, and pets, can be overwhelming for some girls," teased Peter. "You don't have to answer right now."

"I wouldn't want to be a distraction on your business trip, but if it's okay I would love to go. I haven't been there in forever."

"Distraction? Are you kidding? You will convert a dull trip into a great time. A geek like me knocking around Sin City with a stunner like you?" said Peter. It typically cost Peter hundreds of dollars to get a girl naked in his hotel room.

"You are always quick with flattery…too quick, probably. You should show more self-confidence. You have a lot to offer. Compliments are nice, but their potency wilts when they are overused."

"Whatever…it's my nature. A wilted rose is still a rose," said Peter, not understanding her.

After lunch Peter returned to work while Ashley Charles took a long walk through Old Town Alexandria. Some of the durable homes, churches, and museums have looked the same for two hundred years. The long-lasting district made Ashley wonder how our culture became disposable so quickly. At an Internet café Ashley sent the Owl an email regarding the Vegas trip, although she had a suspicion he already knew about it.

LOS ANGELES, CALIFORNIA

As the day's chaos settled down, Agent Gunnlick couldn't get out of his mind the reckless manner in which Director Morgan Higgins was conducting this operation. Truth be told, Ambrose didn't like or respect Morgan, but he felt a professional obligation to try to help him mitigate future damage. "When are you going to notify the local PD? It's a common courtesy. How come we aren't sharing much of anything with the Bureau?"

"Not yet. I guess you don't understand how budgets are allocated in Congress. Why share my spoils with other agencies? I've done all the legwork and taken all the risks," said Higgins.

"Running under-the-radar would be an understatement. You are off radar and armed with missiles of self-destruction. All of us are on the same team. Maybe they can help?" reasoned Agent Gunnlick.

"I know, I know…post-nine-eleven law enforcement agencies are supposed to work together as a single team. After decades of autonomy the idea that budget rivals are going to seamlessly form one super-duper crime-fighting force is overly optimistic. Old habits are hard to shake, especially in an era of recessionary cutbacks. What if COED has a mole somewhere? Then what?" asked Higgins.

"Come on, Morgan. That's highly unlikely."

"It's too late to use conventional protocol. This thing has been handled off the straight and narrow from the get-go, which gives me the freedom to operate on common sense, not outdated procedures. That's why CIGARS is set up to have flexibility," explained Higgins as if he was talking to a child.

"And the collaboration you have going with a soiled lobbying firm? How about the CI, Jack Welker…the one recruited from a psychiatric institution… the one that needed to be bailed out of jail?" added Agent Gunnlick.

"You have to be crazy to be an informant. It's an extremely dangerous game Welker's playing," said Higgins. "Anyway, I've done nothing illegal. Dang it, Gunnlick, worry about yourself, will ya? Go make a profile or something. Leave operations to people with street experience."

"Yes, sir."

As Agent Gunnlick retreated, there was an added confidence in his posture. It was the walk of a man with a clear conscience. *I tried to help you, Higgins. Whatever befalls you when this is over is no longer my concern.*

HOOVER DAM, NEVADA/ARIZONA

"Look at that thing. The Hoover Dam is a concrete example of America's fixation with manipulating nature. It's the familiar argument of weighing people against places. Clean kilowatts and water storage for humans versus…submerging an ecosystem and incarcerating a river," said Scott Horne.

"Remote river canyons didn't offer any other obvious streams of revenue."

"Building dams became vogue during the first half of the twentieth century because their construction created jobs while generating power for the people as part of the New Deal," he said, slowing almost to a stop as he eyed the curb and the railing.

"Thanks, teach, but I'd bet I know American history better than you. The primary goal was flood control. What did Lake Mead, and later Lake Powell, really accomplish? They encouraged the arid Southwest's population to swell to ill-conceived proportions. Housing farms and their symbiotic franchise gardens bloomed in the desert like…wildflowers after a rare rainstorm. Except freeway waystations aren't aesthetically unique or beautiful," said Jack, fanning the rant.

"An apt analogy, because just like wildflowers…those developments will eventually die, too," said Scott. "Current levels of water usage will not be possible during the decades-long droughts that historically occur. There are no other rivers to dam or aquifers to tap."

"I'd like to believe that local governments will shift policy towards water and energy conservation. Electrical utilities can switch to solar and wind power…painfully local sources of clean potential energy. Humans were using wind power thousands of years ago. The issue of water conservation will be trickier," said Jack.

"Those lucky enough to have disposable income are going to have to voluntarily adapt their lifestyle to the realities of our planet, not the other way around. The several billion who struggle with poverty can't be held accountable for their dirty habits. It's up to the haves to alter the polluting ways of the have-nots. The poor are just trying to survive, but they can help themselves out by having fewer kids," said Scott. "Most importantly we need a negative population growth."

"NPG? I like that," said Jack.

Night had erased the blue water, brown dirt, and rock hills, but the bypass bridge and the dam alone made a dramatic scene.

"This place is a paradigm of human technology versus gravity and water. The sheer amount of steel-reinforced concrete arching across this slot canyon is an engineering and public works marvel. The off-white monster has an Art Deco styling, adding an aura of glamour. The Hoover Dam has paid for itself and continues to generate and sell kilowatts while rationing water to downstream farmers and population centers," said Jack.

Unable to walk across the dam at night because of security regulations, Jack and Scott drove across to the Arizona side and then back to Nevada. After the big climbing turn, Scott pulled over onto the right shoulder and silenced the engine. On Scott's last visit, construction crews bravely toiled at great height under bright light. Scott gazed at the newly finished span. "I remember spotting this dam from an airliner as a kid. Even though I didn't understand how heavy water is, I knew it had to be strongest man-made thing I had ever seen," reflected Scott.

"This is a very odd, almost cartoon-ish scene," said Jack.

"While watching *The Simpsons* as a teen, I had no idea that real-life America was drastically more absurd. Springfield seems charming and wholesome in comparison. It's strange how life unfolds. Twenty years later and here I am, an enemy of the state."

"It's not too late to call the whole thing off," offered Jack Welker, reminding Scott of that fact.

"It is too late. I don't care what happens to me…these greedballs need to pay," said Scott. "The Feds know something is up, but not what. They might even think I want to attack the actual dam, *Monkey Wrench Gang* style."

"After your latest stunt in LA they are on guard for sure. Let's split; this place is starting to give me the creeps."

"The great Jack Welker is going on record as being scared…again. This is starting to be a disturbing trend," said Scott referring to the mountaintop in Alaska.

"Say what you will, but you and I are facing…different challenges in this thing. I demand that you take me to the neon lights and destructive women immediately, or I'll jump on a red-eye to Central America," said Jack, trying to use sarcasm as a distraction.

"You would never get to the plane. You'd be at Gitmo getting waterboarded in no time, but that's immaterial. You aren't going anywhere. You're in too deep," said Scott, responding to the joke with something wittier. "It smells like a hard-bar night, doesn't it?"

"Don't embarrass yourself with dumb statements. Every night in Sin City is a hard-alcohol night. That's the only way to fully enjoy Vegas. Dressed to kill, flush with cash, and souped," explained Jack as he swung his body over the welded-shut door using the roll cage.

"You are rich now?" asked Scott.

"You're rich, sucka. Let's ride."

Shortly after arriving, Jack quietly disappeared while Scott was preoccupied with a bevy of bombshells. Jack headed east on Flamingo toward center stage and then turned north on Las Vegas Blvd. While cruising down the strip, Jack felt like he'd climbed into a video game. He asked the driver to drop him off at a specific liquor store. After paying the cabbie, he walked over to a filthy payphone and carefully grabbed the receiver with his T-shirt. He dialed a local number with a rolled-up dollar.

"I'm there," Jack said simply into the receiver. He hung up, relieved to be done with the germ receptacle.

He entered the business and instantly became comforted by the bulk booze displays. The aisles were lined head-to-toe with distilled relaxation. The playful bottles huddled in platoons patiently waiting to assault his equilibrium. This drug outlet dealt in the government-sanctioned intoxicants of alcohol, nicotine, caffeine, and refined white sugar.

The alcoholic requested a couple pints of tequila and his first pack of squares in three years. To the chagrin of the owner, he cracked open a bottle and took a deep pull. Stepping back outside into the nighttime oven, Jack spotted the dreadful duo of J and J Doe parked front and center. *That was too fast. They're shadowing me full-time for sure. Or they might be working closely with the Feds already.*

Jack got into the car without a word and proceeded to light a cigarette, because he didn't know where they were going and whether or not he could smoke there.

"I didn't know that you smoked," said Jane, breaking the strained silence.

"There are a lot of things you don't know about me," responded Jack, trying to get a rise out of John. Benzodiazepines and the tequila had nullified his anxieties. He acted foolishly.

"That is precisely what worries everybody," John stated.

"Johnny…it's an unjust, imperfect world," deadpanned Jack impishly.

She tried her hardest, but Jane couldn't contain a minor fit of laughter. Even the sourpuss John had to smirk. They drove eastward a short distance to a recently foreclosed medical office off Sunset Blvd where Jack was led into a waiting room. Shortly thereafter an exhausted Bill Jones entered the room sporting a sagging posture and countenance. The elderly man appeared to have aged ten years in the past few weeks.

"I hope you have some answers for me, son. We've bet the farm on your information. Our contact in the government has been leaning on us real good," said Jones in an imposing voice, reverting back to the tactic of verbal intimidation.

"All I can control is my own behavior. I'm the one under the most pressure. Your problems are itsy-bitsy compared to mine. My life is at stake. They would kill me so fast, if they knew about this," pointed out the snitch, unwilling to be bullied.

"That may be true, but Applied Leverage is also very exposed. Let's not make any major mistakes, and we'll both come out of this smelling like roses," pleaded Jones.

"Applied Leverage is exposed. However, with your legion of lawyers… bottomless pockets…salaried henchmen…and cozy relationship with government, you are in a much better position to defend yourself. I am an island…out there all alone, surrounded by dangerous predators," complained Jack.

"You are not alone," said Bill reassuringly.

"I understand I brought that upon myself when I voluntarily contacted you. Trust me, I don't need any extra motivation to make this work," admitted Jack. "Getting to what matters… I am now positive the attack involves the Hoover Dam. Not an attack against the dam directly, but it's definitely in the mix somehow."

"Are you sure?" asked Jane in an expectant tone.

"We drove straight to the dam even before stretching our legs. I'm sure you already know that. I brought some recordings I made of me and Horne, but unfortunately he's still keeping everything tight-lipped. This whole situation is extremely sketchy."

"How is your mental state? Are you sleeping well? Are you hearing any voices?" asked John Doe. He was the only one who had the stones to address the questions that were on everyone's mind.

"What did you do, Johnny boy? Go online and take a psychiatry crash course?" asked Jack seriously. "Mentally I'm fine, just nervous about getting caught in the crossfire. The reason I am boozing every day is to make it seem as if everything is normal," explained Jack. "Although it seems like the people in this room don't believe anything I say. Everybody is under tremendous stress."

Judging by instinct Bill Jones believed the things Jack was saying, but there was just too much on the line. It was time to spread out the liability. "Jack, I know you made it clear that you wouldn't work with Feds, but at this point there is no other option. Jack Welker, I would like you to meet Morgan Higgins."

Looking over his shoulder, Jack watched a middle-aged man dressed in khaki slacks and a crimson button-up stride out from the shadows with the confident gait of an athlete. The development wasn't surprising, but the circumstances caught Jack off guard. "You appear to be alone. I figured the government would run out of patience with the old arrangement and force a meet, but I envisioned the moment I finally had to deal with the Feds as more of a SWAT-raid type of atmosphere. Where are the troops?" asked Jack.

Director Higgins knew the ins and outs of conversational tactics and ignored the comment. His experience with confidential informants had taught him that blatant flattery is usually a good place to start. "On behalf of everyone at CIGARS and America in general, I commend you for courageously taking action against these sadists. It's not easy to betray your friends, but anyone who invites you to participate in terrorism is not your buddy. You have chosen your only viable option. We all appreciate the sacrifice you have made."

"I want to make sure everybody gets what they deserve," said Jack honestly.

"Well said. What is the timeline looking like?" asked the lawman.

"It's at least a couple of days off, I'd say. More like three or four. Scott always keeps details obscure. He doesn't completely trust anybody. I know for a fact that the rest of the team arrives the day after tomorrow."

"This team you speak of...it's Curt Joddell, Scott Horne, you, the three Canadians, and who else?"

"Byron Richardson, the New Zealander. He's the primary helicopter pilot, although Scott's pretty good in the Eurocopter, too."

"That's it? What about Mick Nolls? What is his role? What is your role?" asked Higgins.

"I don't know anything about Mick being a part of this. I haven't seen or heard anything about him. Scott and Curt are obsessed with secrecy. On the sailing trip down the coast, we went skydiving every day. I suspect that is somehow involved," theorized Jack.

"I don't understand," said Higgins.

"Part of the escape plan maybe? Or it might just be a way for us to lose surveillance? Scott thinks you have been following him, but that hasn't fazed or deterred him. He believes law enforcement is hemmed in by regulations, but he's worried that you might arrest him at any moment."

"When did he start thinking that we were tailing him?" asked Morgan. "I knew we should have backed off Horne earlier."

"We were in Los Angeles the first time Horne said something to me about being followed, but he assumed it was because of the drug seizure. He looked for aircraft the whole drive out here. I assume you have the car bugged?"

"Don't concern yourself with those types of details," advised the lawman.

"I need to feel like there is some chance of me surviving if things go haywire," confessed Jack.

"Their plan is never going to have a chance to develop. As soon as we have physical evidence of their murderous plot, we're going to take everybody down," said Morgan trying to calm the turncoat.

"I hope you're right, because we've already lost the advantage of surprise. I suggest you focus on off-site methods of snooping. If Horne catches your agents again, he might go underground. The only thing that will accomplish is to temporarily divert an attack. But he'll still be running around with the same malicious intent, and the next time they'll be more careful. We have to get them this time around," suggested Jack.

"I couldn't agree more. You seem smart enough to recognize that your information is the most crucial part of the whole shebang. Do whatever it takes to get him to confide in you," encouraged Higgins.

"I'm trying. That reminds me, there is something I need to talk to you guys about," confessed Jack.

"Anything," said Jones, who had been quietly listening to the conversation from the corner.

"Scott asked me to get some under-the-counter drugs…Oxys, Xanies, K-pins, the popular stuff. Problem is…I don't know anyone around here. Should I risk doing it myself, or what?" asked Jack. After the words left his mouth, Jack almost laughed aloud at the absurdity of the request.

"I can't help you there, but I am sure Bill can have somebody take care of that. We can't have you getting in trouble on the street with the local police," said Higgins.

"That's what I was thinking," seconded Jack with no delay, trying to sound serious and help them ignore the ludicrous situation.

"This is asinine. Tell him we can't obtain any drugs. Frankly there is too much at stake," pled John, adding his perspective without solicitation. John knew he would likely be the mule that had to procure Jack's drugs.

"Settle down, John. You don't understand the bounds of Horne's world. Jack is the one on the inside and knows better than we do how to deceive his peers. Drugs are common among the wealthy. That's always been the case," tersely replied Bill Jones. "We'll take care of it, Jack. I know an accommodating doctor…make a list."

"Thanks," said Jack relishing the taste of the unorthodox manipulation. The pills were for him.

Eastern Pacific Ocean

Curt and the Canadians were using the aluminum-hulled inflatable to cross the channel to Santa Barbara for some much-needed socializing. They all looked forward to at least seeing some female flesh. The boys had even shaved for the event.

"This blanket of advection fog is adding difficulty," commented Curt.

"It's fine, we have a handheld GPS to navigate with," said Evan.

"That won't stop a giant cargo ship or barge from mowing us down accidentally. Without radar, the prudent thing to do would be to turn around and return to the *Arana* because visibility is sketchy," said Curt as a test.

"Quit clowning around. If I have to swim ashore, I'm going to hang with some girls tonight," responded Lyle. The stupendous lights of a platform were becoming visible through the dense milk.

"What is that?" asked Evan.

Curt said, "It's a giant drill press. An oil rig. It's the former vice prez's summer home."

"That's Insaney's place? I would've thought he'd returned to his home galaxy by now. That thing is a monster. It must be thirty meters off the water," said Will.

"More," guessed Curt. "The fog was so thick I didn't see anything until we were five hundred feet away from that glowing steel island."

For most anyone else, the trip ashore would have been a jaw-clenching affair, but these guys regularly found themselves in risky situations. The sea-level cloud simply added a bit of welcome excitement.

LAS VEGAS, NEVADA

Waiting curbside at McCarran, Mick eyed the newly freed air travelers intently. As single women passed by, they smiled initially at his stretch limo and designer threads, but it was his good looks that made the smiles linger a few seconds longer. Having recently explored the Iguaçu, Redwood, Yosemite, Sierras, and Death Valley preserves, Mick felt out of place physically and ideologically. Additionally he'd been sick about what the future held for Marianne, and not only because of his relationship with her. *She doesn't represent anything COED is fighting against. She is an engineer on a dam built thirty-some years ago that presently creates loads of clean power. If I discover Marianne's physical safety is in jeopardy, I will be forced to pull the plug and get her out,* decided Mick. *I feel silly in these expensive tailored clothes Scott sent me.*

Marianne retrieved her luggage and headed outside. She felt downtrodden, parched, and a little hung over. The endlessly circulated air during the long hours of jet travel had dried her out from within.

The engineer looked up and saw a different man from the one who'd left Brazil a few weeks prior. Now Mick looked like one of the bankers she'd mocked as a young girl in Geneva.

Preened and polished in a three-piece suit and gaudy sunglasses, Mick cut a dazzling figure that Marianne found less attractive than the rough-hewn version. "Pardon me, do you know where I'd find the unkempt bloke I recently had a fling with? What happened to Mick?" asked Marianne.

"I'm trying to fit in with my new surroundings. No warm embrace for me?"

After a quick, clumsy kiss, she became further convinced that something was amiss. "What's wrong? Is there another woman? If there is…just be honest with me," said Marianne.

"It's nothing like that. I get uncomfortable in this city," replied Mick supplying only part of the truth.

"Then why are you here?" asked Marianne with a frown.

It was a question to which he had no answer. "I came here to be with you," said Mick being honest, but his reply didn't address the heart of the question. "Anyway, welcome to the desert. They say it's a dry heat, and humidity is indeed low. However, with daytime temperatures in excess of a hundred degrees, it seems as if you are being cooked by the radiation. The slow roast enables casinos to separate disoriented visitors from their monies more easily," he said trying to lighten things up.

"What's with the car and driver?" queried Marianne. "I heard Las Vegas is surreal, but this is asinine."

"Don't you remember? I have a close friend who just opened a service? You agreed to use his company for the trip out to the Hoover?" said Mick overcoming nerves that nearly made him stutter. "I guess he also wanted to pick you up from the airport in style."

"That makes no sense whatsoever. Nobody is paying him for the trip, right? Then why would this person also send a giant car to drive us across the street? It's a bit peculiar to me," Marianne stated, pointing toward the heaps of hotels a short distance away.

"The truth often doesn't make sense. My buddy is trying to build up a favor reservoir with me. He has ambitions of becoming a movie producer. I think the jetlag has soured your normally chipper disposition. Let's get a couple's massage," offered Mick.

"That sounds more like it. It's as if I boarded an airliner in Brazil and was transported to another dimension. The strange buildings I saw from the plane should have been the first clue to the sideshow that awaited me on the ground," said the confused and exhausted traveler.

Santa Barbara, California

The overpriced rental house provided a perfect setting for a big party. The large property sat on the south side of Del Playa Drive on an oceanfront bluff. The temperature at nine P.M. registered a comfortable sixty-eight degrees Fahrenheit.

The intro to the beat started with some sticking before the drummer went into an extended tom roll punctuated by sharp snare notes. Fifteen seconds in, she nudged her right foot, did a two-handed symbol crash, and went into an up-tempo one-two. The bassist and guitarist joined in on the next measure. An all-girl hard rock band was on its third original song, but the aggressive ballads had already captured the party's attention. On increasingly unsteady legs, about two hundred revelers were swaggering and swirling in the genesis of a mosh pit. As the song built up steam, so did the slam dancers. The small vortex metastasized into a human eddy with a defined perimeter. From an upper balcony Curt watched the youthful aggression with admiration. He harvested youthful energy and frustration and directed them toward his own purposes. Live music shows were one of the main places he recruited COED volunteers.

The Derels were already drunk and on the prowl. Overflowing with athletic confidence, the boys had the boldness to randomly start conversations. Their goal was to find some girls with similarly carnal intentions that night.

Las Vegas, Nevada

The sleek black machine muscled its way through the clotted promenade. The displays reminded Marianne of Tokyo. "I've seen nests of neon the world over, but Las Vegas is the king of signage," she commented. "Tell me about this city."

"Politicians of this arid and landlocked state adeptly played the hand they were dealt by allowing streams of revenue absent in other...more pious places. The gambling center's early roots were planted by organized-crime figures. It no doubt took the same type of risk-taking moxie to invest in Bugsy Siegel's desert optimism as it did to run a crime syndicate."

"I know that stuff...I meant, what is it like today?"

"*Las Vegas* means *the firewood*. It's an apt description if, by *firewood*, they meant a hedonic city where money is worshipped and taboo is taboo. It's the municipal manifestation of conspicuous consumption," said Mick. "I'm kidding. Vegas is a vacationer's jackpot. The range and quality of twenty-four/ seven activities is unmatched. Ablaze with casinos, restaurants, outlet stores, marquee headliners, and gimmicky attractions...there truly is something for everyone. The sights, sounds, and smells can mesmerize grown-ups and children alike."

"I can see how this place might make you feel young again," she said.

"Yeah, I can see that, too...provided you were a chain-smoking, alcohol-swilling, degenerate gambler as a child," Mick responded.

"To me, casino gambling makes no sense. In the spirit of optimism... I'll keep a free mind. Other than gambling, what brings people here?" said Marianne, glad to be back under Mick's muscular arm but doubting that she would become a fan of this carnival.

"The shows, the shopping, the restaurants, boxing, Ultimate Fighting... the list goes on. Every night here is like a New Year's Eve elsewhere. Partyers are mostly visiting strangers far from home and the prying eyes of friends, family, and coworkers, which spices it up," said Mick.

"What are the clubs like?"

"Multilevel drinking arenas that are so loud you feel the music, while lights bathe you in seizure-inducing effects. Like anywhere else, I guess."

"Yuck," said Marianne. "I am impressed by the crowded sidewalks. Whatever they are doing, it's getting Americans to walk. Where do all these people come from?"

"Pleasure-seekers make the drive from every direction, but I'd say most come from California. Time-conscious or far-flung tourists like yourself jet straight in. Las Vegas is a temple to excess. It's the premier place to flaunt and worship disposable income. It's something that appeals to a lot of people, not just Americans."

"Some of the buildings appear to have been designed by a schizoid child during a temper tantrum," she responded.

"It's a gateless amusement park teeming with drunken American men-children. We should take in some live comedy. Stand-up comedians are my movie stars."

"That sounds interesting. What type of comedian do you fancy?"

"I favor cutting-edge social commentary...a realm headlined by George Carlin. The ability to make someone laugh is a gift, whatever the means, but to educationally entertain a live audience is significantly harder."

Jack and Scott lounged poolside occupying their minds by searching for available women.

"Let's go throw some discs now that it's cooling off," suggested Jack. "I want to do something outdoors, but nothing too strenuous. Drinking J.D. and Coke all afternoon in this searing heat has left me feeling lethargic. I need to get moving."

"Disc golf pairs nicely with consuming adult beverages. We'll play Mountain Crest. That way, afterward we can hit Buzz," said Scott.

"You are in love with suburban strip malls," said Jack accusingly.

"I am attracted to hickory smoke...anyway, you can't judge a business by its strip mall."

"I thought you were more of a strip club kind of guy. And carcinogens are unhealthy," said Jack.

"Thanks for the concern. If I have to breathe city smog, I might as well use smoke to flavor my food. You know what's even worse for your health? Daily drinking and pill popping," rudely retorted Scott, deflecting the lighthearted jab and returning it with a power punch.

"Regardless of its truthiness, that comment was in bad taste. What do you know about hard drinking? Your life is ...exquisitely tailored to your every whim," responded Jack with a sharp tongue of his own.

"My drinking nova peaked in my late twenties. I've battled back from the alcohol abyss several times...making me qualified to critique your ritualized imbibing," said Scott. "I work hard to keep it at a tolerable intensity."

"What do you do? Burn a couple of hundred-dollar bills every time you want a drink?" Jack said.

After laughing a bit, Scott answered, "After a trial-and-error period, I found a compromise that works. It's an approach of general avoidance mixed with beer and wine binges...and the occasional bout of distilled madness."

"Addictions are like snowflakes...no two are alike. Each person's genetics and life circumstances are unique; therefore, addicts can't be objectively measured against one another," said Jack defensively.

"That sounded like an excuse. Own your alcoholism."

"American society is too quick to attack the folks who favor the sauce as selfish and forlorn. Drunks are mocked for being weak-willed, but nobody knows what it's like to be in someone else's head. Alcohol is abused at social events worldwide, yet binge drinking is frowned upon by many in the States. It's hypocritical. There's advertising everywhere...stores, bars and restaurants push drinks."

"It's frequency that's the problem. People who drink every day are hiding from themselves."

"Losers drink to alter their sorry reality, but they would be losers with or without the booze. Don't blame the alcohol," said Jack in a school teacher's manner.

"I agree with that. I'm just messing around anyway. Drink all you want. It's your life...live it however you please. You never know when it's going to end," said Scott earnestly. "Certain people have a drinking solution, not a drinking problem."

"Now you're talking. If an adult is able to function in his particular life and is only endangering himself, what is the big deal? It's obvious when an individual has the type of drinking problem that needs medical attention, but other than that, all these volunteer life coaches need to worry about their own issues."

"Heavy drinking has harsh, devastating consequences, but job stress and bad eating habits do, too. Lack of exercise and fouled food, air, and water are all far more serious and widespread threats to the strength of American society," judged Scott.

"To me danger is a desirable thing. The stimulation involved with risk makes life vivid. Nothing will make you appreciate the small things like almost losing everything. Are the most successful people simply the ones that live the longest? Hardly…it's the person who lives the fullest, most well-rounded life that gets the last laugh."

CENTRAL NEW MEXICO

"Are you enjoying the flight, sir?" asked a chipper flight attendant.

"I'm grateful for the clear-above, visibility-unlimited weather conditions," said Dewey as he stared out his small, doubled-paned oval. I always factor in the direction of travel and available daylight when choosing my seat location."

"That's a savvy move. Seen anything noteworthy so far?"

"From our flight level of thirty-nine thousand feet I can see more than a hundred miles. For the first few hours the view has been pine forests, the Gulf coast, and bayous. Then the grasslands took hold for awhile before the landscape got dry and hilly. Recently the mountains of New Mexico took over. Sightseeing opportunities notwithstanding, this transcontinental flight is testing my ability to stay stationary," admitted Dewey. Against his better judgment, Dewey was on the way to join the chaos in Las Vegas. The tipping point had been the offer of his biggest payment to date. To resist an opportunity like that would have taken a more mature individual than himself.

"Let's see, Orlando to Las Vegas? The flight is already three-quarters of the way over. At least you're in a first-class window seat," said the woman after checking her watch.

"From a cruising airliner humans don't seem as dominant as they do from street level. From above it becomes clear that the destruction is largely limited to roadways. The emptiness gives me hope that maybe the planet isn't completely overrun by the land management techniques and rat-like breeding habits of *Homo sapiens*," said Dewey with a laugh.

"That's one way to look at it. I worry about the environment, too. It seems like the technology exists to solve most of the problems. It's mostly a question of will."

"What needs to happen is for people to squeeze into the cities. Vertically integrate populations to reduce their physical footprint and save energy," suggested Dewey.

"That makes sense. Let me know if you need anything," said the flight attendant before edging away happily.

The several infusions of cash and gold from Applied Leverage had only created a greater lust for riches within his mind's arc, but Dewey's gross indiscretions of integrity didn't go unpunished. At points his conscience was harassed by narratives of remorse to the point of gastrointestinal pain. Although Dewey fantasized about it, he wasn't a sociopath. The hecklers inside his head ignored the fact that planes, motorcycles, and vacations aren't rewards for virtuous behavior. Mixing martinis hadn't provided the kind of money needed for the lifestyle to which Dewey felt entitled.

After a gradual descent the Boeing 757 touched down with a chirp. The assassin strode through the terminal. He chuckled at the fact that the smoker's incubators offered one-arm bandits, just in case the impulse to gamble was too strong to be delayed momentarily. Dewey surveyed the scene with the educated eyes of a seasoned traveler. With pep in their postflight steps, passengers surged into the saffron sunshine optimistic about the near future. In Las Vegas, the vibe on arriving jets is one of hope and excitement and differs from the often-downcast atmosphere of departing airliners.

As a tourist Dewey loved Nevada and its adult-themed activities, gaming temples, and liberal drinking policies. The hoards of attractive women who were drawn to the powerful lights of Las Vegas like a school of landlocked squid were his favorite amenity. Low self-esteem and a hunger for nice things caused some of the ladies to wrap their tentacles indiscriminately around anyone with disposable funds.

It would be foolish for Dewey to stay in a high-profile location, since video surveillance is an accepted doctrine in Las Vegas. Every casino has facial recognition software and other security systems that most international airports would envy. Dewey would be hunkering down at the vacant rental house of an old friend located out by the NASCAR track. The nondescript home languished in foreclosure and was completely unfurnished, but that didn't matter because he enjoyed sleeping on hard surfaces.

The next morning Byron, Scott, Curt, Will, Lyle, and Evan loaded into the EC-135 at the southern terminus of the Strip, where Scott rented a square of tarmac for his helicopter from a flight-seeing business. They took off and flew northwest for thirty minutes across a hilly, barren landscape towards the remote compound of a fellow believer.

"This region is almost completely empty," said Evan after they landed.

"This area has escaped the wrath of development, partly because of its inhospitable nature, but also because of peculiar government goings-on of the past and present," said Scott. "Sizzling hot by day but frosty at night, the rocky expanses of the Nevada Test Site were utilized as a place to test nuclear weapons up until ninety-two. Aboveground atmospheric detonations stopped in sixty-two. Before that, tourists could watch radioactive mushroom clouds blossom from their hotel room balconies on The Strip. Crazy, huh?"

"I didn't know that. Now Vegas makes sense to me," joked Will.

"Nearby Yucca Mountain is the site of a proposed and understandably controversial nuclear-waste storage bunker," added Curt. "To this day the restricted region hosts an ultrasecret base within a base on the southern shore of Groom Lake, known to the public by the cryptic designation Area Fifty-One. It's still the Air Force's go-to site for testing hush-hush aircraft."

By road it had taken Jack about two hours to reach the same hacienda. He took possession of the custom trailer from Sonya, who had driven it from San Diego. The main portion of the assault team and their necessary equipment were finally assembled in a single location.

"This scene makes me simultaneously giddy and apprehensive. My primary concern is that someone will end up dead...but I bury unsettling thoughts. I believe that fears are often self-fulfilling omens. People make mistakes because they are distracted, even frozen, by irrational thoughts about perceived dangers. Let's all stay positive and everything will turn out fine," said Scott, who needed to follow his own advice. "Let's get inside. Hey, Curt, can I talk to you alone for a minute?"

Everybody else went inside. "I'd say the operation is unfolding smoothly, considering CIGARS hasn't brought you in for questioning," said the Owl.

"The drugs Applied Leverage planted on the cargo ship were a curveball, but it hasn't accomplished anything particularly damaging," agreed Scott. "Initially the Derels worried me, but after meeting them and practicing, they have proved to be nothing but reliable so far. To be safe I'm gonna keep tabs on everybody from this point onward."

"We need to trust our team, but since everybody now has a better idea of the plan, let's be extra careful." said the Owl.

Secure from prying eyes, the crew assembled inside a drab steel workshop. They went over the outline in detail, troubleshooting potential problems and choreographing each member's movements. After their individual roles had been thoroughly imprinted, the posse switched their focus into testing the various pieces of equipment, paying special attention to the communication devices.

After finishing preparations inside, Scott invited everyone outside. In the shade of a carport sat a table bedazzled with a buffet of submachine guns. A Heckler & Koch MP7, an HK UMP, a Ruger MP9, and a MAC-10 .45 were waiting for action. A garnish of hand cannons arranged off to the side included a .44 Magnum Ruger Redhawk revolver, a .50 caliber Desert Eagle auto, and two makes of the iconic Colt .45 1911. The guns were perfectly legal in Nevada, but under the circumstances their collective lethality gave the assortment a sinister aura.

"People...not inanimate objects are dangerous. Guns, knives, cars, planes, et cetera, are all perfectly safe without human involvement. Anyways...I love guns and you should, too," said Scott maniacally. "Something about a gun makes you feel good. That being said I realize that firearms usually fail as a method of solving problems between humans."

"What do you mean by that?" asked Evan.

"Pulling a gun out in anger is likely to create a new, more severe problem, but it's tough to tell us good guys we can't have them when the bad guys got 'em," said Scott misleadingly.

"The power of a gun is undeniable. Guns made America and Canada possible. Having mobile shoulder cannons delivering lethal projectiles across long distances gave settlers the upper hand against indigenous peoples. That's why I don't like them. They create inequalities," said Jack.

"Quit being a sissy, Welker. Everybody should take this opportunity to familiarize himself with each and every weapon. Anybody not shooting should be reloading. Don't be shy. We have thousands of rounds," directed Curt. "You never know when your marksmanship will be tested for real. Have a laugh on full auto, but then switch over to three-shot bursts to conserve bullets."

"Submachine guns are designed for up-close, urban combat…allowing a shooter to rapidly spray small-caliber bullets at multiple targets. Today overripe fruit will be the only victims of their heavy-metal projectiles, but try to make each and every shot count. You won't always have boxes and boxes of ammo lying around," added Scott seriously.

Soon the sharp, acrid smell of cordite perfumed the air. For the next two hours it sounded as if a small siege was taking place. Standing up, sitting down, lying down, walking, running, the guys practiced everything over and over until they felt confident pouring lead into a target from every angle and distance. Everyone except Jack Welker had been shooting guns their entire life and knew about aiming, breathing, balancing, and making recoil adjustments. Today they simply had to adapt to the new hardware.

LAS VEGAS, NEVADA

"What have we found out about the limos?" asked Higgins at the abandoned medical office. As time elapsed, their temporary headquarters became tenser and more crowded.

"Both vehicles are registered to a new limited liability corporation which is owned by another shadowy shell company. We are working to uncover the registered owners. The driver's identity is still unknown, but we're tailing him around-the-clock. The facility where he parked the stretch was rented for only two weeks," said the agent, relieved to have a useful answer. "It looks like your informer has been telling the truth. The two limousines sat unused until the short airport trip and haven't been touched since. Last night the bomb squad cleared both cars for explosives or lethal gas systems. We added tracking devices, cameras, and a kill switch. Both limos are effectively ours."

"Good work. I feel better about using those people, knowing we control the cars," said Higgins.

"Nobody is going to get hurt that isn't holding a gun," replied the young agent.

"Do you honestly think they will try to shoot it out with us?"

"Were you watching the same Predator footage as me just now? They are preparing themselves for a shoot-out…no question about it. Sometimes a dog is so rabid that the only choice is to put it down."

"It sure would save the taxpayers a ton of money. No trials, no prison costs. We'll see what they are made of when their plan implodes," replied Director Higgins with a sneer.

SEDONA, ARIZONA

To make a quiet entrance, Ashley Charles opted to jet into Phoenix. She hired a convertible and headed north into Arizona's beautiful high country. The towering formations of umber rock grandstanding above tranquil pockets of ponderosa pines always relaxed her. At a secluded health retreat, Ashley even managed to squeeze a few hikes into her pampering schedule.

Relaxed and refreshed with clear pores and improved focus, she headed toward the Grand Canyon after checking out. Staring out into the void is a visual lesson in the power of hydraulic erosion. Time, water, and gravity have excavated an immense wound in the desert, exposing layer after layer of stratified anatomy. The dramatic view made Ashley feel as small and powerless as a sand speck being swept downstream by the Colorado River. *Too bad I don't have time for a jaunt from rim to rim.*

After gorging her eyes sufficiently, the high-priced saboteur continued through Kingman and toward the Hoover Dam. As she arrived, the last rays of the day were backlighting the bypass bridge. Parking on the Arizona side, the temptress walked out onto the dam to savor the show. Standing on the dam oblivious to Curt's plan, Ashley wondered what fate had in store for her. As the colors drained from the sky, Ashley had a yearning for municipal pleasures. Considering the long mileage and exhausting visuals, she was ready to experience the suite that Peter Zahn had reserved. Driving toward Vegas she subconsciously pressed down on the accelerator. Luxury awaited her at the Wynn Encore.

LAS VEGAS, NEVADA

Early the next morning a disoriented Jack Welker considered his options. Throbbing subwoofers, stiff drinks, strong pharmaceuticals, and repressed fear conspired to alter his heartbeat. The idea that Scott and Curt were watching everybody with a microscope also negatively affected his pulse. All night long Jack and the Derels had found themselves under intense scrutiny. Scott had flown in a group of friends to serve as handlers, because the best way to keep track of everything was to add eyeballs. The posse numbered sixteen and included folks from a variety of life paths. The guys and gals were simply told to come to Vegas with no money and an open mind. Nobody knew anything about the reason behind the get-together.

The night was winding down and Jack needed to rendezvous with Morgan Higgins to relay the new information, but his departure needed to be both believable and justifiable. Scott had assigned a group of five specifically to watch over him. Jack couldn't use a urinal without one of them peeking over his shoulder. His sentries weren't even drinking heavily, closing the door on any drunken mistakes he might have been able to exploit. An escape plan floated to the surface of his idea pool. It was the end of the night and everyone was grouped near the exit making plans when Jack decided to take action. He went up to the first employee he saw and grabbed her roughly on the upper arm.

"This place blows. What a rip-off these watered-down drinks are. I want my money back," said Jack purposely slurring his words. He even sprayed a little spittle on the cocktail waitress for good measure.

The disgusted server broke his grip and waved for security. "That jerk right there just spit on me," explained the livid girl to a beefy security guard who immediately starting speaking in his collar. The guard could see that the man was entangled with a large group.

One of Jack's minders witnessed the ridiculous incident, knew there was going to be trouble, and aimed to avoid it. "What was that, J-Dub? We're ghosts…there are cameras everywhere."

"It's too late. You got my back if something kicks off?" answered Jack with a devious smirk as a half ton of flesh approached him.

"Sorry to bother you, sir. Can I have a word with you over here, please?"

"The customer is always right. Are you telling me that, among all of you, nobody could hack it as a real police officer?" instigated Jack. "Couldn't pass the physical?"

"Could you please come with me while we review the video to see what happened?" asked the hulking guard politely.

"Nah, buddy, you sheds aren't going to frame me with some CGI voodoo. I'm not going anywhere except out of this sorry casino."

The security guard stepped forward to move the situation along. Jack clenched his fist and telegraphed a looping punch. The other three men were on him in a flash. They bound him with a zip tie and forcefully ushered the guest away. Scott had repeatedly told the group not to cause any trouble whatsoever, so everybody pretended they didn't know Jack. As the newly detained tend to do, Jack threw a posthandcuffed tantrum until Scott sternly advised, "Shut up, you idiot. We'll get you out in the morning."

As Jack was led away, Scott was visibly fuming and had a look of disbelief on his face. Jack didn't say anything to the casino personnel or the arresting officers, claiming he would only talk to his attorney. The cops only charged him with "drunk in public" because the video had been inconclusive as to whether he intentionally spit on the girl. Luckily, Jack had had the presence of mind to remove the prescription-less pills from his pocket before initiating the escape. He was booked into the LVPD facility without incident. It appeared that Morgan Higgins had already gotten the San Diego assault charges against him dropped. The intake officer didn't mention anything about him being out on bail. Less than ten minutes after he placed his call, a somber corrections officer came to fetch him. He was taken to a small interrogation room that was plainly furnished with two chairs and a metal table bolted to the floor. Shortly afterward, Morgan Higgins walked in with Jones and another man he had never met.

"Jack, this is Agent Gunnlick. He is working with us on this. He's a COED expert with decades of domestic terrorism experience."

"How's it? Scott's chaperones were shadowing my every move. I had to force the issue to get them away from me, which I managed to achieve without striking anyone. By the way, thanks for getting those charges dropped," said Jack gratefully.

"I've put my career on the line for you, son. Don't disappoint me. We were in the casino's security room watching everything; you did what you needed to do. We told the casino we were there to investigate Horne for drug dealing, in case he knows someone," explained Higgins.

"I don't think he does at that casino, but who knows? The Owl might."

"Who are all those new people…extra muscle?"

"No, they are just there to watch us, I think…and to act as a diversion to confuse you guys," revealed Jack.

"That's good news. We've been having trouble finding out much about them," said Higgins.

"The real good news is that now I know most of the details. We went over the attack today out in the desert," said Jack, pausing for effect. "Curt Joddell had someone lease two limos and set up a fake company. The plan is for Evan to drive the trailer up to the railing of the Hoover Dam so Will and Lyle can each launch a limo over the edge. They are going to bail out and pull a parachute once airborne. Scott, Curt, and I are supposed to provide protection.

We shot thousands of rounds in preparation. Afterward we are supposed to jump off, parachute down, and get picked up by Byron from the buttress."

"Who is supposed to be inside the limos? When is this scheduled to take place?" asked Morgan. He knew the answer to both questions, but he wanted to check his intelligence against what Jack knew.

"I have no idea. My guess is sometime in the next few days. It's soon. Mick Nolls was somehow involved in getting the passengers lined up. That's all I know about that," explained Jack truthfully.

"Where are the guns now?" wondered Bill Jones.

"The first time I saw any guns was today at the compound. We didn't take them into the helicopter when we departed. We also left the trailer there."

"We watched everything from an unmanned aerial vehicle," informed Higgins.

"Thank you for not shooting a Hellfire missile while I was standing there," replied Jack. His ice-breaking comment provoked a sneer from Higgins, a shake of the head from Jones, and a smirk from the new guy.

"It looked to be a very coordinated exercise. Everyone appeared to be focused and disciplined. Tell me this, why would three young men who have never shown a propensity toward violence want to help Scott Horne murder a bunch of innocent people? They'll be on death row afterward…all the money in the world won't change that," said Ambrose Gunnlick, compelled to speak up and ask some tough questions.

"Simple. Curt has them convinced it's a no-permit stunt for a big-budget ski movie. The Derels were told that the limousines are equipped with parachutes like the ones used by small aircraft in an emergency. I guess they decided three hundred thousand US dollars apiece was worth spending some time in jail. That's where the money went that Scott transferred in LA," explained Jack.

"What about the machine guns?" Ambrose said with impatience. "I'm finding it difficult to believe your story about parachuting limousines."

"They thought we were just shooting for fun. They don't know that Scott intends to bring them with us on the day of the launch," answered Jack immediately.

"That crafty mug…suckering young men into ruining their lives for his own lunatic agenda," remarked Bill Jones. "Do we have enough evidence to take them down, Morgan? Everyone in our camp wants to get this thing over with as soon as possible."

"What evidence do we have that's admissible in court? We have mounds of circumstantial evidence, but that's it. The testimony of a witness recently treated at a psychiatric facility isn't going to cut it," said Morgan Higgins.

"Juries convict people on circumstantial evidence all the time," said Jones.

"Yeah, people with public defenders. Horne's big-money defense attorneys would shred what we have. We need physical evidence…a recording or video of them clearly discussing the attack. I hate to say it, but we probably should wait until the assault to apprehend them. That way we can catch them with the guns and the trailer together on the dam. Plus they will be all dressed up for the occasion. Then we will have 'em," predicted Higgins.

"That sounds awfully dangerous for me. Scott and Curt will start shooting when they realize it's a trap. When this began, Scott promised me more than once that he wouldn't be taken alive. Suicide by SWAT," explained Jack. "I understand you don't have a good enough criminal case yet, but if you want me to take part in a dodgy operation like that it's going to cost somebody some big money."

"You'll have to talk to him about that," replied Higgins gesturing toward Bill Jones. "We'll leave you two alone, since I'd rather not hear the particulars. Jack will be released from the blotto grotto at eight in the morning, so it's going to be a long night of planning. I'll go get some food for us," said Higgins. The two law enforcement agents left the room.

"I am going to need one hundred thousand dollars delivered to a third party before you throw me back into the fire."

Bill balked at first, but quickly realized that they really didn't have much of a choice. "I'll make a call."

The following morning Mick Nolls pinned Curt Joddell down and convinced him to take a stroll. They planned to meet in front of the City Center's abstract and angularly beautiful shopping mall. Pacing back and forth while processing the available pieces of puzzle, Mick spotted Curt among the passersby not wearing a disguise. "Look at you! Going for the hiding-in-plain-sight approach?" asked Mick. *Does he suspect his days are numbered?*

"Hey, Mickey, how has this weather been treating you?" said Curt.

"Save it. I have never experienced stress of this magnitude. Normally I'm a casual drinker, but lately I've started drinking every day by noon," said Mick.

"In Vegas that isn't uncommon," noted Curt. "Let's get moving. The idea of walking it off has usefulness beyond playing fields and sports injuries. Any tough situation is improved by a brisk, steady exercise. The movement, airflow, and change of scenery allow for more rational reflection...while the body is distracted."

"While I have never seen a dark side from you...it's become hard not to ruminate on the unknown. I mean, how well do I really know you? Or anyone else, for that matter?" asked Mick.

Calmly, Curt pulled a tangerine from his pocket and began peeling it.

"What is going on?" demanded Mick.

"What do you mean by that? This is an insanely complicated undertaking filled with moving, living variables. Don't you think I'm under the grip of stress, too? I can't have every person involved knowing every little detail...especially people like you, who are playing limited roles," said the Owl.

"I respect that, but unless you can vouch for the well-being of the engineer, I can't continue to help you in good conscience. I've crafted a beautiful life for myself, and I'm not ready to throw it all away on blind instructions," dictated Mick.

"The plans for the limousine trip to the dam are already set in concrete, right?" asked the Owl.

"Yeah, but...."

"Then you should get out of here. I mean it. Take off. Your job is done," said the Owl convincingly.

"If I leave, Marianne is coming with me," said Mick immediately.

"That's the kind of supreme selfishness that could ruin the hard work and sacrifice of dedicated people across the globe. Don't let your fear override your common sense," warned the Owl.

The heat and stress, combined with the loaded statement, provoked an uncontrollable impulse deep inside Mick Nolls. Involuntarily, Mick grabbed Curt by the lapels and shook him violently. "Listen, chump. Nothing is going to happen to Marianne. If it does, I will spend my fortune hunting down and killing whoever had anything to do with it," threatened Mick, flooding with anger. "Did you hear me? Do you understand what I said to you?" Eventually he released Curt and stood rocking from foot to foot waiting for a reply, but nothing came forth. "Actually I'm not going anywhere. I am going to be riding in one of those limousines. If something happens to us, you are the world's foremost coward," yelled Mick before storming off. He had almost attacked Curt full-force and caused an even bigger scene. In hindsight, that might have been a simple, but effective, way to derail the proceedings. The further Mick walked, the calmer he became.

The blacked-out tint of a nearby minivan hid an arsenal of eavesdropping equipment. In the early phase of the investigation, everything had been done off the record. Since CIGARS had no judicial consent, they couldn't legally present any of that material in a trial.

"Finally we have warrants."

"I'm pleased with the quality of the audio component, considering the ambient noise. Hard evidence that can be used in a court of law is what Director Higgins needed, and we just provided a solid start."

"Good work. The boss is going to love this. It connects Joddell to the vehicles and clearly illustrates that he is the one pulling strings and calling shots."

"COED is getting sloppy. I remember when the Owl would stay offline for months at a time and only travel at night. What a turnaround. Like he said, the stress is getting to him."

That evening Scott walked into the penthouse and saw Curt basking in bluish light. "You look entranced. I thought you avoided the loser's campfire?" teased Scott, although he recognized the voice emanating from the box.

"Jon Stewart lampoons the establishment while providing useful bits overlooked by the pop news. The Daily Show is a lush island of journalistic creativity…in a sea of regurgitation," said Curt defensively.

"Mainstream media doomsayers have struck fear in a graying populace by effectively using melodramatic music and bold graphics, but talking heads talking dread have lost their credibility. I like PBS because there are no advertisers to appease," said Scott.

"BBC more than holds its own, but the most informative newscaster of this era uses comedy as his bait…reeling in viewers with crisp, witty observations," said Curt.

"The usefulness of the twenty-four-hour a day news cycle was demonstrated by the across-the-board failure to in any way predict an impending economic collapse," stated Horne while staring out at the neon. "Did those ladies leave?"

"Yeah."

"Dang," said Scott. He motioned for Curt to follow him.

"I was about to jump into the pool," said Curt.

A minute later, Curt and Scott peered down beyond the water with awe. "Regardless of my faith in modern engineering, it's exhilarating to be swimming while cantilevered hundreds of feet above the ground. Apparently the architect envisioned a swimming pool with a diving board complex," said Scott.

"What did you think of Jack's little stunt?" asked the Owl.

"Typical J-Dub. The escape that alcohol provides is Jack's main priority. Add pills to the stew and he gets sloppy. When people are in a twisted headspace they make mistakes, but I still trust him," said Scott optimistically. "The casino incident isn't the most pressing issue on my list of worries."

"What about Mick's outburst?"

"Typical Nolls. Have you seen the pictures? The woman is stunning, and Mick falls in love easily. I mean, that's why we sent him. That is the one aspect of this nasty bit of business that really bothers me," said Scott.

"The Mick situation?" asked the Owl, surprised by the admission.

"His job is done. I thought for sure he would have disappeared by now."

"It can't be helped. I offered him a chance to escape and he declined," responded the Owl coldly.

"Honestly, I'm more nervous about my own fate than Mick's, but at least I know what I'm getting into," said Scott reflectively.

"I couldn't trust him with the truth. I've got no regrets about what we're doing. You have to fight evil with evil."

"When the lights go out, I'll be proud of the life I lived," said Scott truthfully.

"That's the idea. When confronting injustice, good people are forced into doing bad things," explained the vigilante.

Peter Zahn arrived in Las Vegas with no forewarning about his specific role. The only clue was that Bill Jones had asked him to become an expert in the field of unmanned aerial vehicles. Other than that, the hacker tried to maximize his off time.

Ashley exited the pool and playfully let water drip onto Peter's warm skin. "Wake up."

"I'm soaking in UVs while watching the other guests stare at you."

"I can't blame them."

"There's no need for me to get nervous about the leering of others. You seem to be attached to me."

"What's the plan for the next couple of days? I thought this was a business trip."

"Tanning is serious business. Do I need to remind you that I work full-time in a windowless basement?"

"Yuck. Can we go flight-seeing later this afternoon? Purty please? It would be romantic," promised Ashley, pouting her lips exaggeratedly.

"Sounds like a plan. For now I want to sunbathe. Go shopping or something if you're bored."

"I'm bored."

"There's cash in my wallet on the bureau in the bedroom."

"Do you think that money can solve everything? You really believe that, don't you?" Ashley paused for drama and then added, "And you'd be correct. Money remedies most problems, and the rare thing that it can't outright solve, it salves. But along with new money come new, unforeseen problems. Something has to fill the void left by the old problems."

"That's true to an extent…as far as blanket opinions go. Look, it's not like I had this innate lust for money when I was a small child. Our market society force-fed me greed. After a couple of decades I acquired a taste for it. With extra coinage come new challenges, but they pale against the rigors of being destitute. When people think of rich versus poor, they visualize material items… homes, cars, clothes, jewelry, stuff like that. The most important advantage of having money is the ability to access quality medical, mental, and dental health care. Healthy food, too, and a dark, quiet place to sleep," summarized Peter, regurgitating one of his at-the-ready topical discourses.

"I agree with you on that. You are a lot smarter than you look. To show you I appreciate the value of a dollar, I promise to truly enjoy and embrace each and every minute of my shopping spree." With that final spark of sarcasm, Ashley gracefully spun on her heel and headed for the wallet.

"How are you holding up, honey?" asked Morgan's wife, Cindy, over the phone.

"The last couple of days have been taxing. I'm having nightmares where COED dominates the shootout like those infamous Hollywood bank robbers. I constantly visualize the upcoming takedown and all the things that could go wrong. How is everything on the home front? Are the kids behaving?"

"The children are fine. Don't worry about us. You should stay focused on keeping your team safe."

"First and foremost I am committed to protecting lives, but if everything works out like it should…I will finally have some national name recognition," said Morgan.

"Everybody likes to receive credit for a job well done."

"I don't want to get ahead of myself, but this is the big break we have been waiting for."

"Well, back east we're all proud of you and we love you."

"Okay, I'd better get dressed. See you soon. I love you, too."

Lately Morgan Higgins hadn't been sleeping soundly. Whenever he had a quiet moment his mind was obsessed with details of the operation, but the encouragement from his wife gave him a boost. Morgan couldn't shake out of his mind the image of the limousines flying off the dam. When he thought about it lucidly, both scenarios were totally irrational. The bad guys would be in custody before the limos arrived on the scene. As far as a shootout was concerned, the FBI's vaunted Hostage Rescue Team was on the way. They had been called in to conduct the takedown. Three gun-toting terrorists presented no match for them.

The FBI's Hostage Rescue Team landed at Nellis Air Force Base under a sky chock-full of stars. The base is located about ten miles northeast of the Strip on the same street, Las Vegas Boulevard. The team was given a vacant hangar to use, and they obsessively checked and rechecked their sophisticated equipment. The assembled marksmen knew nothing of their upcoming mission. They had simply received a page demanding their presence. The FBI mandates that the HRT must be ready to deploy within four hours of a call. Any queries about quarry were shut down by the team leader with no explanation.

A blacked-out Suburban with no decals slowly entered through the large hangar doors. The big vehicle stopped and Director Higgins exited displaying a physical confidence. The nation's top SWAT team looked upon the smiling grill of Morgan Higgins with dismay; most knew of his reputation as a careerist and politico. To the tip of the spear, Higgins embodied government's lightly shrouded corporate romance. Inside the Beltway, the CIGARS director coddled people in power and was known as a self-promoted rising star.

Higgins called the team leader over for a private conference. "Hey, Phillips, I feel so much better with you guys here. Thanks for moving so fast on this," he said humbly opening the conversation with a gesture of respect.

"I heard you guys have been on this case for weeks. Why the short lead time?" asked Phillips. "I'm annoyed by the vague background information we've received."

"It couldn't be helped. We have a confidential informant on the inside, but Scott Horne and Curt Joddell kept him in the dark detail-wise until yesterday."

"Where and when are we going to take them into custody?"

"That's the tricky part. We need to wait until the last minute if the convictions are going to stick," admitted Higgins.

"What does that mean?"

"I will explain everything to you in due time, but first let me address the team," advised Higgins, already walking toward the group. "Can I have your attention, please? I am Director Morgan Higgins of CIGARS and together we are going to make history tomorrow. The short version is that a band of terrorists is planning on executing about twenty innocent people in the morning. We're not going to let that happen. These guys are armed to the teeth and have vowed to not be taken alive."

Perched atop the Wynn casino a man paced about his suite nervously. "It's going to be a showdown at the dam after all. Morgan's driving this thing and that's what he's decided," explained Bill Jones. "I wanted to fill you in on the latest details before I try to catch some shut-eye. It's out of our hands, Alan."

"I've changed my rationale about that. I think that's the best way to do it, too. You, Peter, and the Does are going to watch the proceedings from the Predator module. That way we will know what's going on in real time. I have already arranged it with Morgan," said Alan Reynard.

"Is that a good idea? I'd rather leave town right now."

"No. It's all planned out. Just do what you're told," said Alan with a tinge of guilt.

"I can't wait for this whole ordeal to be over and done with. It will be worth it in the end," stated Jones while eyeing the bags under his eyes in the hotel mirror.

"Stick with the plan and everything will work out fine. Only contact me in a serious emergency. I really appreciate the things you have done for me over the years. I know I don't express that often enough. Get some sleep. You'll need it for tomorrow. Goodnight," said Alan Reynard.

For his part, Jones was a ball of anxiety. There was something amiss and he knew it, but he couldn't interpret what his mind wanted to tell him. His subconscious screamed out, but Bill Jones's waking senses brushed it off as pregame butterflies.

The Great Basin spun eastward until the chemical fireball appeared over the reddish-brown mountains. The sun doesn't rise per se. In fact, it only appears to be climbing as Earth rotates on its vertical axis daily. Only one-half of the planet receives radiation at a time. There is nothing for the solar energy to reflect off except the moon, sometimes.

The pink, purple, red, and orange hues gave an aura of grandeur befitting the suite. The song "Black Sabbath" blasted from the stereo adding an eerie tone to the scene.

"I hope you haven't been up all night," Curt called out.

Contorted mid-pose on the balcony, Scott replied, "I'm an insomniac; the sunrises I catch are late nights that spilled over. I spent last night contacting friends and family, then I slept like a baby…a baby that ingested three milligrams of Xanies and then slammed a few beers," replied Scott with a smile.

"I thought the profiteering element of health care had soured you on pills?" asked Curt.

"Getting some sleep was imperative, and my mind was throttled up. I hate to admit it, but there are situations when prescription drugs are the best option. How are you feeling?" answered Scott.

"I haven't slept adequately in days, but last night I, too, resorted to pharmaceuticals. A couple of V's chemically forced the issue," admitted Curt.

"Good. I'm feeling this. No regrets whatsoever. Let's go bury these fools."

"We could still cancel this thing," said Curt.

"Yeah, right," said Scott with a chuckle. "In my heart I have a deep sense of pride now that we're in the final stretch. That said...I'm struggling with the consequences of what we're about to do. But I'm a stubborn optimist."

"I was just testing you," confirmed Curt. "This may sound corny, but I think this stunning sunrise is a nod of approval from Mother Earth."

"It's good to wake up early and be on the healthy side of a sunrise every now and again," said Scott, calmly while on the inside things were getting less and less tranquil.

An hour later the team rendezvoused at the heliport. Filing no flight plan, Curt, Scott, Jack, and Byron headed south under visual flight rules. After leaving McCarran's airspace Byron turned off the device that helps ground radar installations pinpoint an aircraft's altitude and dropped down to the deck. It didn't matter how hard they tried to hide, the chopper had been fitted with a tiny satellite beacon and the unmanned Predator was already in the air.

The inexplicable was happening. Debilitating poison had rendered Higgins and the Hostage Rescue Team inert. Members of COED had secreted canisters of sarin gas where the lawmen were waiting to conduct their takedown. In all directions men were gasping and choking, trying to fight off the toxin.

Lying against the railing immobilized, Morgan Higgins watched helplessly as the first limousine approached the launch ramp at thirty miles per hour. The black stretch gracefully sailed into the air in slow motion. After the wheels left the ramp, the engine screamed as the vehicle flew out of sight. Morgan Higgins's spirit shattered into a hundred pieces. As he continued watching, the maniac driver exited the cascading vehicle and threw a chute. The second limo raced into his field of view seconds later and flew off into oblivion.

Both drivers made a clean exit and had good openings. The first limo crashed onto the concrete with a sickening sound. The second devastating impact rang out soon afterward. He peered down at the two smoking wrecks at the base of the dam. Morgan had just watched his whole world collapse around him. Struggling to fight off the poison and regain his motor skills, he saw Scott Horne and Curt Joddell laughing as they approached him, firing.

HOOVER DAM, NEVADA

"Wake up, Morgan!" shouted Agent Gunnlick, tired of seeing the director's haunted sleep. "You're having another nightmare."

"I'm up. Could somebody please get me some coffee? How long was I asleep?"

"Ten minutes. It's time to get serious."

"This time COED planted poisonous gas. I watched as the limos were smashed into a thousand pieces," admitted Higgins. "I can't catch a nap without being terrorized."

"You know that's impossible. We have control of the vehicles and the dam, Morgan. That's not going to happen. You should eat something…it's going to be a long day," suggested Agent Gunnlick.

"I'm too excited to eat," replied Higgins.

"We've had the compound under surveillance ever since the other day. COED never went back there to retrieve the guns."

"They have other guns," said Higgins.

The CIGARS team had set up their base of operations immediately west of the dam in an employee parking lot. Their command post was a converted bus crammed with gadgetry.

270

The FBI's Hostage Rescue Team was ready to rock and roll. They had been thoroughly briefed by a high-ranking Bureau official this morning. What the team had learned sounded bizarre, but the sharpshooters weren't empowered to question policy. The HRT were trained to put holes in the bad guys and save the good ones. They left the decision-making to office-bound bureaucrats in expensive suits.

The Predator's control module had been relocated to a remote cell antenna site southwest of the Hoover Dam off Highway 95. Director Higgins had assured the others that Bill Jones was waiting it out back in Vegas, but he had slipped away from his casino in the early hours. The Applied Leverage crew was on-site to watch the show live. Bill, Peter, and the Does were eager to see how tough the COED activists were when the bullets started flying.

Will and Lyle spent the night in Kingman, which meant they had to get an earlier start than their brother, Evan. Their job required them to be in a different location than the launch ramp. The elder two brothers each had a street-legal dirt bike as their personal transportation and were already nearing the Arizona checkpoint.

The crew-cab dually and the off-axis trailer were hidden together in the workshop of a COED sympathizer in Boulder City. Evan had spent a long, lonely, sleepless night aboard a houseboat on Lake Mead. After preparing his gear, Evan used his last few moments of free time to mentally visualize every aspect of his role, over and over. The troubleshooting session was aimed at thwarting any gut-wrenching second guesses. At precisely the right time he jumped into a rental car and headed toward the launch ramp.

Byron dropped Scott, Jack, and Curt off southeast of the dam near Highway 93. In a dusty field sat a brand-new black-on-black six-speed WRX STI outfitted with run-flat tires and bullet-resistant glass. The rally car made few concessions to street friendliness. Scott and the boys jumped in, did a few donuts to tone down the shininess, and tore onto the blacktop with tires squealing.

At that moment back in Las Vegas two sparkling limousines picked up sixteen passengers in front of the MGM Grand. The Itaipu Binacional employees and Applied Leverage's lobbyists, including Alan, Jr., loaded into the deluxe motor carriages and departed on schedule. A fleet of plainclothes agents formed a loose ring around the caravan.

"Way to go on the free ride, Marianne," remarked a lobbyist.

"Thank him," responded the Swiss engineer pointing to Mick.

"It remains to be seen…how free this will turn out being," replied Mick truthfully. Before getting into the limo, Mick hadn't liked the demeanor of the young athletic driver; the kid seemed nervous. His mind flashed with alternating visions of mayhem and relief. It was tempting to make an exit as Curt had suggested, but Mick couldn't bring himself to abandon Marianne. A part of him still trusted the Owl, but to be safe Mick had taken a precautionary measure. He'd added a letter to his Last Will and Testament outlining what had happened, with detailed instructions on how to settle the score with Joddell and Horne.

Inside the CIGARS command center, agents were concerned about the missing launch ramp. Using a feed from the Predator they could see Scott Horne, Curt Joddell, and Jack Welker progressing northwest along the highway closing in on the dam. The two Canadians on dirt bikes were accounted for. The beacon showed the helicopter parked about four miles south of the dam. The limousines were en route, but the ramp was missing in action. Director Higgins was about halfway to a coronary when the radio call finally came in from a black-and-white in Boulder City.

"A black Ford pickup towing a motocross jump just passed me at the casino going eastbound on ninety-five. Only saw one male passenger," said the officer.

That call was the predetermined signal for everybody to get into their pre-assault positions.

All traffic headed toward the dam in either direction was subject to a cursory inspection by security officers. It wouldn't be smart to pull up to the checkpoint wearing parachutes, so they'd stashed them in the trunk. At the wheel as they queued up at the eastern checkpoint, Scott rolled the window down and said, "Here we go, boys. I know we're keyed up, but try to relax."

The security officer briefly stared at the WRX and waved it up. "Good morning. Where are you guys coming from?" asked the deputy looking into the ride curiously.

"Kingman…we toured the Grand Canyon yesterday. Now we are headed back to Vegas," answered Scott in a friendly fashion.

"Thanks…go on ahead." The man watched the black car slowly drive away before toggling the radio's transmit button. "Horne, Joddell, and Welker are on-site with unknown weaponry. Black sedan."

On the Arizona side, Scott pulled off just uphill of the dam. The men quickly jumped out of the car to climb into their parachutes. The parking lot had a smattering of cars, but was empty of people except for Will and Lyle, who were waiting on motorcycles.

"Anybody see a dam around here?" Scott yelled to the Canadians.

Will and Lyle rode over to the WRX and got their chutes from the trunk. After Scott had safely attached the leg loops, waist belt, shoulder straps, and chest connector, he grabbed a cell phone from the car and used the walkie-talkie function. "Where are you, buddy?"

"I just passed through the control point. Nothing is amiss yet, far as I can tell," said Evan.

"Pull off on the shoulder and get your chute on…you know what to do," encouraged Scott.

Cars containing the general public were no longer allowed to enter from either direction; all of the new vehicles contained armed law enforcement officers. Director Morgan Higgins and the HRT had been monitoring their radio chatter. "I understand the importance timing will play in subsequent court battles, but protecting the lives of my men is always my primary concern. Don't let Joddell and Horne meet up with the truck. We'll take them down separately, like we planned," decided Higgins.

The Director put on his last piece of body armor and grabbed his AR-15. He toggled the radio, "These terrorists are armed and dangerous. Shoot to kill. Red Team, take down the truck when it's even with the parking structure. Blue Team will converge on the dam group like we practiced. Be safe, everybody."

Scott slid back into the driver's seat, "I guess there's no need for seatbelts. There's no turning back now. It's time to take a few deep breaths." He eased onto the roadway followed by the two motorcyclists.

The graceful, off-white water-stopper clashed with the brilliant blue sky and reddish-brown earth. A thick calcium collar ringed the shoreline. The water level of Lake Mead was low.

"What a great day to make a statement against these power mongers. Remember, don't make any unnecessary moves. Let's go make some headlines," said Curt.

For Jack Welker the moment held a different kind of anxiety. In short order, he would be exposed as a traitor. He was mostly at peace, but he struggled with guilt from selling out, even though the guys he'd betrayed had brought it on themselves.

Everyone on the law enforcement side was wound tight, but they were excited; the wait was over. When the vehicle and two motorcycles edged out onto the dam's lip, Red Team put itself into motion. With armored personnel carriers as their shield, the phalanx charged out from the Nevada spillway. From the Arizona side, two armored cars closed off COED's escape route, as did the snipers. Seconds later just up the road, several units surrounded Evan and the launch ramp.

Instantly Scott recognized the trap and pulled over. The Owl was already moving before the car stopped. They stepped outside to confront the lawmen.

Morgan Higgins ran out in front of the others and away from the protection of the vehicle. He saw three men wearing parachutes throw their doors open and aggressively step out of the car. Predictably, Jack Welker separated himself from the other two. Scott Horne and Curt Joddell were now only one hundred fifty feet away. His trigger finger trembled in anticipation. Instinctively Morgan's training took over. He pulled the trigger. The machine gun's hammer went back and forth three times in a blink. The gunshots broke the tension. The spent shells landed on the roadway with a jangle. Inexplicably, Morgan didn't hear the HRT shooting. "Something isn't right. Oh, no," he whispered to himself as fear flooded in. The split-second clarity impacted him with the force of a hammer blow.

It happened so quickly that Scott Horne didn't have a chance to react. He simply looked down at his body and was elated to see it still intact as a dumbfounded Higgins struggled to come to terms with the circumstances. "Add two counts of attempted murder to the long list of crimes you committed with Applied Leverage," taunted Scott brandishing only a video recorder.

Double-crosser Jack Welker laughed and smiled at Higgins with empty hands. "Things aren't always what they seem, Higgins. You suckers shouldn't have believed anything I said. I used a bunch of lies to get Applied Leverage to contact the authorities, but you abused your power on your own. We've documented on video and audio all the laws you've broken," said Jack.

As he heard the words Morgan Higgins understood that his recurring visions of the operation going terribly wrong had come painfully true, but in a different way than he had foreseen. The answers to his nagging questions were delivered with the subtlety of a landslide.

"Put the gun down, Morgan…it's loaded with blanks. Don't even think about going for your pistol…they're duds, too," suggested the only other CIGARS agent present.

After turning around slowly, Morgan saw that Ambrose Gunnlick and the FBI troops were pointing their guns at him and not at the bad guys. Higgins decided he liked his chances in court because others had broken the law while entrapping him. He'd have an opportunity to flip on Reynard and reduce his sentence. Better still, maybe he could find a legal loophole to squeeze through. "This isn't over," Morgan promised everyone as he was led away in handcuffs.

"I'll see you in hell," responded Jack with a grin.

Horne reached over and shook Agent Gunnlick's hand for the very first time. "I told you he'd shoot," said Scott.

"How do you know him?" asked Jack.

"Nancy Watkins's best friend, Marissa Ehrlich, has a brother who is a federal prosecutor. He knew of Agent Gunnlick's spotless integrity and put us in contact," explained Scott.

"To play it safe, our relationship was known only to us. We never met," said Ambrose Gunnlick.

"I suspected you had an inside source. You are too selfish to have done this without a net," teased Curt.

"Only I knew the full extent of the sting. I harbor no guilt about my method of revenge. Applied Leverage and Morgan Higgins had sunk themselves with boundless confidence," said Scott smugly.

"So you brought the FBI in?" Jack asked Agent Gunnlick.

"Mister Horne's Plan B was his friend Ernie Vargas, a former judge. He was the conduit to the FBI," said an FBI official.

"I knew Ernie Vargas would contact the authorities. I sent him physical evidence documenting the various stages of the setup. The Amsterdam escape, everything Mick did, Jack's fake boardwalk skateboard assault, the conversations with Bill Jones, the cash payoffs from Applied Leverage, video of someone planting the drugs on my ship, my reckless financial transactions, and the casino incident...were all staged. My idea was to let Alan Reynard hang himself based on the lies of an informant. Morgan Higgins was unlucky enough to be Alan's law-enforcement connection."

"How did you know Reynard would contact Morgan Higgins?" asked the FBI man.

"My private investigators had seen them together enough times for me to feel confident that was who Reynard would turn to," said Scott.

276

The Canadians finally made their way over to the group. "I'm confused by this, but relieved, too," said Will speaking for the three.

"Well, you no longer have to commit a slew of felonies. You will never understand the crucial decoy role you three unwittingly played to perfection," said Scott.

"We told them this whole thing was about riding the motorcycles off the ramp into a BASE jump," Curt explained to the group.

"I'm going to let you keep the full payment so long as you give me some wingsuit lessons. I hate getting all chuted up for nothing. Can we at least jump off the bypass bridge?" Scott asked the bigwigs.

"Of course...you can't. And you'd better not try to jump it some other time," threatened the local police chief.

"All dressed up with no place to jump," said Curt sourly.

With permission from the authorities, Scott radioed Byron instructions to pick them up in the east parking lot. "I need a stress-relieving jump before we head to the FBI building in Las Vegas to make official statements," said Scott. "I'm sure nobody is looking forward to piecing together a chronology of the events. Unfortunately someone will have to be left out. The helicopter doesn't have enough seats."

After several knockout rounds of ro-sham-bo, Evan was the unlucky one who had to forfeit some free-fall.

At a mountaintop several miles away Bill Jones, Peter Zahn, and the Does had watched in absolute horror as Morgan Higgins was led away in handcuffs. As the scene developed Bill Jones spoke up, "It's clear that Scott Horne and Jack Welker have duped us with an elaborate scheme. My life will never be the same. My wife and children will never forgive me," he lamented while recounting the laws Reynard and Higgins had ignored. "The Feds are probably on the way."

"Thankfully I had the sense to have Higgins relocate the control module at the last minute. In the pre-raid confusion nobody knew its new location except for the Director," stated John. Everybody in the module watched from the Predator as the HRT remobilized and headed toward them. They saw

Horne's helicopter swoop in and land in the parking lot. "Zoom in on their faces, operator," ordered John.

The three-man Predator team was as confused as the Applied Leverage crew about what had happened. Everybody could clearly see the jovial mood that prevailed as the conspirators celebrated their coup against Applied Leverage and Morgan Higgins.

John reached behind his back and produced a handgun and aimed it at the shocked crew. "Don't move, guys...it's not worth it. Zip-tie them, Jane," ordered John. Using the priceless element of surprise, they easily disarmed the operators. John then pointed the barrel at the back of the pilot's skull.

"John...what do you think you're going to accomplish?" Bill Jones demanded.

"I'm going to settle the score. After their helicopter takes off, fly the drone into the rotor," John commanded the pilot.

"Sir, I can't do that," responded the young man without hesitation.

The butt of John's pistol slammed against the pilot's scalp with a thud. The laceration began to ooze before he hit the floor. With each heartbeat, blood would surge out in a slow wave.

"You said something about being able to fly this thing, Peter?" queried John Doe, still holding the gun menacingly.

"That helicopter has a much faster cruising speed than the Predator, but I'll have an altitude advantage and they won't know it's coming...plus they're weighed down and the doors are off. They have no visibility behind them. They literally won't know what hit them," boasted Peter, fearing John Doe at that moment more than anything.

Against their better judgment, Bill and Jane failed to intervene. Bill rationalized that if everybody in the helicopter were deceased, a forthcoming trial might be winnable. It was a wishful and delusional thought train, but in an emergency the brain will grasp at any raft of salvation, no matter how flimsy.

"I'll go outside and make sure the guards don't get suspicious. I'll be waiting in the car," said Jane as she slipped out of the module.

Wordlessly, John went over and locked the door behind her.

Inside the helicopter Scott, Jack, and Curt talked about their success.

"I would love to have been present for the takedown of the Applied Leverage goons, but that wouldn't have been appropriate. We'll watch the footage of it later on," said Scott.

"Do you think they will go quietly?" wondered Jack.

"It depends on the circumstances. Let's find out," said Curt deciding to contact his eyes-on-the-ground with the two-way. Ashley Charles had been tracking Peter Zahn with a tiny device she'd placed inside a pair of his shoes. Curt put his two-way to his lips, "How is it going at the module?"

Ashley's voice crackled over the handset, "I've been trying to reach you! Everybody from Applied is still inside the module. Where are you? Where is the assault team?"

Noise inside the bird made it hard to hear. The doors had been taken off the helicopter. "The Feds aren't there yet? What? Please repeat that," said Curt nervously.

"Nobody has arrived. They moved to a new location right before the assault," Ashley yelled.

"Call nine-one-one and ask them to relay your location to the FBI," screamed Curt into the phone.

"Wilco...I'll call ya back."

"Okay," said Curt from inside the maelstrom of the chopper's cabin. He put his headset back on and relayed the disturbing news to the others over the intercom.

"I say we land the helicopter until we know it's safe," yelled Jack. "Trust me, Byron...you won't see the thing coming. The Predator's signature will be tiny. It's designed to defeat military systems. The radar in this thing is child's play."

"Come on, worrying again? Don't you think Homeland Security has people guarding their multi-million-dollar toy?" asked Scott.

Jack peered out the doorway into the void and spotted a paved road four thousand feet below. He unbuckled his seatbelt, put his right foot over the edge halfway and said, "I'm positive that if John Doe is in the control module, we are in jeopardy. I'm outy."

Abruptly Jack threw off his headset and dove out of the aircraft. The unexpected shift in the helicopter's weight and balance startled Byron. Fearing that the Predator had hit them, he smiled when he saw Jack missing from the backseat.

After leaving the aircraft, Jack rolled unto his back and searched the sky through amber-tinted goggles. The polarized lenses helped him spot the subtle, gray skin of the UAV. It was in a dive and about two miles behind his friends. The Predator was noticeably gaining on the helicopter. *That was a cowardly move…only saving myself. I should have forced Byron to take evasive action.*

"One of them bailed out. They saw us somehow," stated Peter. "Strangely, the chopper hasn't altered its course or altitude. So far the remaining occupants have stayed inside. I only need twenty more seconds and they will be toast," said the guest pilot.

"Come on, baby," said John Doe.

Back in the chopper Scott was thinking aloud, "I'm trying to figure out why Jack was motivated into bailing. I have no doubt that Welker was honestly scared. Byron, bust a one-eighty…let's check our six," ordered Scott. "Jack is the only one who spent any time with those kooks."

As the helicopter banked into an aggressive descending turn, Lyle spotted it. "Jack was right. That robot gone wild is chasing us…three o'clock high, around a thousand meters out."

"Everybody out right now!" demanded Byron. "There's no reason to have you guys onboard…you're dead weight," said the Kiwi, who wore no parachute. He likened it to a driver wearing a crash helmet.

Lyle and Will didn't need any more coaxing than that. They gladly launched their bodies out of the chopper in half a flash.

"Land the thing, mate. It's replaceable…you're not," pleaded Scott as he edged his way toward the windy abyss. Scott knocked off his headset and leapt into the troposphere.

"Thanks for the ride," said Curt Joddell before he leapt headfirst through the door. "Be careful."

With seven hundred pounds out of the helicopter, Byron had improved his chances of outmaneuvering the smaller, lighter drone. With the doors off, he wasn't as fast or maneuverable as normal, but unlike the fixed-wing drone, he could hover and fly in any direction.

"Talk about bad luck," complained Peter. "Maybe they were planning on jumping there anyway?"

"No way. They saw us or somehow figured out we were here," said John. "Go after the chopper anyway."

Byron spooled up the turboshaft to maximum thrust with a twist of his wrist and vectored toward the Colorado River. *If you want to destroy my baby…you'll have to do it midair. Let's see if your RC plane on steroids can follow me through a river canyon."*

When he got to the edge of the canyon, Byron rolled in aggressively like a snowboarder carrying into a halfpipe. When Byron noticed that he was pulling away from the flying machine too quickly, he throttled back to draw the Predator in close.

Eons of restless snowmelt and gravity had carved a chasm into the desert and in the process created an obstacle course. Millions of dollars of machined metals and composites had been painstakingly assembled, only to have a couple madmen engage in a high-stakes game of follow the leader.

As they navigated through the twists and turns, Byron swung back and forth and from side to side to keep tabs on the Predator. He descended to less than a hundred feet off the water and slowed down considerably to let the persistent pest creep up to within a hundred yards.

"Maybe he's running out of gas or he's trying to land?" asked John anxiously. After seeing the others leap out of the helicopter, his hopes of revenge had mostly fizzled out.

Considering it was his first try, Peter Zahn was pleased with his skills. As he piloted the slot with dexterity, he decided it was the perfect time to dive in for the kill. It was too late. The last thing he saw on the monitor was the sleek Eurocopter in front of him in a vertical climb, and then the screen went fuzzy. The unmanned spy plane disintegrated into hundreds of pieces when it struck sandstone at over a hundred miles per hour.

"Nice work, Peter. We can add 'destroying government property' to our growing list of felonies," dryly quipped Bill Jones. "It is truly over. The air inside of this module seems to be devoid of oxygen."

"Let's get going. I marked the map where Welker jumped out. He did this. I'm going to kill him," pressed John Doe, who didn't have an ounce of quit anywhere in his makeup.

The goon squad spilled out of the module with the disgusting aftertaste of defeat. They had played right into COED's hands and were now wanted by the FBI. Everyone had bulletproof alternate identities and hidden funds, but living on the run is a dead end. Compared to their previous lifestyle, it would be a dreadful existence. The dejected posse climbed into a dark-blue BMW M6 and tore off in a cloud of dirt with Jane Doe at the wheel.

Ashley Charles had called the authorities and included a description of the car. Watching them leave, she suspected they wouldn't get far. Without warning, the luxury car disappeared inside a fireball. Shards of molten metal splayed outward at supersonic velocities, the concussion hit her a split second later. The passengers of the car were pulverized instantly and never knew.

The violence of the explosion shook Ashley's emotional nucleus. Although she had been involved in some sordid affairs, she had never been exposed to a decimation of that nature. The singed carcass of the luxury auto lay at the edge of a blackened crater.

It had just happened directly in front of her, but Ashley didn't want to believe she had just witnessed the end of Peter Zahn. Three salty tears slid down her shocked face. *Peter was tied to a bad lot, but he didn't deserve that.*

The assassin stared at the carnage with a composite reaction. He was stuck in the guilt-morass associated with slaughtering defenseless humans, but he also felt relief about erasing his ties to Bill Jones. *That's the end of it. No longer am I going to be a merchant of destruction.*

Dewey reached into his pocket and pulled out a phone to notify Alan Reynard with a text to his personal line. Dewey intended for the record of the message to be used in court. He wanted to see Alan Reynard rot away behind bars.

To find Bill Jones' boss, Dewey had used the archival power of the Web. First he had narrowed it down to five companies where Jones might work. Then he had researched those companies. Eventually, he had been able to find a picture of Bill Jones with Alan Reynard in a magazine.

After carefully crafting his arguments, Dewey had secretly contacted Alan Reynard. He had used Alan's own sense of self-preservation as the crux of the pitch. Why endanger Applied Leverage to protect a few people? In one swoop Alan could be free from the looming threat of Bill, Peter, or the Does ever becoming government witnesses. Eventually Dewey had convinced Alan that he was leaving too many loose ends and that a car bomb would be blamed on COED anyway.

"Talk to me," answered Curt after feeling the phone vibrate.

Ashley was calling to relay the news. "Curt, they're gone. The car disintegrated. It must have been an ultra-powerful car bomb."

"Whoa! What the heck are you talking about?"

"All four of them are dead...Peter, Jones, and the couple. I'm staring at a smoldering crater right now. You better not have been behind that!" screamed Ashley in a screechy voice that betrayed a rare note of panic.

"I promise I didn't have anything to do with it. Get out of there…the bomber may still be nearby," encouraged Curt before closing the call. "All of them are dead…blown up in a car bomb. Reynard realized how exposed he was and did some preemptive damage control," said Curt angrily, breaking the bad news to Scott as he folded up his parachute.

"Well, that's just great. That's devastating. He has ruined all our hard work. With Bill Jones, the Does, and Peter Zahn unable to testify, Alan Reynard's cabal of lawyers will place the blame on them…and argue that the whole gig was the work of an overzealous and paranoid security chief and his secret minions," worried Scott.

"Not the bomb. He'll try to blame that one on us," suggested Curt.

"We've got nothing to hide. I hope the perp did something that leads back to Reynard," said Scott. "I can't believe I didn't foresee something like this happening, especially considering that slime ball."

NORTHERN VIRGINIA

The incinerators in the basement of the building were working overtime as briefcase-sized servers were being thrown into the inferno whole. There wasn't that much to burn. Applied Leverage had always taken extreme care not to leave paper or digital tracks. Seized evidence was the least of Alan Reynard's problems as he sat in his palatial office, terrified. He morosely watched the progress of the motorcade on closed-circuit video cameras and tried to deduce what had happened. Everything he had built had been flattened in seconds. *Why is the FBI already here? Something has gone terribly wrong. Was Bill working with the government? Why did the Hunter set me up?*

The crux of the riddle came to him belatedly. The whole thing was a sting from the get-go. He didn't know how or why, but Alan had been expertly tricked into making foolhardy decisions that had unraveled decades of hard work. The FBI was now inside the building, which meant Alan didn't have much time to consider his options. *With Bill, Peter, John, and Jane gone, there is nobody left to point the finger at me. Why is the FBI already gunning for me? Do they know what really happened to Nancy? Did Roger turn on us? Is a single text message enough to connect me to the car bomb?*

Unable to imagine a tolerable resolution, Reynard pulled out the ornate gold box that held an acquittal. He stuck the implement into his mouth and triggered it. The cyanide tasted like unripe almonds and immediately went to work on destroying his respiratory system. Soon Reynard felt dizzy, and he went into convulsions before he collapsed onto the floor. By the time the FBI reached his regal office and broke down the door, Alan Reynard had escaped.

BAHIA, BRAZIL

The fiery sun beat down and, together with the muggy tropical air, transformed those on deck into a languid mass. Ice-cold cocktails contributed to the stupor. The anchored vessel sat in a deep channel only a hundred meters from the action. Perfect head-high swells of seawater were colliding against a submerged reef. The surf session had rapidly turned into "The Jack Welker Show." He was taking off the deepest on the biggest waves.

"Outside," called out someone excitedly.

Constantly repositioning himself against the current paid off once again. He was the only one in a favorable location to snag a wave from the set of the day. Once in the right location, Jack leaned back, grabbed his board, and spun one hundred eighty degrees. Now facing the same direction as the approaching swell, Jack began to paddle rapidly in order to catch the wave as it passed. As the water under him steepened, Jack added a burst of frenetic strokes. When he began to accelerate down the seawater slope, he popped up off the board, planted his feet with authority, and hooked a bottom turn.

Since water doesn't compress, the swell was pushed upward by the reef. The lip thinned until gravity forced it to gracefully fold over, one section at a time. Racing across the face, Jack found himself too far from the breaking part of the wave. He shifted his weight back and stalled until he was tucked in the pocket and completely covered up. He inched his feet forward to speed up and keep pace with the rotating cylinder of water.

As it collapsed, the wave spit Jack out of the tube in a flurry of spray, as if it wanted him to succeed. As he kicked out, Jack triumphantly raised his arms as spectators on the sailboat shouted their approval.

To reward the bravery of his accomplices, Scott had borrowed a single-hull, blue-water yacht from a close friend. The thirty-five-meter schooner featured exquisite craftsmanship and functional elegance at every level. All of the main contributors to the sting, excluding Ambrose Gunnlick and Ernie Vargas, had journeyed south to celebrate. Scott Horne, Erin De Sousa, Curt Joddell, Ashley Charles, Sonya, Jack Welker, Jasmine, Byron Richardson, Marissa, Mick Nolls, Marianne, and the Derelicts were staying on the vessel. On an extended sailing trip, Scott figured a boat can never have too many bikini-fillers, so he'd invited two of the unwitting participants. The eyewitness from the faux skateboard attack and the spittle victim from the casino accepted his apologies and the free trip.

The squad paddled in for an alfresco lunch of fresh-harvested shellfish and grilled yams. Tropical fruits had been rapidly whittled into edible bits by the surf guide.

"What's in these?" asked Marissa.

"*Cachaça* is the local firewater…it's made from sugar cane and is the engine of the *Caipirinha*. You take generous amounts of crushed lime, sugar and ice, and add the sauce," said Jack.

286

"It's a refreshing method of losing one's balance," said Marianne.

"Here's to exploring Earth with great friends...and searching for the most elusive port of call inner peace and happiness," said Scott. "I'm buzzing from that session. Although I snagged a few choice barrels, I'll give it to Jack on that last one," he admitted reluctantly.

"Of all the amazing experiences I have enjoyed on this planet...a tube ride is tops. Gliding through a horizontal seawater tornado and getting shot out at the last second...is the most epic," said Jack.

"I'd like to propose a toast to Scott...for coming up with a nonviolent method of revenge," stated Curt. "Everyone here should be proud of the part he played in what turned out to be one heckuva diversion, but my MVP award goes to Jack Welker...he's the one who risked the most."

"The immensely talented Jack Welker is currently available for any of your sabotaging needs. I also do birthday parties and motivational speeches," said Jack.

"I have to warn any potential employers that he doesn't work cheap," said Scott. "I also have to mention the essential role that Mick Nolls filled... although he nearly lost his faith in us toward the end."

"What can I say? I found something I cared about more than helping you nut-jobs," said Mick grabbing Marianne.

After a while, Scott pulled Curt in close. "I'm surrounded by my best friends under ideal circumstances, yet I can't help but ruminate on the deaths I caused. Neither time nor revenge has eroded the shame."

"It's impossible not to analyze how you could have done this or that differently," said Curt reassuringly.

"In hindsight I never should've approached Nancy Watkins in the first place. My brain-dead maneuver of using Zell's phone is tougher to cope with. At least we succeeded in avenging their murders by dismantling the Applied Leverage empire."

The distinctive melody of an old aircraft's engine disrupted the banter. "It's getting louder, but I can't spot the plane," said Curt.

From behind a rocky headland a WWII ocean-rescue seaplane flew ultra low. "Grumman Albatross. It looks as if it's going to set down, but they're too fast and the swells are too heavy."

Everybody stood up from the table when the plane zeroed in on them and aimed straight toward the boat. With growing concern, the guests stared across the water at the large propellers closing in from only four hundred meters away.

"Jump!" said Jack before he leapt over the stanchion cables on the lee side.

Nobody else jumped into the water. Scott walked over to the edge and leered at the plane. It was already close enough to see the two men in the front. The bulky plane didn't deviate from its collision course and was only seconds from impact.

"Could people loyal to Applied Leverage have moved that fast?" Scott asked Curt. The large chunk of speeding metal was now only seconds away. "Get in the water and dive deep!" screamed Scott with conviction. The others took his advice and jumped into the sea, but Scott wasn't going anywhere.

At fifty meters and roughly one second from impact, the big seaplane jumped upward, narrowly avoiding the rigging that supported the mast. The noise was forceful. Turbulence spun off the big wing and shook the boat.

As the plane approached, Scott tried to recognize the pilots, and what he saw frightened him.

"I need to get hold of myself. I'm imagining things. The sun and surf must be screwing with my head," said Scott. Envious at the fine stunt, he watched the plane head offshore. His confused guests reboarded the sailboat.

"I must admit that was quite a flyby…best one I have ever seen. Who was that?" asked Curt, who hadn't jumped either.

"Zell's ghost," answered Scott. Everybody watched the Grumman splash down off in the distance, out where the waves were calmer. "Can someone go out there in the dinghy? Tell that joker he almost hit the forestay."

"I'll go," volunteered Erin De Sousa.

"I'll go with you," Marissa chimed in.

"Take a couple of shotguns," suggested Jack in a serious tone.

Everyone returned to the table to resume lunch. Much laughter and gesturing went into recounting their personal thoughts and actions throughout the aborted kamikaze run.

After an interminable wait, the Grumman took to the sky, but this time the big girl climbed up to three hundred feet and wagged its wings as it passed overhead. Scott finally saw the rigid-inflatable bobbing back toward the sailboat. He grabbed a pair of binoculars and could just make out a familiar frame. As it got closer, Scott recognized the style of hat and rushed to judgment. When the tender came within range of the naked eye, Scott lowered the binoculars.

More than anything, he wanted to confirm his wishful suspicion. To his utter dismay Scott recognized the elderly man as Erin's father, Mark De Sousa. At close range his physical resemblance to Zell was slight, but from a long distance it had been plausible. Dejected, Scott became angry with himself for letting his emotions run wild without proof of anything. Scott had forgotten that premature celebrations only serve to strengthen the agony of defeat.

Marissa, Erin, and Erin's dad boarded the vessel. Scott pretended to be excited about Mark's arrival, but everyone knew something was amiss.

"Hey, Scott. Long time no see. I see that your fortune survived the Yanks destroying the world economy," said Mark.

"All the big money-makers obviously were using smoke and mirrors. Enron should have been a big clue about the level of deception possible... Worldcom...Tyco."

"What do you think happened?"

"Short-sighted Wall Street greedmongers recklessly gambled with borrowed money. The last straw was the mortgage crisis. It exposed their get-even-more-rich-even-more-quickly schemes. Then the insurers couldn't insure."

"Where were the regulators and auditors...or whistle-blowers?"

"Ask Mick; he's a banker. People got caught up in the hype, or maybe they worked on commission. A giant bonus is a giant motivator to look the other way. The short-selling...credit-default swaps...mortgage-backed securities...

absurd debt-to-asset ratios…the level of risk taken with other people's money infuriates me. Financial products bring short-term prosperity to a selected few, but they disrupt actual businesses that serve a purpose," said Scott. "Nobody cares about how they make money anymore. No thought is given to creating jobs or protecting the environment. They just want profits, and they don't want to do anything to earn them."

"It's been a slow recovery. As you know, I work in the UK's financial industry. The way I see it, the government has to create opportunities for the unskilled portion of the work force. Improve the revenue stream of that segment of society and it's found money. Low-income workers spend their money on commodities and services, out of necessity," stated Mark.

"Poor people start small businesses which the rich businesses try to destroy. I'd like to see everything transition to being done on a smaller, more local scale. Bring back cottage industries and specialization. Anyway, I'm not feeling very social right now. Tell you what, later on you can ask me all the annoying questions you want," said Scott, transferring his anger onto the nearest recipient.

After making a few excuses for him, Erin followed Scott down to his quarters and gently rapped on the hardwood door. "I'm sorry, Scott…I should have warned you that my dad was coming, but I didn't think you'd throw a hissy."

"I like your pops…that's not the problem I'm dealing with right now. I've been in the sun too much; I need a nap."

"Okay, suit yourself…act like a moppet," Erin replied through the door.

For hours, Scott concentrated on finding sleep, but several times his mind played tricks. Whenever he cleared his mind enough to shut down, he'd hear a voice on deck that sounded exactly like Zell's distinctive baritone. He heard someone walking up to his door.

"Sorry to bother you, but you have an urgent call," said Erin.

"Who is it?" barked Scott.

"The caller wouldn't say, but he insisted it was an emergency," she explained calmly.

"At what point did I start accepting random phone calls?" Scott asked. "I am beginning to wonder if I need to find a new assistant." He grabbed the satellite phone handset and then slammed his cabin door. "Scott Horne."

"Why did you do that to me?"

"Who is this? Is this a joke?" Scott demanded. The caller's voice sounded just like Zell's.

"I thought we were friends."

Mind racing, Scott had the presence of mind to check the caller ID. What he saw sent him spiraling into a rage. The LCD showed that the call was coming from his auxiliary satellite phone. Scott couldn't believe someone on the boat was intentionally provoking him.

Hyperventilating, he grabbed the door, swung it open, and stormed up the wooden stairs to search the deck in the gathering dusk. There was a group sitting in the rear cockpit, but they looked innocent. On the prow, he spotted the culprit holding a phone to his ear.

"You think you're funny, chump?" asked Scott, skipping up to the bow intending to strike the prankster.

"Do you hang up on all your friends?"

For several seconds, Scott Horne feared his eyes were lying to him in the low-light conditions. In front of him was Zell Fergusson. Immediately Scott went up and grabbed his face to feel if it was a mask.

"Is this your idea of foreplay?" enquired Zell.

"It's you! It's really you...I can't believe it. In my entire life I have never been so confused...or excited! I thought it was you flying that Grumman!" yelled Scott.

"Did you like that? I thought I'd show you my old age hasn't affected me in the way you suggested," said Zell. "I noticed that you stayed on deck."

"Zell...I'm terribly sorry about making that call from your phone. I'd like to apologize."

"Everybody makes mistakes from time to time. It goes without saying that a brash young idealist like you is going to make them more often," teased Zell. "On a serious note, I'm real proud of the way you handled those suits."

"Thanks, I appreciate that. We'll talk about everything later. For now, let's celebrate…I feel like I'm dreaming," said Scott.

"Why don't you dream me up a cocktail?"

"Let's go celebrate ashore…there's tons of driftwood on the beach," said Scott.

Hours later on a long and narrow beach a ball of fire cast a romantic light. The molten embers and deep yellow flames made patterns dance across the rain-dimpled sand. The pyre burned hot and orderly since there was no shortage of Type-A fire tenders. On the firm sand of the tide line, Jack, Jasmine, Mick, and Marianne were engaged in a hand-walking contest. Erin De Sousa and Byron Richardson strummed acoustic guitars over a bongo beat laid down by the surf guide.

"Mastering fire was a crucial step in our evolution," said Curt. "Without fire it's dark, cold, and lonely. Cultivate a flame and you have light, heat, and companionship."

"When I stare into a fire it just feels right…like I'm meditating. I think there's an ingrained impulse somewhere in our DNA that draws us into its glow," said Ashley from inside Curt's arms. The couple had reconnected following the chaos.

Slightly away from the main group, Zell and Scott took the opportunity to catch up. "What happened that night?" asked Scott.

"Applied Leverage sent some barkeep to break into my house to snoop around. I surprised the rascal and shot him twice in the chest when he tried to make a run for it," explained Zell, mimicking his shooting motion. "Guy was wearing body armor. We tussled on the ground a bit. He stabbed me in the arm, which got me going. I started knocking the snot out of him. Then he zapped me with a stun gun. Pretty tough guy."

"Zell, don't take this the wrong way, but I guarantee that man was there to kill you," stated Scott.

"Then why didn't he do it when he had the chance? He bound me up and dragged me out of there unconscious before he torched the place. I woke up the next day at a trapper's cabin near Talkeetna Pass," said Zell.

"All alone?"

"No. He was there with me. We figured out it was you that had led the lobbyists to me that morning. At that point, we didn't know who had hired him."

"How long did the guy stay there? Do you know where to find him now?"

"He spent that night at the cabin and then took off...said he'll contact me after everything blows over," answered Zell.

"After he left, why didn't you call me or tell the authorities you were alive?" asked Scott. "I didn't need to suffer through...dual clouds of death guilt."

"He and I decided it'd be safer if the people who had hired him thought I was gone. And I knew that, if you thought I was dead, it would motivate you," Zell admitted with a wink.

"This stranger tried to kill you and you decided to team up with him?"

"Well, as it turns out, he didn't try to kill me...didn't even bring a gun. It would be more accurate to say he saved me," explained Zell.

"Saved you from a fire he started? That's nonsense; you're suffering from Stockholm syndrome or something. I'd bet he's the one who placed the car bomb."

"He's a private investigator, not a soldier of fortune. I doubt I'll hear from him again. Word is that COED was behind that explosion," Zell confided.

"What? No way...that bomb screwed up my plan. I swear we had nothing to do with it...Curt would never do anything like that. Why would I have gone to all that trouble if we planned to kill them afterward anyway?" said Scott. "The only good thing is that it saved me, Jack, and Curt from testifying in federal court for weeks on end and dealing with the gotcha media. The sad part is that Alan Reynard's partners have already been cleared of wrongdoing. How that is possible...I don't know."

"I don't even understand what happened, really," stated Zell.

"Nobody does," said Scott, lying.

"How did you come up with the idea of using Jack as a…mis-informant against Applied Leverage?" wondered Zell.

"I had been investigating them for almost a year and hadn't had any success trying to get someone hired there. After they killed Nancy, I decided to use their own paranoia against them. I kept hearing about informers getting away with saying anything and thought I'd use that as our in. The night you got kidnapped, I came up with the idea of sending Jack to Applied Leverage with a fish story," explained Scott proudly.

"What's your next move, kid?" asked Zell. "I'm eager to see how this ordeal has affected you."

"Sail off into the sunrise. I'm going to spend the next couple of months exploring and surfing…free diving with my pole spear. After that, I'll relax for a while…maybe become a regular on Virgin Galactic," said Scott.

"You mean to tell me you got my cabin burned down and nearly got me killed for nothing? That's what's wrong with America…the younger generation's got nothing but quit in them. You do one productive thing and then it's back to being a playboy?" demanded Zell.

"Come on! Don't you think me and my friends deserve a break? At great personal risk, we destroyed one of the worst for-hire power-peddlers. Life goes quick…I intend to maximize my stay," said Scott honestly.

"You need to change your perception. There is more to life than just enjoying it. You could accomplish meaningful things if you worked hard. For you to devote your talent and resources to taking elaborate vacations is… unacceptable. In this time of uncertainty, America needs people like you to effect positive change," said the older, wiser man.

"To be completely honest, my loyalty is to the natural world. I'm a planet patriot," said Scott. "We need to address our disposable culture and negate the trail of devastation left in our society's wake. On the bright side, the children of the Great Depression matured into the greatest generation…guys like you. I believe this economic downturn will positively affect today's youth."

Reservoir of Corruption.com

------------------------------ ✂

Reservoir of Corruption.com

------------------------------ ✂

Reservoir of Corruption.com

------------------------------ ✂

Reservoir of Corruption.com

------------------------------ ✂

Reservoir of Corruption.com

------------------------------ ✂

Reservoir of Corruption.com

------------------------------ ✂

Reservoir of Corruption.com

------------------------------ ✂

Reservoir of Corruption.com

------------------------------ ✂

Reservoir of Corruption.com

------------------------------ ✂

Reservoir of Corruption.com

------------------------------ ✂

Reservoir of Corruption.com